THE BLIGHTED FLAME

INASSEA CHRONICLES
BOOK ONE

P. A. PEÑA

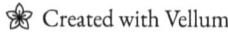

CHAPTER
ONE

It could be anywhere. Concealed within a painting. Hidden behind the face of a statue. Under their very feet. Each step Virgil took was slow. Methodical. He kept his shoulders squared and his back straight. His hands were at the ready in anticipation of the slightest bit of provocation.

It was dark save for the glimmers of moonlight fighting their way through fog laced windows, and a wisp of fire hovering in the air. The thick must of centuries of history flooded Virgil's nostrils. The nightly halls were a stark contrast to their daytime counterpart. Just hours prior the museum bustled with attendees. Now it lay barren, its only occupants the curator, the hunter, and his prey.

"Are you sure the fire is absolutely necessary?" Mr. Bicksby stammered as he followed behind Virgil.

"I am," Virgil replied, keeping his eyes forward. His tone was low, just barely above a whisper. "And please refrain from speaking unless it's absolutely necessary."

"R-right."

Virgil glanced back over his shoulder and lowered his brow. Mr. Bicksby swallowed the lump in his throat and covered his mouth.

The two men stood in sharp contrast to one another. Mr. Bicksby was short at five foot five, and wore a gray tailored suit complete with a tie and cufflinks to match. Virgil, on the other hand, stood at six foot three. He was dressed casually in a black trench coat, white t-shirt, black jeans and buckled boots.

Mr. Bicksby looked around, analyzing each exhibit to ensure it was still pristine. "I hate to be a bother," he whispered, his hand curled around his lips. "But the fire—"

"Is both necessary and under control," Virgil interrupted with a bite in his tone.

"I'm sure it is. It's just if visibility is an issue, we have plenty of lights."

Virgil waved his hand. "Like I said before, I need this fire to detect the phantom, and if we turn on too many lights it might not appear at all."

"Right," Mr. Bicksby said placing a hand on Virgil's shoulder, "but you see—"

Virgil's eye twitched as he stopped and turned around. "We've already been over this, Mr. Bicksby."

Sweat was beginning to form around the curator's forehead, and his hands were unsteady. "Forgive me. It's just we've been lucky enough to keep business going even with the phantom problem, but if anything were to happen to the exhibits—"

"I already know. That's why I'm taking extra care while working this job. Speaking of which, if you insist on tagging along, I really need you to—"

"I'm sure you will be careful, but accidents happen and given your profession we're honestly a little cautious."

Virgil took a deep breath, forcing his words down his throat. His patience waned thin, along with the urge to conceal that fact.

"I-I mean there's nothing wrong with being a hunter," Mr. Bicksby blurted out, his face reddening. "It's just, we were really hoping to hire a Crusader for this job."

"Let me guess." Virgil rolled his eyes. "The Alliance didn't have time to spare for something so insignificant."

The curator cleared his throat. "Well, they didn't exactly put it like that."

"Oh, I'm sure they made it sound really nice."

"R-right," Mr. Bicksby said with a shake of his head. "Are you absolutely positive you can handle this job? You know. Without damaging anything."

Virgil looked Mr. Bicksby in the eye, placing his hand on the curator's shoulder. "Look." He flashed a smile. "I may not be an 'esteemed Crusader,' but I am a professional 4-Star hunter. I swear to you no harm will befall the museum under my watch. However, and I'm trying to say this as delicately as possible, perhaps you'd be more comfortable waiting in the security room. When I finish the job, I'll—"

"Oh no." Mr. Bicksby puffed out his chest as he removed Virgil's hand from his shoulder. "What kind of curator would I be if I let a pyromancer roam around my museum alone?"

A frown crept onto Virgil's face as he covered his eyes with his palm. *Why do I do this to myself?* he thought. "Okay. What's it going to take for you to let me do my job in peace?"

A gust of wind barreled down the hall, sailing past the two men. The sparkling wisp of fire fluttered Virgil's coat and dragon tooth necklace.

"W-what was that?" Mr. Bicksby stuttered. A slight chill overtook the hallway.

Virgil smirked as he turned around. "That's what you hired me to kill." He firmed his jaw with determination, and he became weightless as his body surged with energy. He hovered off the floor and directed harsh instructions to Mr. Bicksby. "Go to the security room. I'll come for you after I've slain the phantom."

"Wait!" Mr. Bicksby cried, reaching out for Virgil. "I'm coming with you."

It was too late. Virgil sped down the hallway in pursuit. Weaving through the air, he followed the foul trail of aura left behind by the phantom. It was fast and its movements erratic, but Virgil kept up the chase. In no time, he found himself within striking distance.

Virgil's temperature rose as he gathered his mana into his hands. Flames erupted around them like roaring campfires. He waved his hand, and a wall of fire appeared in front of the phantom.

Cornered, the creature turned to face Virgil. Although its tattered cloak concealed its form, bits of flesh shown through the many rips in the fabric. Its brownish-green skin appeared to be dry and cracked.

"I've got you now!"

"What are you doing?" Mr. Bicksby shouted between tired breaths as he approached.

Virgil spun around. "I told you to stay out of this."

The phantom entered a stone sculpture of a man dressed in long flowing robes. It began to glow, and with a cackle, it brandished its fists.

Virgil groaned as he held out his hand towards the sculpture. "This is getting dangerously close to not being worth it."

"Stand down," Mr. Bicksby demanded. "It's taken our prized masterpiece hostage!"

Virgil didn't respond. Instead, he closed his fist, and the statue burst into flame. Mr. Bicksby gasped and put his hand over his mouth. "What have you done?"

The sculpture began writhing, and its wail echoed throughout the hallway. Slowly, it returned to its original form. The phantom burst out of the statue and thrashed around in the air, but no matter how hard it shook, the creature couldn't quell the fire consuming it. Before long, there was nothing left but a pile of ash on the floor and the pungent smell of burnt flesh in the air. Virgil released his fist, and the flames disappeared. His temperature returned to normal, and his mana stabilized.

"You must be out of your goddamn mind!" Mr. Bicksby shouted as he marched in front of Virgil. His face was livid, red with rage.

"Mr. Bicksby," Virgil said as calmly as he could.

"I knew it was a mistake to keep you on this job. I just knew you'd be nothing but trouble. It's a miracle you didn't burn the entire museum down!" The curator's finger furiously waved just inches from Virgil's face. "I hope you don't expect to get paid for this. After I'm through with you, you'll be lucky to ever find work in this city again!"

Virgil groaned as he pointed towards the sculpture. "You might want to inspect things before you blacklist me. I'm sure you'll find everything is in order."

Mr. Bicksby pursed his lips as he turned around. His eyes grew wide and his mouth fell open. "I-I don't understand," he stuttered in disbelief. He walked over and circled the sculpture, only to round it again. "There were flames everywhere, but there isn't so much as a scratch on it."

"I told you I would be extra careful. A good pyromancer can burn an entire forest to the ground, but a great one will burn just a single tree."

"R-right. I do recall you, uh, mentioning something like that." Mr. Bicksby cleared his throat once more as he adjusted his tie. "It appears I've underestimated you. Please accept my sincerest apologies."

"Don't worry about it," Virgil replied as he tucked his hands into his coat pockets. "I'm just glad I could help."

After receiving his compensation, Virgil left the museum for the city night. Liron wasn't the largest city in the Diamond Nation, but it was sprawling nonetheless. Limestone buildings were spread across the valleys and cliffs, and a series of anti-gravitational platforms made traversing the city easier for those not gifted with flight. The streets were desolate; however, the void was something Virgil had grown accustomed to. A stiff breeze tousled the ebony waves flowing through his hair, and a layer of goosebumps coated his bronze skin. He pulled out his silver pocket watch. Midnight was fast approaching, putting a stir in his step.

It didn't take long for Virgil to arrive at his destination. Petra's Joint was far from ragged, but no one who lived a conventional life would ever rest there. The lot was fairly small, consisting of about fifty rental units, a shack of an office, and the motel bar. Despite the lack of paint, cars lined the parking lot in somewhat decent rows, and a flickering sign illuminated the area in bursts.

Virgil entered the office. It was nearly desolate, the only things filling the space being a desk, a computer, and a clock. Virgil approached the elderly woman sitting at the computer. A seemingly infinite number of wrinkles creased her face. "Truesdale," she said, not bothering to turn her head from the computer screen. "Glad to see you made it back in one piece. I was worried those books would bore you to death."

Virgil chuckled. "It was a museum, Petra. Not a library."

Petra scoffed, still clicking away at her keyboard. "Does it really matter? They're both boring as all hell, and can't pay worth a dime."

"Maybe, but somebody has to help them. Right?"

"Whatever you say, kid." Petra finally took her eyes off her screen. "As long as you have my money, I don't care how you waste your time."

Virgil shook his head as he reached into his coat pocket. "I suppose that was my cue, huh."

Petra grinned as she took Virgil's payment. "If you're looking for subtlety, go try one of them stuffy ass hotels." She thumbed through each bill before placing them in her desk. "Is there something else I can help you with?"

"There is. Do you happen to have any new leads?"

"Sure do." Petra returned her gaze to her computer screen. "There's a farm offering top dollar to be rid of their demon problem."

Virgil shrugged. "Do you have anything involving witches?"

"If I did, I would have told you. You know witches are an elusive breed."

"Yeah," Virgil groaned. "I know. If you do hear anything—"

"You'll be the first to know. Assuming you have the cash, of course. I am running a business here."

Virgil left the office and made his way over to the bar, currently uproarious with a myriad of individuals swapping stories over bottles of booze. There were two floors in the building. However, the second floor was a mezzanine, allowing patrons on the top floor to see those on the bottom. The ground floor housed tables, while the top was reserved for things such as dart boards, pool tables, and arcade cabinets. The bartender's station was at the back wall of the first floor. There was a mass of shelves, each filled with bottles of liquor.

The collection of spirits was impressive, but the real draw of the bar was the massive board that hung on the wall above it, nearly six feet tall and twenty feet long. It was entirely digital, with the screens sectioned off in squares. Each held either text, images, or a combination of both. Finally, there was a line of text at the very top of the screen. It was the only text to ever stay constant on the board and consisted of a single word repeated over and over again: *Bounties!*

Virgil walked through the bar. A number of the patrons stared at him. Some addressed him, while others simply nodded. Virgil smiled and continued walking. He was careful not to linger for too long. Doing so invited conversations he was never willing to have.

"Ah, Virgil," the barkeep said as he approached. "Welcome back."

"Thanks, Phil." Virgil claimed a spot along the counter's edge.

Phil's wrinkled cheeks carried a sort of puffiness that made his demeanor seem jolly. Despite his age, his snowy white hair grew in abundance—so much so, he needed to tie it down with a series of rubber bands. "So," he began as he prepped a glass for Virgil, "how was the hunt?"

Virgil shrugged. "It was all right. Could have dealt without the chaperone." Phil laid the glass in front of Virgil. He then reached for a bottle of tequila from the top shelf. "Actually," Virgil interrupted. "Could you pour me a glass of scotch tonight?"

"Of course. If you don't mind me asking, why the change?"

"I'm celebrating."

Phil grabbed a bottle of scotch. "It went that well," he said as he filled the glass.

"It's my brother's birthday." Virgil answered. His tone was somber, and his words nearly choked him. "He would have been twenty-eight today."

The barkeep frowned. "Would have been, huh. So that means he's no longer with us."

Virgil nodded as he brought his drink to his lips. "I imagine so. It's been ten years since he left home."

"Really." Phil raised a brow. "If that's the case, isn't it possible your brother's still alive? I mean, you don't know for sure, right?"

In one gulp, Virgil swallowed his drink, not so much as wincing as the bitter brown nectar nipped at his throat. He took in a deep breath, and frowned. "No," he said, his tone definitive. "He's been gone far too long. When you're a hunter, silence always means death." He set down the empty glass and pushed it away. "How much do I owe you?" Phil slid the glass back over and began to pour another round. "I-I'm sorry," Virgil stuttered. "I only wanted one."

Phil gestured Virgil to take a seat. "These are on the house."

As Virgil sat down, Phil grabbed another glass, filling it just as he had the first. "What's your brother's name?"

"Danny," Virgil answered.

"Listen up everyone," Phil called out. The bar fell silent, until the only sound was the light flickering from the parking lot. "Tonight," Phil continued as he raised his glass, "we drink to Danny Truesdale. Whether he be on the road, or in the heavens, this one goes out to him."

Virgil couldn't help but smile as he raised his glass. He brought the liquor to his lips once more. Again, he swallowed it whole, but somehow it tasted better this time around.

The bar resumed its joyful chatter and Virgil set his glass down on the counter. "Thank you," he said. "That really meant a lot to me."

"Don't mention it," Phil said with a smile and wink.

"Please forgive me," Virgil heard from behind him as a hand came to rest upon his shoulder, "but I couldn't help but overhear you before. You're a hunter. Yes?"

Virgil turned around to find a nymph standing behind him. He was male, as evidenced by the fin upon his head, and was nearly six feet tall. His skin was scaly and as white as chalk, which only accentuated his ocean blue eyes. He wore a black suit tailored to a T, not a single thread out of place.

"I am," Virgil answered. "Is there something I can help you with?"

"Oh, I hope so. My name is Orlando. I serve the Newton estate as head steward. I'm afraid Miss Newton requires a hunter's services."

"What's the job?"

"Miss Newton has recently attracted the ire of a nefarious individual and—"

"No, thank you," Virgil said hastily. "Sorry if I got your hopes up."

Orlando paused at the curtly response. "Pardon my forwardness, but you haven't even heard me out."

"I don't need to. I never accept bodyguard work."

"I see," Orlando said as he moved next to Virgil at the bar. "If it's an issue with money, I assure you, you will be well compensated."

Virgil shook his head. "I don't care about the money. That line of work tends to linger on longer than I prefer. I hope you understand."

The nymph exhaled as he prepared to walk away. "I do. I'm sorry to have disturbed you."

"Don't worry about it, and I hope you find what you're looking for."

"As do I. I only hope we can find adequate protection before the witch makes her move."

Virgil perked up as Orlando walked away. "Wait." He stood, nearly knocking over his chair in the process. "Did you say 'witch?'"

Orlando stopped and turned around. "That is correct. Quite a nasty one, in fact."

Virgil grinned, unable to contain his excitement. "In that case, you have yourself a bodyguard."

"Are you sure?" Orlando asked tilting his head. "I can't guarantee just how long your services would be required."

"Oh, I'm sure. If a witch is involved, I'm your man."

CHAPTER
TWO

Virgil sat in the back of a black sedan alongside Orlando. The car was fitted with tinted windows, and it glided through the night like a hot knife through butter.

"Do you mind filling me in on the situation?" Virgil asked. "It'll help me prepare for the job ahead."

"Of course," Orlando replied. "What would you like to know?"

"Well, for starters, do you happen to know who this witch is?"

"Does it really matter? An assailant is an assailant. Correct?"

"That's true, but the more information I know, the better I can protect my client."

"I see. Unfortunately, we do not know the witch's identity."

"How do you know this is a witch, then?" Virgil asked, tilting his head.

The nymph flashed a smile. "I assure you, we are dealing with a witch. We recently sent out a squad of hunters to handle the problem. We could only recover one of the bodies, but the corpse reeked of lost magic."

Virgil frowned. "I imagine I'm not the only hunter hired for the job then."

"Not exactly. We plan to hire a full protection detail for Miss

Newton. About ten or so hunters in total. However, we've found that many hunters share your position on bodyguard work. We'll continue to keep looking for additional help, but at the moment, you're the first to agree."

Virgil's frown shifted to a grin. "That's good."

"I beg your pardon," Orlando replied, as he looked over the eager hunter.

Virgil cleared his throat. "It's nothing. You can call off your search for hunters. I'll be all the muscle you'll need."

Orlando chuckled. "Is that so? That's mighty brazen of you. If you're looking for a higher payout, there are certainly less dangerous ways to go about it."

"Like I said before, money doesn't concern me."

"Then what do you care about?"

Virgil paused as he turned his attention to the window. "It's personal. I do have one last question, though. What has Miss Newton done to provoke this witch?"

Orlando expelled a quick puff of air. "And what makes you think Miss Newton initiated this confrontation?"

"Witches are nearly extinct and would sooner run than fight. If one is gunning for Miss Newton, I wager they must have a pretty good reason." Virgil turned back to face Orlando, awaiting his answer.

The nymph looked at Virgil, shifting his lips to the side as he thought. "Let's say you're correct," he began. "Is that going to be a problem?"

Virgil shook his head. "I have no sympathy for witches."

Orlando frowned.

"Is something wrong?" Virgil asked.

"N-no," Orlando said hastily. "But I'm afraid I must keep you in the dark. However, if the terms of the job are unsatisfactory, please refrain from accepting it. We will hold no ill will against you for doing so."

Virgil crossed his arms and took in a deep breath. His mind was flooded with doubt. The job was beyond sketchy, and with each passing moment, it grew shadier. Still. It was the first lead on witches he had gotten in months.

"I'm still in," he said. "I would just like to be as prepared as possible, is all."

Orlando smiled. "I'm glad we could come to an understanding. We should be arriving shortly."

Virgil looked out the window as the car approached Newton Manor. The grand estate consisted of a limestone mansion and various other smaller structures. It was enveloped in a massive gate that erected high into the air, of which there was only one entrance. This was guarded by a security checkpoint in the form of a small shack and motorized blockade.

"Where are the guards?" Orlando said as the car pulled up to the blockade.

Virgil reached for the car door as he looked to Orlando and the driver. "You two stay in the car. I'll check things out."

"I will do no such thing." Orlando exited the car as well.

With Orlando close behind, Virgil walked over to investigate the security booth. He peered through the window, but there was nothing but blood, and tatters of fabric spread across the floor.

"Oh dear," Orlando said, his hand covering his mouth. "We have to check the manor. Miss Newton is in danger."

"It isn't safe here," Virgil said. "Hurry back to the motel. I'll secure Miss Newton, then rendezvous with you there."

"I'm not leaving." Orlando puffed out his chest. "I am the head steward of this estate. To abandon it in such a crisis would be an indignity worse than death."

Orlando opened the window and flipped the switch to release the blockade. "Billiam," he said as he approached the driver. "Once we reach the estate, I want you to remain in the car. We must be ready to leave the moment we retrieve Miss Newton."

Virgil took to the air. "No. I'll fly ahead and bring her back. It'll be faster that way."

Virgil flew off toward the mansion, not bothering to wait for a response. He approached the front doors, or rather, the lack thereof. Each of them had been battered open and were littered with damage. One hung on by a single hinge. The other rested in pieces on the floor. Splatters of blood dotted the pummeled walls and torn carpet.

Virgil steadied his mind and began his search. Even if Miss Newton was clinging to life by a thread, her aura would still be present in the world. It would barely be detectable, but it would be present nonetheless.

With each empty room, Virgil's nerves stirred that much more. Apart from his own aura, he could only feel Orlando and Billiam.

Virgil made his way up the foyer stairs. As he rounded the corner, a bright light flashed down the hall. He rushed over as the white flare faded away, and burst into the room. The bedroom had been ransacked. A woman lay on the floor draped in a short shimmering pink bathrobe covered in blood.

"Orlando." She grimaced. "Is that you?"

Virgil approached the woman, examining her closely. *Something's not right*, he thought.

"Orlando hired me," he said as he knelt down next to her.

Slowly, Miss Newton opened her eyes. They were teary and hemorrhaged, but what Virgil noticed most of all was how dull and hollow they were. He closed his eyes and focused his mind on the woman's aura. It was faint, but still more than enough to confirm his suspicions.

"M-Miss Newton," Orlando whimpered as he entered the room. "What has she done to you?"

Orlando began to approach, and Virgil rose to his feet, turning towards the nymph. A mass of fire swirled around his fists. "Don't come any closer," Virgil barked.

Orlando paused, bewilderment clear on his face. "I beg your pardon?"

"You heard me."

"We don't have time for this," Orlando said, taking a step forward. "Miss Newton is—"

Virgil closed his fist, and flames swirled around Miss Newton. Her body burned like coal in a furnace; however, she didn't even blink.

"She isn't real," Virgil said, his glare piercing as he raised his hand to Orlando. "I'll only say this once more. Stay back, or I will kill you."

Orlando paused as he looked at Virgil. He then laughed, placing a hand on his hip. His entire demeanor switched. No longer was Orlando's posture poised and elegant. Instead, he stood loose, his shoulders relaxed. "All right. All right. You win. Go ahead and turn the flames off."

Virgil tensed, his eyes narrowing. "I'll turn them off once you explain yourself. Of course, that implies I like your answer."

"Fair enough," he replied, raising his hands. "I suppose this looks pretty sketchy, but come on. You've got the sharpest aura perception I've ever seen. Better than some deities, in fact. I mean, do you sense any malice in my aura?"

Virgil remained silent, watching the nymph for the slightest bit of movement. He scanned his aura, and reluctantly quelled his flames.

"Thank you." Orlando lowered his hands. "To answer your question, I brought you here to test you."

Virgil paused. "What do you mean test me?"

Orlando gestured towards the door. "Why don't we take a seat in the dining room? I'll explain everything over a cup of tea."

Virgil followed Orlando downstairs. No words were spoken as Orlando prepared the teapot. Virgil analyzed his every move, but despite his efforts, he couldn't figure the nymph out. There wasn't a drop of ill intent in Orlando's aura. Even so, something about him lit Virgil's nerves on fire.

"All right," Virgil began as the two men sat down at the dinner table, a full tea set between them. "Start talking. Who are you really, and what are you testing me for?"

Orlando picked up the teapot and began pouring. "Friendly word of advice, kid. Try sticking to one question at a time. You're more likely to get answers that way."

"You're stalling."

Orlando smirked. "Just imparting wisdom."

Virgil's eye twitched. "You know, I'm about five seconds away from either leaving or burning your scaly ass to a crisp. You wanna guess which one I'm leaning towards?"

Orlando grabbed his cup of tea. "That's not funny. We nymphs burn quite easily. Like grilled cheese. Easy to learn. Impossible to master. Dangerously delicious." Virgil's hands burst into flames. "Okay, okay. I got it. No more dicking around. You have to understand, though. It's hard to resist when you Truesdales make it so easy."

Virgil's flames grew more turbulent. "You make it sound like you know me, but I know for a fact we have never met before."

"Not you in particular, but your old man and I go way back." Orlando coughed as he fiddled with his collar. "Seriously though. I'd appreciate it if you put the flames out. Not really a fan of being baked alive."

"Prove it."

"That necklace around your neck isn't just some pretty tooth for show. It's a Dragon's Treasure. The Fang of Kayveon to be specific. It's a catalyst used to amplify magic. It used to be Danté's."

Virgil scoffed, turning his flames up even higher. "Not good enough," he said. "Anyone who's heard of my father knows the Fang of Kayveon was his treasure."

Orlando's breaths were beginning to grow heavy. "Okay. How about this then? It wasn't always his. It used to belong to a friend of his. A friend of ours. Once she died, he inherited the fang. He wore it every day until the day he died and then you inherited it." Virgil fell silent, the magnitude of Orlando's words overwhelming. "Okay, so maybe I guessed on that last part, but the rest is all true. Could you please—"

"S-sorry," Virgil stuttered as he recalled the flames. He picked up his teacup and took a sip. Usually, he would have inspected it for poisons, but his mind wasn't exactly in its usual state. "You knew who I was all along, didn't you?"

Orlando steadied himself, taking a deep breath. "I did. Danté and I were friends for a long time. We worked more jobs together than I can remember. Of course, that was before I joined the Crusader's Alliance." Virgil sighed as he set his cup down and slid it forward. "Is something wrong?"

"No," Virgil replied. "That just explains a lot. You're a Crusader."

"I am. In light of everything, I gotta say, you exceeded my expectations. Oh, and the name's Orlando Knox, Queen of the Crusader's Alliance. Diamond Division."

Virgil's eyes drifted towards the nymph's fin. "Queen?"

"It's just a rank. We're not gender specific."

"Whatever," Virgil said with a shrug. "Just what does the Alliance want with me? I've always hunted within the bounds of the law."

"I'm so glad you asked. One of my duties as a queen is to nominate a new applicant to take the Crusader's Exam. You know. Keep young blood circulating into the organization."

"I see. So this whole bodyguard charade is just your way of vetting potential applicants. If you couldn't tell the woman was a fake, you have no business joining the organization. Right?"

"Not quite," Orlando said as he took his cup and brought it to his lips.

"Then what is it?"

Orlando took a sip and set his cup down. "As I said," he continued. "You exceeded my expectations, but I never expected you to perform as well as you did."

"What does that mean?" Virgil asked, his eyes lowered.

Orlando held his hand out and three humanoid water forms appeared on the table. Two of them stood next to one another while the other lay on the table. "Normally, I would have merely judged how you reacted to the staged attack." The water began to move, mimicking the prior events. "I never expect people to spot Miss Newton is just a conjuration of mine, but you were able to figure it out, and quite quickly I might add."

Virgil remained silent and skeptic.

Orlando sighed as he waved his hand, dispelling the water. "Anyway, are you familiar with the Crusader's Exam?"

"Familiar enough."

"Well," Orlando said, gesturing towards Virgil, "you should know that it takes an individual of incredible caliber to be considered for sponsorship. In all my years of running this test, you're the first to ever decipher that Miss Newton is just a fabrication. Your ability to perceive an aura is uncanny."

Virgil folded his arms. "I take it that means you want to sponsor me then. You want to serve me up to the Alliance and see if I'm fit enough to be their latest dog?"

Orlando pouted. "I wouldn't put it like that, but I'm sensing a little bit of hostility here."

"You say you know my family, right?" Virgil rolled his eyes. "There's a reason my father never mentioned you."

Orlando nodded. "Okay, I deserved that. Danté and I didn't exactly end on the best of terms. Still. You have more raw talent than anyone I've ever seen. Sure, you're rough around the edges, but with the proper guidance, there's no limit to the amount of good you can do in this world."

Virgil laughed before unfolding his arms and leaning forward. "And what about the people who the Alliance never has time for, because their problems aren't the world's problems? I think they would agree that I can do plenty of good in the world without taking orders from anyone."

"That may be true, but take it from someone who's been there before. You can do so much more when you're more than just one man in the fight."

"You know, you are terrible at convincing people to sign away their freedom. I don't need or want to join some superhero team to continue doing the same thing I'm already doing."

"Look," Orlando began, "I get it. I used to be a hunter like you. Like your dad. Hell, your brother too. I used to think I was making a real difference in people's lives, and one day, a hard truth made me realize I could be doing so much more. As much as I wanted to, I couldn't do it alone. I joined the Crusader's Alliance looking for allies to strike up real change, but do you know what I found when I made it there?"

Virgil sneered as he leaned back into his chair. "A leash?"

"A family."

Virgil was taken aback. His mind filled with memories at the mere mention of that word. It was something he thought about nearly every day, but he hadn't felt it since he was a boy.

"If none of that interests you," Orlando continued, "then consider what the Crusader's Alliance can do for you. If you become a Crusader, you'd have a near-limitless pool of resources to draw from. There'd be no more traveling aimlessly. No more wondering when or where your next meal is going to come from. No more risking your life for a payout just to make it one more day and do it all over again."

"You make it sound so simple," Virgil said, snapping back into focus on the conversation. "Tell me, what's the difference between risking my life for myself and putting my life on the line for an organization where I'm just another drone in the hive?"

The room was deathly silent as each man looked the other in the eye. Orlando chuckled and reached into his suit pocket. "The answer is hidden right there in your question." He pulled out an envelope and slid it across the table. "I can't force you to accept the opportunity, but you'd be making a grievous mistake leaving an offer like this on the table. At any rate, I hope you at least accept this. Consider it payment for indulging me tonight."

"Thank you." Virgil took the envelope, stashing it in his coat pocket.

"If you happen to change your mind, meet me at the bus station tomorrow at noon. Registration for the exam doesn't close until Friday, but I'm afraid the registration site is a two-day bus ride from Liron. If I don't see you tomorrow, I'll assume the answer is still no."

Virgil departed, leaving with Billiam back to Petra's joint. As Virgil rode in the back seat of the car, he pulled out the envelope and counted his payment: five thousand dollars in crisp hundred-dollar bills. He couldn't help but beam at the cash in his hands. It was the most significant payout he had seen in a while, and more than enough to continue his witch hunt. If only he had a clue where to search next.

The rumbling in his gut begged him to hightail it to the nearest restaurant and gorge himself. He had certainly earned it after the night he had. Experience, however, directed Virgil to ease the tension in his muscles with a hot bath. The mere thought of hot running water was nearly intoxicating.

After cleaning himself up, Virgil filled his stomach with eggs and sausage at a nearby diner and returned to his room at Petra's. If he hadn't had been awake for nearly a day, he would have considered doing some recon work to figure out his next move. Since keeping his eyes open had become a more difficult task than breathing, Virgil elected to get some much-needed shut-eye instead.

CHAPTER

THREE

Virgil stood still as a corpse in a graveyard, his eyes focused on the door in front of him. It was made of cedarwood, and there were no fancy designs or insignias. It didn't have a window or anything special carved upon it. All it had was a simple black doorknob, rounded and smooth. He stared intently at the door, but then again, there wasn't anything else he could look at. Except for the door, Virgil was stuck in an abyss with darkness as far as his eyes could see.

He had been there many times before. More than he cared to remember. There used to be a time when Virgil would avoid opening the door. He once turned his back to it and walked away. He walked for what seemed like hours, but the moment he turned back around, the door was there as if he hadn't taken a single step. Another time he tried to destroy it, but no matter how hot he made his flames, it remained unharmed, beckoning Virgil to release the terrors held within.

With each passing moment, his heart pounded harder until it thumped in his ear like clashes of thunder. He reached for the doorknob, his hand trembling. Slowly, Virgil opened the door, revealing a bedroom he knew all too well.

The room was small, consisting of just a bed, a chair, and a night-stand. In the bed lay an old man, brittle and decrepit. His skin was just a few shades lighter than Virgil's. However, it was nearly void of life. The man could barely keep his dark brown eyes open, and it was clear his life hung by a single worn-out thread. His white hair was thin, the feeble strands separated by rough patches of skin. In the chair sat a boy. He was a younger, much more foolish Virgil.

Virgil sucked in a deep breath, trying his best to keep his knees from wobbling. It felt as if the walls were closing in, and yet, they hadn't budged. He shook his head and turned to leave. Per usual, the door was gone, leaving Virgil no other option but to stand there and watch. He held his breath. He hoped doing so would also hold back his tears, but of course, that never worked.

"How are you doing?" the younger Virgil asked, his words nearly strangling him.

Reluctantly, Virgil turned around.

"I don't want to talk about me," the old man said, wheezing. "Tell me, son. How are your studies?"

The younger Virgil paused for a moment. "I haven't been keeping up with them," he confessed. He couldn't lie to him. Not after what happened. "I've been looking for a cure. I think I'm getting close." A frown emerged on Dante's face. "What's wrong?" Virgil asked.

"I don't want you to spend your life taking care of me. You'll be eighteen soon. You should be—"

"I'll take care of you until I'm eighty if I have to!"

Dante paused, his breaths shallow. After a brief moment he finally spoke. "What kind of life would that be?"

The young Virgil looked away, his attention falling on a picture frame resting on the nightstand. It was of a middle-aged man and two boys. The man and one of the boys resembled each other significantly, while the other was taller and a shade darker. They all had smiles painted across their faces. The taller boy was holding a fish he had caught on a line, and the happiness emanating from the photo was undeniable. The longer he stared at the picture, the wetter his cheeks became. And yet, the young Virgil couldn't bring himself to pull his eyes away.

"Please don't cry," Danté said, reaching for the young Virgil's face, but they might as well have been oceans apart.

The young Virgil did his best to suck in his tears. "I'm fine," he said, as he took his father's hand. "I promise, Dad. I'm going to make you better again." He waited for a response, but nothing came. "Dad?" Gently, the young Virgil prodded Danté's shoulder, but to no avail. "Dad!"

The walls faded away revealing the infinite darkness. Virgil watched through tear-filled eyes as his younger self panicked, trying to save Danté. In the pit of his heart, Virgil hoped things would be different this time. Even if it was impossible, he wanted to see his father restored. Just once would be enough.

"Such a tragedy," a devilishly tender voice rang out from the darkness.

Virgil turned around to find a woman standing there, her petite frame clad in robes decorated with ancient runes. Her white skin was lightly tanned and she had green snake-like eyes.

"Cecelia," Virgil said, a monsoon of anger and hatred boiling inside him. His hands became immersed in roaring infernos. "This is all your fault!"

Cecelia laughed. "Are you sure about that, little boy?"

Virgil raised his hand, unable to contain his wrath any longer. Something tugged on his coat. He turned to find a young boy holding his coat tail. "Danny?"

"It was you," the boy said softly. "You did this."

"No. I didn't. I—"

"You did this," the boy continued, his voice deepening until it was no longer human. "You did this. You did this! YOU DID THIS!"

Virgil's eyes shot open. His harsh breaths echoed through the room, drowning out his racing heart. He didn't need to check to know the walls were scorched. The scent of roasted wood filling the air was evidence enough. Virgil wrestled the blanket off his body, desperate to escape the sweat-drenched bed. He stood, but unsteady legs sent him back to the bed with a thud. He sat, elbows firmly set in his thighs, as he cradled his face with his hands.

"Not again," he said, his voice hoarse.

Virgil forced in a breath of air as he twirled the Fang of Kayveon between his fingers. Slowly, his heartbeat lessened its ravenous pulsing. Despite this, however, he couldn't shake Orlando's words echoing in his mind.

"I couldn't do that to him," Virgil said, shaking his head as he stood up.

He made his way over to the shower and stripped down, telling himself he'd be fine. He repeated it again and again, but no matter how many times he echoed those words, he couldn't steady his nerves. He moved at the pace of drizzling honey as he turned on the water. Thoughts of his family ran through his mind.

"I have to move on from here," Virgil said to himself as he rubbed the bar of soap into his washcloth. "Maybe Sofield. Danny was last seen there after all. Maybe I missed something." He let out a hefty sigh. "No. Cecelia would never go back there."

Virgil rubbed the washcloth across his chest, pausing when his fingers touched his scar. Eight years had passed since Cecelia dealt him that blow. In all that time, its presence had yet to fade. Virgil stared at his chest. The disfigurement pulled at him. With every ache, it was like she was there, taunting him.

Once dressed, Virgil left his room. This time, however, he had his satchel with him. As a traveling hunter, it wasn't much—a few changes of clothes, some emergency rations, and a stack of maps he had collected along his journey. Virgil headed over to the motel bar and perused the bounty board. He prayed someone had posted a job relating to witches in the time he was away, but of course, it was still as sparse as it had been the night before. He tried Petra next, but to no avail. With no other option, Virgil began combing the streets for leads.

It hadn't been more than an hour before he rested on a park bench. He told himself it would only be for a minute, but one minute became two, and two became four. Before he knew it, he had been there for a half hour, hopelessly lost in thought.

"What should I do, Dad?" Virgil asked. He breathed deep and

cradled his face in his palms. "If I joined them, it would only be for a little while. Just until I can make things right like I promised. Would you hate me if I did that?"

Bells chimed in the distance, prompting him to check his watch. It was half-past eleven.

"It would be worth it, right?" He took hold of his necklace. As he looked at it, he nodded. "It's got to be worth it."

Virgil rushed over to the bus station. Just as he had said, Orlando was standing on the platform to board the bus to Ekrham. The nymph had ditched his suit. Instead, he wore a weathered vest, jeans, and a pair of steel-toe boots.

Orlando beamed as Virgil approached. "I was hoping I'd see you again. Good thing I grabbed you a ticket. You almost didn't make it."

"Just a minute," Virgil replied. "I haven't agreed to anything yet."

"Okay. However, and I'm not trying to be a dick here, the bus will be departing like now, so I really need an answer."

"I just want to make a few things clear before I sign my life away."

Orlando pursed his lips. "You make it sound like a death sentence, but go on. Ask me anything you like. Just please, make it snappy."

"You said that as a Crusader, I'd have access to a nearly limitless pool of resources. Right? I assume this includes privileged information not accessible to the public."

"Certain information is locked behind rankings, but yes." Orlando reached into his vest pocket and pulled out a glistening black card. He showed it to Virgil, revealing the bright gold C.A. printed on the card along with Orlando's picture and a white gem in the bottom right corner. "In addition to that, you get one of these. A Crusader's license is proof of your accomplishment and servitude to the Alliance. This card grants you full access to businesses and services worldwide. Of course, there are limitations and budget constraints. However, purchases made with your license are almost always approved."

Virgil nodded. "Now answer me this. What exactly is the price I would have to pay to enjoy those perks?"

Orlando paused, gathering his thoughts as he stroked his chin. "I'm not going to lie to you, Virgil. The price is steep. As a licensed Crusader, you would be tasked by the Alliance to carry out missions.

While it may sound like a continuation of everything you've been doing as a hunter, make no mistake. This is the big leagues. Every assignment given to you will be of significance, and there will be no room for debate. And that assumes you make it through the exam. Hundreds lose their lives every year attempting to secure their spot in the Alliance."

Virgil fell silent, allowing Orlando's words to sink in.

"This is the last call for the bus bound for Ekrham," a voice on the loudspeaker called out. "Please find your seats and prepare for departure."

"One last thing," Virgil said. "I'm looking for someone. Someone I owe a great deal of suffering."

Orlando rubbed his neck. "I was afraid of that. The way your ears perked up at the mere mention of a witch. Look. There will be periods where you can do as you please, but you will always be at the beck and call of the Alliance. With the resources they can provide, there's no doubt you'd have a much greater chance at fulfilling your quest. However, you may also miss the opportunity to find the peace you're looking for altogether."

"All right." Virgil turned his attention to the bus. "That's all I needed to hear. Let's go to Ekrham."

CHAPTER
FOUR

Virgil sat across from Orlando. The bus to Ekrham was moderately empty, and it moved along the highway at a steady speed. The scenery was gorgeous, filled with rolling cliffs and vast mountains off in the distance. Despite this, Virgil knew he couldn't last two days staring out the window.

"So, Laughing Squid." He turned towards Orlando. "What's the Crusader's Exam like?"

Orlando chuckled. "You noticed my code name, huh."

"Yeah. I'm assuming you all have one. I hope I don't get saddled with something so embarrassing."

"I'll have you know my code name is amazing, but to answer your question, it's against the rules to discuss the details of the exam. Past, present, or future."

"Of course it is," Virgil said, rolling his eyes. "Well, you're a queen. Right? I imagine that ranking must be pretty high, especially considering it's your responsibility to round up new meat."

"It's up there," Orlando said as he leaned back and crossed his leg over his knee. "Assuming you make it through the exam, you'll get a rundown of the hierarchy then, but I could break it down for you if you'd like."

Virgil leaned forward. "I'm all ears."

"I guess the best place to start would be the divisions. The Crusader's Alliance is broken down into four of them: Diamond, Onyx, Ruby, and Amber. Each division is a representative of their respective nation that makes up the Alliance. Crusaders are then classified by their rank, with each rank having a set of duties and responsibilities."

"How many ranks are there?"

"Six. From lowest to highest, you have the pawns, the knights, the bishops, the rooks, the queens, and finally the kings."

"Like chess," Virgil replied with a nod.

"Precisely."

Virgil leaned back in his seat and stroked his chin. "So you're one step from the top, huh. Impressive."

"You sound surprised," Orlando said. "But I'll take that as a compliment. It's the responsibility of the rooks to actively seek out nominees every year. As a queen, I have to scout out new recruits every three years. Of course, the kings have the authority to nominate applicants as well, but that's extremely rare."

"And what about when you're not recruiting?"

"Then I'm carrying out missions for the Alliance. I can either work on my own or lead a team of lower-ranked Crusaders. Serve as their mentor and whatnot. Mostly though, my job involves working with my king."

Virgil smirked. "Is a longer leash a privilege reserved for the queens and kings?"

"No, smartass." Orlando rolled his eyes. "Rooks have the same options as queens. The only real difference between them is their level of responsibility and the fact that queens are appointed by their king. Each king has two queens in their service, but there is no limit to the lower ranks."

"Interesting. So, do you prefer to work alone? I mean, you don't have a team with you."

Orlando fell silent, turning his attention to the window. "Yeah," he said slowly. "Something like that."

"I'm telling you he's real," Virgil heard from a group sitting just a few rows ahead of them.

"And I'm telling you he's just made up," his friend retorted. "There's no such thing as the Scarlet Mage."

"And there goes another one," Orlando groaned as he turned in the group's direction.

"Tell me about it," Virgil agreed. "You have no idea how many hunters I've run across searching for that pipe dream. Frankly, I wish it would just die already."

"Oh, no. The Scarlet Mage is very real. We've confirmed his existence, although it is my duty to head over and assure them that there's no such thing."

"Wait," Virgil said, "the Scarlet Mage is real?"

"Yes. You do know what confirm means, don't you?"

Virgil huffed. "Obviously. But if the rumors are true, then why is the Alliance pretending they aren't?"

"That is beyond my paygrade. If I had to guess, though, I'd say the Alliance wants to avoid mass panic."

"Are you serious?" Virgil asked. "You don't think people deserve to know a mass murderer is on the loose?"

Orlando pointed to the ceiling. "Like I said. It's above my pay grade. Besides, is it really so bad to keep the knowledge to just a rumor? Don't you think people would sleep better at night thinking that there might be a boogeyman out there as opposed to knowing there is one?"

Virgil fell silent. As much as he wanted to argue against Orlando's point, he couldn't deny the value of letting the populace rest at ease in blissful ignorance.

"Well," Orlando said as he rose to his feet. "Excuse me while I go tend to my Crusaderly duties."

Virgil scrunched his nose. "Crusaderly? Please don't tell me I'll have to start saying corny shit like that."

"Yeah. It sounded a lot better in my head."

Virgil returned his gaze to the window, and Orlando walked over to the group ahead. "Who would have thought the rumors were true?" Virgil said to himself. He smiled. "Perhaps when I'm done with this Crusader business, I'll track him down myself. With a payday that big, I'd never have to work again."

"You don't get it, mister," a man up front said. "Not only is the Scarlet Mage real, but I hear he's working with witches now."

Virgil perked up as he turned his attention to the group ahead.

"Listen," Orlando began, "I understand what you're saying, but without evidence—"

"I have evidence."

Virgil rose to his feet, promptly making his way over. "What did you say?" Virgil asked, interrupting the men.

"This is my partner, Virgil," Orlando said, flashing a smile so blindingly fake it was painful. "I was just telling these concerned citizens that they really shouldn't be running off making baseless claims. Right?"

Virgil looked over to the man. "I don't know, Orlando. This man seems pretty convinced to me. What's your name?"

"Johnny, sir," the man replied. "It's an honor to meet you both. I've always wanted to be a Crusader."

"Trust me," Virgil replied. "The honor's all mine. You were saying that the Scarlet Mage is working with witches?"

"Yes. I was traveling on vacation in the Onyx nation. Seeing the islands and whatnot. While I was there, the embassy had Esteras Island blocked off. I was really hoping to see it. Luckily the embassy refunded my ferry ticket and hotel room, so everything worked out, I guess."

"So the Scarlet Mage was spotted on Esteras with witches?"

"Oh no," Johnny continued, "it was far worse than that. I overheard one of the healers who tried to treat the wounded."

"Wounded?" Virgil said, "Sounds like there was an altercation."

Johnny nodded. "From what I overheard, it sounded more like a massacre."

"I hate to say it, but what you describe doesn't necessarily prove that this was the Scarlet Mage, or that witches were involved."

"I'm not finished yet. Apparently, the embassy tried to interrogate the hunter. He described seeing a figure draped in a red and black cloak, and his face was covered by a mask. When they tried to press the matter further, the hunter snapped. 'Keep the blood away.' That's all he said, over and over again until he, well, you know. According to the healer, a malicious aura was left imprinted on the hunter's body. One that could only be caused by lost magic. I mean, the black and red cloak. The mask. The blood. The aura. That's gotta mean that this is the Scarlet Mage. Right? And he's been learning lost magic from witches?"

Virgil smiled and patted Johnny on the shoulder. "Thank you for the information. I'll be sure this gets back to my superiors."

Virgil and Orlando returned to their seats. "And just what was the meaning of that?" Orlando asked.

"I was curious as to what he had to say," Virgil replied. "Weren't you?"

"Yeah, but you all but confirmed the presence of the Scarlet Mage for them."

"That may be, but it was valuable information worth gathering. In the end, I was just doing my job and gathering intel on potential threats for my superiors. Speaking of which, the Scarlet Mage is rumored to be working with witches and was last seen on Esteras Island."

Orlando couldn't help but chuckle. "I'm not your superior yet. You still have a long road ahead of you."

Upon arriving in town, Orlando took Virgil straight to the registration site. The building was quite small, blending inconspicuously with the shops and businesses around it. A single worker sat in the tightly confined space. He was a half-elf, as evidenced by his pointed ears, but lack of whimsical brightly colored hair.

"Ugh," the half-elf said. "I was hoping I wouldn't see you today."

"Damn, Franchesko," Orlando replied, holding out his hands as they approached the counter. "I thought we were cool."

"Yeah, yeah, we're cool. That isn't going to win me the pool, though. I thought for sure you were going to strike out this time."

Orlando laughed. "Haven't you learned by now? You never bet against the Squid."

"Right," Franchesko said unconvincingly as he turned his attention to Virgil. "Are you sure you're ready for this?"

"I am." Virgil nodded.

"And do you, Orlando, swear to the ability of this applicant by offering your sponsorship?"

"That is correct," Orlando replied.

"You know I have to hear you say it."

Orlando raised his right hand. "Yeah, yeah. I solemnly swear that Virgil Truesdale is capable of taking the Crusader's Exam by his own merit."

Franchesko reached into his desk and pulled out a stack of papers. "All righty then." He handed the documents to Virgil, along with a pen. "Go ahead and fill out these forms. They're nothing special. Just some basic info on yourself, and a waiver stating you understand the Crusader's Exam could result in property damage, bodily harm, psychological trauma, dismemberment, disability, or death."

Virgil looked down at the stack of papers. He paused as thoughts of his family coursed through his mind.

"Is everything all right?" Franchesko asked.

"Y-yeah," Virgil stuttered.

"Listen, if you don't think you're up for it—"

"Virgil's more than capable of taking the exam," Orlando said, placing his hand on Virgil's shoulder and giving it a firm squeeze. "You wouldn't be trying to influence his decision for your own benefit now, would you?"

"Please," Franchesko said with a roll of his eyes. "I'm not that pressed to win the pool. I'm just saying if Virgil here was to give up so easily, he surely isn't Crusader material."

"You needn't to worry about that," Virgil said as he picked up the pen. "I'm more than capable of passing the exam."

"Well, look who's beaming with confidence all of a sudden."

Orlando chuckled. "Yeah, the kid's a real firecracker. Gets it from his dad. At any rate, I have to get going. I probably won't get to speak to you again until after the exam, so knock 'em dead."

Orlando left the registration office, leaving Virgil to finish up his paperwork. The pages were not only long but long-winded. In no time at all, Virgil zoned out, mindlessly filling out the blank spaces. He then paused as a particular page snatched his attention, and his heart sank.

"Is something wrong?" Franchesko asked.

"N-no," Virgil stuttered. "I just. I don't have a next of kin to notify if I die."

"I see. I'm so sorry to hear that. You're welcome to put down a friend's information instead."

Virgil remained silent, his eyes still fixed on the empty line.

Franchesko frowned. "So, no friends then either. Ummm. In that case, you can leave it blank."

The tiny room seemed to be getting hotter, and the walls much closer. Virgil turned his attention back to his application. He burned through the rest of the forms as quickly as he could, and handed them over to Franchesko, who gave them a once over and placed the paperwork into a folder. Franchesko then reached into the cabinet behind him and pulled out a crystal as clear as freshly blown glass. The gem was about the size of a golf ball, and was ridged around its surface.

"Are you familiar with teleportation crystals?" Franchesko asked.

Virgil nodded.

"Good. That makes these instructions much shorter. This crystal has been set to allow transport to one specific location. It won't be active until noon tomorrow, and it only contains enough mana for one use. When the crystal glows blue, use it, and it will take you to the testing grounds. You only get one crystal, so if you happen to lose it or it breaks, then you're disqualified from the exam and will have to try again next year."

Virgil took the crystal with haste, and slipped it into his coat pocket. After thanking Franchesko, he left the registration building. His heart raced, and sweat pooled on the back of his neck. He looked down to the Fang of Kayveon and begun to twirl it between his fingers. He took a deep breath, allowing the crisp air to fill his lungs.

"Don't worry, Dad," he said. "I won't forget what you taught me. I promise. As soon as she's dead, I'm leaving the Alliance."

CHAPTER

FIVE

Throughout his travels, Virgil had never been to the Diamond Nation's capital. Not only was it the largest city in the nation, but it was also the most technologically advanced. Ekrham had long since done away with utilizing a traditional power grid. Instead, it used a mix of solar and thermal energy, and when that fell short, sorcerers filled in the gap.

Ekrham was split into seven districts with the biggest being the business district. It was better known as downtown Ekrham and was always lively with a mix of locals and tourists. During the day the streets were full of businesses and boutiques selling their wares, and at night, the district throbbed with a blend of music and neon lights. For hours Virgil wandered downtown Ekrham, allowing his curiosity to be his guide. When he had his fill, he retired to a hotel he had stumbled across while exploring.

The Grovallia stretched high into the sky and was adorned with a mass of gold and glass. Virgil entered the building through a set of grand revolving doors. The lobby was sumptuous, decorated with various pieces of furniture too beautiful to actually sit on comfortably. The carpet was bright red, embroidered with golden tassels, and an enormous chandelier hung from the ceiling. It illuminated the room like hundreds of glowing stars captured in crystal bulbs.

Virgil turned his attention to the lobby attendant, and immediately caught a look of disdain. Despite this, he continued his approach.

"I'm sorry," the attendant began, his tone condescending, "but if you're looking to use a phone—"

"I'm not," Virgil replied. "I'm looking to book a room for the night. A king-sized bed if you have it."

"Pardon me, but are you sure you wouldn't be more comfortable at another establishment?"

"Probably," Virgil admitted. "I usually don't go for these 'fancy' establishments, but things are kind of changing in my life right now, so I figured fuck it. Why not give this a shot?" The attendant's eyes widened, his mouth hanging open in stunned silence. "So, do you have a room available?"

The attendant forced a smile as he turned his attention to his computer. After clicking away at the keyboard and mouse, he looked back to Virgil. This time he bore a more sinister grin. "I'm afraid we only have one room available with a king-sized bed. Our diamond suite. It's the absolute pinnacle The Grovallia has to offer."

"Sounds good. How much is it?"

"It will be three thousand a night plus taxes, as well as an additional thousand-dollar deposit. Try not to be too discouraged. As I said, the diamond suite is the most luxurious suite in the nation. Nobles from across the land travel to Ekhram just to spend a single night here."

"Seriously," Virgil said as he reached into his pocket and proceeded to sort out the payment. "It must really be something then." He handed over the stack of bills.

The attendant's face had begun to turn red, and sweat formed upon his brow. "Well, I . . ."

"Is there a problem?" Virgil asked.

"N-no, sir. Please forgive me. I'll just need a quick moment to prep your room."

Fumbling over his computer keys, the attendant put Virgil into the system. With everything squared away, he handed Virgil his room key along with instructions to his room.

The diamond suite was elegance in its purest form. The moment Virgil stepped into the room, he was greeted by two women. One was human, tall and slender. Her white skin was tanned, and her hair was brown with curly locks. The other was an elven woman with gray skin. She was short and muscular with purple hair that fell to the middle of her back. Both women wore the same uniform: a glimmering white maid outfit equipped with golden bows.

The room itself was massive. A large hot tub in the shape of a diamond was embedded in the middle of the floor. Its rims were golden, and its porcelain was as white as freshly fallen snow. An eighty-inch tv stretched across the wall. Several paintings surrounded it. A full bar lined the western wall, and opposite that was a patio equipped with a private pool and several tanning chairs. A set of white oak wood doors sectioned off what must be the bedroom.

"Greetings, Mr. Truesdale," the women said in unison, their right hands clasped over their left. "How may we be of service?"

"Excuse me?" Virgil said as he placed his satchel on the floor.

The elven woman rushed over to Virgil in a panic. "Please allow me to get that for you, sir!"

"We are your assigned maidens," the other woman explained. "It is our job to fulfill your every desire during your stay at The Grovallia. Should you need anything at all, please do not hesitate to ask."

The elven woman returned, having placed Virgil's bag in the bedroom.

"Thank you, miss, uh, I'm sorry. I forgot to ask for your names."

"Our names?" the elven woman gasped.

"Yeah. What are they?" The women fell silent. It looked as if the elven woman was about to cry. "I'm sorry," Virgil said. "I didn't mean to offend you."

The human woman erupted in laughter, gripping her sides as if to keep them from splitting. On the other hand, the elven woman simply smiled, tears running down her cheeks.

"Don't apologize," the elf said. "You've done nothing wrong."

Virgil pursed his lips. "Then I'm afraid I'm terribly confused."

"I've been working at this hotel for eight years now," the human began, finally managing to pull herself together. "Naomi's been here even longer than that. In all our time here, no one has ever asked for our names. We're always just 'the help' or 'you there' or 'you with the tight ass.'"

Virgil paused, his eyes wide. "You can't be serious."

"I'm afraid so," Naomi replied. "The Grovallia attracts nobles of the highest class. We've come to know that such types care very little for those of us who live a life of servitude."

"That's awful."

"It is," the human woman agreed. "Which is why I must thank you, Mr. Truesdale. Oh, and my name is Talia."

"Yes," Naomi joined in. "Thank you for bringing a bit of joy into our day."

"You're both welcome," Virgil said with a smile. "And please, just call me Virgil."

"All right, Virgil," the women said in unison. "How can we be of service to you?"

"Point me to the best steak restaurant in town."

They recommended the hotel steak house located on the top floor of the hotel. After leaving a generous tip for the women and instructing them to make full use of his room while he was away, Virgil left to go grab a bite to eat.

The crowd outside the restaurant was daunting. Two enormous pillars made of marble stood on both sides of the host's stand. A red carpet bearing the same design as the carpet in the lobby led up to the stand. Potted palm trees, genetically modified to be more compact, stood every few feet along the carpet.

Virgil stood, patiently awaiting to approach the host's stand. A fine mist burst from the trees, causing Virgil to take a small step backward. In a wave, the salty scent of an ocean breeze overtook his nostrils, and he couldn't help but smile.

Finally, it was Virgil's time at the host's stand. He requested a table for one, which he was refused.

"What's the problem?" Virgil asked.

"I'm sorry, sir," the host said. "But we can't reserve a table for just one person. It's our busiest night of the week."

Virgil sighed. "Okay. Would it be possible to place an order and have it sent to my room?"

"I'm afraid not. You'll have to return to your room and place an order for room service there."

"I can't just do it here? That seems needlessly complicated."

"Pardon the intrusion," a man said behind Virgil, "but I couldn't help but overhear your dilemma."

Virgil turned around to greet the man. He had black medium length hair that was bouncy and full bodied. His eyes were light blue like chiseled sapphires, and his skin looked pale and smooth to the touch. He wore a black collared shirt under a burgundy sweater and a gold band around his right pinky.

Another man, just as tall as Virgil, stood to the first man's right. His skin was white as well, but much rosier. He had long red hair and a jawline strong enough to crack steel. He wore jeans, boots and a brown tee shirt. A black rope necklace hung loosely around his neck, but what was most notable about the man was the tattoo on his right arm. It was a black dragon stretched across his bicep, breathing fire.

To the first man's left stood a third man, although he was considerably shorter than the other two. He wore a pair of black shorts and sandals with white socks and a collared short-sleeved shirt. He had brown skin, and even though his eyes were closed, he looked directly where Virgil was standing.

"My name is Lucious," the man said. "The gentleman on my left here is Chad, and on my right is Fynn. I believe we can help you with your dinner problem."

Lucious stepped forward and stood next to Virgil. "My friends and I have a reservation for three," he said to the host. "I assume it wouldn't be too much trouble to add one more to our table." Lucious then turned to Virgil. "If it's all right with you, of course."

"Thank you for the offer," Virgil said, raising his hand, "but I'd hate to intrude on your evening."

"Nonsense," Lucious exclaimed. "Tonight's a guys' night out. You are a guy, aren't you?"

"I-I am. I guess if you insist, I—"

"Splendid!"

"All right then, Mr. Wright," the host said. "Just give us a moment to prepare the table for you."

Within no time, Virgil, Lucious, Chad, and Fynn were sitting at their table. It was set with a clean cream-colored linen sheet, and the chairs were wooden with thick fabric cushions. A mass of floating chandeliers lit the room, and a pianist off in the distance provided a tranquil ambiance.

Virgil did his best to try and blend in. He kept his order simple: a ribeye cooked medium well, mashed potatoes, and a bed of steamed vegetables. When prompted for a wine selection, he simply repeated what the other men were having—Cabernet Sauvignon imported from the Amber Nation. Virgil tried to only speak when spoken to, which turned out to be easier than expected. The longer the conversation went on, the more it became apparent these men came from noble families.

"You know, Virgil," Lucious said, after emptying his glass of wine, "you've been pretty much quiet the entire evening. I suppose you must be the strong silent type."

Virgil flashed a smile. "Something like that. Really, though, I've been engrossed in your conversations. It sounds like you guys lead quite interesting lives."

"Don't let him fool you," Chad said as he cut into his steak. "Most of the time, Lucious just likes to hear himself talk."

"I do not."

"You kind of do," Fynn joined in. He took a sip of wine, only to shudder at the taste.

Lucious grumbled. "I do not. But even if that's true, and that is a big *if*, I assure you, it only means I have truly important things to say." Virgil couldn't help but chuckle as he reached for his glass. "At any rate," Lucious continued, "I'll have many more stories to tell once I become a Crusader."

Virgil nearly choked on his wine; half because of the sour taste, and half from shock. "You're taking the exam?"

Lucious took his dinner cloth and blotted a splash of wine on the tablecloth. "We all are," he replied.

"I'm sorry," Virgil said his cheeks beginning to flush. "I didn't mean anything by it. It's just, you guys don't strike me as the type who would be taking the exam."

"Oh, you're quite wrong about that. There are tons of noble families within the ranks of the Crusaders. After all, there isn't a more noble profession in the world. The men in my family have been Crusaders for generations."

"My family doesn't go as far back as Lucious's," Chad said. "But the Willinghams have served the Alliance for multiple generations as well. It's basically a rite of passage."

"Yes," Lucious said. "Our red-haired lummox here is the only one of us who comes from a family without Crusader lineage."

"Hey!" Fynn exclaimed. "I'll be starting my family's service this year. And I told you not to call me that."

"Oh, stop it," Lucious replied. "You don't even know what that word means."

Chad began laughing, however, Fynn pouted. "I may not know what it means," he replied. "But I know it isn't good."

"Whatever." Lucious turned his attention back to Virgil. "There's actually something I wanted to talk to you about concerning the Crusader's Exam. I have a proposition for you."

"No, thank you," Virgil said, signaling the waiter for his check.

"You haven't even heard what I have to say." Lucious set his silverware on the table. "Hear me out before you turn me down so hastily. The Crusader's Exam is, no doubt, going to be a challenge for everyone. I'm not saying any of us can't handle it, but it would be more beneficial if we all, say, watch each other's backs."

"And what makes you think I'm even taking the exam?"

"Don't deny it," Chad said. "I read your aura. Under normal circumstances, anyone with your levels of mana being here wouldn't be too suspicious. However, given the registration site is in Ekrham this year and the exam is tomorrow, there's no way someone of your caliber is here coincidently. I'm willing to bet my trust fund you're a last-minute applicant."

"That's very perceptive of you," Virgil said, nearly impressed. "But if you couldn't tell, I prefer to work alone."

"I'm not saying we work together per se," Lucious said. "I'm just saying maybe we don't work against each other. And who knows? Perhaps once we get into the thick of things, you might find you could use some support."

The waiter came around and dropped off Virgil's check. He promptly pulled out cash, leaving his payment and tip. "The answer is still no." He stood. "I do appreciate you helping me out, though."

Lucious stood up to meet Virgil eye-to-eye. "Are you sure about this? I can be a powerful ally, but an even more formidable adversary."

"Yeah, I'm sure."

CHAPTER
SIX

Virgil awoke the following day, eagerly awaiting the teleportation crystal's activation. At the stroke of noon, the gem began to radiate in a twinkling blue glow. Virgil squeezed it and declared his intentions in his mind. A blue light began to envelop his body. It grew brighter until the light became blinding.

The ocean in the distance and the sand beneath his feet when the world reformed around him indicated he was far from Ekrham. Numerous people began to appear around him. Each of them varied in size, appearance, race, and species, but one thing was abundantly clear. Virgil was woefully underprepared. Many of the applicants had an assortment of bags, no doubt filled with potions, tools, or whatever else might come in handy.

There was a vast structure a few hundred feet away. The building looked to be made of ash wood and contained a hand full of windows. The entrance was propped open, and a table with a seated attendant was set up in front of it. A box filled with white envelopes lay on the table, and next to that was a set of three clipboards fixed with paper.

Virgil funneled into the line forming at the attendant's table. A gentle tap on his shoulder alerted him to the person behind him.

"Excuse me," the woman said. "That necklace. It wouldn't happen to be the Fang of Kayveon, would it?"

The woman had powder blue skin with ears that came to a fine point. She wore a lavender tunic embroidered with black lace along its edges. The tunic fell just short of her knees, and she wore a pair of black tights and boots that both complimented her outfit and were suited for combat.

"It is," Virgil answered reluctantly.

The elf grinned. "You must be a Truesdale then."

"Did you just say Truesdale?" the man in front of Virgil asked, spinning around.

A head perked up in the line, and then another, all to the tune of chattering whispers.

"Um," Virgil stuttered, as he pointed forward. "I think the line is moving."

The man turned around and progressed further, and Virgil did the same.

"I'm sorry," the elf whispered, tapping Virgil's shoulder once more. "I didn't mean to bring any attention to you."

"You're fine," Virgil whispered back. "I'm kind of used to it."

"My name is Olivia. Olivia Abernathy."

"I'm Virgil. You kinda already know my last name."

Olivia smiled. "I gotta say, I'm shocked to see someone from such a well-revered hunter family taking the Crusader's Exam. You must be the black sheep of the Truesdale clan."

"I could say the same thing about you. You don't see too many full-blooded elves outside of the Emerald Garden."

Olivia tucked a strand of her flowing pink hair behind her ear. "You got me there. My family left our homeland generations ago. We are pretty far removed from the ancient elven traditions."

"Please keep the line moving," the attendant shouted.

Virgil turned around to find that it was his turn to approach the table. "Good luck in the exam," Virgil said before walking away.

"You too."

"Sorry about that," Virgil said to the attendant as he walked up to the table.

"Mmm-hmm," she replied, her interest clearly below zero. "Place your bag on the table. Oh, and your necklace, too."

"The necklace stays with me." Virgil said placing his satchel on the table.

"Not if you want to take the exam. Catalysts are strictly forbidden during the first phase of the exam. Don't worry. Your belongings will be returned to you upon your success or failure. Should you die, however, your items will be shipped to the next of kin listed on your application."

Reluctantly, Virgil removed the Fang of Kayveon from his neck and set it on the table. "So, there's going to be multiple phases in the exam then. Just how many are there?"

"That is classified information, Mister?"

"Truesdale. First name Virgil."

The attendant took a look at one of the clipboards. She checked off Virgil's name and waved her hand over his belongings. A black void appeared, swallowing the necklace and satchel before disappearing just as quickly as it arrived. The attendant began searching through the box of envelopes. Once she found the package stamped with Virgil's name, she handed it over.

"You're all checked in. Go ahead and enter the hall. The commencement ceremony will be starting shortly. You're free to wander around the building all you like, but try not to stray too far. And don't open your envelope until you're told to."

Virgil nodded, and the attendant gestured him inside. "I suggest you mingle among the other applicants. You never know when you might need an ally."

"Thanks for the advice." Virgil walked toward the doors. "But I'll be fine on my own."

He entered the building and made his way down a long corridor. There were several doors and hallways on each side; however, he kept walking, uninterested in any particular path. That is, until he came upon a massive showroom. There were round tables spread out and decorated with blue tablecloths. Enchanted flowers glowing like fireflies sat on each of the tables and featured an assortment of colors. Like the building itself, the chairs at each table were made of ash wood. Apart from the way Virgil had come, there was only one other exit, a massive double door on the opposite side of the room.

It didn't take long for Virgil to find a spot along the wall. He placed his back to it and began observing the crowd. He tried his best to stay focused on identifying potential threats, but that proved to be a futile endeavor. Before Virgil knew it, a group had surrounded him, each of them enamored by the fact that he had been raised by the infamous Danté Truesdale.

"What was he like?" someone in the crowd asked.

"He was normal, I guess," Virgil stammered.

"Really?" someone else chimed in. "I would have thought he'd be like super strict. Was he your master? I bet you trained with him every day."

"Well, I wouldn't exactly say it was every day."

"Is it true your dad took out an entire demon's nest with a single blast?" a third person called out.

This went on for what felt like eons, testing the very limit of Virgil's patience. Finally, a dimming of the lights ushered in silence, and a wave of relief washed over him. A woman of average height phased into the room through a white void that appeared from thin air. Everyone's eyes fixed on her.

A pair of silver eyes blinked behind her thick rounded glasses, and she wore a white collared shirt, black slacks, and a charcoal gray trench coat buckled at the waste. Her gray hair was reminiscent of polished steel, and her skin was a dark brown. Had it not been for the band holding her hair, it would have certainly cascaded down her back in rippling waves.

From the moment she entered the room, the atmosphere had shifted. The air had become thick, nearly tangible. Virgil swallowed hard, and the hairs on the back of his neck stood on end. Her aura was overflowing. It was something he had never encountered before. And yet, there was no doubt in his mind. He knew exactly what she was.

"Welcome to Akata Island," the woman said, her tone poignant and dignified. "My name is Roxanne Fullbright, but I'm better known as The Silver Sabre. For those of you who don't know, I am one of the kings of the Crusader's Alliance as well as royal advisor to the Diamond Nation."

For a moment, the room erupted into clusters of whispers. With one stern look from Roxanne, silence overtook the room once more. "The role of a licensed Crusader is not to be trifled with. It is not a job. It is not a profession. Taking on this mantle means taking on a duty more significant than any other oath, commitment, or responsibility you could possibly imagine. We Crusaders shoulder the weight of the world, facing the terrors that seek to plunge our existence into calamity. We battle the darkness so that the innocent may cherish the light."

The crowd hung in awe of Roxanne's every word. Except for Virgil, who stood, patiently waiting for the speech's end.

"Over the coming weeks, you will be challenged in ways you never dreamed possible. We are going to push you to the absolute brink, and just when you think you've gotten your bearings, we are going to throw you over the edge. There are over two hundred applicants this year, each endorsed as being the best our nations have to offer. While there is no limit to how many of you will be accepted, make no mistake. The competition will be fierce, and I assure you that no amount of training you have done will have prepared you for what you are about to face."

Roxanne paused as she scanned the room, sizing up the applicants in a broad sweep. "The exam is broken up into multiple phases. As you are already aware, the use of catalysts, charms, et cetera, is strictly forbidden during the first phase of the exam. We have set this restriction so we can gauge your abilities without any enhancements or alterations. Anyone caught using a restricted item will be expelled from the exam and prohibited from ever retaking it. Each of you has been given an envelope detailing your starting position on the island. At that location, you'll find an additional envelope detailing a specific item you are tasked with hunting down. You have until sundown to acquire it and reach Akata Castle, located in the northern quadrant of the island."

Sounds simple enough, Virgil thought, as a smile crept onto his lips.

"One last thing. Everyone here has at least one other person after the same item. I want to make it perfectly clear. It is entirely within the parameters of the exam to appropriate another examinee's item. It should go without saying, but let me remind you that you all have signed waivers acknowledging the danger present in taking the exam. Be prepared to guard your life at all times during active phases of the exam."

The crowd erupted into a flurry of whispers once again. Only this time, they were much more rambunctious.

"Preparations for the first phase are nearly finished. Once they are complete, a siren will ring on the island. At that moment, you are to open your envelopes and report to your designated starting position. If you are not there when the siren rings again, you will be disqualified from the exam. No exceptions. Good luck, everyone, and may the Great Deities illuminate your path."

CHAPTER
SEVEN

Roxanne turned to leave. Despite the applicants clamoring to ask her follow-up questions, she conjured another void and stepped through it. A number of Virgil's admirers left, obviously shaken by the revelation of the exam's first phase. Unfortunately, only the most intrigued and callously annoying remained. Virgil excused himself under the guise of needing to find a restroom.

He walked through the halls of the building, tuning his aura perception to find an area to be alone and clear his mind. He rounded corner after corner, finally coming to a halt. There were several distinct auras present in each room, but one of the two auras in the room at the end of the hall ignited Virgil's nerves.

The aura felt anxious and turbulent. He could sense it was human, just like he could sense something was amiss. He took a deep breath as his brows drew closer together. Making matters worse, three men were on guard outside the door—three men Virgil already had the misfortune of meeting. Uncertain, Virgil pressed forward anyway, determined to aid whoever was inside the room. After all, he was his father's son.

As he drew closer to the door, Lucious, Chad, and Fynn turned to greet him.

"Just what are you doing here?" Lucious asked, his tone as frigid as his eyes.

"I'm only going to say this once," Virgil said. "Step aside."

"And if we refuse?"

Virgil tightened his fists. "Then I'll have no choice but to make you."

"You're quite the tough guy," Chad said with a snicker.

Fynn scoffed as he cracked his knuckles. "Don't worry. I'll make sure Paisley isn't interrupted."

Chad slugged Fynn in the arm. "You just don't know when to stay quiet, do you, dumbass?"

"Don't call me a dumbass," Fynn said, rubbing his shoulder, his wind ripped from his sail.

"Then stop acting like a dumbass."

Lucious stepped forward and locked gazes with Virgil. "It doesn't matter. Virgil is going to walk away and go about his day. After all, he has an exam to prepare for."

Virgil heard rumbling in the room behind Lucious, followed by faint crying. "Is everything all right in there?" he shouted.

"Nothing's wrong," a woman called out. "Please. Just go away."

"See," Lucious said. "Nothing's wrong."

Virgil lit his fists ablaze. "Open the door, Lucious."

Fynn grinned. "I can take care of this." He stepped forward.

Lucious raised his hand, halting his friend. "Listen to me. I want to make one thing perfectly clear. The only reason we invited hunter filth to dine with us is because of that fang hanging around your neck."

Virgil ground his teeth, balling his fist even further. He opened his mouth to speak, but Lucious cut him off. "It's my fault, really. I should have known a hunter wouldn't have been smart enough to recognize a golden opportunity to escape the worthlessness of their existence. Nevertheless, your time will come soon enough. For now, I suggest you walk away, and relish the fact that you're actually allowed to take the exam."

Virgil took a deep breath, steadying his nerves. "I can either put you all down, or you can leave willingly. What's it gonna be?"

The hallway fell silent as Virgil and Lucious glared at each other. Lucious smiled, flashing a set of pearly teeth. His eyes still fixed on Virgil, he knocked on the door. "We're leaving, Paisley."

Virgil recalled his flames as a woman burst through the door. She narrowed her dark blue eyes as she sneered at Lucious. The anger within her was unmistakable. Even her white skin was tinged with shades of red.

"Are you serious?" Paisley said, the frills of her black dress and long chestnut hair bouncing with each dramatic motion. "We're really just going to—"

"We are," Lucious interrupted as he walked away.

Paisley stood firm, planting her boots on the floor. "I'm not leaving," she said.

"Fine," Lucious replied, not bothering to look back. "Have fun dealing with the hunter then."

Paisley stood for a moment, watching Lucious as he got further and further away. Finally, she began to walk after him. "Sweetie, wait."

"See you on the battlefield," Chad said, as he walked away.

Fynn stepped up to Virgil, and they locked eyes. "We won't forget this."

"Neither will I," Virgil replied.

Virgil entered the room. It was empty except for the woman on her knees on the floor. Her hands covered her face. Virgil walked over, and she looked up at him. Tears welled up in the corners of her gray eyes.

Virgil extended his hand. "It's okay," he said with a smile. "You're safe now."

"You didn't have to do that," the woman sniffled as Virgil helped her to her feet. "But I'm grateful you did."

The woman brushed the dirt from her dark blue jeans. She adjusted her knee-high boots along with her suede jacket and made sure the silver cross was intact around her neck. Her white skin was lightly tanned, and apart from a couple of slight bruises, she appeared to be fine.

Virgil tilted his head to look her over. The woman's aura was stable now, but still, something wasn't right. It was almost as if . . . his eyes widened as the truth hit him full force.

"What is it?" The woman looked herself up and down.

"N-nothing!" Virgil said abruptly, realizing he had been staring. "Well, your hair is a bit messy is all."

The woman ran her fingers through her waving white tresses, sliding each of them back into place.

"My name's Virgil," he said holding out his hand.

The woman giggled as she took Virgil's hand. "I know," she said. "You're kind of famous around here. Everyone's been talking about the Truesdale taking the exam."

Awesome, Virgil thought. *The exam hasn't even started, and everyone already knows my name.*

"My name is Aurelia Bryant. It's nice to meet you."

"It's nice to meet you too. Umm. Feel free to tell me to mind my own business, but why was that woman attacking you?"

Aurelia shrugged. "Beats me. I suppose she doesn't like me."

"It seems like it's a lot worse than that. Do you have a prior history with her?"

"I just met her not more than an hour ago." Aurelia began twiddling the tips of her fingers. "Well, I did knock her over, but it's not like I meant to. I tried to apologize, and I thought she took it well. I guess that wasn't good enough."

Virgil shook his head. "I'm beginning to see these noble types don't really care for us too much."

"Yeah. It sounded like you've had a run-in with them before. It wasn't too pleasant, huh."

"Well, it wasn't nearly as bad as what you just went through, but those pricks did manage to sour a perfectly good steak dinner."

Aurelia giggled once more. "I guess we have something in common then."

"I suppose we do."

Aurelia's eyes widened. "Oh, no."

"What is it?"

"My brother—I said I'd only be gone for a minute. He's probably worried sick."

"Is that all? Let's go find him. He's probably back in the show-room waiting for you."

Aurelia shook her head. "I couldn't possibly bother you further. I'm sure you have to prepare for the exam. It'll be starting any minute now."

"I'll be all right. Like you said, the exam will be starting any minute. I might as well head back now, and there's no reason why we can't walk together."

And of course, if I have company, people might leave me alone for once.

Aurelia and Virgil returned to the showroom, and she spotted her brother almost instantly. He was not only taller than Virgil, but bulkier as well. His complexion matched his sister's, and he wore an olive-green vest over a black long-sleeved thermal shirt, which paired well with his cargo pants and boots. His brown hair was short, and a handful of locks swooped across his forehead. As soon as he saw them, he began fighting his way through the crowd to make it over.

"Really quick," Aurelia said, turning to Virgil. "Please keep this incident between the two of us."

"Okay," Virgil replied slowly. "Mind if I ask why?"

Aurelia sighed. "My brother can be, umm, challenging. It's best if he doesn't know what happened."

"Sure. I promise I won't say a word."

"Logan," Aurelia gushed as her brother approached.

"Aurelia. You were gone for some time. Is everything all right?"

"You worry too much," she replied with a wave of her hand. "I'm perfectly fine. Look who I ran into, though."

Logan looked past his sister, his amber gaze studying Virgil like a textbook. "Virgil. Right? You're the late Danté Truesdale's son."

"Yeah," Virgil replied, rubbing the back of his neck. "Apparently, I'm all anyone's been able to talk about around here."

Logan stepped closer to Virgil. "You don't look all that special to me."

Virgil tensed up, clenching his fists. *What's this guy's problem?*

"Do you have to be so prickly?" Aurelia whined. "If you keep this up, we're never going to make any friends."

"What?" Logan looked back at his sister. "I'm just saying he looks like a normal guy. The way people have been talking, you'd think he was a dragon or something."

Virgil laughed. "I'm definitely not a dragon."

"My apologies," Logan said, extending his hand. "As my sister will tell you, I have a nasty habit of putting my foot where it doesn't belong. My name's Logan Bryant."

Virgil took Logan's hand, and instantly regretted it. Logan's grip was like a boa constricting its prey before swallowing it whole.

"It-it's a pleasure to meet you," Virgil stuttered, praying his fingers would endure the exchange.

A siren rang, echoing throughout the building. The double door swung open, revealing a vast jungle.

Logan released Virgil's hand. "It appears it is time to get things underway. Good luck to you."

"Y-yeah. You too." Virgil massaged his aching fingers.

Logan then turned his attention to his sister, placing his massive palm on her head. "Don't overdo it, okay. I'll see you on the other side."

Aurelia nodded and walked away. "Stay safe, you guys."

Virgil waved off the duo and pulled out his envelope. He was designated to begin the first phase of the exam in the western swamp of Akata Island. His instructions were to look for a flag with his name written on it.

Without hesitation, he exited the hotel and flew through the jungle as fast as he could, weaving between trees and vines. As Virgil crossed the edge of the jungle, he staggered at the stark shift in climate. Just a few feet behind him grew a vibrant wilderness with lush trees and abundant wildlife. Now Virgil found himself pelted by a barreling blizzard. There was nothing in sight but a snowy wasteland, although he could barely see more than a few feet in front of him.

"They're really going all out for this," Virgil said, shivering. "I bet the entire island is enchanted like this."

Virgil focused his mana and coated himself in a layer of thermal energy. Warmth enveloped his body along with a faint orange glow. As he moved through the icy winds, he hoped he could avoid the frozen tundra. While it didn't take much energy to keep from freezing to death, it was still a drain on his mana reserves nonetheless.

Virgil blazed through the frozen wasteland, and cheered when he finally crossed over into a murky swamp. However, that quickly faded as the pungent smell of the bubbling gases flooded his nostrils. Virgil scanned the swamp, elated once he came upon his flag sticking out of a rotting tree. He grabbed the envelope attached to it and stood still, staring at the white rectangle. This was it: phase one of the Crusader's Exam. He didn't know how many phases would come next, or what challenges each of them would bring, but what he did know was he had no other choice than to surpass whatever the Alliance had in store.

CHAPTER

EIGHT

The siren rang again, and Virgil tore open his envelope. Within it, he found a syringe along with a mere six words written on the paper: *The Blood of a Desert Wraith*.

Virgil smirked, already assured of his victory. He ascended high into the air, leaving the confines of the swamp until he had a clear view of the entire island. Within no time, he identified the desert biome. To his surprise, though, he found no castle. Shrugging it off, he descended back to the ground, overjoyed that he wouldn't have to travel through the tundra again.

In less than an hour, Virgil reached the desert. A massive wave of heat overtook him and sweat began to drip down his neck.

"All right," he said to himself. "Find the hunting ground. Get the blood. Move on to the castle."

Slowly, he flew over the ground, searching for blood-soaked sand. Desert dwellers often used this tactic to avoid a gruesome death, but for Virgil, the reddened sand served as a target identifying his prize. For a while, there was nothing but golden sand, cacti, and the occasional scorpion or two for as far as he could see. Despite this, he remained calm and focused on his breathing.

Finally, he found a section of sand tinted red with blood. Bones and scraps of clothing were scattered upon the ground. It was clear the remains were human, but the empty syringe in one skeletal hand was proof that despite just starting, the exam had already claimed a victim.

Virgil bowed his head, paying his respect with a brief moment of silence. He then positioned himself in the air and focused his mind. With a deep breath, Virgil pooled his mana into his chest. As he exhaled, a barrage of flames rained down, baking the sand. The fire continued to grow in intensity until the sand began to liquefy. Before long, the wraith sprang out, prompting Virgil to rescind his flames. The wraith let out a frightful wail, nearly splitting Virgil's eardrums in two. It was almost twice as big as he was, with claws that curved outward. Its skin was ash gray, clashing heavily with its beaming green eyes, and its body was long and lanky.

Keeping his eyes on the creature's toxic claws, Virgil fell back. It would only take a single misstep to render his body no more useful than a sack of meat. The wraith howled once more as it moved towards him. Fire burst around his hand as he raised it towards the creature. He closed it into a fist, and the wraith fell to the ground. It thrashed about wildly as its head was caught in a whirlwind of fire. The stench of rotten flesh sizzling filled the air as the wraith cried out in anguish. He roasted the creature's head until there was nothing left but a charred skull.

Virgil released his grip, and the fire vanished. With his syringe in hand, he approached the lifeless wraith. He took its arm and carefully examined it for the proper vessel. Once he saw it, he pushed the needle in deep and siphoned out the black liquid.

With a relaxing exhale, Virgil checked his watch. He had roughly four hours of daylight left. Even with so little time remaining, he was confident there'd still be plenty of time to make it to the castle. He found himself in a forest after leaving the desert. Luckily, this was the final biome he needed to clear before reaching the northern mountains. Trees grew everywhere, and the forest teemed with life. The melody of birds chirped overhead as he weaved through the trees. Squirrels clamored for nuts. Rabbits ran around, chasing one another. Memories began to overtake his mind, and he welcomed them with open arms. He came to a stop, returned to the ground, and tucked his hands into his pockets.

"I really wish you guys could see this," Virgil said to himself, tears building in the corners of his eyes. "You'd really like it. It looks just like the forests back in Arythbelle."

Virgil continued his way through the forest, allowing his mind to travel deeper and deeper into his memories. It was certainly foolish, but how could he not? His favorite pastime had always been camping with his family.

He smiled as warmth billowed from the pit of his chest. "Remember how I used to bother you to take Danny and me out into the forest? I'd ask you nearly every day until you said yes. Oh, or how about the time we caught those bottlenose bass? They were so big." He stopped. The warmth faded and frown overtook his face. "It's been so long. I don't even know if you guys would still enjoy camping."

He reached for his necklace, only to come up empty-handed. "Right. It's just me."

With a sniffle, he wiped the tears from his eyes and took flight. "You're doing it again." He shook his head, as if the act would dispel the dark thoughts invading his mind. "You know it wasn't his fault." He picked up his pace. "He had to go. He was eighteen. You know this. It wasn't his fault."

Virgil continued through the forest, desperate to escape its borders. Perhaps if he could just leave the foliage behind, his thoughts would stop gnawing at him.

A sharp pain burrowed into his shoulder and jolted him backward as he clenched his jaw against a hiss. He stopped and looked over to find a chunk of ice lodged deep in his flesh. A stark freezing sensation pulsed from the wound, making Virgil's skin ache. Before he could even react, another icicle assailed his skin, followed by another. One by one, they pelted him until ten shards of ice decorated his chest. Blood oozed from around the ice and soaked into his shirt.

"Careless," a smug and pretentious voice called out. "Absolutely careless." Virgil looked ahead to find Lucious walking towards him, accompanied by Fynn and Chad. "I thought you'd be able to dodge at least some of my attacks," Lucious said as he raised his palm. "It seems your abilities have been greatly exaggerated."

Lucious fired off another icicle. It flew through the air with blinding speed. Wincing at the pain in his chest, Virgil caught the shard. A raging inferno engulfed his body, turning the ice into nothing more than puddles of water.

Virgil took in a deep breath, refocusing his fire into his hands. "It figures you degenerates would try to ambush me and take my item." He studied the three men carefully. "So, which one of you is it?"

"We've actually already collected our items," Fynn boasted, cracking his knuckles.

"We finished up hours ago, in fact," Chad added. "Now, we're just having a little bit of fun."

"I wouldn't exactly call this fun," Lucious said begrudgingly. "Crushing these pathetic hunters doesn't pose any challenge. I'd say we are more fulfilling our civic duty as noble Crusaders."

"And what is that supposed to mean?" Virgil asked.

"Come now. Are you really that dense?"

With a wave of his hand, Chad summoned a black void. From it fell a multitude of pillaged items.

"You see," Lucious continued, "your kind has no business joining the ranks of true nobility. Therefore, it's up to us to ensure the Crusader's Alliance remains as pure as possible."

Virgil's stomach tightened, and his nostrils flared. "My kind," he said, his blood beginning to boil. "So, you mean to tell me you've been preying on hunters, all because we weren't born with a silver spoon up our ass like you."

"Think of it more as additional screening. Frankly, I'm not sure why you care anyway. We all know how much your family hates the Alliance."

Virgil scoffed. "You're right about one thing. I couldn't care less about the Alliance, but we all have hopes and dreams invested in this exam. Who are you to take that away?"

Lucious grinned. "There's no one better for the job."

Virgil looked towards each of the men. He could feel his skin getting hotter with each second that passed. His muscles were tense, and he wanted nothing more than to rip these pompous assholes to shreds. Lucious signaled his friends to fan out.

"Dragonic Eruption," Fynn said as he held out his palm.

Fynn's hand began to glow orange, and an orb of fire appeared above his hand. From that flame emerged a flock of ten dragons. Each one was thick, made entirely of fire, and five feet long.

From the corner of his eye, Virgil saw Chad place his palms together. As he pulled them apart, a sword formed in mid-air, and Chad took hold of his weapon.

Lucious prepared to fire off another flurry of icicles. "I hope you put up more of a fight than the rest of your ilk."

Virgil focused in on Lucious and bolstered the fire around his hands. The flames were intense, but they paled in comparison to the pleasure that would come from shoving Lucious's face into the dirt. Seconds felt like hours as Virgil waited to see who would be the first to act. Nature itself seemed to be on hold, until finally his bloodlust got the better of him. He dashed forward, heading directly towards Lucious.

"I take it back," Lucious gloated, "you're not careless. You're downright stupid!"

Lucious fired off his bolts of ice one after another. Virgil weaved through the air, dodging each shard and closing the distance between them. Chad erected a metal barrier to guard his friend, but his efforts were in vain. Virgil altered his trajectory and headed straight for Chad. Chad raised his sword and projected another barrier.

Virgil cocked back and threw his punch with all his might. His knuckles collided with the barrier with such tremendous force, it shattered entirely, along with the blade. Virgil's fist drove into Chad's jaw, sending him tumbling across the ground until a tree finally broke his momentum. Fire surrounded his unconscious body.

Virgil doused the flames covering Chad and turned his attention to the other attackers, only to find three of Fynn's dragons in his face. He didn't even have time to think about dodging before they slammed into his body. The dragons exploded into a violent burst of fire. Even with a resistance to pyromancy, he couldn't withstand the full blast. Virgil grunted, flinching as the flames kissed his skin. As the blast subsided, he stood, battered, heaving in as much air as he could. His clothes were singed in several places, and smoke trailed off of his body.

"You idiot!" Lucious shouted at Fynn. "Why didn't you send them all? We had him!"

"Th-three usually does it," Fynn stuttered.

"He's a pyromancer, you imbecile. You honestly thought three of your little fireballs were good enough?"

"They're not fireballs," Fynn grumbled.

"I don't care if they were fucking frisbees! If you have a shot, you don't half-ass it."

"Whatever," Fynn said as he replaced his missing dragons. "You had a shot, too, you know."

"What was that?"

"What's wrong?" Virgil interrupted as he raised his palm to the air. Despite his injuries he bore an intense grin on his face. "Don't tell me you've lost your cool over a trashy little hunter."

A ball of fire formed above the men. It looked as if a second sun had appeared above them. With a snap of his fingers, the swirling inferno plummeted to the ground, splitting into a countless number of smaller fireballs.

Lucious fired off a volley of ice shards in response. As the shards connected with the balls of fire, clouds of steam filled the air, making visibility murky at best. Fynn waved his hand. His dragons converged in the sky and began to fly in a circle. Their flight created a vortex, pulling the steam away from the battlefield.

Why did he have to be an aquamancer? Virgil thought as he readied his defenses. He then turned his attention to Fynn. *If I can just eliminate him, I can focus on Lucious.*

Virgil charged towards Fynn, his fists covered in flames.

"Another frontal assault," Fynn said as he readied an attack.

His dragons swooped at Virgil head-on, forcing Virgil to change his flight path. He flew through the air with the dragons hot on his tail. From the corner of his eye, Virgil saw an object hurling in his direction. Lucious had fired another barrage at him. Virgil tried his best to dodge the ice, but he couldn't shake them all. An icicle clipped his leg, tearing his jeans and slicing his flesh. On its own, Lucious's attack wasn't enough to inflict significant damage. However, the strike caused just enough drag in Virgil's flight to allow one of the dragons to catch up. As the dragon sunk its fangs into Virgil's leg, it exploded.

Virgil cried out, and a searing pain shot through him as he hurtled to the ground. Anticipating the worst, he concentrated his mana and erected a barrier of fire around himself. The remaining dragons piled onto him, setting off a symphony of explosions. The sky lit up with fire, and the trees swayed back and forth.

Virgil crashed into the ground, and his barrier vanished. His body was smoldering, covered with a multitude of burns and bruises. He pulled himself to his feet as Fynn and Lucious closed in on him. His knees buckled as he stood up. He drew in a deep, painful breath.

Fynn let out a hearty laugh as he summoned more dragons. "I like this guy. You don't go down easy, do you?"

"Not at all," Virgil said, between gasps. "That's quite a signature you have there. I've never seen a pyromancer use his magic in such a way. It's a shame you keep such bad company."

"Why don't you show me your signature? I'd love to see what someone with your reserve of mana can produce."

Virgil summoned fire around his hands once more. "I hate to disappoint you. But I'd rather not reveal my secrets."

Fynn reached over, petting one of his dragons. As he rubbed it, its flames grew in intensity. "In that case, I'll just have to burn it out of you."

"Stop toying with him!" Lucious commanded. "I swear you're like a fucking dog. No, that'd be giving you too much credit."

"S-sorry," Fynn stammered.

"I'm tired of playing games." Lucious clenched his fists. "I'll show you what a real signature looks like."

Lucious's aura began to swell and billow outward. He then placed his palms together with one on top of the other. "Glacial Beast!" He slid his palms across one another, then locked his fingers in place. A sphere of ice began to surround his body, spreading quickly until it covered him entirely.

"You're in for it now," Fynn said, recalling his dragons. "No one's ever beaten Lucious's signature."

The sphere continued to expand until it hit tree height. It took a new shape, sprouting tentacle-like tendrils from its base and forming a large beak. There were eight tentacles in total, each flailing, knocking trees over with ease.

Lucious lifted one of the ice kraken's tentacles high into the air. "Let's see you get back up after this!"

Virgil took off to retreat and regroup. A blur whizzed past him. Against his better instincts, he stopped and turned back around. Logan stood there, looking up at the frozen beast. His fists were wrapped in an elegant pair of gloves. Each glove was adorned with a golden lion's head on the back of the hand. Glistening rubies were encrusted in the eyes, and the mouths were stretched wide. Despite the size difference between himself and the kraken, Logan stood unwavering.

"GET OUT OF THERE!" Virgil shouted, but Logan didn't so much as budge.

The kraken's tentacle came crashing down on top of Logan. However, he not only caught the massive limb, he lifted the beast and began swinging it around as if it were weightless. With a mighty roar, Logan released the kraken, forcing it to collide with Fynn.

Logan turned to Virgil. "I'm surprised," he said, clearly brimming with confidence. "When we met, you didn't strike me as the type of man to run away from a fight."

"I wasn't running," Virgil replied as he approached Logan. "I was merely repositioning."

"But of course." Logan gave Virgil a once-over. "Don't take this the wrong way, but you look terrible."

"Yeah, I feel that way too."

"You should let me finish these two off. Start making your way to the castle."

The smart thing to do would be to take Logan up on his offer. Virgil's body throbbed. Even with the rush of adrenaline coursing through him, his muscles twinged, pleading for him to rest. "Sorry, but that's not exactly an option." He then pointed over to Fynn and the kraken who had yet to get back up. "However, if you feel like you have to do something, go ahead and take care of the redhead for me."

Logan's brow raised. "Are you sure about that? It's going to be quite difficult for you to overpower an aquamancer, and you're not exactly firing on all cylinders there."

The kraken rose up and began charging towards Virgil and Logan. It was evident from its rampaging nature that Lucious was furious.

"I'm sure," Virgil confirmed, not a shred of doubt in his tone. "I owe this prick a proper beating."

The kraken focused in on Logan. "Do you honestly think you can just toss me around like a rag doll and get away with it?" It cocked back and swung its tentacles at Logan once more.

Virgil lifted his hand, summoning a wall of flames between Logan and the tentacle, melting the ice upon collision. "Don't worry about him. Like I said before, I'm going to beat some humility into you."

CHAPTER

NINE

The ice kraken chased after Virgil like a raging bull. It had been several minutes since Virgil and Lucious had begun their solo bout, and Logan left to deal with Fynn. Virgil still had plenty of mana at his disposal, but his body ached. He had no choice but to push the pain out his mind and push forward. If he didn't and took another blow from Lucious, it would likely be his last.

"What's the matter?" Lucious goaded. "Where's all that bravado you had a minute ago?"

"Don't worry," Virgil said, grinning as he looked back. "I still got it."

"You insolent little shit," Lucious summoned a massive wall of ice, and Virgil took a sharp right to avoid a head-on collision. He stopped, managing to dodge a tentacle by mere inches. With nowhere to go, he spun around to face Lucious.

I've got to end this before—

The wall of ice came crashing down behind Virgil. Only it was no longer ice. Lucious had changed its state into liquid. The enormous wave of water swallowed Virgil. He held his breath as the liquid tossed him around, but before he could gather himself to retaliate, Lucious converted the water back into ice.

Virgil felt cold, and his vision was blurred. He couldn't move, and the pressure closing in on him was immense. He could feel his heart beating in his chest. There was only one way out. He focused his mana as best he could and surrounded himself in fire. The ice began to shift as it melted, giving Virgil a bit of leeway. A stark chill overtook Virgil, and the ice began to reform. Lucious must have been fortifying the ice jail. Virgil doubled down. His flames exploded in intensity and change into an azure blaze. In no time at all, every bit of ice Lucious had conjured was gone.

The radiant blue fire shimmered, and the air grew thicker as Virgil's aura rippled around him. His body felt like one enormous bruise pulsating in pain with every beat of his heart, but he stood tall, fighting to keep his legs from buckling under his own weight. He looked at Lucious, who was drenched in sweat and breathing heavily. "You've run out of mana," Virgil said with a smirk as he recalled his flames.

"I see you're all wrapped up here," Logan interjected as he approached Virgil.

"Yeah," Virgil replied, loosening up, careful not to move too drastically. "We're done here."

He looked over towards Logan, his eyes instantly drawn to the carnage left in his wake. Chunks of rocks were scattered about, and trees were uprooted everywhere. Fynn lay on the ground, clutching his mangled right hand. "I, uh, see you've finished your battle as well."

Logan walked over to Lucious. "Your friend tells me you have collected the fang of a two-tailed fox. Please hand it over without issue. There's no honor in beating a man who's already been defeated, but if you refuse me, I'll take it by force."

Lucious blinked at Logan. He looked exhausted and was barely able to point to their pilfered loot. Logan walked over and picked up the fang, tucking it away into his vest pocket. As he did, his lion gloves disappeared from sight.

"Thank you for complying peacefully," he said as he looked back to Lucious. "Your friends require serious medical attention. I suggest you assist them before they incur any permanent damage."

With the battle over, Virgil and Logan continued heading north.

Initially, Virgil tried to walk normally, but the physical strain on his body proved to be too much. Instead, he levitated just inches above the ground. The two men traveled in silence, the unfortunate side effect of not being in the same party, but heading to the same destination.

Virgil looked over at Logan, whose attention was fixed on the path in front of them. "Thank you," Virgil said, more bluntly than he had intended.

"Hmm?" Logan replied.

"I-I was just saying thank you. I wasn't sure how I was going to defeat both of them at the same time. If you hadn't shown up when you did—"

"Don't mention it."

The men fell silent again, allowing awkwardness to overtake the air once more. "Virgil," Logan began without taking his eyes off the path in front of them.

"Yeah."

"I must speak with you honestly, and I pray you understand what I have to say. I never intended to aid you in your fight with those nobles. At least not at first."

"What do you mean?" Virgil asked.

"When I discovered what my item was, I knew my only chance to succeed would be to take it from another examinee. The thought of it sickens me even now, but it is an indignity I must endure to make sure I move onto the next round with Aurelia."

"I imagine it would be hard to track down a two-tailed fox if you can't detect aura signatures. It must suck to be mana-less."

"Your battle stirred up quite a commotion. I was merely checking to see if my item was present at the battle."

"I see," Virgil replied. His eyes widened and he turned to face Logan. "Wait. What if you found out I had it?"

Logan paused for a moment and let out a heavy breath. "It's my job as Aurelia's brother to protect her from harm. I know my sister through and through, and although you two have only just met, I can tell that she has taken a liking to you."

"If you say so. Like you said, we've all only just met. I mean, you guys do seem cool and all, but it's not like we've gotten to know one another."

Logan chuckled. "I agree, but I've known my sister for a very long time. I can tell she sees you as a friend and ally. As such, Aurelia would have been furious with me, but I would have taken the fang by force if you refused to hand it over."

"That's understandable. We do what we have to for our family. That's why you're taking the exam, then?"

Logan nodded. "Becoming a Crusader has always been her dream. I've tried to convince her that there are other safer, more practical ways for her to help people. But she is insistent on taking this path. As much as it pains me to see her subject herself to such anguish, I've come to realize I could never keep her away from this. My only option is to catch her should she fall, reaching for the stars."

"That's very noble of you. If you don't mind me asking, what is your dream?"

"My dream?" Logan replied, as if the thought had never once run through his mind.

"Yeah. Surely you must want something for yourself?"

Logan paused for a moment, allowing silence to creep back between them. Virgil turned his attention forward, believing himself to have offended the man.

After a brief moment, Logan broke his silence with a definitive tone that left no room for misinterpretation. "What I want is inconsequential."

"I see. Well, I hope you change your mind about that one day. Having a dream is a wonderful thing. No one should ever feel like what they want doesn't matter."

Logan stopped in his tracks so abruptly Virgil didn't even notice until he was a few feet in front of him.

"Is something wrong?" Virgil asked as he turned around. Logan stood still. Virgil could nearly see the gears turning in his head as he thought. "Logan?"

"Yeah," he said, snapping back to reality as he looked to Virgil.

"Are you okay?"

Logan resumed walking. "I'm fine," he said. "Let's get a move on. The sun will set before you know it."

As Virgil and Logan rounded the bend of the forest trail, the castle came into view. It was huge, making it evident that sorcery obscured it to the human eye from an aerial view. It appeared to be made entirely of cobblestone and hardwood, and consisted of many wings, court-yards, and terraces. Four main battlements rose high into the sky, each with an insignia carved into the stone and a colored banner waving in the wind. When connected, they formed the shape of a triangle.

On the western battlement, a white banner with a circle was carved into the stone. Within the circle, several carved swords rained down from the sky.

Like the western battlement, the northern battlement had a circle engraved in the stone. However, this circle's line waved back and forth, like a pebble tossed into a lake. Inside the waving circle was a roaring wave, and next to the insignia was a black banner.

A hexagon was carved into the stone of the southern battlement. There was a red banner next to the insignia, and a flame carved inside of the hexagon.

Finally, in the center of the triangle stood the final battlement. Upon its stone surface was a square engraved next to a yellow banner. Within the square a range of mountain peaks had been carved into the stone.

As Virgil and Logan approached the castle gate, they were greeted by a familiar voice. "You made it!" Aurelia gushed as she ran up to the two men. She took both of them in her arms, hugging them tightly.

"Of course, I'd make it," Logan said as he patted Aurelia on her head. "I promised we'd become Crusaders together. Didn't I?"

Virgil tried to speak, but Aurelia's grasp proved to be too much. He barely had the strength to continue breathing. There was no way he could fight off her affection.

"You did, but still. I always do the tracking. I was worried you wouldn't be able to make it through. Virgil must have helped you."

Logan rubbed his neck as he looked away. "Not exactly."

"Virgil," Aurelia continued. "Are you all right? You haven't said a word."

. . .

Aurelia let go of the two men and Virgil collapsed onto the ground, his eyes fluttering. Her words echoed in his mind, but he struggled to make them out.

"Virgil!" she cried out. She then turned her attention to Logan. "What happened?"

"He had a scuffle with that Lucious fellow and his comrades," Logan explained. "By the time I arrived, Virgil was already pretty banged up. We managed to defeat them, but—"

"YOU LET HIM KEEP FIGHTING?"

"I told him I'd handle it, but he refused."

Aurelia exhaled. "Just help me get him inside before it's too late."

Aurelia proceeded to lift Virgil up, but Logan stepped forward, assuring her he had it. Logan lifted Virgil into the air and propped him over his shoulder.

"Hold on, Virgil," Aurelia said as they entered into the castle grounds. "Just hold on."

Virgil opened his mouth to speak, but his words turned unintelligible. With each passing second, his vision became hazier, until finally darkness overtook him, and he slipped into unconsciousness.

CHAPTER
TEN

The moon's light shone brightly, bathing the forest in an eerie crimson glow. Tension thickened the air as Virgil watched his younger self skulking through the trees. It was clear he was pursuing someone.

His target wore a long coat, rugged jeans, and a t-shirt. His dark brown eyes were a near match to his long flowing hair, and he stood nearly six feet tall. His skin was just a few shades lighter than Virgil's, complemented well by the black tooth necklace hanging from his neck. The man ran with intent, quickly and quietly sweeping the forest. He was searching for something. Or perhaps, someone. Although the young Virgil couldn't keep up with the man's intense speed, he could feel the faint imprints of aura the man left behind, making it easy to safely follow him.

A rancid mass of aura off in the distance swirled with a mix of hatred and contempt. The feeling alone was enough to stand young Virgil's hair on end, but the fact he was heading toward the source of it made his skin feel like lightning was traveling across it.

Young Virgil slowed his approach. The mass of aura was just beyond a pile of bushes. He tip-toed closer, keeping his body low to the ground. The man was there, but what drew young Virgil's attention was the wooden altar. A young woman rested upon it, and a much older and withered woman leaned against it. The old woman didn't move. Her eyes had rolled to the back of her head, and her mouth hung open. Dozens of candles hung in the air like wayward spirits. Each of them was adorned with green sigils matching the carvings in the altar, and they pulsed rhythmically.

The young woman was stunning and as bare as the day she was born. While her white skin looked to be supple and lightly tanned, it wasn't without flaw. The same runes were carved into her chest and stomach. The young woman rose to her feet and stretched. Although blood drizzled from her wounds, she appeared unfazed.

The man raised his right hand towards the woman, and a flurry of fire swirled around it. "Answer me this," he began, his voice hard and steady. "Are you the witch known as Cecelia Holland?"

The young woman looked her body over, paying no mind to the man's demands. Her hands began to glow a bright blue, and she ran her fingers across her body. Where they touched her wounds, her skin closed, leaving no trace she had ever been injured at all. Her fingers approached her chest, and she took hold of her breasts. Smiling, she gave them both a gentle squeeze. "I must say," she said, "I picked quite the cutie this time around. I'll certainly be able to have a good time in this body."

The man's necklace began to glow, and his flames grew tenfold, turning from their orange hue to a bright white. "Answer me!" he shouted.

With a wave of her hand, the young woman summoned clothes that formed around her figure. In a matter of seconds, she was draped in a green dress and a black hooded cloak concealing her bouncy, sandy blonde hair.

The young woman looked at the man, her shimmering eyes like polished emeralds. "You haven't really given me much incentive," she replied. Her words slid off her lips like silk. "In fact, it seems to me like no matter what I say, you're going to kill me."

The man let out a hearty laugh. "I suppose that's fair. Let me make it worth your while then. If you happen to be just another random witch, you have my word I'll grant you a quick and painless death."

"And if I happen to be this Cecelia you're looking for?"

"If that's the case, I'm going to spend hours melting every inch of flesh off your bones."

The woman gasped, covering her mouth. "Oh dear," she cried, but despite the harshness in the man's tone, she spoke almost playfully. "You're quite the brute, aren't you? How can you say such a thing to a poor defenseless woman?"

"I'm beginning to lose my patience."

The young woman paused for a moment as she looked the man over. "All right," she said. "You've found me." She raised her hands forward, and they began to glow a bright green. Her eyes changed from their perky demeanor to a menacing scowl. "Now what are you going to do about it?"

The man grinned. "One last question while you can still think coherently. Do you remember a young man named Daniel Truesdale?"

"Daniel?" Cecelia perked, "Ah, the young alloster. Yes, I remember little Danny."

The man trembled as his flames grew wilder. "You have no right to call my son by that name!"

"Oh! So you're little Danny's father. I must say you're looking a lot more accomplished than your son. I guess the apple doesn't always fall near the tree."

"You know," Danté said, his eye twitching, "I think I'm going to start with your tongue. Let's see how slick your mouth is after I turn it into a pool of bubbling flesh."

Young Virgil shot up from the bushes. His fists were balled, and tears flowed from his eyes. His gaze held on Cecelia. "IT WAS YOU!" he shouted. "YOU TOOK DANNY AWAY FROM US!"

"Virgil," Danté said, his face full of shock as he turned to his son. "What are you doing here?"

Cecelia turned her attention to the young Virgil. "What do we have here?" she said intrigued. "Is this another son of yours? How precious."

Despite his father calling out to him, young Virgil's attention remained fixed solely on Cecelia. He coated his hands in fire. "You're going to pay for what you've done to my brother."

Cecelia laughed. "Is that so, little boy. And just what makes you so sure I've done anything to him at all?"

"Get out of here, now!" Danté called out.

Young Virgil tightened his fist. "I have every right to be here. I want to see this bitch burn for what she's done."

With everything he could muster, young Virgil fired off a ball of fire at Cecelia. Raising her hand into the sky, Cecelia summoned an enormous creature reminiscent of a bear, made entirely of wood. The bear absorbed the blast, and as the wood turned to ash, the glow surrounding Cecelia's hands intensified. "You should have listened to your father."

Cecelia fired off a blast of sorcery that illuminated the night sky in a burst of green light. Young Virgil's eyes widened as the wave of magic speeded towards him. His legs trembled and his stomach lurched, but he refused to run away. He had to stay and make Cecelia pay for tearing his family apart. He raised his hands in the air and erected a barrier of flames. Closing his eyes, he braced himself for the impending attack.

CHAPTER

ELEVEN

Virgil's eyes burst open, his heart racing as he thrashed about.

"Take it easy," Aurelia said, placing her sparkling blue palm on Virgil's chest. "You're safe now."

Virgil looked up to find Aurelia looming over him. She was smiling, and her hand was cool to the touch, soothing his skin like a wet rag on a hot summer's day. Virgil took a deep breath, followed by another. As Aurelia gently swayed her hands from side to side, calm began to return to him.

Virgil looked to his hands. "I didn't burn you, did I?" His voice was hoarse, and it pained him to ask. Still. He had to know.

"Of course not," Aurelia replied. "What would give you that impression?"

Virgil looked around to find they were in a small room equipped with a bed, a table, and a couple of chairs. Logan slouched in one of the chairs, fast asleep and snoring vigorously.

"It doesn't matter," Virgil said as he laid back and rubbed his throat. "Where are we exactly?"

"This is your room. Or at least it will be once you pass phase two. Roxanne was nice enough to let me treat your wounds in here."

"I see."

"Yup. Now sit up a bit and open your mouth."

"E-excuse me?" Virgil coughed.

"I said sit up and open your mouth."

"No, I heard you just fine. What do you want me to do that for?"

Aurelia groaned. "Just do it. You are thirsty, aren't you?"

Virgil looked at Aurelia. Beyond the suppression in her aura, he couldn't sense anything amiss. With reluctance, he obliged.

"Was that so hard?" she asked, as she twirled her finger in a circle. A small orb of water formed above Virgil. Aurelia flicked her finger downward, and the sphere began to drizzle into Virgil's mouth. The crisp, ice-cold water instantly soothed Virgil's parched throat.

"You said this will be my room after I complete the second phase." Virgil laid down again. "So, does that mean you two have already made it through?"

"Logan has, but I haven't gone yet. It's a good thing you woke up when you did. Roxanne said they would move us towards the end of the list, but if you hadn't woken up by the time they came for you, they'd have no choice but to disqualify you."

"I take it I've been out for a while then?"

"Not too long. Just a couple of hours."

"How many is a couple?"

"About five. No, wait. Six. It's almost midnight."

Virgil gasped. "Are you serious? That's more than just a couple."

"I don't know why you're surprised." Aurelia's tone turned stern. "Logan told me what happened. What were you thinking, trying to take on three mages at once? You're lucky I was able to get to you when I did. I may be a trained aquamancer, but I'm not a miracle worker." Virgil averted his eyes. "I'm serious," she continued. "You could have been severely injured, or even killed. Did you at any point consider the consequences of your actions? What would you have done if Logan hadn't shown up?"

"It's not like I asked them to ambush me," Virgil blurted. "I didn't have a choice."

"You always have a choice. Nobody was forcing you to stay there and fight."

Virgil tightened his fists. "Running away wasn't an option. Not after what they did."

"Oh, really. Then tell me, what was so important that it compelled you to do something so stupid?"

Virgil looked up at Aurelia. They locked gazes, prompting Virgil to scoff and turn away once more. "You wouldn't understand."

Aurelia reached over and placed her hand on Virgil's cheek. Gently, she guided his eyes to meet hers. "I think you'll find I'm a lot more understanding than you're giving me credit for."

For a moment, Virgil laid there looking up into Aurelia's eyes. His stomach began to turn and his chest tightened. "Lucious and his friends," he began. "They were stealing items away from hunters so they'd be disqualified. They eliminated twenty of us by the time they got to me. I couldn't just run away and let them go unpunished for destroying people's dreams like that."

Aurelia was now the one frozen in silence.

"I'm sorry," Virgil continued, although he wasn't quite sure why he was apologizing. "I shouldn't have been so reckless. Regardless of the situation, it was stupid to take them all on."

Aurelia broke her silence. "No. You're not stupid, and I'm sorry for saying so. It was very brave of you to fight for people you'll probably never even meet. I'm sure they would appreciate it." Aurelia's hands stopped glowing, and she took a step back. "You're all set now. Just try not to get so banged up next time. Okay?"

Virgil sat up on the edge of the bed and looked his body over. He was ache-less. No, it was more than that. There were no cuts. No bruises. No burns. If it hadn't been for his tattered clothes, a casual observer wouldn't have been able to tell he had been in a fight at all.

"This is incredible." Virgil rose to his feet. "You must have been trained extremely well. You've even restored my mana. Thank you."

"It was nothing." Aurelia took a seat in the empty chair.

"It's absolutely something. You spent five—no, six hours tending to my wounds. I definitely owe you one."

"It was nothing. Really."

That's when he noticed it. His satchel and the Fang of Kayveon were sitting on the table. Virgil walked over and picked up his necklace. He slid it around his neck, and a reassuring comfort washed over him.

"So," he said as he walked back over to the bed and sat down. "What do we have to look forward to in the next phase of the exam? I imagine your brother must have said something before passing out."

Aurelia shook her head. "The Alliance swore him to secrecy, and Logan would never break an oath he's made."

"I see. Your brother is quite an honorable man. Has he always been this way?"

"Ever since we were kids. He's always tried to be like our father. Whenever I'd feel frightened, he would pat me on the head and tell me everything was going to be all right. Just like our dad used to do."

Virgil smiled. "I know what you mean. My dad was the same way. If he was around, you just knew everything was gonna be all right."

"I don't know what I'd do without Logan. He's all I have left now."

Silence crept into the room, as Aurelia's words rang in Virgil's mind. Aurelia gasped and she covered her mouth. "Oh, no."

"What's wrong?"

"I'm so sorry," she said bowing her head. "I'm such an idiot. Here I am talking about my family, while you're all alone. Please forgive me for being so insensitive."

Virgil laughed. "You have nothing to be sorry about. You're a saint compared to those assholes at the docks."

"Excuse me?"

"Yeah. Before this whole exam even kicked off, I had my own band of groupies. They just wouldn't let up with questions about the famous demon slayer Danté Truesdale. Not a single one of them could take a hint to fuck off."

Aurelia giggled. "Be that as it may, I should have—"

"Don't do that. I've really enjoyed talking to you. It's been a treat I don't get to enjoy often."

"Really? Don't you have any friends back home?"

"Nope. Honestly, I don't really have a home, either. Well, not anymore anyway."

"I'm sorry to hear that. It sounds incredibly lonely."

Virgil sighed as he shrugged. "I've gotten used to it. Even as a kid, it was kind of always just my family and me."

"Well," Aurelia said as she held out her hand. "I hope you consider me to be your first friend. Oh, and Logan, too."

Virgil looked at Aurelia. Her smile was as wide as the ocean blue, and she radiated a sense of warmth and comfort Virgil had long since forgotten existed. A series of loud knocks on the door interrupted them. A kurara man stepped into the room. His skin was tan, and his black beak curved downward. He wore a pair of black slacks that were wide enough at the bottom to accommodate his talons. The wings on his back were made of brown feathers, and he was without a shirt.

"I'm glad to see you're awake, Mr. Truesdale," the man said. "We weren't sure if you were going to make it in time."

"No worries there," Virgil replied. "Nothing's going to keep me from passing this exam."

"Of course. My name is Kaenara. If you would please follow me, I'll escort you to the testing room."

With a wish of good luck from Aurelia, Virgil left with Kaenara. In no time, the two men were standing in front of a set of wooden doors. Kaenara gestured Virgil to open it. He didn't budge. His hair stood on end. Beyond the door were pools of aura, potent and overwhelming. They were staggering, nearly pulling the air out of his lungs, and Virgil hadn't even entered the room yet.

CHAPTER

TWELVE

"Is everything all right, Mr. Truesdale?" Kaenara asked. "If you'd like to forfeit—"

"I'm fine!" Virgil said sharply as he reached for the door.

Virgil pushed the doors open and stepped through. Dim candlelight coming from the many sconces on the walls lit the room. A long rectangular table sat in the middle of the room. Three people sat on one side, with an open chair on the other. Virgil recognized Roxanne sitting in the middle of the three, but the other two were a mystery.

Sitting to Roxanne's right was a mountain of a man with light brown eyes, and dirty blond hair. He was the tallest among them and quite muscular. It looked as if he could crush steel balls between his bronze biceps. Despite his grand physique, he wore a white long sleeved collared shirt, a black tie, and neatly pressed black slacks.

To Roxanne's left sat a nymph. She was almost as tall as the man, but quite slender. Her only curvature came from the fullness of her breasts. She wore a simple black t-shirt and a pair of tight blue jeans. Her skin was pale, scaly, and tinted pink, which contrasted heavily with her inky black eyes. Her ears were webbed, and behind her, a long tail waved to and fro. At its tip was a fin in the shape of a crescent moon.

As Virgil approached the table, his knees wobbled.

"Go ahead and take a seat," Roxanne said.

Virgil complied, pulling in his chair as he sat down.

"You already know who I am, but allow me to introduce you to the others. On my right, we have Clayton Stone, the Amber Mountain, and to my left sits Cordellia Love, the Black Wave."

Virgil swallowed the lump in his throat. "It's nice to meet you," he said, his stomach twisting into knots. "Er, both of you. It's nice to meet you both."

"Please try to relax. The second phase of the exam is merely an interview conducted by the kings of the Crusader's Alliance. Unfortunately, we are short a king, but that's typically the case with Aiden."

Virgil let out a breath of relief and his stomach loosened. Clayton's eye twitched. It was slight, and if Virgil hadn't been paying close attention, he'd have missed it. "I'm glad to hear that I won't have to fight any of you," Virgil confessed.

"Goodness no," Cordellia exclaimed, covering her mouth as she laughed.

Clayton, on the other hand, found no such amusement in Virgil's comment. He sat, still as a boulder, staring through Virgil as if he were examining his very soul.

"We'd never test our applicants through direct combat," Roxanne explained. "Doing so simply wouldn't be a fair assessment of your abilities."

"So, all we're going to do is sit here and talk?" Virgil asked.

"Correct," Cordellia answered. "You see, Virgil, the role of a Crusader is one that comes with a great deal of duty and responsibility, as well as pain and sacrifice. As the leaders of the Alliance, we have to ensure that we promote those who are not only physically capable of carrying that burden but also mentally capable as well."

"All right then," Roxanne said. "Now that we've gotten the formalities out of the way, let us begin your interview. We've each read Orlando's dossier. He obviously thinks very highly of you. If accepted, he estimates you'll make queen. Assuming an opening presents itself, of course."

"Orlando's praise must be taken with a grain of salt," Clayton said, his voice stern. "Let us not forget about his relationship with the Truesdale family."

"You make a good point," Cordellia replied. "But Orlando has proven himself on numerous occasions despite being so eccentric. I trust his judgment."

"Agreed." Roxanne nodded. "However, I'm much more interested in Virgil's performance thus far. We noticed you have the ability to levitate. That makes you a natural born pyromancer."

"Yeah. I was born on August 14th, 3216. The year of the—"

"We know," Clayton interrupted. "We have your application, remember."

"Right," Virgil said, his stomach beginning to twist once more. "You already know that."

"So," Cordellia began, "how long have you been levitating?"

Virgil shrugged in his seat. "I don't know exactly. I guess for as long as I can remember."

Clayton grunted. "I noticed you showed no effort to hide your talent during your battle." He folded his arms. "In fact, you've shown no regard for secrecy whatsoever. You do know that by doing this, you telegraph your weakness as a pyromancer?"

"I-I do."

"So, are you arrogant, or just foolish?"

Virgil paused for a moment as he gathered his thoughts. He took a deep breath, and steadied his nerves as best he could. "Neither," he replied. "The way I see it, I have to overcome my enemy regardless."

Clayton smiled, prompting Virgil to do the same. "I see," Clayton replied. "You're both."

As quickly as it came, his smile faded. Virgil opened his mouth to say something, but his words were cut off by Roxanne. "Orlando also reports that you're quite adept at reading and detecting aura signatures. Apparently, you're the only sponsor he's had who could see through his test."

"As I said before," Clayton interrupted, "Orlando's praise cannot be taken at face value."

Cordellia turned to Clayton. "You're being too critical again. If it were up to you, we'd never recruit any new Crusaders." Clayton grumbled and leaned back in his chair. "Virgil," Cordellia resumed, giving her attention back to him. "Tell me what you think about our auras."

"I've certainly never felt anything like them before," he answered. "The auras pouring out of you all are remarkable."

"Is that all?" Clayton asked with a roll of his eyes. "If so, Orlando greatly exaggerated your abilities."

"Well, I'm sure you are deities. It's the only way you could exude such powerful auras. On the other hand, well, you and Roxanne aren't completely deity. It's like you're auras have been, I don't know, diluted."

"Diluted!" Clayton exclaimed, his nostrils flared. "You dare use such language to refer to divinity?"

Despite Clayton's disapproval, Cordellia couldn't help but burst into laughter.

"I-I'm sorry," Virgil stuttered, his face reddening. "I didn't mean any disrespect."

"You're fine," Cordellia said as she pulled herself together. "You're right on the money. Clayton and Roxanne are not full-blooded deities."

"That's quite the aura perception," Roxanne joined in. "Detecting aura is a difficult task in itself, and the aura produced by a deity is by far the hardest to pick up on. Not only could you pick it up, but you're able to determine that it isn't fully deity as well. Tell me, Virgil. Can you tell what the other pieces are?"

Virgil looked over to Clayton and instantly regretted it. Clayton was still fuming, and his glare was so piercing, it felt as if Virgil were sitting inches from the sun.

"Virgil?" Roxanne said.

"S-sorry," Virgil said as he turned back to Roxanne. "I'm afraid I can't. Your auras are just so overwhelming."

"Go ahead and try," Cordellia said. "Really focus your mind."

"If you insist." Virgil closed his eyes.

There they were. Three seas of aura. Virgil felt like a piece of driftwood caught amidst a raging tsunami. A yellow aura kept mostly to one area but darted around itself like a spinning top. A black aura was the most turbulent, swaying back and forth, almost melodically. The final white aura, was stagnant and unmoving, but domineering nonetheless. Virgil focused more intently, trying his best to pick it all apart. Sweat formed upon his brow, and his body began to tremble.

"Don't push yourself too hard," Roxanne said, breaking Virgil's concentration. "What we're asking you to do is something not even we can accomplish."

"Yes," Cordellia added. "We didn't expect you to succeed, but thank you for trying anyway. I'm sure that with proper training and guidance, your abilities can be improved dramatically. I also think that even now, you would do well as a Crusader."

"Agreed," Roxanne said. "We could use your aura perception in a variety of different applications. Interrogation. Tracking. Threat detection—"

Clayton huffed. "Enough with the small talk. I say it's time we get down to what this is really about. Tell me, boy. Why do you want to become a Crusader?"

The question was simple, and yet, it gave Virgil pause. Of course, he knew the answer, but he couldn't very well just say it. "Why do I want to be a Crusader?" he repeated.

"Precisely. Let me explain something to you. There are three types of people who take our exam: those who wish to uphold justice, those seeking fame and fortune, and those in search of vengeance. Which one are you?"

Virgil remained silent, unsure of how he should respond.

"The only wrong answers here are those that are not the truth," Cordellia said, her voice the essence of tranquility.

Virgil took in a deep breath and braced himself. "I'd like to tell you that I want to uphold justice," he began, "but in all honesty, I'm seeking vengeance."

Clayton sat up in his chair. "Go on."

"A witch took everything from me," Virgil resumed, his chest feeling tighter the more he spoke. "I think about it every day. It'd be a lie to tell you anything different, but the truth is it's too late to save my family. However, as a Crusader, I can spare others from the same suffering I've endured."

Clayton rolled his eyes. "As I expected. The typical hunter response."

"Clayton!" Cordellia scolded. "Don't you think you're being a bit harsh?"

"Not in the slightest."

"Cordellia's right," Roxanne said. "Loss isn't easy to overcome. We can help Virgil—"

"You two are far too soft," Clayton interrupted. "These hunter types are all the same. They are loose cannons and foolhardy to their core. The Alliance cannot afford to employ a trigger-happy mage more concerned with putting a witch's head on a pike than upholding peace."

Virgil bit into his tongue. It was painful, sure, but he sincerely doubted he could convey his feelings in a way that wouldn't incite violence. Instead, he sat as still as he could, trying with all his might to ignore the rage bubbling inside him.

"I don't blame him for it," Clayton continued. "It's just the way hunters are."

"That's enough!" Roxanne said. "You're taking this way too far. You know the Alliance has no quarrel with hunters so long as they work within the bounds of the law."

"Perhaps it would be best if you remove yourself from the interview," Cordellia suggested.

"I will do no such thing," Clayton replied. "I am a king just as you are. If I'm not here, I shudder to think what riffraff you two will pass."

Roxanne glared at Clayton, her eyes narrowed to mere slits. "Are you questioning my competence?"

Clayton didn't budge. "Anyone with common sense can tell this boy is not Crusader material. In this first phase alone, he has shown a clear disregard for his own safety, poor decision-making skills, foolishness, and worst of all, arrogance. I firmly believe that if he were to become a Crusader, we'd be lucky if he only gets himself killed."

The room fell silent, Clayton's words hanging in the air. Virgil wanted desperately to speak up. Not to defend himself, but rather, to declare that the Alliance could kiss the entirety of his ass as he strolled out the room. Still, he sat, his fists shaking under the table.

"As I said, I don't blame Virgil for the position he's in. I mean, just look at his father. Are we really so quick to forget how much havoc Danté wrought in his search for his missing son? Can we really expect his lineage not to be as much of a nuisance as he was?"

Virgil shot up from his chair, filled with a raging fury. Blue flames wrapped his hands and lit the room with an azure glow. "Don't you dare speak ill of my father in my presence!"

Clayton stood up as well, his stone-cold gaze fixed on Virgil. His brown eyes turned to a glowing golden yellow. "You'd best quell those flames, boy, lest I show you why I'm king of the Amber division."

As he stared into Clayton's eyes, he wanted desperately to burn Clayton's mouth shut. Nothing would have pleased him more than to see smoke billowing from Clayton's jaw, but he knew it wouldn't be worth it. Grinding his teeth, Virgil recalled his flames and turned to walk away.

"Virgil, wait," Roxanne said.

He didn't respond.

"Let him go," he heard Clayton say. "We're done here."

Virgil exited the room. As he slammed the door behind him, Kaenara approached him.

"That was quick," Kaenara said. "Allow me to escort you back to your room."

"Don't bother," Virgil snapped. "I can find my own way."

He stormed off, but Kaenara followed behind him. "I'm afraid I can't do that."

With a quick turn of his head, Virgil looked back at the kurara, his nostrils flared. Kaenara stopped dead in his tracks, clearly paralyzed by Virgil's gaze. Without saying another word, Virgil pressed on into the night. Alone.

THIRTEEN

Virgil entered his room, finding it empty. He lay on his bed and mulled over his options. Rage clouded his thoughts, bubbling inside him like pools of lava pushing against the earth's surface. His breathing was heavy and slow, and his skin was hot to the touch.

"I should have never come here. Dad hated these people for a reason." He stood back up and began pacing the room. "I need to get out of here. If I make it to the beach, I can fly to the nearest island."

Virgil then stopped and placed his hands over his eyes. "Of course, I have no idea where that is. Or where I am. Never even heard of this shithole before today. It doesn't matter." He walked over to the table. "If I pace myself, I can fly for days with a full mana pool."

He reached for his satchel and paused. A block of ice rested on his bag. It was carved into a series of letters that read *Congratulations, Virgil!*

Virgil smiled, and his nerves unwound a bit. "I can at least say goodbye."

With his bag in hand, Virgil left his room. He focused his mind, searching for Aurelia's aura signature. In no time at all, he found it and began making his way to her. He sauntered down the hall, making slower and slower progress until finally, he stopped altogether. He stared down the empty hallway. "She'd only try and talk me out of it. It's best if I just leave."

Virgil turned around and began looking for the central courtyard. Having been unconscious for his first trip through the castle, it took a while for him to reach his destination. The courtyard was huge and decorated with four rows of flower beds. One row was black, another yellow, one red, and the last one white. In the middle of the grass field sat a huge fountain adorned with four sculptures spouting water.

A tiger with long blade-like spikes running down its spine faced west. A tortoise with a massive shell faced north and, facing south, a phoenix beat its mighty wings. Finally, a dragon sat in the middle. It was humanoid in shape, and had no wings.

Virgil walked along the stone path, stopping just short of the fountain. "All right," he said, tightening his fists. "I know you're hiding over there. Why don't you just come on out?"

"Huh," a woman said from the other side of the fountain. Out stepped Olivia, a bewildered look on her face. "Oh, Virgil. It's just you. You scared me. I thought you were one of the kings." She took notice of the satchel draped over Virgil's shoulder. "Wait. You're not leaving, are you?"

Virgil resumed walking. "I am," he said, blunt as a wooden club.

"What for? Don't tell me you're giving up already?"

"Yup. I was crazy to think I needed their help."

Olivia walked after Virgil. "Well, that's really a disappointment, then."

"It's really not. Coming here was a mistake."

"That may be," Olivia said, a hint of intrigue in her tone. "Or perhaps you're making a mistake now."

Virgil rolled his eyes. "I doubt that. I shouldn't be here, and the Alliance doesn't want me here. They made that abundantly clear."

"Why do you think that? Did something happen?"

Virgil forced a chuckle. "Oh yeah, something happened, all right. Now, if you excuse me, I'd really like to—"

Virgil felt a tug on his sleeve and stopped. As he turned around, he opened his mouth to tell Olivia off. However, he found himself incapable of doing so. Virgil searched for the words to say, but all he could focus on was how her hazel eyes twinkled in the moonlight.

"Why don't you tell me what happened?" Olivia said as she pulled Virgil over to the fountain. "I'm sure you're blowing things out of proportion."

Reluctantly, Virgil placed his satchel on the ground. He sat down on the fountain's edge alongside Olivia, and explained what had happened in his interview.

Olivia laughed. "That does sound pretty terrible, but it's nothing to worry about."

"Are you kidding me?" Virgil exclaimed. "I almost assaulted a king of the Crusader's Alliance. If that's not bad enough, he's also half-deity. I think worrying is the least I can do right now."

"Well, it's actually worse than that. Clayton's grandfather is the Great Deity of Earth, Olmir."

Virgil took a deep breath as he closed his eyes and pinched the bridge of his nose. "Thank you for clarifying that," he said with a sarcastic flair. "It's a miracle I was able to walk away alive."

"Well, I wouldn't say that."

"And why not? Clayton's family is literally responsible for birthing Geomancy into the world. He could have crushed me into dust if he wanted to."

Olivia held up her finger. "Exactly. Honestly, I'm a bit surprised you haven't figured it out yet."

A puzzled look overtook Virgil's face. "Figured what out?" he said.

"Duh. The second phase of the exam is still going on."

"What makes you say that?" he asked, still failing to grasp what the elf meant.

"Just think about it for a minute. You were in a room alone with three kings. If they wanted to, it'd be no effort at all for them to boot you off the island. The fact that you're sitting here with me is proof the exam isn't over for you."

Virgil pursed his lips. "Let's say you're right. If this really isn't over, then what's the point of it all? What exactly am I still being tested on?"

Olivia stood up and took a few steps forward. "They told you, didn't they?" she asked as she turned around. "I imagine they gave the same speech to everyone. Their whole rhetoric about making sure they only accept applicants who could mentally withstand the pressure. If the kings manage to get you all frazzled up and you run away, then how can the Alliance count on you when things get really tough?"

Virgil paused as he pinched the bridge of his nose once again. He didn't want to admit it, but she was right. He had been put to the test, and he had failed. Olivia picked up his bag and handed it to him.

"Thank you," Virgil said as he took it. "I owe you one."

"That one's on the house," Olivia replied, flashing a smile.

Virgil stood up and draped his satchel over his shoulder. "Guess I really lucked out finding you out here. What are you doing out so late anyway?"

"Oh, nothing much. I know I shouldn't be out wandering the castle at night, but I had to get another look at this courtyard. It's just so beautiful, and I didn't really get a chance to look at the flowers when I first arrived."

"I see. You must really like flowers then."

"Guilty as charged. Typical forester, right."

"Yeah," Virgil said with a frown. "I suppose so."

Olivia gave Virgil's shoulder a playful shove. "Ugh. Don't give me that look."

"I-I'm sorry," he stuttered, his face heating. "You just caught me off guard. I mean, I've never cared about revealing the sorcery I was born with, but I know others guard that secret with their life."

Olivia rolled her eyes. "This isn't a battle, Virgil. You don't have to be so serious."

"I know. It's just. You really shouldn't reveal information like that. Not unless you're prepared for the disadvantage that brings."

Olivia frowned as she looked at Virgil. However, her frown quickly turned to a grin, and an uneasy chill ran up Virgil's spine. Olivia leaned in close, so close in fact, she was merely a breath away. Not a word was spoken as the two stared into each other's eyes.

Virgil's face burned hot, and his mind raced. All he could think about was the luminescence of Olivia's eyes. The sweet scent of berries that hovered off her body. Her breasts that filled the folds of her tunic in just the right way.

Olivia grabbed Virgil's shirt. She pulled him even closer, and his heart pounded vigorously in his chest like drummers in a marching band. Just as their lips were about to touch, Virgil closed his eyes, awaiting the beauty that would be his first kiss. Olivia tilted her head, missing Virgil's lips and hovered right next to his ear.

"You have to learn to lighten up," she whispered.

Slowly, she ran her fingers across his cheek as she walked back towards the castle. "I'll see you around," she called, her tone soft and inviting. "Hopefully, you'll be a bit more relaxed next time we meet."

Virgil watched Olivia as she walked away, mesmerized by the gentle swaying of her hips. For a moment, he considered going after her. But just what would he say? What would he do when he caught up to her? Ultimately, he sighed and began making his way back to his room. As he walked, bathed in the moon's light, he couldn't contain the grin on his face.

FOURTEEN

L ight beamed on Virgil, jarring him awake. He turned in bed, pulling his blanket closer to his face. Usually, Virgil didn't mind an early start to the day. However, after the previous night's episode, he found it difficult to wind down and get some rest.

He stared at the wall, begging his mind to go back to its peaceful slumber. Surely, they would be coming for him. He needed to enjoy this moment of rest before the start of the next phase, but he might as well have been asking the sky not to be so blue. That's when he noticed it sitting on his table: a box that hadn't been there before he laid his head down to rest.

"When did that get there?" He pulled himself out of bed.

As he sat up, his ears perked, and he clenched his fists. The box was cardboard and had the Alliance insignia printed on the side. Virgil approached the table cautiously.

"Could the third phase already be underway?"

He prodded the box. Nothing. Again, he poked, only this time a little harder. Still nothing. Virgil relaxed his guard. The box burst open in a shower of sparks and fire. Virgil jolted backward and braced himself. Quickly he raised his hand to the box, preparing to reduce it to ash. The fire that had sprung from it began to take shape. It morphed into a series of letters that read: *Congratulations On Making It To The Third Phase!*

Virgil rolled his eyes. "You've got to be kidding me."

He approached the table and his congratulatory message faded away. Virgil peered into the box, finding a note addressed to him. It contained instructions telling him to suit up, report to the banquet hall for breakfast, and at eight o'clock sharp, the third phase would commence. Virgil continued rummaging through the box. There were several sets of clothing, although each set was the same. Virgil damn near flinched. He wouldn't be caught dead wearing a tracksuit, especially one with a massive number four sewn into the back. Not to mention, the Crusader's Alliance's insignia was just as gaudy on the front.

"At least it's black," he said as he pulled out his watch.

His eyes nearly burst from their sockets. Eight o'clock was fast approaching. Virgil stripped down, letting his clothes fall wherever they landed. With his uniform on, he charged out of his room. A quick scan of the castle revealed a collection of auras gathered in the distance.

"Please don't be late," Virgil said to himself, his heart pounding furiously in his chest as he flew through the halls.

They were empty, allowing him to throw caution to the wind and fly as fast as he could. Of course, that also meant that Virgil was the only one not in attendance, and it would be that much more noticeable when he finally arrived. Virgil rounded the corner and came to a screeching halt as he crashed into a wall. Or at least that's what it felt like.

"I'm sorry," a golem said. "I didn't see you there."

The golem had to be at least seven feet tall. He was quite round, with thick forearms, and his tan skin looked to be as dense as stone. His eyes were a light blue.

Virgil massaged his shoulder. "No," he said looking up at the behemoth towering over him. "It's my fault. I should have been paying attention to where I was going."

The golem reached down. "How about we split the difference?"

"Sure," Virgil said as he got back up on his feet. He levitated once more. "I hate to hit and run, but I'm running a bit behind." He began to fly away when he was halted by the golem grabbing his arm. "What is it? Not to be rude, but I'm kind of in a rush here."

"You know where the banquet hall is, right? Could you tell me how to get there? I'm afraid I'm lost."

In his haste, Virgil hadn't even noticed the golem was wearing the same jumpsuit as he was.

Virgil turned to leave again. "Sorry. I can't exactly give you directions, but I'll leave a trail for you." He flew away, and in his wake, a trail of heatless flames hovered over the stone floor.

Virgil made it to the banquet hall. As he approached the door, he checked his watch. Six past eight. He entered the hall and to his surprise, it was disorderly, without a king in sight. The applicants were spread across the room, sitting at tables. Each wore the same uniform: the men in black, white for women. The scent of breakfast lingered in the air, although all of the food had been cleared from the room.

Virgil looked for an open seat. Before he could find one, Aurelia waved him down. Naturally, Logan was sitting there with her. Virgil weaved his way through the tables, making his way over. "What did I miss?" he asked as he took a seat.

"Nothing yet," Aurelia answered.

"Really? The note said eight sharp, didn't it?"

"It did," Logan said, his arms folded together. "It appears the kings are running late."

"Did you sleep well?" Aurelia asked.

Thoughts of Olivia flashed through Virgil's mind, and his heart skipped a beat. "I-I slept okay."

The group sat, waiting for the start of the third phase. The hall was boisterous, but Virgil's table had fallen eerily silent. Logan was as still as a rock, his eyes closed. Aurelia, on the other hand, was nervously twirling the cross around her neck. Virgil sat, quietly scanning the room and analyzing the crowd.

You have to be ready, he thought. *You nearly failed the last phase. Don't let it happen again.*

"There are a lot fewer people here," Aurelia said softly.

"I count seventy-five," Virgil replied.

Aurelia's eyes widened. "Really? You actually counted them all?"

"Of course. Who knows what the kings have in store for us? We may have to fight some of these people."

"Or each other," Logan added.

Once again, the group fell silent, until Virgil spoke. "Right. Or each other."

A white void appeared, and the room filled with three over-whelming auras. Roxanne and Clayton stepped through the void, accompanied by a kurara man. He was average in height with crimson red eyes, an orange beak, and matching talons. His black skin bore tints of gray here and there. However, his hands and ribs were red in color. Feathers surrounded the base of his neck, and sprouted in a crown like a mohawk. Both were the same shade as his eyes. He was shirtless, showing off a set of hardened muscles, but sported ripped black jeans with a gray fade, and his wings consisted of large gray feathers.

"Good morning," Roxanne said as the group took their place at the head of the hall. "Please forgive us for the late arrival. Before we get things underway, allow me to introduce you all to the final king of the Crusader's Alliance. This is—"

"Thanks, sweetheart," the kurara began, "but I can introduce myself." He stepped forward and held out his arms. "I hope you'll forgive me for missing your first two phases of the exam, but we can't very well expect the world to keep itself safe. My name is Aiden Alabaster, better known as the Crimson Wind."

Aiden snapped his fingers and a whirlwind of flames shot through the room. They captivated the crowd as they collected at the ceiling in a radiant ball. It burst open, and beautiful embers fell to the floor like sparkling bits of confetti. The crowd erupted in a myriad of cheers and whispers, and Aiden grinned.

Clayton sighed as he pinched the bridge of his nose. "Are you done with the theatrics?" he groaned. "You've already made us late enough as it is."

Aiden didn't respond. Instead, he continued indulging in the roar of the crowd. Roxanne stepped forward.

Aiden opened his beak to speak, but with a twirl of his finger,

Clayton encased Aiden's beak in stone. "You've done enough show-boating for the day, sweetheart."

The crowd laughed, but a sharp look from Roxanne quieted them down. "Back to business," she started again. "Aiden and Clayton will be assisting with the third phase of the exam, and before any of you ask, no, you will not have to fight either of them."

"Phase three will be conducted as follows," Clayton joined in. "Each of you will be thrust into what we call the Network. Roxanne will be voiding each of you to a different entry point. The goal is simple. All you have to do is make it out."

"There will be two methods to do so," Roxanne added. "By default, you will be voided out of the Network once twenty-four hours have passed. If you're still alive and conscious when that happens, you will be passed onto the next phase. Alternatively, if you can find an exit point, you can escape the Network. Both methods are equally valid."

All right! Virgil thought. *This should be an easy win.*

"One last thing," Aiden said, finally managing to melt the muzzle off his face. "For this phase, you are allowed to group together. Feel free to party up with as many people as you like, but know that for each member of your group, your required survival time rises by one day. And yes, it still counts if you decide to group up while inside the Network."

"Choose wisely how you would like to proceed," Clayton said. "The third phase will begin in one hour."

Aurelia turned to Logan and Virgil. "This should be easy enough," she said.

"I was thinking the same thing," Virgil agreed.

Logan scoffed as he unfolded his arms. "Let's not get ahead of ourselves."

"Come on, Logan," Aurelia said with a nudge of her elbow. "Each of us could easily handle this on our own. If we group up, I know we'll finish this challenge in no time at all. I bet we even finish first."

"Don't forget about what Roxanne said. We may not be fighting Aiden or Clayton, but they're involved in some way. It isn't wise to assume this phase will be easy."

Aurelia turned to Virgil. "I'm sure we got this. Right, Virgil?"

"Y-yeah," Virgil stuttered, looking away. "I'm sure it will be a piece of cake."

"Are you okay?" Aurelia asked. "You look nervous."

Virgil turned back to face Aurelia. Her face was full of concern. *Just be honest with her,* he thought. *It's best if you handle this alone.*

Aurelia's gaze was soft and comforting. The longer he sat there looking into her gray eyes, the harder it became to force his words out. Finally, he spoke. "I, uh, I'm just hungry is all." Virgil stood up. "I'm gonna go see if I can snag a leftover biscuit or something. You two want anything?"

They declined, and Virgil left the table heading towards the kitchen in the back of the room.

You're such a coward, he thought with a shake of his head.

Virgil was in luck. The kitchen staff had yet to discard of a bowl of croissants. Virgil grabbed a few along with a glass of lemonade. As he made his way back to the table, Virgil bit into the flakey goodness. It was just the right amount of buttery, making Virgil wish he had gotten there on time to taste the pastry in its prime. The lemonade was chilly on his tongue and fell spectacularly in the middle of sweet and sour. However, as the beverage made its way down his throat, it began to grow colder and colder until it felt as if Virgil was swallowing a mouth full of ice.

Virgil's heartbeat quickened as he tried to pull the glass from his lips, but it was no good. The lemonade was frozen solid and stuck to his skin like candy to a wrapper. He looked around in a panic, searching for whoever was responsible. After a few quick glances, he saw Lucious standing off in the distance gripping his sides in laughter. Virgil's eye twitched and his nostrils flared. He took in a deep breath through his nose, and exhaled, releasing a stream of blue flames from his throat and melting the frozen beverage.

"Was that too cold for you?" Lucious taunted as he approached Virgil with Fynn and Paisley at his side. Chad, however, was nowhere to be seen.

"You just don't know when to quit, huh?" Virgil replied. "Weren't you embarrassed enough after phase one?"

"I admit you caught us off guard back in the forest, but I assure you, it won't happen again."

"Yeah," Fynn jumped in. "You better hope we don't run into you in the Network."

"That would suck," Virgil confessed, "I really would hate to dish out the same ass-whooping twice."

Fynn smirked as he flexed his knuckles. "This should be fun. I hope Logan will be with you. I owe him for breaking my arm."

"What are you smiling for, you oaf?" Lucious said, popping Fynn in his arm. "I swear, as long as you can get a good fight, you're happier than a pig rolling about in its own filth."

"What's wrong with wanting a good fight?" Fynn asked, rubbing his arm. "And I told you to stop talking to me like that, or—"

"Or what?" Lucious interrupted. "You'll stop being my friend? Stop being so dramatic, and focus on the task at hand."

"I was kinda hoping you'd be disqualified in phase two," Virgil said. "You know, on account of being an insufferable dick. I see the system has failed us all. I guess being a noble excuses you from being a decent human being."

Paisley stepped forward, boldly standing in front of Virgil. "You have no right to speak of nobility that way. Not as a hunter, and definitely not after what you and your friends have done."

Virgil let out a quick puff of air. "That's funny. Last I checked, it was you and your friends who started this."

Paisley's eye twitched and her face reddened. "No, that bitch started this. Walking around here like she's hot shit. The nerve of her to look down on me. Like she's so much better."

"This is far from being over," Lucious said. "Chad's been eliminated from the exam, and it's all your fault. We won't rest until we make this right."

"He's going to be disowned for failing the exam," Paisley added. "Do you have any idea the amount of shame you've brought upon his family?"

Virgil laughed. "Do you have any idea the amount I don't care?"

"We'll see just how funny you think this is in The Network." Lucious said, turning to walk away. "You'd better be ready."

CHAPTER
FIFTEEN

The hour ended, and the kings rounded up the teams. One by one, Roxanne enveloped them in a white void, and they were gone in an instant. Before long, it came time for Virgil, Aurelia, and Logan.

As quickly as they left the banquet hall, they reappeared in a room. Or at least that was what Virgil believed it to be. Nothing but darkness surrounded them.

"I got it." Virgil summoned three wisps of fire.

The trio looked around, finding that they had been transported underground. Jagged rocks, moist to the touch, jutted from the walls. Unlit torches lined the walls, and while there wasn't much of note in the cavern, one thing stood out like a sore thumb. A massive stone door waited on the other side of the cave, with ancient runes written upon it in red ink.

"The door's over here," Aurelia said, pointing in that direction.

"Wait just a minute," Logan said.

"Why? Is something wrong?"

"We shouldn't leave this room. We only need to outlast the timer to pass on to the next phase, and this room presents no immediate danger."

"You're joking," Virgil joined in. "You really want us to camp out in this room for three days? There isn't anything here. We'll starve before time runs out."

"We'll be fine. It won't be pleasant, but—"

"Speak for yourself. I've only had a handful of croissants for breakfast."

"Frankly, that's your own fault for being late, but even on an empty stomach, you can survive three days without food and Aurelia can provide us with plenty of drinking water."

"I'm with Virgil," Aurelia said. "We may not know what's outside this room, but this phase will go a lot faster if we try to find the exit."

"Or we could all die the second we try and open that door," Logan replied.

Virgil rolled his eyes as he placed his hands on his hips. "Don't you think you're being a bit dramatic?" he asked.

"I don't do dramatic," Logan said, flashing Virgil a cold, dry look.

"If you say so. What makes you think that door leads to certain death?"

Logan pointed to the door. "It's written right there."

"Oh," Virgil said, rubbing the back of his neck. "Is that what that says?"

Logan groaned. "You didn't know? It's ancient dragonian."

Virgil rolled his eyes once again. "No, I didn't," he sneered. "Forgive me for not studying ancient languages in my abundance of spare time."

Aurelia giggled.

Logan shot her a stern look. "Don't you dare laugh," he scolded. "You couldn't read it either. You've been neglecting your studies again."

"Neglect is such a harsh word," Aurelia said, her cheeks reddening as she turned away.

"Well, if we're going to be stuck here," Virgil began as he raised his hand, "we might as well turn on the lights."

"DON'T!" Logan shouted.

It was too late. Virgil had already closed his fist, lighting each of the torches along the walls, and filling the room with light. The cave began to shake violently as chunks of rock dislodged from the ceiling. Aurelia surrounded the group in a massive bubble, preventing the stones from crushing them. After a brief moment, the rocks stopped falling, and Aurelia dispersed her bubble.

"S-sorry about that," Virgil said.

"It's fine," Logan said with a heavy breath. "Just don't touch anything else."

"Guys," Aurelia said, pointing to the ceiling.

Water began to pour from the newly formed holes. It started out slow, but with each second, it picked up in speed.

"This isn't good," Logan said.

"Don't worry," Virgil replied, summoning flames around his hands. "This I can handle."

"Don't bother. Assuming this water will continue running until the third phase is over, you'll only end up depleting your mana." Logan placed his hand on his chin as he looked up at the ceiling. He turned to his sister. "Do you think you can freeze the holes shut?"

Aurelia frowned. "I can try, but I'm still struggling with conjuring ice. I could probably do a couple, but not all of them."

Virgil turned his attention to the door. "Looks like we don't have a choice then."

Logan took in a deep breath, and summoned his gloves. "You two stand back. I'll open the door."

"No," Virgil protested. "I'll open it."

"Don't worry about it. I'm the strongest, so the duty should fall unto me."

"No. It was my mistake, so it's my responsibility. And who cares if you're stronger. I have more mana."

Logan's eye began to twitch. "I don't have any mana. Remember?"

The two men stared each other down, unwilling to surrender. The cave shook once more, only this time it was accompanied by a gust of wind. Virgil and Logan turned to face the door to find it open, with Aurelia standing before it.

"Aurelia—" Logan called out.

"Don't even bother," she interrupted. "We would have drowned waiting on you two to stop bickering."

Virgil and Logan walked towards Aurelia, but a monstrous growl halted them in their tracks. A humongous beast came into view, towering over the group. Red scales covered its entire body, and its black eyes were haunting. Its overgrown fangs curved out the corners of its mouth, and its limbs were as thick as tree trunks.

"That's a wyvern," Virgil said, his eyes wide. "I've never seen one so close before."

"You're never going to see another one if we don't do something about it," Logan said.

Virgil balled his fists, intensifying his flames. "Right. Get back, Aurelia. I'll handle this."

Aurelia stood still, unresponsive to Virgil's instruction. She raised her hand towards the wyvern, and it charged at her. Aurelia didn't budge as water shot out from her hand. The result was blindingly fast, so much so, Virgil missed it entirely, leaving him perplexed at the gaping hole appearing in the wyvern's chest. The creature slumped to the ground, causing the cave to shake one last time.

Aurelia turned around and smiled. "Let's get a move on, shall we?"

The group stepped through the stone doors, and Logan pulled it shut behind them. There was nothing but a long tunnel in front of them. With no other option, they pressed on, traveling through the tunnel for what seemed like hours. As they walked, they made small talk, swapped stories of past hunts, and told jokes.

"All right," Logan said. "I have a tattoo, my middle name is Wilber, and I'm naturally a blond."

"Oh, this is an easy one," Aurelia said.

"Of course you'd say so," Virgil scoffed. "You've only known him your whole life."

Logan chuckled. "That doesn't excuse you from guessing."

"I know," Virgil whined. "I'm going to go with your middle name is Wilber."

"What? Do I look like my middle name is Wilber? That was clearly just a decoy."

"Or it was too embarrassing not to be true."

"But if that's the case, why would I share that information?"

Virgil groaned. "Fair point. So, you're really a blond then. I would never have guessed, but I can totally see it."

Aurelia burst into laughter while Logan simply covered his eyes. "My god," he said. "You're really bad at this."

"You're joking," Virgil said in disbelief. "You have a tattoo. You?"

"I do. Why does that surprise you?"

Virgil shrugged. "I don't know. You just seem so uptight."

"I am not uptight."

"You are, and now you have to show me."

Logan's brow raised. "And just how do you want me to show you I'm not uptight? Better yet why would I—"

"No," Virgil said, shaking his head. "I meant your tattoo. You have to show me your tattoo."

Logan's face began to blush. "I certainly do not."

"Yes, you do. If you tell someone you have a tattoo, you are obligated to then reveal said artistry. It's the law."

A blank expression washed over Logan's face. "I know for a fact that is not the law."

"Stop being a baby," Aurelia joined in. "What was the point in paying all that money if no one's ever going to see it?"

Logan looked at his sister. Her expression was stern and unwavering. "Fine," Logan said as he stopped, "but I'm only doing this once, so you better make sure you get a good look."

Logan pulled up his shirt, revealing the artwork that had been painstakingly inked into his flesh. A mural spanned across his back. There were two knights clad in regal armor surrounded by a sea of skulls. Although the tattoo was only in black ink and various shades of gray, the detail was impeccable. One knight faced left, looking as if he were leaping into the air to strike the very sun itself. The other knight faced right and was on one knee. She had her shield raised and her lance at the ready.

Logan pulled down his shirt. "All right, that's enough of that."

"I don't know why you're so shy," Virgil replied. "That right there gets the badass seal of approval. If I had ink like that, I'd never wear a shirt."

Aurelia giggled. "Wouldn't you get cold?"

"Nope," Virgil said as he enveloped himself in a warm orange glow. "I'm a walking space heater."

A scream echoed through the tunnel, causing the group to look ahead.

Virgil took to the air. "Come on," he said as he flew off. "Someone's in trouble."

"Wait!" Logan shouted, but there was no stopping Virgil.

CHAPTER
SIXTEEN

Virgil stood in a room, paved with smooth stones. It was illuminated by several torches, and four paths stood before him. Each was marked with runes and had arched frames. Virgil closed his eyes and focused his mind.

"I'll just assume you didn't hear me back there," Logan said, as he and Aurelia approached him, riding on a wave of water.

Virgil opened his eyes and headed down the path to the far right. "This way," he said.

Aurelia and Logan followed suit.

"Have you considered this is a trap set by the Alliance?" Logan asked.

"It's not," Virgil said, his voice stern and certain. "Someone I know is in trouble up ahead. She doesn't have much time."

"All right, then. Be ready, you two."

Virgil smirked. "You're not gonna lecture me again?"

"This is different. Someone's actually in trouble this time."

"Well, color me shocked."

"Don't worry. There's still plenty of time for you to fuck something up."

A closed set of stone doors fast approached. With a wave of her hand, Aurelia sent Logan ahead. He summoned his gloves and punched the doors, bursting them open. The group entered the room to find a mass of vegetation. Mushrooms as tall as trees were everywhere, and vines hung down from the ceiling. Swarms of bees the size of boulders hovered in the air, each of them bigger than Logan. The hum of their wings echoed in the air like chainsaws. They had two heads, each equipped with rows of razor-sharp fangs.

"Olivia!" Virgil shouted.

"Oh, hey, Virgil," she replied as she turned around, her words slurred. "Fancy meeting you . . ." She fell to the ground, and the bees closed in on her.

Aurelia raised her hand toward Olivia and a wave of water formed around Olivia's body. The wave picked her up and pulled her out of the fray. Virgil clenched his fists, unleashing an inferno upon the creatures. Those that weren't burned to crisps were ripped apart by Logan, leaving pools of entrails on the floor.

When the last bee was no more, Virgil turned his attention to Olivia. Her face was pale, and a veil of sweat hung over her brow. She squirmed on the ground, grunting in pain. He looked down at the hole in her uniform. Her stomach was exposed, revealing an oozing gash. Blood pooled onto the floor, and the wound glowed purple. Aurelia was on her knees, hard at work treating Olivia's injuries.

Virgil bit the inside of his lip. "How is she?" he asked, as if he didn't already know how dire the circumstances were.

"It's not good," Aurelia answered. "She's been poisoned. I can treat her wound and keep her fever in check, but that's about it."

"We can suck the poison out," Logan suggested. "Try to keep it from spreading further."

"No," Virgil began, his voice beginning to crack. "Those were neuro bees. Their poison can be absorbed into the body regardless of the contact surface. We'd only be poisoning ourselves if we tried."

"How long does she have?"

"Keeping her fever down will buy some extra time, but the fever won't matter once her organs start to fail."

Olivia opened her eyes and met Virgil's gaze. "Virgil," she said faintly. He knelt beside her, the familiarity of the moment plaguing his mind. She reached for his hand, and he took it. "Go. Go on," she stuttered. "You don't have to stay, and watch me die."

A dull ache in the pit of his stomach prompted him to hold her hand tighter. "You're not going to die," he said, trying his best to reassure her, but the feeling of déjà vu was haunting.

Olivia tried to laugh, but it turned into a cough. "You're lying." Blood dripped down the side of her mouth.

Virgil reached down and wiped away the blood. He forced a smile as he cradled Olivia's cheek in his hand. She was burning up, causing Virgil's stomach to knot up that much more.

"I hate to say it," Logan said. "But she's right. If we can't stop the poison—"

"What if I freeze her?" Aurelia suggested.

"First off, that's crazy, and second, your ice sorcery is shaky. Remember?"

"Yes, but I'm sure I can encase her at least halfway." Aurelia looked to Virgil. "Will that buy us enough time to figure something out?"

"Maybe," Virgil replied, keeping his eyes on Olivia. "It'll certainly buy us more time, but it's impossible to tell how much. Olivia's aura is nearly gone already."

Aurelia held both of her hands over Olivia's body. "It's better than nothing."

"Don't I have a say in this?" Olivia asked between heavy breaths. "All you're doing is wasting your mana. Nothing is going to keep me from dying now."

Flashes of his father played in his mind. He looked down at the wound once more. The flesh around it was becoming discolored, and radiated a foul odor.

"You're not going to die," Virgil repeated, his voice emboldened. He placed his hand over Olivia's stomach.

"Just what are you planning to do?" Logan asked.

"I'm going to burn the poison out of her."

"And that's even crazier than her plan. Do you know how precise you're going to have to be to pull that off without causing significant damage in the process?"

Virgil ground his teeth. "I know that, but if I could just get rid of the poison, Aurelia can handle the rest."

For a brief moment the group remained silent, before Aurelia backed up. "He can do it," she said.

Logan turned to Olivia. "And you're okay with this? I can't imagine how painful it's going to be, not to mention, if he slips up, that's it."

"I'm gonna die anyway, right?" Olivia replied.

"Fair enough," Logan said, taking a step back.

Virgil took a deep breath and tried to steady his nerves. "All right. Everybody, please keep quiet for a moment."

Virgil emptied his mind of everything except Olivia. Her body. The blood flowing through her veins. The poison. Flames swarmed around his hand as he held his palm over her stomach. Slowly he closed his hand, and a faint orange glow radiated from Olivia's wound.

Focus, he thought. *Only burn the poison. Just the poison.*

Sweat formed upon Virgil's forehead and trickled down his face. His body was tense and heavy as if his bones were made of steel. Still, he kept his mind focused on the task at hand.

You can do this. You have to do this!

Virgil trembled. His skin grew hotter, and smoke trailed from his body. Logan opened his mouth to speak, but a quick glance from Aurelia halted the words in his throat. The orange glow grew in intensity, so much so, it looked as if an oven burner had been stuck in the elf's flesh. Olivia squirmed, crying out as her face contorted in agony. Despite this, Virgil pressed on, pushing her voice out of his mind. After about a minute, he released his fist and fell backward. His breath was labored, and his clothes were drenched in sweat.

"You did it," Olivia said between breaths.

Virgil wiped the sweat from his forehead. "Try not to speak. Aurelia will make sure you're all right physically, but it will take a while to shake off the effects of the poison."

His words were useless. In that brief moment, Olivia slipped out of consciousness.

Aurelia looked to Virgil and smiled. "I knew you could do it."

Virgil rubbed his neck, his cheeks flushed. "We're not out of the woods yet," he said. "She'll need to wake up by tomorrow."

"What do you mean?" Aurelia asked, bewildered.

"You remember the rules, right? You need to be both alive and conscious when your timer's up. I'm assuming Olivia's not grouped up with anyone considering she's here by herself."

"That might not be the case," Logan joined in. "She may have been scouting ahead for her group. Or perhaps in helping Olivia, we inadvertently added her to ours. Whatever the case, though, I think we're all in agreement we should stay put and guard her until she wakes up."

Virgil nodded as he looked at Olivia. "I-I'm sorry, you guys," he stuttered.

"What?" Aurelia said. "Why are you apologizing?"

"You two shouldn't be here. I've made the exam so much harder for you. I knew I should have just done this alone."

Aurelia walked over to Virgil and extended her hand. "None of this is your fault."

"Yeah," Logan added. "Had you have not rushed in, I would have."

Aurelia looked back at her brother. "I would have definitely gone in first."

"If you say so. In any case, this is what it means to be a Crusader. Right?"

Virgil looked up at the two siblings. While the physical features shared between them were few and far between, they had one thing blatantly in common. Both of them bore a smile, bright enough to light the darkest night.

"Yeah," Virgil said. "That's what it means."

SEVENTEEN

Aurelia and Logan scouted the area, gathering whatever resources they could find. Meanwhile, Virgil took another chunk of bee flesh. He removed the poisonous gland and roasted the meat. It wouldn't be the tastiest meal, but it would provide nourishment nonetheless. Against Virgil's protests, Logan arranged wood for a fire, and Aurelia strung together leaves into makeshift beds.

Their work done, the four of them rested around a roaring fire. Virgil remained awake, keeping watch over the group, while the other three were out like broken lights. The room was quiet. The only sounds to be heard came from the cracks of wood in the campfire, and the almost melodic drum of Logan's snoring. Virgil looked at his watch. It had been nearly fourteen hours since entering the Network.

Virgil returned his gaze to the fire and twirled the Fang of Kayveon between his fingers. "I've come really far, Dad. I don't know how much farther I have left, but I hope I'm making you proud." A frown washed over his face. "Who am I kidding? I'm sure you hate me for being here." Virgil hunched over, tucking his knees into his chest. "I'm such a disappointment."

Aurelia rustled. She turned again and again until finally, she lay flat on her back. "These rocks are going to be the death of me," she groaned.

"At least it's only for a couple of nights, right?"

"I suppose that's the silver lining. Still, a woman needs adequate beauty sleep."

Virgil smiled as he sat back, stretching his legs out.

Aurelia sat up, turning to face Virgil. "What?" she asked.

"I didn't say anything."

"Obviously. What were you smiling for?"

Virgil tilted his head. "Are you telling me I can't smile?"

"That depends on why you were smiling," she replied, her eyes narrowing.

"It was nothing. Really."

"It was enough to smile."

"All right, fine," Virgil sighed. "I just thought it was funny is all. You don't really strike me as the kind of woman who cares about beauty sleep."

"Oh, really," Aurelia said, her tone raising. "Am I not dainty enough for you, Virgil? Too man-ish for your tastes?"

Virgil's cheeks turned red. "That, that's not what I meant."

Aurelia giggled. "Relax, Virgil. I'm just yanking your chain."

Virgil exhaled in relief. "Right. You got me."

"Of course I did. You make it too easy. You have to learn to lighten up."

Virgil looked over to Olivia, checking once again to make sure she was still breathing. "Yeah. That's still a work in progress."

Aurelia followed Virgil's gaze over to Olivia. "She's cute. Where'd you meet her?"

"Here on the island. Back at the docks. Wait. Did you say she's cute?"

"Yeah. What? You disagree?"

"N-No," Virgil stuttered, his face growing redder still. "I mean, she's attractive. Yeah. Attractive."

"Am I making you uncomfortable?" Aurelia laughed. "That's adorable."

"I'm not uncomfortable," Virgil said sharply as he turned his attention back to the campfire.

"Right," Aurelia said. "Well, I wish you well in your romantic endeavors. Can't say I'd be looking for love in a place like this, but then again, you never really have control over these sorts of things."

Virgil chuckled. "Trust me. Love is the furthest thing from my mind."

"Please," Aurelia said with a roll of her eyes. "I saw the way you were looking at her when she was going to die. The way she was looking at you. You two looked like you were ripped straight out of a movie."

"You've got it all wrong. Nothing is going on between us." Aurelia remained silent, staring at Virgil with a blank, unconvinced expression. "Well," he continued. "We did almost kiss the other night. But not really. I don't think she meant it. Yeah. She wasn't serious."

"Let me ask you this. Did she look you in the eyes?"

Virgil nodded. "Right before she leaned in, whispered in my ear, and walked away."

Aurelia grinned. "Oh yeah. She wants you. That's flirting 101."

"Really? How do you know?"

Aurelia waved her hand. "Some women just know these things. Trust me."

The thought of someone actually wanting him made Virgil's chest feel full, and he couldn't help but smile. It was something he hadn't felt before, and he welcomed it. However, the feeling was fleeting, as thoughts of Olivia lying on the ground, dying, flooded his mind. The look on her face. It was just like his father's.

"You okay?" Aurelia asked.

"You're wrong," Virgil replied, snapping to his senses. "I wasn't looking at her like that. She reminded me of somebody. I don't know. Seeing Olivia like that. I couldn't just let her die."

"Oh," Aurelia replied, shock washed over her face. "Was it your father?" Virgil nodded, the words too painful to let escape from his lips. "I'm so sorry to hear that," she continued. "It's agonizing to relive such traumatic experiences."

Virgil shrugged as he bit the inside of his lip. "I'm okay. You get used to it."

Aurelia looked Virgil in his eyes. Her gaze was soft but firm. "No, you don't. Sure, it gets easier over time. Eventually, you think about it less and less, until one day, it doesn't cross your mind at all. Then a week goes by. Or a month. Maybe even two. But sooner or later, something happens, and in an instant, you're right back there all over again. And somehow, it's like you never even left."

Virgil swallowed the lump in his throat. Truer words had never rung so clearly in his ears. He had nothing to say. Nothing he could contribute. In one fell swoop, Aurelia had encapsulated his life for the past several years. It was haunting having someone so new to him seem to know him so intimately, and yet, hearing those words from her set his heart at ease.

Aurelia stood up and made her way around the fire. She sat down next to Virgil, their legs pressed to one another. She placed her arms around him. He didn't know which was warmer: his cheeks flushing red, or her embrace as she held him just tightly enough. Whichever it was, he didn't care. Comfort washed over him in a barreling wave. He wasn't in a dank and dreary cave anymore. He wasn't battling monsters or fighting for his life. He was there with her. His friend. His first friend.

Aurelia pulled back, meeting Virgil's gaze. "It's okay to go back to those dark places. Just make sure you don't stay there for too long. Okay?" Virgil smiled, his mind still unable to form a coherent response. Aurelia returned the smile, giving Virgil's shoulder a gentle nudge. "And if you ever need someone to haul your ass out of there, you can count on me to come through."

"Thank you," Virgil replied. "You don't know how much that means to me."

CHAPTER

EIGHTEEN

Virgil awoke in a peculiar mood. He couldn't have been asleep for more than a few hours, and yet, he felt renewed. He sat up, rejuvenated, as he wiped the sleep from his eyes.

"Look who's finally awake," Olivia said.

Virgil perked up at the sultry sound of the elf's voice, and his heartbeat quickened. "I could say the same thing about you," he said, yawning. "How are you feeling?"

"Much better, thanks to you."

"You don't have to thank me. I did owe you one, after all."

Olivia chuckled. "I don't think a pep talk equates to saving my life."

"Maybe not, but who said it has to?"

"I guess you have a point there."

Virgil looked around. They were alone, causing his stomach to do a series of small flips. "W-where's Aurelia and Logan?"

"They went on ahead to do some scouting. I volunteered to stay behind and watch over you. After everything you did yesterday, we didn't want to wake you."

Virgil stretched. "Well, I appreciate the gesture, but we should head out. I'm sure we can catch up if we hurry."

Olivia stood up and walked over to Virgil. "Or," she said as she sat down beside him, "We can stay here. Just the two of us. They'll be back soon enough."

Virgil's cheeks burned red, "I-I suppose we could do that too," he replied, his voice cracking a bit. He cleared his throat, and leaned back onto his palms. "It's probably a good idea for you to take it easy anyway."

"So, how much longer do you think we'll have to go?"

"In the exam? I don't know."

"We must be getting close. The applicants have been cut down quite a lot."

"I hope so. We're down to just seventy-five now."

"Geez," Olivia said, with a stunned expression. "Did you really count everyone?"

Virgil rubbed his neck. "Why is everyone so shocked by that?"

"Because not everyone walks around so defensively," Olivia said, laughing. "What have I told you about relaxing?"

"I know," Virgil replied. "Trust me. It's easier said than done."

"And why is that?"

Virgil leaned forward, placed his hands in his lap, and let out a heavy sigh. "It's just the way things are. I am a hunter, after all. Or was a hunter, I guess."

"There are lots of hunters here, myself included, and none of us are nearly as wound up as you. What's really the reason?"

Virgil looked over at Olivia. Even in the dimly lit cave, her eyes still shimmered, inviting him in like a burning fireplace on a cold winter's night. "Do you really want to know?"

"Of course. I wouldn't have asked if I didn't."

Virgil paused, letting his eyes fall upon the floor. "I've never really shared this with anyone."

Olivia placed her hand over Virgil's. Her skin was soft and warm to the touch. The hair on the back of Virgil's neck stood on end, and his heart pounded just a little bit faster than before. "That doesn't have to change," she said. "We can end the conversation right here if you want."

Virgil shook his head, returning his eyes to Olivia's. "No. I don't mind. This 'relaxing' stuff is just so new to me. I'm still getting used to it." Olivia remained silent, patiently awaiting Virgil's words. "Everywhere I go, everyone always talks about my father. Once people realize we're related, they always assume he was grooming me to be this fantastical sorcerer."

"That's a fair assumption. Right? I mean, if my parents were even half as powerful as your father, I wouldn't have needed to seek out a master to teach me."

"I know. I'm not saying anyone is wrong."

"Well, what are you saying, then?"

Virgil tensed up a bit as memories of his father coursed through his mind. "The truth is, everyone always has that envious look in their eyes. Like they'd do anything to be in my shoes—to be the son of the infamous demon slayer, Danté Truesdale." Virgil looked down at his trembling hands. "They don't know the pain I've had to endure. The training sessions that felt like they'd never end. Feeling like such a failure 'cause—"

"Failure?" Olivia said with a raised brow. "What do you mean? You're one of the most powerful pyromancers I've ever seen."

Virgil's eyes widened. He had nearly said too much. Olivia reached over and placed her hand over Virgil's once more. A chill ran down his spine, causing him to retreat into himself.

"Virgil," she said, soft-voiced.

"I-I'm sorry," Virgil said quickly, his stomach feeling as if it had been run through a blender. "I. I just. I feel like I'll never be as strong as my dad." Virgil forced out a chuckle as he rubbed the back of his neck. "I mean, he left pretty big shoes to fill." He continued laughing, as if in doing so he might actually believe the lie himself.

"Yeah," Olivia said slowly, "I can see what you mean. You shouldn't worry so much about that. You're still young. You have plenty of time to make it there." Olivia's gaze fell to the black fang dangling off of Virgil's neck. "Besides. You do have that backing you up. I'm sure it helps a lot."

Virgil looked down at the Fang of Kayveon and took it between his fingers. *Not as much as you'd think,* he thought.

"Ah, you're awake," Aurelia said as she and her brother walked back into the room.

Virgil smiled, relief washing over him as he rose to his feet. "I am. So, what's the situation?"

"We've made our way through a couple of corridors and found a door," Logan said. "Apart from that, there is nothing out of the ordinary. As Olivia is still with us, it appears that she is now deemed to be part of our group. While that does add an additional day to our wait requirement, we are perfectly capable of camping out the remainder of our time here."

"Should have known you would say that."

"And I assume you would like to press our luck a third time?"

Virgil shook his head. "Not at all. Sure, that door could be the exit to this place, and we do have strength in numbers; however, I agree with you. Olivia should be resting, so whatever path offers the least resistance is fine by me."

"That's very kind of you to think of my well-being," Olivia said. "But I'm more than capable of pulling my own weight."

"Perhaps we should put it to a vote then?" Aurelia suggested.

"Sounds fair," Olivia replied.

Logan groaned. "Sounds unnecessary. It's plain to see what the outcome will be."

"Oh, really," Olivia said. "And what would that be?"

Logan shrugged. "Three votes for camping out here. One vote to press onward."

"Are you sure about that?"

"I—"

The cave began to glow a bright yellow around its borders, and shook violently. The floor crumbled, and the group plummeted into an unyielding abyss. Rock and debris fell all around them. The only light to be found came from the ominous yellow glow.

Virgil steadied himself in the air and searched for his friends amidst the chaos. His eyes darted around like a fly trapped in a bottle. Blue light burst through the darkness, and a pool of water appeared. No. It was more like a lake, suspended in the air. The liquid swallowed everything within reach. Virgil looked around, quickly spotting Aurelia. Her hands glowed blue like beacons in the night. Virgil scanned for Olivia's aura, and while he couldn't lay eyes on her, he could feel her, and that was enough. But where was Logan? Virgil continued his search, only to find stone and rock everywhere he glanced.

He has to be here.

Virgil fixed his eyes on the last object suspended in the water. It was too far away to make out clearly. He propelled himself forward as best he could, fighting against the drag of water against his body. As he made it closer, his heart sank. It was just another piece of rubble.

Virgil turned to Aurelia. They locked gazes. He pointed downward, and her eyes grew wide. She released the water around Virgil, allowing him to plummet once again. He kept his arms close to his sides and channeled everything he had into his flight. The sharp wind pulled against his face as he searched through the falling debris. A light glowed at the bottom of the abyss, the ground fast approaching.

Come on! Where are you?

Finally, he saw Logan, unmoving among a group of rocks. Virgil rushed over to him, dancing around chunks of earth, took hold of Logan, and staggered.

"Why the fuck are you this heavy?" he said, wincing as Logan's weight pulled at his muscles.

Logan didn't respond. Although he was breathing, his eyes remained shut. Virgil took another look down. He was running out of time. He held onto Logan as best he could, and propelled himself upward. It wasn't a foreign endeavor to be flying with a passenger. However, Virgil struggled to keep both of them afloat.

A rock slammed into them with a thud, and Virgil lost his grip. He took in a deep breath, ignoring the pain billowing within him as he steadied himself in the air. Virgil focused on Logan once again and darted down. As he wrapped his arms around Logan, he pulled him in close and locked his fingers. This time, he made no effort to keep them floating and instead focused on dodging debris.

"Wait for it," Virgil said. "You have to time this just right."

The ground below was in full view, no longer just a light in the distance. In mere moments, the two men would be reduced to nothing but puddles of flesh, bone, and blood.

"Just a little bit longer. Three. Two. One. One and a half. NOW!"

Virgil poured his mana into his flight. They slowed down more and more, but it wasn't enough. They crashed and tumbled across the ground. When they finally stopped, Logan had Virgil's left arm pinned under him. Virgil couldn't help but scream as he squirmed under the immense weight. Boulders fell from the air shaking the ground around him as they hit the floor. Through pain filled grunts, Virgil gathered all the strength he could muster and pushed against Logan's body. It wasn't much, but he managed to maneuver Logan just enough to free his mangled arm. Virgil's eyes welled with tears as he turned over onto his stomach.

"You're not finished yet," Virgil said, grimacing as he forced himself off of the ground with his good arm.

He looked up at the cavalcade of rocks coming his way as his broken arm dangled in the air. Virgil planted his feet into the ground and raised his right hand. It ignited in blue flame, and a vortex of fire shot out above him. The fire extended outward, blooming out like a flower. The rocks burned away into nothing more than dust the instant they came in contact with the sapphire blaze. He kept his inferno roaring until the crashes of stone stopped, and all he could hear was his body's desperate gasps for air and the violent beating of his own heart.

Virgil fell onto his back, and whimpered as sharp pain echoed throughout his body. His arm throbbed as if it had its own heartbeat. Despite this, he lay on the ground, smiling, relishing the fact that he was still alive and a competitor in the exam. Two large orbs of water came into sight above Virgil. He opened his mouth to call out, but it was too painful.

"Are you two all right?" Aurelia asked as their feet touched the ground, and the water dispelled from around them. Again, Virgil attempted to speak, only to cough up blood the second his lips parted. Aurelia rushed over to Virgil's side, and he nudged his head as he tried to point at Logan. "I know my brother," Aurelia said. "He'll be all right. You, on the other hand, are several different kinds of fucked up."

"She's right," Olivia said as she joined them. "You're cute and all, but right now, you look like you've been run through a meat grinder."

Virgil smiled, overjoyed by the fact that his earlier awkwardness hadn't seemed to dissuade her. Of course, smiling was all he could manage to do. The more he tried to move, the more it felt as if his chest would rupture.

"Just keep still." Aurelia's hands glowed blue as she began to rub them across Virgil's body. "I have to keep you from choking on your own blood."

"I'll take a look around," Olivia said. "See what this room has to offer."

Virgil glanced over to watch Olivia leave. The room looked nothing like the cave that came before it. It was massive and adorned with marble floors and giant pillars. The ceiling had reformed leaving the boulders scattered around the only evidence of the previous quake. A multitude of doors was spread around the room, and everything was polished and pristine.

Aurelia's touch felt invigorating. As she worked, Virgil could feel his strength returning to him. With each passing minute, his breaths became more manageable, and his aching body relaxed just a little bit more.

"It's going to take some time to mend your broken bones," Aurelia said, "but I'll fix you up as good as new."

"Thank you," Virgil said as he looked up at Aurelia.

"You don't have to thank me."

"I do. This is twice now you've saved me."

"Friends don't keep track of these things."

"I suppose that's true."

"Besides," Aurelia said, frowning. "It's my fault you two are in this mess."

A wave of confusion washed over Virgil. "How do you figure that?"

"If I had caught my brother, you wouldn't have had to dive in after him." Tears began to well in the corners of her eyes. "You're both hurt because of me."

"You can't take the blame for this."

"Yes, I can."

"I won't let you."

"Why not? I could have—"

"Because, well, because friends don't keep track of these things. Are you trying to tell me we aren't friends?"

Aurelia's face began to fluster. "N-no. I just—"

"Then it's settled," Virgil said with a smile. "I'll stop counting all the times you bail me out, and you're not to blame for this. Honestly, you're getting the better end of the deal."

Aurelia returned Virgil's smile, the tears in her eyes subsiding.

"What happened?" Logan said, his words groggy as he sat up. "Did we get hit with an earthquake or something?"

"Sort of," Olivia said, making her way back over to the group. "I imagine that tremor was Clayton's doing."

Virgil rolled his eyes with irritation. "Of course it was."

"Is everyone okay?" Logan asked.

Aurelia chuckled. "It's funny you'd be the one asking that. You were knocked unconscious. Virgil had to fly in and rescue you. He pretty much broke himself to do it."

"He did?" Logan replied, shock written on his face as he looked at Virgil lying on the floor.

"I did," Virgil said smugly. "Speaking of which. Is your ass made of steel or something?"

Logan's face reddened. "Have, have you been checking out my ass?"

Aurelia and Olivia burst out into laughter. "What?" Virgil replied, "Of course not. Why would you think that?"

"You specifically mentioned my ass. Why would you say it like that?"

"W-why would you take it like that?"

"How else was I supposed to take it? You're talking about my ass."

"I obviously didn't mean it like that. And stop saying ass. You're making this weird."

"*I'm* making this weird?" Logan exclaimed. "You were talking about my ass!"

Virgil turned to the girls, who were still deep in laughter. "You two knew what I meant. Right?"

"I'm not touching this one," Aurelia said, fighting back the fit of giggles that consumed her.

"Yeah," Olivia joined in. "You two are on your own."

"I guess you could say they're 'ass out' then," Aurelia quipped.

"Look," Logan began. "I'm willing to forget this whole thing happened. Just promise me you won't be checking out my ass anymore and—"

"I haven't been checking out your ass!" Virgil shouted.

CHAPTER
NINETEEN

Olivia and Aurelia had yet to stop laughing. Virgil and Logan, on the other hand, were silent. Their faces were red, and they refused to make eye contact. A set of stone doors across the room slid open, revealing three figures, and Virgil's expression soured. Lucious, Paisley, and Fynn waltzed into the room with grins stretched across their faces.

"Well, what do we have here," Lucious said.

Olivia moved in front of Logan, forming a blockade. Aurelia continued her work, keeping her attention focused on Virgil. He tried to lift himself up and winced in pain.

"Be still," Aurelia demanded.

Virgil opened his mouth to speak, but his words were cut short by Logan. "Sit tight," he said as he walked towards Lucious and his crew. "I'll handle this."

Fynn cracked his knuckles as his eyes locked with Logan's. "Don't you worry about him. I'm the only one you need to be concerned with."

Logan stopped just a few feet short from their aggressors. "Listen up, and listen well. There is no need for us to fight, and to be perfectly honest, I'd rather not harm any of you. If you would be so kind, please walk away and leave us be."

"Not a chance," Fynn said with a smirk. "I've been itching to settle the score between us."

"Likewise," Paisley said, looking past Logan to Aurelia. "I've been dying to get my hands on her again."

Logan's expression twisted to one of bewilderment. "Are you referring to my sister?"

Paisley looked at Logan, the contempt clear in her eyes. "Is your sister that stuck up bitch over there who thinks she's better than me?"

Logan turned around to find Aurelia nervously tending to Virgil's injuries. He sighed as he returned his attention to Paisley. "What business do you have with Aurelia?" Logan asked, his eyes glaring.

"Are you deaf?" Paisley continued. "I said I need to get even with her. That bitch had the nerve to knock me right over. Like I was nothing."

"It was an accident," Aurelia said.

"Like hell it was!"

"If my sister said it was an accident, then it was an accident." Logan's tone was menacing as he looked down at the brunette. "Leave now, or I will break each and every one of you."

Lucious laughed, drawing in everyone's attention. "My word, you're so chilling." He then raised his hand, calling forth a swarm of ice shards. "Still. You're not nearly as cold as I can be."

Lucious fired off his icicles, his aim solely focused on Virgil. With a flick of her wrist, Olivia summoned pillars of wood shielding them.

Once again, Virgil tried to get up but was held down by Aurelia. "Let me up," he pleaded.

"Not a chance," she replied. "They can handle this."

"But I'm the one he wants."

"And?"

"What do you mean, 'and?'"

"I mean, what does it matter if he wants to fight you? You have a broken arm and several fractured ribs. There isn't a chance in hell I'm letting you get up and do anything."

Virgil fell silent, biting his lip as he turned his attention to the scuffle.

Paisley dashed for Aurelia, but Logan took hold of her arm. Without so much as blinking, he threw Paisley backward with tremendous force. It was a miracle he didn't rip her arm clean off. She clashed against a marble pillar, and gasped as the air was forced from her lungs. Slowly, Paisley got back up, her breathing heavy, but ready to fight nonetheless. Logan walked towards her, but a fiery dragon cut off his path.

"I told you," Fynn exclaimed. "I'm your only concern right now!"

Logan scoffed as he summoned his gloves. "You know, you're really starting to annoy me."

"Good," Fynn said. "I hope that means you'll give me a good fight then. You'll be happy to know I've done my homework. I won't be caught off guard by your dragon's treasure again."

Paisley moved in on Aurelia.

Virgil pointed. "Behind you!"

Aurelia nodded as she took her hands away from Virgil. She then touched the tips of her fingers together and closed her eyes. "Cerulean Effigy."

Aurelia's body became enveloped in a glowing blue liquid. The water swirled around her skin before springing off of her body. It began to morph into shape, and in a matter of seconds, it was the spitting image of Aurelia, down to the very dimples in her cheeks.

"You fucking coward," Paisley sneered.

She threw her hand forward, summoning a massive fist made of stone from the ground. The fist was blindingly fast, but the doppelganger was faster. Aurelia's clone held its palm to the fist, and a burst of water shot forward, shattering the rock into rubble. Paisley's eye twitched as she sent out fist after fist, only to have them crumble to pieces.

"We don't have to do this," the clone said. "We could—"

"SHUT UP! I don't want to hear your bullshit. Just shut up and fight me."

The floor under the clone's feet began to shake. Six stone spikes erupted from the ground, piercing the clone in various places. Two through the legs. One through the hand. Two through the chest. And one through the eye. The clone didn't so much as flinch as the stone skewers invaded its watery flesh.

"Do you really hate me that much?" the clone asked. Paisley exhaled in frustration, the gravity of her attack's ineffectiveness clearly weighing on her nerves. The clone raised its hand, and bursts of water shattered the spikes. "I'm sorry to have made you feel this way. I hope that you can find it in your heart to forgive me one day."

Paisley's eyes widened as she balled her fist. "This is exactly the shit I'm talking about. Don't you dare act so high and mighty. You're not better than me!"

"Why don't you be a dear and move aside?" Lucious said as he stared down Olivia.

"Why don't you go and fuck yourself!" Olivia replied as she raised her hands towards Lucious. "On second thought. I get the feeling you do enough of that already."

Lucious laughed. "My, my, I didn't know elves could be so feisty. We'll have to do something about that mouth of yours. After I finish up with Virgil—"

Two bulky hands made of wood erupted from out of the ground at Lucious's feet and took hold of him. A wooden creature like a hulking ogre rose up. Its eyes glowed green, and white flowers sprouted from its wooden flesh. The beast slammed Lucious into the ground, pinning him to the stone floor.

"The only way you're getting to Virgil is if you go through me, and trust me, you're better off—"

An icicle formed above Lucious and pierced the creature's skull. "I know," Lucious began as the creature faded from existence, and he rose to his feet, "I'm better off fucking myself."

"Well, I was gonna say taking your flunkies and leaving, but that's your call."

"You know it's unfortunate," Lucious said, dusting off his shoulder. "Being underground with so many support pillars around, there's no way I could use my signature sorcery here."

"That so," Olivia sneered. "Afraid you can't win without it?"

"Oh no," Lucious replied, a devilish grin painted on his face. "This just means your defeat will not come swiftly."

The battle raged on with everyone giving it their all. That is, everyone except for Virgil. He instead lay on the ground, forced to merely watch as his friends fought for their lives. Every so often, he'd squirm about, desperate to throw himself into the fray.

"If you don't stop moving, I'm going to chain you to the ground," Aurelia scolded.

"I'm sorry," Virgil replied, his eyes restless, "but it's tough to just lie here while everyone is fighting around me."

"Trust me. It's not nearly as difficult as holding her back and healing you at the same time. I'm trying to work as fast as I can, but it's going to be even more of a pain if I gotta restrain you too."

"R-right. I promise I won't move again."

"Good."

Virgil's eyes widened, and he quickly raised his hand in the air.

"Damn it, Virgil!"

A mass of fire formed around Virgil and Aurelia, blanketing them in flames. Chunks of stone rained down upon them like a rockslide, but as they hit the fiery blaze, they dispersed into nothingness. "I'm sorry," Virgil grimaced. "But—"

"I know. Just, just don't move again."

That's when he noticed the strained look on Aurelia's face. He returned his attention to the fighters, unable to bear her tired expression. Aurelia's clone was holding its own, but its form had become sloppy. It was less detailed than before. Its movements slowed, and its reflexes were dulled. Logan was on the defensive, continually weaving between pillars, seeking cover from the fire Fynn rained down upon him. Olivia, on the other hand, had Lucious at a stalemate. A horde of wooden soldiers surrounded him, rushing him down one after another. Despite the onslaught, he kept the ice flowing, shredding Olivia's minions like paper in a blender.

The room began to glow a bright red, just as the room before it had shone yellow. Mounds of fire shot out from the ground and into the air. There were far too many of them to even bother counting. In a matter of seconds, the room felt as if it were suspended in a bubbling volcano. Even Virgil found the steadily rising temperature unbearable. He winced in pain as he tried to sit up, clutching at his ribs.

"Stay down," Aurelia said, her breaths heavy.

Virgil grunted as he forced himself up. "There's no time for that." The heat burned his throat. "Listen up," he shouted as well as his simmering vocal cords could manage. "Aiden's going to cook us alive if we don't do something about it."

Lucious fired a shot of ice at Virgil. It hadn't even made it halfway before Virgil melted it away.

"Really," Virgil said.

Lucious raised his hand, prepping another attack. "Don't think for a second our circumstances have changed."

Fynn approached his comrade. "Virgil's right, Lucious. You know I'd love to keep the battle going, but we don't stand a chance in this heat, and that goes double for Paisley. She doesn't have any resistance to pyromancy like we do."

Lucious looked at Paisley. Her hair was frizzled, and she struggled to keep her eyes open. He looked back over to Virgil, his brow furrowed. "Fine," he said. "We'll settle this another time then."

The pillars of fire began to move, gathering into a circle. They piled onto one another and grew into a cluster of flames. One after another, the pillars assimilated into the cluster until finally, they combined into one massive blaze. The fire took on a new shape. Four arms sprouted from the base, followed by two legs and a horned head. A long serpentine tail whipped through the air as the creature let out a ferocious roar.

Fynn's eyes glistened. "Now that's a beast."

"Oh, shut up," Lucious sneered.

"Are we going to have to fight that thing?" Paisley asked.

"It looks like it," Aurelia joined in.

"I wasn't talking to you."

Logan stepped forward. "I'll handle this," he said, flexing his fingers. "If I can manage to get ahold of it, I can nullify it."

"You really think O'Drakka's Fists will work?" Fynn asked. "My dragons are one thing, but this creature was conjured by a deity."

"Deity or no, it was born of magic."

Lucious waved his hand, and an avalanche of water fell upon the creature. The fiery behemoth shrieked in pain, and it quickly turned its attention to Lucious.

"Didn't you hear me?" Logan said.

Lucious kept his focus on the beast. "I may have held off on exterminating you lowly hunters, but don't think that changes your status. I'd rather die than take orders from one of you, so just run away and leave this to the professionals." He sprang into action, launching a full assault on the creature.

Fynn turned to Paisley. "Try to find us a way out of here."

"I'm not going anywhere," Paisley said, her words barely escaping her lips. "I can—"

"If you stay here, you're going to die," Virgil said. "I can feel your aura. You really don't have much time left."

"Come on," Olivia said. "We can look for an exit."

Paisley clenched her jaw before huffing and leaving with Olivia.

"You might as well join them," Logan said as he began walking towards the battle. "Your assistance is not needed here."

"Don't be foolish," Aurelia said. "We can help you close the gap."

"If you don't want to help them, then get back to healing. Whatever you do, just keep out of my way."

Virgil and Aurelia stood still, taken aback as Logan entered the battle.

"What should we do?" Aurelia asked.

Virgil paused for a moment. Aurelia had done much to restore him, but his chest still throbbed with a dull ache, and his left arm remained limp.

"There's no way in hell I'm sitting this out," Virgil said. "Logan's just going to have to deal with that."

Aurelia nodded. "I was thinking the same thing. So, what's the plan?"

Virgil raised his hand to the creature and steadied himself. "You already said it."

His aura began to swirl as he summoned a mass of fire around the flaming beast. As the flames merged with one another, it was nearly impossible to distinguish Virgil's flames from the creature itself. In fact, the fire only seemed to be adding to the creature's body.

Lucious whipped around towards Virgil. "Are you daft?" he exclaimed.

Virgil continued pumping out his fire, paying no mind to Lucious.

"Virgil!" Logan called out. "What part of 'keep out of my way' didn't you understand?"

Virgil remained focused. The beast hulked around, thrilled to be invigorated with such a tribute.

Logan approached Virgil, his fists clenched. "Stop this at once before—"

"Just be ready for your opening," Aurelia said.

The beast prepared its massive fist to strike, raising it high in the air above Lucious. He threw another wave of water at the creature, but it didn't so much as flinch as it punched. Virgil closed his fist, and the beast stopped. Another second later, and Lucious would have been nothing more than a pile of ash and bone. *Perhaps I shouldn't have stopped it,* Virgil thought. The creature paused, trembling in place. All eyes fell to Virgil as he stood quivering. His knees were buckling, and his hand was shaking as sweat dripped from his brow.

Lucious was pale, his eyes misty with disbelief. Logan was as well. As a matter of fact, the only one not floored by Virgil's display was Aurelia. Instead, she smiled as if she had already known what the outcome would be before the die was ever cast.

Virgil tightened his fist further, and slowly the beast retracted into itself. It fought hard against Virgil's will, bucking back and forth. Virgil kept up the pressure. Falling to one knee, he kept his fire roaring, trapping the beast. Aurelia knelt behind him, propping him up to keep him from collapsing. Before long, the creature was confined to a sphere of fire suspended in the air.

Virgil's breath was shallow, and his arm wavered in the air. His body begged him to release his hold on the beast. He took in a deep, pain-filled breath. He hoped the air, even if scorching, would help him keep his composure, but his grip was still slipping and his eyesight fading.

"What are you waiting for?" Aurelia shouted.

Logan turned his attention to the fiery sphere of death, snapping back into the battle at hand. In one fell swoop, he leaped into the air, his fist aimed at its center. As his glove pierced the sphere, sparks rained down to the floor. The jewels on his gloves glowed bright, and just like that, the beast was gone, leaving the room eerily silent. Logan returned to the ground, recalled his gloves, and made his way over to Aurelia and Virgil.

They were a mess, although Virgil was much worse off. Aurelia held him up, wrapping her arms around his chest as he gasped for air. He was nearly limp, his face was covered in sweat, and he struggled to keep his eyes open.

Logan stopped just short of Aurelia and Virgil. "Is he dead?"

"I'm still kicking," Virgil said softly.

A shard of ice whizzed by Logan. As it plunged itself deep into Virgil's broken arm, he flinched in pain and sucked in a breath. Slowly, he looked up and opened his eyes to see Lucious approaching them.

CHAPTER

TWENTY

Virgil held out his hand towards the shard sticking out of his arm. He tried to summon a fire strong enough to melt the ice but failed.

"What the fuck is your problem?" Aurelia shouted as she pulled the shard from Virgil's arm. The ice sliced her hand. She hissed, blood trickling down her fingertips as she tossed the icicle on the floor.

"I held up my end of the bargain," Lucious said. "The conjuration is gone, and now we're going to pick up where we left off."

Paisley joined her boyfriend. "You can leave," she said, pointing to Olivia. "But we're going to finish what we started with these three."

Logan summoned his gloves once again and stood firmly to block their assailants. His eyes traveled across each of them, waiting for someone to make the first move.

Fynn stepped forward, turning to his friends. "Just hold on a second. None of us are exactly in fighting condition. This really wouldn't be a satisfying victory."

"You imbecile," Lucious scolded. "I don't care about something so trivial. All I want is to make him regret ever stepping foot on this island."

"He can't even defend himself, Lucious."

"Again, I don't care. As long as he's still awake, he'll receive no mercy from me. Now move out of my way, before I lose my temper."

Fynn fell silent.

"You heard him," Paisley joined in. "Or are you just too slow to get it?"

"That's always a possibility. Fynn is a dumbass after all. Perhaps we should just—"

"I told you to stop talking to me like me that!" Fynn interrupted, a vein nearly bursting from his forehead.

Lucious laughed. "Exactly my point. I was talking about you, not to you."

Fynn tensed up as he stared at Lucious, his fists tightly wound into balls.

"Stop looking at me like that," Lucious demanded. "Have you forgotten my family practically owns yours? With one phone call, I could have your father ruined."

Fynn's eyes widened as he unclenched his fists. "You wouldn't."

"I think we both know I would. That's the problem with new money. There are no roots. No stability. It would be a shame too. Your father showed such promise. And to think it would all go to shit because one idiot doesn't know when to just shut his mouth and move two steps to the left."

Virgil struggled to stand. Aurelia tried to protest, but Virgil waved her off and continued to pull himself up. "You know," Virgil said between breaths, "every time I think, well damn, there's just no way this guy could be any more of an enormous cunt, you somehow manage to prove me wrong."

"Virgil," Fynn said as he turned around.

Virgil could barely breathe. Everything hurt, from the slightest hair on his head to the skin between his toes. It took everything he had just to rise to his feet, but he stood as tall as he could. His knees wobbled, and it felt as if they would give out at any moment. Even so, he kept his eyes fixed on Lucious.

"That's what I like to see," Lucious said, flashing a devilish grin. "This tough guy act is going to make crushing you so much more satisfying."

The room began to glow red once again. Just as before, pillars of fire began to shoot from the floor.

"Are you fucking serious?" Lucious said as he jumped backward to avoid a pillar.

Virgil collapsed, Aurelia just barely managing to break his fall. "We can't fight another one of those things," she said.

"We won't have to," Olivia replied. "I'm pretty sure we found the exit over there." She pointed to a stone wall off in the distance. Lucious, Paisley, and Fynn were already making their way over.

"Okay." Logan walked over to pick up Virgil. "Let's get a move on before—"

The room shook as its borders pulsed, alternating between shades of red and yellow. Stone pillars shot out of the ground and began combining with the fire. Before long, there were dozens of humanoid creatures spread around the room.

"This doesn't look good," Aurelia said.

"How are you two doing on mana?" Logan asked.

"We'll manage," the women said simultaneously.

Virgil perked up as best he could. "I can—"

Logan hoisted Virgil up over his shoulder. "You'll do nothing but keep yourself alive." He then turned and looked at his sister. "When we make it out of here, we're going to have a serious conversation about what's been going on here."

The creatures made their move, closing in on the group. Olivia summoned a mass of wooden soldiers to battle the horde. As Logan moved, he pushed the monsters out of his way. With one touch of his glove, they crumbled. Aurelia summoned waves of water that carried the monsters away. She kept them coming one after another, but it was only delaying their assault.

Across the sea of molten monsters, the group could see Paisley fiddling with the wall. As the stone slabs shifted apart, a bright light shone through the cracks. Explosions echoed through the room as Fynn held the creatures back. The final slab lifted, revealing a white void. Lucious wasted no time stepping through it, and Paisley followed suit. Fynn continued backing up, covering their escape. He turned around to find a wall had been conjured, cutting off the escape route.

A creature took hold of Fynn's head. Muffled screams escaped his lips as the creature slammed his face into the wall. The beast tossed him onto the floor, blood gushing from his mouth, and the monsters began to crowd around him. Aurelia raised her hand towards Fynn.

"What are you doing?" Olivia exclaimed. "We have our own problems to worry about."

"He's going to die if we don't do something," she replied.

"Again. That's not our problem."

"I'm making it our problem." Aurelia summoned a wave of water to sweep away the creatures surrounding Fynn, but a giant explosion erupted from the pile. Chunks of rock flew everywhere as smoke filled the air. Embers formed in the sky above Fynn, each of them morphing into a tiny dragon. They looked to be no bigger than a sparrow, but they were countless in number. As the dust settled, Fynn stood tall, his feet firmly planted into the ground.

"BRING IT ON!" Fynn shouted, his nose crooked and blood spraying from his lips.

With a snap of his fingers, the dragons descended onto the battlefield. One after another, the dragons collided with the creatures and explosions echoed throughout the room. The walls began to tremble. The group made their way through the carnage, bobbing and weaving past fire and stone flying in every direction. Fynn remained focused on his task. Even as they passed him, he continued his onslaught, unleashing his fury on the lifeless creatures.

"I swear," Logan said as they approached the wall. "All of you pyromancers are so short-sighted."

"I resent that," Virgil murmured.

"Okay," Olivia said. "Do any of you know geomancy?"

Logan placed his hand on the wall. In an instant, it crumbled, revealing the void.

"Right," Olivia said. "Magic gloves."

Logan turned around and called out to Fynn. It was impossible to tell if he couldn't hear Logan over the explosions, or if he simply didn't care to listen. Either way, he didn't so much as budge in Logan's direction.

"Just leave him," Olivia said. "If we don't make a run for it now, this entire room is going to collapse on us."

"Logan, we can't—"

Logan exhaled as he took Virgil off his shoulders. "I know, Aurelia. Just make sure he gets to safety, and I'll see you on the other side."

"No." Virgil returned to his feet. "We're not leaving without you." He tried to take a step, but his knees buckled, and he fell into Aurelia's arms.

"You've done plenty," Aurelia said as she and Olivia propped Virgil upon their shoulders. "You just focus on getting some rest."

Virgil opened his mouth to protest but stopped when Logan held out his hand in front of Virgil's face. With a flick of his finger, Logan thumped Virgil's forehead, and he was knocked out cold.

CHAPTER

TWENTY-ONE

Virgil's mind stirred. An all too familiar sensation danced across his chest. "Aurelia," he said softly.

"Try again," a woman laughed.

Virgil's eyes burst open to find Cordellia towering over him, her glowing blue hands caressing his body.

"Cor-Cordellia," Virgil stuttered.

"Yes?"

Virgil looked down. Only a white sheet separated his bits from the open air. "I'm naked," he said, his face burning red. "Why am I naked?"

"You're not naked," Cordellia replied, her tone quite aloof. "You have a sheet."

"I don't know about you, but that's still naked where I come from."

Cordellia laughed. "You were absolutely filthy. If I was going to heal you properly, something had to be done."

"Surely it couldn't have been that bad."

"It was. Now try to relax. After all, you have nothing to be embarrassed about."

Virgil covered his privates with his hands. "What, what is that supposed to mean?"

"Sorry," Cordellia replied, laughing once again. "Bad choice of words. Although."

Virgil fell silent, completely mortified. He felt as hot as an oven, and was getting hotter with each passing second. *Why couldn't I just stay knocked out?* he thought.

Cordellia reached over and placed a hand on Virgil's shoulder. "Don't get so wound up," she said, flashing a smile. "I'm only joking, but I do need you to be more still." Virgil laid back, trying his best to ignore the gnawing feeling of being exposed. "Clayton and Aiden went a little overboard this year." She sighed. "I suspect you're to blame for that."

"Me?" Virgil said, taken aback. "Why would I have anything to do with that?"

"Isn't it obvious? You've sparked their interest."

"I suppose Clayton makes sense. I can feel his contempt for me from across the room, but Aiden, I've never even spoken to him."

"I get why you feel that way, but Clayton doesn't hate you. In fact, I wager he respects you a great deal. Aiden, on the other hand, can't stand you at the moment."

Bewilderment had yet to leave Virgil's face. "I don't understand. What did I do to him to make him so upset with me?"

"You bested him in the exam. Caused quite an uproar in doing so actually."

"That doesn't make any sense. Sure, I held Aiden's conjuration back for a few seconds, but I'd hardly consider that besting him. If anything, he should be pissed at Logan."

"Don't sell yourself short. Logan would never have been able to land a hit without your help. You, if only for a brief moment, were able to hold back Aiden's fire with your sorcery and willpower alone. Of course, if Aiden had been using his full strength, I doubt you would have been able to pull off such a feat. Still. The fact remains that you were able to do something that few applicants have ever accomplished."

"Is Aiden really that petty? I thought the entire purpose of the exam is to recruit the strongest candidates possible. Surely, he must know that this is bound to happen eventually. More than once, even."

Cordellia burst into laughter. "You sure don't hold your tongue, do you? It's almost as if you're not talking to a king about her ally of equal stature while we're judging your every move."

Virgil swallowed the lump in his throat. "F-forgive me. I'll choose my words more carefully."

"You needn't be so nervous around me," Cordellia said with a smile. "Just a word of caution for the others. I'm sure you've learned already to mind your manners around Clayton, but Roxanne can be a bit of a wild card. It's best to err on the side of caution with her. And Aiden, well, I'd just steer clear of him for now if I were you. That should be easy enough. He's awful busy these days. I fear if you were to meet before he's had a chance to forget about things, you would certainly come to blows."

"Thank you," Virgil said. "I'll be sure to keep that in mind." Virgil paused for a moment as the gravity of her words set in. "Cordellia, can I ask you something?"

"You want to know why I am helping you," she replied. "You're wondering why I didn't have Aurelia heal you, or one of my staff. And of course, I have no obligation to give you any advice."

"Y-yeah. How did you know that?"

"I was born with the talent of clairvoyance. Depending on the circumstances, I can see probable outcomes up to twenty-four hours into the future. But you're incredibly easy to read. Like an open book."

"Oh. I suppose that makes sense. I'm sure all you kings were born with talents."

Cordellia shook her head. "Not all of us. It's quite a rarity to be born with such a gift. To answer your question, though, the answer is simple. I like you, Virgil. Quite a lot, actually."

Virgil's face flustered. "You do?"

Cordellia burst into laughter, stopping her work entirely. "Not like that. Don't get me wrong, you are easy on the eyes, but I'm already spoken for. What I meant was I like what you are for the Alliance. I think you're a much-needed breath of fresh air."

Virgil grinned. "It's good to hear at least one of the kings favor me."

"Don't let that go to your head. The exam isn't over yet." Three evenly paced knocks rang on the door. "Right on time," Cordellia said. "You may enter."

"Pardon my intrusion," Aurelia said as she entered the room. "But . . ." Aurelia's brow raised. "Is he naked?"

"He has a sheet." Cordellia replied as she turned to face Aurelia. "Although, I've been told that doesn't count."

"A-Aurelia," Virgil stammered as he squirmed on the table, making sure the sheet was still covering him. His cheeks were flushed red once again. "What, what are you doing here?"

Aurelia closed the door behind her and began walking towards Virgil and Cordellia. "I'm here to check on you, of course. Oh, and I brought you a change of clothes, too." She set the clothes on the side table. "I figured you'd need something new since your uniform didn't exactly make it out of the Network in one piece."

"As much as I'd love to stay and continue this," Cordellia said, "I have some urgent matters to attend to." She turned to Aurelia. "I'm entrusting you to finish Virgil's care. I've already done the bulk of the work, so it shouldn't be much longer."

"Yes, ma'am," Aurelia replied. "You can count on me."

"Before I go, though, I want to show you something."

"What is it?"

"A spell, of course. I did ask you to finish healing Virgil, didn't I?"

Aurelia's eyes lit up. "You're really going to teach me a new spell? Like seriously?"

"I am. To be honest, I'm a little shocked someone with your skill in aquamancy hasn't learned it yet, but of course, stranger things have happened. The spell is called Saint's Breath. It's essentially a more powerful version of the Healing Touch spell, but with a purification effect as well. Very useful for counteracting curses, hexes, and even some forms of lost magic."

"How's it done?" Aurelia asked.

"It's quite similar to the Healing Touch actually. First, you'll want to focus your mana into your chest. Take a deep breath, allowing positive and tranquil thoughts to fill your mind and exhale. Allow me to demonstrate."

Cordellia took in a deep breath and her chest swelled with air. She then closed her eyes as she leaned in over Virgil. She exhaled, and a blue mist coated Virgil's body.

"As you can see, a proper casting of the Saint's Breath is not only more potent than the Healing Touch, but covers the target entirely, allowing for much faster healing."

Cordellia was right. The soothing mist caressed Virgil's body like a plush blanket. His body tingled, but the feeling was fleeting, as Cordellia dispersed the mist.

"There are significant drawbacks however," Cordellia resumed as she began walking towards the door. "For one, you can't focus the healing, so more intricate work isn't suitable for the spell." Cordellia opened the door before looking back at the duo. "And remember, you must keep tranquil thoughts." Aurelia nodded, an eager grin stretching across her face. "No one will disturb you for about three hours. I imagine that should be plenty of time for you two to finish up here."

Cordellia stepped through the door, leaving Virgil and Aurelia alone.

"All right," Aurelia said as she spun around towards Virgil. "Let's get started." Aurelia took in a deep breath and prepared to exhale only to stop when Virgil raised his hand.

"I know you're excited and all," Virgil said. "But can I please put some clothes on first?"

Aurelia looked down at Virgil. Her cheeks turned red as she sheepishly released the puff of air she was holding on to. She walked over to the side table where his uniform lay. "Are you sure you want these? You look so comfortable."

Virgil nodded. "I'm sure. I wouldn't exactly describe a mere sheet keeping my meat and veg tucked away as comfortable."

Aurelia giggled as she handed Virgil his clothes and turned around. "Did you say meat and veg?"

"Yeah," Virgil said, uncovering himself and standing up. "You know. My—ugh—package."

Aurelia rolled her eyes, as evidenced by the bob of her head. "I know what it means, Virgil. I'm not twelve. I'm just saying who refers to their dick and balls as their meat and veg?"

Virgil blushed as he pulled up his boxers followed by his pants. "Well, I was trying to be, you know, modest."

"Sure. You were a gentleman and a scholar."

"Okay," Virgil said as he reached for his shirt. "I'm decent now."

Aurelia turned around to face Virgil and her eyes grew wide. She looked as if she wanted to speak, but couldn't find the words to do so.

"Is everything okay?" Virgil asked as he pulled his shirt over his head.

"I'm fine," Aurelia said, snapping back to the conversation. "Go on and lie back down."

"So." Virgil lay on the table. "Is the third phase over yet?"

"Not yet. There are a few teams still navigating the Network. Roxanne estimates that phase three should be over by the end of tomorrow at the latest."

"That's good. We have some time to relax before things get hectic again."

Aurelia nodded as she took a deep breath. She closed her eyes and exhaled. A faint blue mist cascaded over Virgil and enveloped his body. It wasn't nearly as potent as Cordellia's, but comforting nonetheless.

"Is Fynn okay?"

The mist faded just as quickly as it had come. "Fynn?" Aurelia said, taken aback.

"Yeah. Last I remember, he was moments away from death and too stubborn to care."

"He's doing okay. He went kicking and screaming, but Logan pulled him out of the Network and Cordellia's staff patched him up."

Virgil breathed a sigh of relief. "And what about Logan?"

"He's doing well. He wasn't nearly as banged up as you and I were."

"No," Virgil said with a shake of his head. "That's not what I meant. How's he doing since finding out about Paisley?"

Aurelia paused, her eyes trained on the floor. "Oh. He's pretty much acting how I expected he would."

"I take it that's a bad thing."

"It is what it is." Aurelia shrugged as she looked back at Virgil. "He's upset now, but he'll get over it. He always does."

"And how are you feeling?"

"I don't know. I mean, I'm okay. I hate keeping secrets from him, but sometimes, I feel like I don't have any other option. Logan can be so stubborn sometimes. Like no matter what, he knows what's best for me. It can be so frustrating. You know?"

"Have you told him this?"

Aurelia forced out a chuckle. "Why bother? Nine times out of ten, he's right, and I just end up looking like a dumbass little kid again."

"Even if that's true, you should tell him how you feel. Things won't change if he doesn't know he's upsetting you."

"I suppose you're right."

"If you want," Virgil continued. "I can talk to him with you. Perhaps together—"

"No," Aurelia said sharply. "That's a bad idea."

His eyes narrowed as bewilderment washed over Virgil's face. "And why is that?"

"It just is. You're sweet to offer, but I can handle it on my own."

"Well, if you change your mind, I'm more than willing to back you up."

Aurelia conjured the Saint's Breath once more. This time the mist was thicker and much more vivid.

Virgil opened his mouth to speak, but the words wouldn't come. He knew what he wanted to ask. The question was burning through his mind like a flaming arrow. And yet, he couldn't bring himself to let the inquiry escape his lips. He locked eyes with Aurelia, and quickly turned away. Virgil swallowed the lump in his throat, and took a deep breath. "Is, uh, how is Olivia?"

Aurelia grinned, her eyes lit with excitement. "Boy, I thought you were never going to ask. She's doing well. Cordellia's healers took care of her. More importantly though, she asked quite a bit about you."

"She did?" Virgil asked, his stomach fluttering as he turned back to Aurelia.

"She did."

"Well, what did she ask? What did you say? What did—"

"Easy there," Aurelia replied. "We'll get to it. She asked a bunch of personal stuff, which obviously was just a ploy to get to know your likes and dislikes. I told her what I could, but most importantly, she asked if you and I were a thing. I told her no, of course."

Virgil took in a deep breath as relief washed over him, and he couldn't help but grin.

Aurelia giggled. "You've never done this before, have you?"

"Is it really that obvious?"

"It is, but I suppose it doesn't matter." Aurelia winked at Virgil. "You've got me in your corner after all." Her gaze drifted down towards Virgil's chest. A frown stretched across her face, and the mist disappeared again.

"What is it now?" Virgil asked.

"Nothing," Aurelia said, her tone low. "I just, I was thinking about your scars."

Virgil looked down at his chest, and thoughts of Cecelia, the vile witch responsible for dealing him that blow flooded his mind. He forced a smile. It was all he could do to keep the rage from boiling inside him.

"I'm sorry," Aurelia said. "I didn't mean to stare before. They just look so painful. I couldn't imagine living through an injury like that."

"This is nothing. My father got the worst of it."

"Can you tell me about it?"

"About what part?" Virgil asked.

"About everything." Aurelia placed her hand on Virgil's chest. "I get the feeling you're holding on to a lot of pain and suffering. You don't have to carry that alone. I can help you."

"Ah," Virgil replied with a smirk. "You mean like letting me help you with Logan?"

Aurelia leaned on the edge of the table and sighed. "Okay, I walked right into that one. How about this? If you let me help you, then I'll let you help me. Sounds fair, right?"

"I suppose that works," Virgil said as he sat up alongside Aurelia.

"I swear, by the end of this exam, I'm not going to have any secrets left."

Aurelia rolled her eyes. "You say that like it's a bad thing."

"I'm not sure I'd call it a good thing."

"Quit stalling," Aurelia prodded.

"Okay, okay."

Virgil revealed everything. His brother's disappearance. The witch responsible. His failure to make her pay for what she had done. What his shortcomings had cost him. What they cost his father. As he spoke, his shoulders eased up. It was as if he had been saddled with a thousand weights, and with each word that left his lips, another weight disintegrated.

"I'm not sure what happened after the light," Virgil said. "I blacked out, and my memory still hasn't come back after all these years. I don't know if it ever will. What I do know is that I woke up sometime later, and Cecelia was gone. I remember my chest feeling as if it had been doused in gasoline and lit on fire." Virgil tensed up as he rubbed his hand across his chest. "Even now, I can feel it stinging sometimes. It's like my skin is burning from the inside out."

"That's terrible," Aurelia said.

Virgil nodded. "My father got it so much worse. He was so strong, and he held on for so long, but even he couldn't keep the curse at bay forever." Tears formed in the corners of his eyes, and his hands began to tremble. "He was my hero. He was everything I wanted to be, and in the end, he wasted away." Tears poured down his face. Aurelia leaned over and placed her arms around him, holding him tightly. "I tried for so long to cure him. I took him to see specialist after specialist. I tried every elixir you could think of, but nothing worked. In the end, my only hope was to track down Cecelia and force her to undo her curse before it was too late."

"But you couldn't find her in time."

Virgil nodded, his tears coming to a halt. "I'm still looking for her, and the Crusader's Alliance is going to be my ticket to her doorstep. When I finally find her, I'm going to repay her for all the suffering she's caused. The one thing that saddens me is that I'll only get to kill her once."

"Will that really make you happy?" Aurelia asked.

"What do you mean?" Virgil asked as he pulled back. "Of course it will."

"I mean killing Cecelia isn't going to bring your family back. Do you really think it will make you feel any better?"

Virgil paused for a moment as he looked down at his necklace. "I don't know, but it's a damn good place to start."

TWENTY-TWO

V irgil sat in the banquet hall, his mouth flooding at the sight of the feast spread out before him. A symphony of smells flooded his nostrils. There were cheese-covered eggs scrambled to perfection, bacon with crispy edges and soft, chewy centers, powdered toast with fresh vanilla, and a tall glass of ice-cold lemonade. He dug in, the thought of waiting another moment a complete and utter travesty.

"Must you eat like an animal," Logan said from across the table, a cup of coffee in hand.

"Look," Virgil said between bites of egg and toast, "last time I was here, I only had a couple of lukewarm pastries. I'm making up for lost time."

Aurelia giggled as she nudged Virgil's ribs with her elbow. "Don't talk with your mouth full."

Logan tilted his head. "You two are more chummy than usual."

"Not really," Virgil said after swallowing a gulp of lemonade. "If anything, you're more grouchy than usual."

"I'm not grouchy," Logan grumbled.

"If you're not grouchy, then I'm not eating the best damn

powdered toast in the world." Virgil took his fork and dipped a piece of toast in a pool of syrup before taking a bite. "Mmm. Yeah. Just as I thought. These are savagely delicious."

"I think what Virgil is trying to say," Aurelia said between giggles, "is that you seem on edge. Is everything all right?"

"I'm perfectly fine," Logan replied. "I'm sure that after our talk yesterday, everything will straighten itself out."

"About that. There's something I want to talk to you about."

At the head of the banquet hall, a white void appeared, and Roxanne entered the room. By now, the applicants had grown accustomed to her grand entrances. They turned quiet almost instantly and awaited her instruction.

"Good morning," Roxanne said. "I hate to interrupt a good breakfast, so I'll try to make this as brief as possible. It brings me great pleasure to announce that we are entering the fourth phase of the exam. In years past, we've implemented more phases, but this year's exam has proved to be much more grueling than anticipated. Truth is, if we follow our normal protocol, we fear none of you will make it to the finish line. And so, I'm certain you will also be happy to know this will be the final phase of the exam."

The crowd erupted in jubilee.

"Hold your excitement," Roxanne said, raising her hand. "I'm not finished. Per usual, the final phase of the exam is a mentorship. You will each be grouped into teams and assigned a rook or queen level Crusader. Once again, you are free to form your own teams, however, if you are unable to do so, we will group you together into a team of at least three. Under the guidance of your mentor, you will develop your skills, learn exactly what it means to be a Crusader, and get first-hand experience working in the field."

Wait, Virgil thought. *Does that mean?*

"Yes, you heard me correctly. As of right now, you are all probationary Crusaders. Congratulations."

The crowd exploded into a celebration much more boisterous than before. There wasn't a body still seated.

"All right," Roxanne said. "I have one last announcement to make.

As an introduction to the fourth phase, we will be holding a tournament. Each of you will be pitted against another in a series of one-on-one battles to determine who among you is the strongest. Now, I'm sure you're wondering, what's the point of this if you're already probationary Crusaders? Well, the reason we have this tournament is to determine your starting rank in the Alliance." The crowd was silent as everyone hung off Roxanne's every word. "For those of you who don't know, the Crusader's Alliance is broken up into ranks. At the bottom, we have the pawns, followed by the knights, then the bishops, then the rooks, then the queens, and finally the kings. As I've already stated, you've all been accepted as probationary Crusaders, so if you'd rather not fight, we won't force you to do so. However, know that you will be starting out at the bottom of the heap, and thus, missing out on crucial opportunities. The tournament will consist of four rounds. Our tournament winner will be crowned rook, the semi-finalists bishops, the quarter finalists knights, and everyone else Pawns."

This is it, Virgil thought. *Orlando said rooks get to work on their own. I'd have to report to a queen, but still. If I win this tournament, I'll be in the perfect position to finally hunt down Cecelia.*

"You'll have three days from now to prepare. On the morning of the tournament, you will find instructions in your rooms detailing where to gather on the island. For those of you who choose not to participate, please enjoy everything we have to offer here in the castle and patiently await the tournament's completion."

With that, Roxanne left, and the banquet hall fell into an uproar.

"We did it," Aurelia said, her smile brimming ear to ear. "We're Crusaders, Logan. Just like Mom and Dad."

Logan shot Aurelia a cold, domineering stare, and the joy drained from her face.

"That was a little uncalled for," Virgil said, his brows lowered. "Your sister's excited. You should be too."

"I'm ecstatic," Logan replied, dry as a bone.

"You have a funny way of showing it."

"Shouldn't you be going off to do some training? I imagine you'll be gunning for the top spot, after all."

"Of course, but no. I'm probably going to just relax. The best thing I can do is clear my mind after all of the stress I've been through. I'm sure you two could use a break too."

"I don't think so," Logan said with a laugh. "Aurelia and I will be deep in training."

Logan began to walk away but stopped when he noticed Aurelia hadn't budged. "Aren't you coming?" he said as he turned back around.

"I think some rest right now would be good," Aurelia said, her tone low, almost inaudible.

"Now is not the time for that. Have you forgotten how shaky your ice conjuration is? There are several techniques you can improve upon before the start of the tournament."

"Dude, we just went through a lot in the last phase," Virgil said. "I think she'll be fine if she slacks off for a day or two."

"Forgive me," Logan said. "But we are not people who care to throw caution to the wind and hope for the best."

Virgil clenched his fists, as he ground his teeth. "And what is that supposed to mean?" he asked, as if he didn't already know the answer.

Logan glared at Virgil. "It means what you think it means."

"You guys are making too big a deal out of this," Aurelia said, walking towards her brother.

"Aurelia—"

"Logan makes a good point, Virgil. We could have avoided some dangerous situations if I had a better grasp of aquamancy. There's plenty for me to work on, and it will only help me better prepare for the tournament."

Virgil paused for a moment as he looked at Aurelia, and then to Logan. "If that's really what you want to do, then fine. But please don't think you have to."

Aurelia flashed a smile. "I'll be fine," she said. "Why don't you see what Olivia's up to? Perhaps you two could spend some time together. You are running out of time, after all."

"What do you mean?"

"Well, after the exam, I imagine we'll be going our separate ways.

If you don't establish a bond with her now, then you might not get another chance later."

Virgil nodded as he exhaled. "That's an excellent point."

"You got this." Aurelia winked. "Remember, she already likes you. Just be yourself, and you have nothing to worry about."

TWENTY-THREE

Virgil walked through the halls of the castle. He had locked onto Olivia's aura signature and was on his way to her location with a bouquet of flowers he had scrounged together from the various gardens spread around the castle. The closer he got, the more his heartbeat ramped up, and his nerves seized up like rusty locks.

"This is stupid," he said to himself. "You don't know what you're doing. You've never had a girlfriend before. Hell, you've never talked to a woman before." He stopped, frozen in place. A hard lump swelled in the back of his throat, and his stomach turned. "You're going to make an ass out of yourself. You're going to look like a fool again, and this time you won't be so lucky." Aurelia's words echoed through Virgil's mind. "She thinks I can do it," he said as he resumed walking. "Yeah. She'd know."

Virgil stopped again, and frowned. "But what if she lied to me?" He shook his head and continued walking. "She wouldn't do that."

Virgil rounded a corner, and Olivia came into view. As he walked closer, he prepared to call out her name but quickly stopped. He ducked behind a nearby pillar and concealed his aura as best he could.

What is she doing? He thought as he poked out his head.

There she was, examining the wall carefully. She was focused and intent, only, the wall was barren. It wasn't even intricately designed.

Okay, this is weird. It's almost as if she's looking for something, but nothing's there.

Virgil came out from around the pillar. "Olivia," he called out. "How's it going?"

Olivia turned around in a panic. "Oh, it's you," she said, relieved. "You've got to stop sneaking up on me like that."

Virgil pursed his lips. "Afraid I was a king again?" he asked.

"N-no. Not this time." Olivia took note of the flowers in Virgil's hand. "Are those for me?"

"They are."

"They're beautiful. Although, I don't think the Alliance would appreciate you picking their flowers."

"I can see that. What were you doing here?"

Olivia's face began to look flustered. "Nothing."

"Really? It looked like you were searching for something."

Olivia paused, looking Virgil in his eyes. She exhaled and turned away. "Okay. You got me. I'll tell you what's going on, but you have to promise not to say anything."

"I'm listening."

Olivia turned back towards Virgil. "I'm serious. What I'm about to tell you could put everyone on the island in danger."

Virgil tilted his head. "What is it?"

Olivia took a deep breath, and exhaled. "The Scarlet Mage is here."

Virgil paused for a moment, her words hitting him like a slap to the face. "That's not funny," he said, his shoulders tensing. "You shouldn't joke about something like that."

Olivia's eyes began to water. It looked as if the air had been snatched from her lungs. "I wasn't joking, Virgil. And honestly, I'm a little hurt you think I would."

Virgil paused again, allowing Olivia's words to sink in. He looked at the elf. She was trembling, and the fear in her eyes was unmistakable. "I'm sorry," he said as he rubbed his forehead. "I just, I wasn't expecting that."

"And what exactly were you expecting?"

"I don't know. Definitely not that. Where is he now?"

"I thought I had the mage cornered down this hallway, but as you can see, he managed to slip away. I couldn't tell if it was sorcery or a hidden passage or something, but the wall opened up and he ran inside."

"What makes you so sure the person you saw was the Scarlet Mage?" Virgil asked. "Perhaps you saw an attendant or something. An old castle like this is bound to have hidden passageways."

Olivia reached into her pocket. "Well, I did startle him and he dropped this before he escaped." She pulled out a small canvas pouch covered with sigils and bound with string. Virgil's heart skipped a beat as he looked at the bag in her hand. "I'm not sure," Olivia continued. "But I think this is a hex bag. Of course, I'm not an expert and I've never actually seen one before, but—"

"No," Virgil said, his tone low. "You're right. I've spent years hunting witches, and that is definitely a hex bag. Still. I don't feel any additional auras here. If he was here, I should be able to feel an imprint of his aura." Virgil pinched the bridge of his nose. "Then again, he's been consorting with witches, so I suppose it's possible he has a way to mask his presence."

Olivia's eyes grew wide. "He's working with witches? How do you know that?"

"I ran across a rumor on my way to registering for the exam, which I guess isn't a rumor anymore. What really doesn't make sense, though, is why would he come here? Especially during the Crusader's Exam. Akata Island is crawling with Crusaders right now. Even the kings are here. There is literally no worse place for him to be right now."

"I have a theory." Olivia raised her finger. "You know about the Crystal Catalyst, right?"

Virgil gave Olivia a blank expression. "You mean the catalyst forged by the Great Deities themselves, said to be the most powerful magical artifact to have ever existed? There isn't a mage alive who doesn't know about it. But the Crystal Catalyst was lost after the Blood War."

"Rumor has it, it's not lost anymore. I've heard that the Crusaders have found it and have stashed it away for safekeeping."

"And just where'd you hear that?" Virgil asked, folding his arms.

"It doesn't matter where I heard it. If it's true—"

"It absolutely matters. Honestly, it sounds like a tall tale tossed around bars."

Olivia groaned. "You're missing the point. Okay. Indulge me for a moment, and let's assume it's true."

"Okay. Assuming this is true, it would definitely be worth the risk in coming here. A catalyst of that caliber could do some serious damage in the wrong hands. And I suppose even if this isn't the Scarlet Mage, someone lurking around the island is cause for concern."

"That's exactly what I was thinking."

Virgil took hold of Olivia's hand. "All right. We have to go notify the kings."

"No," Olivia said, pulling her hand back.

"What do you mean, no?" Virgil said in shock. "We don't have a moment to spare. With or without the catalyst, if this person manages to make it off the island, it's going to be a million times harder to track them down."

"You can't tell anyone about this, Virgil."

"Olivia—"

"We don't know who this person is, or who they may be working with, or even how high this goes. What if we go to a king only to find they've been bewitched? He could be a king waiting for the perfect opportunity to make a clean get away. Going to them could be walking right into a trap, and it would be child's play for them to explain away our deaths. That's why I was trying to catch him in the act, and have concrete evidence to back me up."

Virgil paused for a moment, thinking the situation over. "We should at least tell Aurelia and—"

"Virgil, I mean it. I'd much rather just deal with this on my own, but I'm telling you because I trust you. The more people who know about this, the more dangerous it gets for everyone, and we can't afford to mess this up." Olivia placed her hand on Virgil's cheek, her soft, supple skin caressing his. "Promise me we'll handle this on our own."

Virgil placed his hand over hers. It fit so perfectly under his palm, as if it were created for that very purpose. He looked into her glistening hazel eyes. He could still see the fear and uncertainty held within them.

"Okay," he said with a sigh. "I promise I won't say a word."

TWENTY-FOUR

Three days flew by as Virgil and Olivia worked diligently to decipher who the Scarlet Mage could be. They kept to themselves, although that was easy enough. Since their prior episode in the banquet hall, Virgil hadn't seen so much as a hint of Aurelia or Logan. Every now and again, he would think of them and wonder how they were and if he should go to them. Those moments never lasted long, however, as his mind would always drift to more troubling thoughts.

Virgil and Olivia sat in the stands of a grand coliseum. Despite being hidden deep under the island, the coliseum was huge. The decor clashed heavily with Akata Castle. Several massive hologram projectors floated in the air above the coliseum floor. There was a boxed seating area reserved for the kings, and the stands were made of a sleek metal equipped with cushioned seats.

Virgil studied the crowd, watching for any anomalous behavior. He was hunched over, his elbow planted in his knees and his fingers interlaced over his lap.

"Are you okay?" Olivia asked.

"I'm about as okay as I can be," Virgil replied, tapping his foot on the floor. "I'll be a lot better once we catch the Scarlet Mage."

Aurelia and Logan entered the coliseum, instantly catching Virgil's eye.

"Do you want to go talk to them? You could—"

Virgil shook his head. "I'd rather avoid them until this is over. I don't have to lie to them if we don't see each other."

Aurelia looked up into the stands, scanning them left and right. When she saw Virgil, she waved and began making her way over. Reluctantly, Virgil waved back.

Damn it, he thought, his shoulders tensing up.

Olivia placed her hand on Virgil's back. "It'll be all right," she said. "Just play it cool, and remember the plan."

"Long time no see," Aurelia said as she and Logan joined them.

"Yeah," Virgil replied. "How did training go?"

"It went. You two seem to be hitting things off well."

Olivia smiled as she hooked her arm around Virgil's. "He makes it easy."

Fuck my life, Virgil thought. *This would actually be nice if I weren't tracking down a killer. Or hiding it from my friends.*

"I could say the same thing about you," Virgil replied, forcing a smile.

"You better."

Logan rolled his eyes as he took a seat, a considerable distance between him and Virgil, and Aurelia sat down between them.

"He's still acting grouchy?" Virgil whispered as he leaned in towards Aurelia.

"Unfortunately," Aurelia whispered back. "I don't know what's going on with him. He's usually back to himself by now."

"Well, you just let me know when you want to have the intervention."

"Intervention? He's not a drug addict, Virgil."

"Obviously. He's far too uptight to have ever dabbled in such substances."

Aurelia burst into laughter, drawing everyone's attention on her.

"What's so funny?" Olivia asked.

"It's nothing," Virgil said, trying his best not to laugh.

The lights darkened, leaving the entire coliseum dimly lit except for the boxed seating. A white void appeared, and Roxanne, Cordellia, and Clayton stepped through. They each waved to the crowd before Cordellia and Clayton sat down. Roxanne, on the other hand, stepped forward and prepared to address the crowd.

"Good morning," she said, her voice echoing throughout the coliseum. "For those of you participating in the tournament, I trust you have all prepared yourselves adequately. Before we get things underway, I just want to congratulate you all once again. Each and every one of you has fought valiantly to make it here. Relish in the fact that you are Crusaders. You are the might of our great nations!"

The crowd exploded, and the room nearly trembled from the excitement. As Roxanne raised her hand, the crowd quieted down, awaiting her next remarks.

"Allow me to explain the tournament rules. There will be no time limit for any of the fights today. A battle will only end once a fighter is incapacitated, or someone surrenders. In the event of a double knock out, the fight will resume once both fighters regain consciousness. However, should a fighter awaken before his or her opponent, the unconscious fighter will have exactly one hour to awaken before he or she is disqualified. Finally, and this should go without saying, but we've had problems in previous years, so bear with me, while we may still be conducting the Crusader's Exam, you are all probationary Crusaders and thus are comrades. We expect you to treat each other as such. Have I made myself clear?"

The crowd replied in confirmation.

"Good." Roxanne pointed at the hologram projectors, and they began spitting out images. It was a giant tournament bracket listing everyone's names and who they would be fighting. "Here are your match-ups for the first round. We will be holding the battles for the first two rounds simultaneously, however, the battles for the third and final round will be held one by one."

With a snap of her finger, the coliseum floor began to shift. Metal walls sprouted from the floor, creating eight separate but equally sized arenas. "You have thirty minutes to make any final preparations and report to your designated arena. If you are not there on time, your match will be considered forfeited, so if you intend to participate, please make sure you are there. No exceptions will be made."

Virgil looked at the holograms. His first opponent was Mifune, although that name meant nothing to him. Olivia was to fight Astrid, another person who failed to strike Virgil's recollection. Nevertheless, it was inconsequential to the plan. Logan was slated to fight Fynn. Virgil looked over to the redhead sitting alone across the coliseum, and found a wide grin painted on his face.

Virgil turned his attention back to the brackets, searching for Aurelia's name. When he found it, his eyes widened. She was going to have to fight Paisley.

Virgil looked at Aurelia. She was nearly pale. "Are you okay?" he asked.

"Yeah," she replied. Her hands were shaky, and her tone was shrouded in doubt. "I can't say I'm thrilled about this, but it is what it is."

"Try not to worry about it. You're stronger than her, you know."

Aurelia stood up, and sighed. "Yeah, that's the problem."

Before Virgil could reply, Aurelia walked away, and Logan followed suit.

"Remember the plan," Olivia said as she stood up as well.

Finally, Virgil stood. "Right. Remember the plan."

It didn't take long for Virgil to reach his arena, but it sure felt like it took ages. As he walked, his mind was flooded by a mass of information. No matter how he tried to piece things together, nothing made sense. Who was the Scarlet Mage? Where was he hiding? Was this even him? What if this had all been a misunderstanding?

The arena wall opened up, revealing the battlefield. Virgil stepped through, and the wall closed behind him. Across the battlefield, Mifune did the same, and Virgil studied the kurara closely. Rather than the uniform everyone else was wearing, he wore a suit built for combat. His back was partially exposed to allow room for his wings, but the rest of his body was covered in armored plating with a radiant black sheen. Glowing green lines traced around the perimeter of the armor, and pulsed rhythmically like a heartbeat. An armored visor covered his eyes, glowing just as vibrantly as the rest of his gear. Across his waist lay two straps holding twin swords at his side, and along the straps sat a myriad of pouches.

No mana, Virgil thought. *I suppose the Alliance would have to let him wear his combat attire. Still. It makes sense why I never noticed him before.*

"If you wish to shake hands," Roxanne shouted, "do so now."

Slowly, the men approached one another.

"Is it true?" Mifune asked as they stopped just shy of each other. "You're really Danté's son?"

"Yeah," Virgil replied.

Mifune held out his hand. "I consider it an honor to do battle with you today."

Virgil shook Mifune's hand. "Thank you. I consider it an honor as well."

The two men retreated to their respective sides. Before long, a blaring siren echoed throughout the coliseum. Virgil took his battle stance, engulfing his hands in flame as he stared down Mifune. The kurara did the same, pulling out a single blade, and planting his feet into the ground.

I've got to put an end to this quickly, Virgil thought.

Mifune disappeared. Virgil looked around in a panic.

"Where did he—"

"Behind you," Mifune said, swinging his blade.

With no time to dodge, Virgil braced himself for the impending attack. He expected the sting of metal to slice his flesh, but instead, a blunt club-like object struck his back. Virgil was sent flying, tumbling across the ground. As his momentum slowed, Virgil planted his feet into the ground, managing to finally stabilize himself.

"I'm impressed," Mifune said. "A blow like that should have knocked you out."

"Thank you," Virgil said. "You know. You could have inflicted some serious damage had you armed your weapon."

"We are comrades. I have no desire to harm you any more than I have to."

"I'm glad we share that sentiment. Still. If you surrender to me, I'd gladly accept it."

Mifune let out a hearty laugh. "Do you really think that little of me?"

"Not at all," Virgil replied. "Just trying to save time."

Virgil took flight, flying towards Mifune. Once again, he disappeared. Virgil paused and searched around. Nothing. He spun around, expecting to find Mifune skulking behind him.

"Not this time," Mifune said, reappearing and swinging from Virgil's right.

Virgil raised his forearm in defense. He sucked in a breath, and winced as the blunt sword struck him. Pain reverberated through his body, but Virgil stood firm. He pulled his free hand back and launched a counterattack of his own. Moments before Virgil's strike could connect, Mifune disappeared yet again.

Virgil ground his teeth, his nostrils flared. "This is really starting to get annoying."

"Forgive me," Mifune replied as he appeared directly in front of Virgil. "This will all be over soon."

Before Virgil could respond, Mifune released a flurry of strikes with pinpoint accuracy. It was clear Mifune favored shots to the stomach, but that didn't stop him from striking Virgil's arms and legs. In fact, the only places he didn't hit were Virgil's vitals. Amid the barrage, Virgil tried to counter, but it was no use. Mifune was just as competent at dodging blows as he was at delivering them.

Virgil raised his hand to summon a wall of flames between them. It was all he could think to do to create distance between them, but Mifune swung his blade, smacking it into Virgil's wrist. The fire appeared out of place, utterly ineffective to stop Mifune. He followed up with another vicious swing at Virgil's chest. Virgil gasped, yelping as he was sent flying once again until the wall broke his momentum. Mifune closed the distance and pinned Virgil to the wall.

Mifune pressed his blade up against Virgil's throat. "If this is all you're going to do, then you should surrender now."

"Not a chance," Virgil said, forcing his words out.

"If you won't surrender, then show me what you're really capable of. Use your catalyst." Virgil smirked as he placed his hand on the blade. "What's so funny?" Mifune asked.

"You're the first person to ever ask me to use my dragon's treasure."

Mifune applied more pressure on Virgil's neck. "I wasn't asking."

"I'm afraid I'll have to disappoint you." Virgil took in as much air as he could manage. He exhaled, releasing a shower of fire and forcing Mifune to retreat.

Mifune planted his feet to the ground and tilted his sword to Virgil. "What is it going to take to get you to use Kayveon's Fang?" he asked.

"Why do you care so much?" Virgil asked as he rubbed his throat.

"It's simple. I'm curious to see what the infamous Danté Truesdale's son could do with the legendary fang. I want to see where I stack up in comparison."

Virgil took to the sky, rising high in the air. "I'm shocked," he said. "You didn't strike me as the petty type."

Mifune stretched his wings and took to the air as well. The two men circled each other, keeping their eyes locked on one another until Mifune disappeared. Virgil halted in the air, focusing his senses. Wind gusted from his left, and he turned to find Mifune reappearing in front of him. The kurara's eyes widened as he rose his blade. Virgil planted his foot into Mifune's chest, knocking him back in the air. Virgil quickly gave chase. Before Mifune could retaliate, Virgil thrust his fist into Mifune's face. The kurara plummeted to the ground, grunting in pain as his body hit the metal floor.

Virgil took in as much air as he could. As Mifune swiftly rose to his feet, he reached into one of his pouches. From out of the pouch, he drew four shurikens and launched them at Virgil. In one mighty breath, Virgil exhaled, blanketing the area under him with blue fire. The flames swallowed the metal stars, melting them into useless puddles of liquid. Mifune tapped the armored plating covering his chest, and his body began to glow. As the fire rained down, Virgil couldn't see the kurara, but he could hear his piercing screams of agony. The inferno ceased revealing a charred Mifune quivering in place. His armor had become deformed and misshapen, and the bits of his skin that showed were singed and raw. His visor was cracked, revealing his hard, golden eyes, and his sword was damaged far beyond its usefulness.

"Will you surrender now?" Virgil asked as he returned to the ground.

Mifune threw down his broken sword. Virgil relaxed, but tensed right back up when Mifune drew his second blade. It was damaged as well, but still functional enough for battle.

"That was quite the attack," Mifune said through pain-filled breaths. "You managed to overload my armor with ease. That fang is really something."

"I didn't use the fang."

"What?" Mifune said, his eyes growing wide. "You mean to tell me that blast wasn't boosted by your catalyst?"

Virgil nodded. "I told you I was going to be a disappointment."

Mifune tightened his grip on his sword and smiled. "You did, didn't you. In that case, I guess I'll just have to go for broke."

"Don't be ridiculous," Virgil replied. "You have no chance to beat me now. Just surrender and we can be done."

Mifune charged towards Virgil, his sword raised. Virgil closed his fist, and Mifune's sword burst into flame. He discarded it but reached into another pouch and pulled out a small black sphere, coated in gray lines. Mifune threw the ball at the ground, and a cloud of smoke began pouring out.

Virgil locked his fingers together. "No more sneak attacks."

A fiery blaze encircled Virgil. It expanded outward and kept going until the flames reached the walls. When the smoke finally cleared, Mifune lay on the ground, face down, barely moving.

Virgil walked over to Mifune and crouched down. "You fought well. I'm sorry I couldn't give you what you wanted, but if it makes you feel better, you made me use a lot more mana than I intended to."

Mifune looked up at Virgil. Before he could speak, his head fell, and his eyes closed. The metal wall behind Virgil opened up, and two men rushed in to assist Mifune.

Virgil exhaled. *It's definitely not him,* he thought as he exited the arena.

TWENTY-FIVE

Virgil returned to the coliseum stands. He moved quickly, all while trying his best to act inconspicuously, as if he weren't scanning everyone in sight. Olivia was already seated, and Virgil promptly sat down beside her.

"Are you all right?" she asked.

"I'm a little banged up," he replied. "But it's nothing. I'm more concerned with the mana I've used up."

Olivia leaned against Virgil, wrapping her arm around his. "Try to relax. Everything's going to be all right."

Virgil's shoulders tensed as he watched the battles unfolding on the holograms. There were only three fights still progressing.

Damn it, he thought. *I missed so much.*

"How's the plan progressing?" he asked.

"I lost quickly and effectively," Olivia replied with a twirl of her finger. "No one should suspect a thing."

"Great. So, you got a good look at the fights that have already ended then?"

"I did. Sadly, nobody has struck me as a suspect."

"Same here. Mifune's a Boy Scout." Virgil sighed as he leaned back in his chair. "We still have time to weed out the Scarlet Mage. How has the crowd been?"

Olivia let go of Virgil's arm. "Typical. It seems like everyone's enjoying themselves."

"And the kings?"

"The same. They've had their eyes glued on the fights. Particularly Aurelia's."

Virgil turned his attention to the hologram showing Aurelia and Paisley.

That makes sense, Virgil thought. He scanned Aurelia's aura and bit the inside of his lip. *Keep it together, Aurelia. I know you can do this.*

Aurelia stepped back. Her posture was defensive as Paisley pressed forward. The angry brunette threw punch after punch, each strike aimed at Aurelia's face. Her fists were wrapped in jagged rocks, and a mix of dirt and sweat muddled her skin. Her breathing was slow and cumbersome. Apart from the concerned look on her face, Aurelia was perfectly fine, dodging Paisley's blows with ease.

Paisley shifted her weight, putting her full force behind her swing. Aurelia stepped out of the way and struck Paisley's wrist. Paisley's fist plummeted to the floor, denting the metal.

She looked up at Aurelia, her eye twitching before she got back up and continued her assault. Aurelia took a step back to evade once again. This time however, she tripped over a stone Paisley had conjured behind her. She fell backward, leaving her defenses wide open.

Paisley grinned. It looked like she was fighting back the urge to laugh as she cocked her fist back. Paisley launched her fist at Aurelia, but Aurelia threw her hand up, and a burst of water shot forth. The stream flung Paisley high into the air. She crashed into the ground and sucked in a deep breath as she writhed in pain.

Aurelia's eyes grew wide and her mouth hung open. She got up in a panic and rushed over to Paisley. A large stone hand shot out of the ground and took hold of Aurelia's head. The hand flew through the air and pinned her against the wall. Paisley made her way over. Each step she took exuded arrogance.

Aurelia placed her hand on the stone, and a burst of water split it apart from the inside out. She fell to the ground, desperately trying to fill her lungs with air. Paisley cocked her fist back. Her eyes were filled with vicious intent, not a hint of remorse to be seen.

Paisley's devilish grin turned to terror as she was hoisted into the air. Aurelia had risen to her feet and wrapped her hand around Paisley's throat. Paisley had no time to react. It looked like she was trying to speak, but her words were cut off by Aurelia's intensifying grip. Paisley clawed at Aurelia's hand, desperate to alleviate the pressure crushing her windpipe. Her eyes began to flutter, and her movements became slower.

Aurelia gasped, and she dropped Paisley. To say Paisley was wheezing for air would be an understatement. It seemed oxygen couldn't fill her lungs fast enough. The wall opened up, and two attendants rushed to her side. Slowly Aurelia walked towards Paisley, holding her hand out, but she shot Aurelia a burning look of contempt that halted her. Aurelia spun around and quickly exited the arena.

"That was intense," Olivia said.

Virgil nodded. "You have no idea what those two have been through."

"Apparently not, but we should stay focused on the task at hand."

Virgil nodded. "Right. We can rule out those two."

"Really?" Olivia said. "Paisley's always seemed like a bit of a basket case, and well, you saw what Aurelia just did."

"Paisley's insecure and petty. She's more of a threat to herself than anybody, and Aurelia wouldn't hurt anyone without cause."

Olivia scoffed. "Try telling that to Paisley's windpipe."

Virgil sighed. "You're just going to have to trust me on this." He turned his attention to the remaining battles. His lips pursed as he noticed something peculiar.

"What is it?" Olivia asked.

"Lucious is still fighting."

"And what's so interesting about that?"

"You fought him. He may be a massive dick, but he's a skilled aquamancer."

"And?" Olivia replied. "I'm afraid I fail to see your point."

"Well, I would have expected him to have finished his match by now."

Olivia shook her head. "That's not a cause for concern. Unless you're sensing a malicious aura?"

Virgil shrugged. "Not really. I mean, Lucious's aura is always a little twisted." He looked closer at Lucious's opponent. "Hey. I know that guy."

"You do?"

"Well, sort of. I bumped into him before the start of the third phase."

"Do you think he could be the Scarlet Mage?"

Virgil chuckled. "God no. I mean, I only spoke with him for a second, but he struck me more as the soft and cuddly type."

Olivia rolled her eyes. "Looks can be deceiving, Virgil. We shouldn't rule him out. Or anyone else for that matter."

"I know. I'm just saying. I wouldn't put my money on it."

CHAPTER
TWENTY-SIX

A loud explosion echoed throughout the coliseum, drawing everyone's attention to Fynn and Logan's bout. The two men stood across from each other. They were both panting, almost as if they were racing to see who could catch their breath first. Despite his battered and bruised body, Fynn was smiling ear to ear.

He summoned another dragon and sent it flying towards Logan. However, Logan raised his palm, and caught it with ease. The eyes on his gloves shone bright, and Logan dashed towards Fynn. Fynn retreated backward, but Logan leapt into the air.

Smiling, Fynn raised his palm towards Logan and summoned a swarm of tiny fire dragons. He snapped his fingers, and the dragons darted towards Logan. The eyes on Logan's gloves began to glow once again as Logan pointed his palm towards the dragons. A downpour of flames released from Logan's hand, and although the blast had surely come from him, it felt as if Aiden had been the one to release a blistering inferno. Cordellia gasped as she sprung to her feet. She held out her hands towards their arena, covering it in a shimmering blue dome of water.

His eyes were wide and sweat poured down his face as Fynn

looked up at the fiery blaze raining down upon him. He threw his hands up, veiling himself in a barrier of fire. The dragons were devoured by the divine flames, and before long, Fynn was engulfed as well.

Logan returned to the smoldering ground below. Had it not been for the barrier Cordellia conjured, the entire coliseum would have been in ruins. Fynn trembled on his knees as smoke trailed off his body. Logan cracked his knuckles as Fynn struggled to get back on his feet. His knees buckled, and it was clear he was approaching his limit. Despite this, Fynn wore a smile on his face and chuckled. He said something, but of course, only he and Logan could hear it. Whatever it was, it raised Logan's brow. They exchanged words once more, and both men readied their battle stances, each bearing a satisfied grin.

Logan charged towards Fynn, releasing three fiery dragons from his gloves: the culmination of all his battles with the pyromancer. Fynn summoned a multitude of dragons, far outnumbering what Logan had tucked away. With a flick of his wrist, Fynn launched his assault on Logan. The dragons flew through the air, two of Logan's colliding with two of Fynn's. The remaining dragon, however, weaved through the chaos, managing to slip within range of Fynn. He braced himself for impact.

However, the dragon dove into the ground just a few feet from him. Fynn took a step back, clearly in shock, his vision obstructed by the explosion swirling in front of him. Logan emerged from the fire, his fist balled, smoke trailing from his charred body. There was no time to dodge. Logan slammed his fist into Fynn's jaw. Fynn flew backward, the sheer force of the blow drawing blood from his mouth. He slammed into the wall and slumped onto the floor.

Logan stood tall, the flames around him subsiding. As his gloves disappeared, the wall behind him opened up, and two attendants rushed into the arena.

"I knew you could do it," Virgil said smiling.

"Looks like you've loosened up a bit," Olivia replied.

"I guess. I'm just happy to see them both make it through."

"Whatever you say. I'm just happy to see you've finally relaxed."

"So am I," Aurelia said as she took a seat next to Virgil.

"I wouldn't go that far," Virgil replied. "The tournament is far from over."

"You really want to win, huh."

Virgil turned away back towards the holograms. "Yeah," he replied, his tone low. "It's all I can think about."

Olivia nudged Virgil's arm. "You're such an overachiever."

"So," Aurelia said. "Who's left fighting?"

Virgil pointed towards the final battle. "Just those two."

Lucious and the golem were still going strong. Or rather, Lucious was. The golem looked exhausted. Layers of frost coated his body, and cuts plagued nearly every inch of his skin. He could barely keep his left eye open, and the other was swollen shut. Blood soaked his clothes, or at least what was left of them. The golem's uniform was torn and frayed from the onslaught of attacks he had endured.

"I'm surprised they're still going at it," Aurelia said.

Virgil shook his head, clenching his jaw. "Lucious is just toying with him."

"You think so?" Olivia asked.

"Definitely. There's no reason why he couldn't have ended this a long time ago."

Lucious sent three balls of ice towards the golem. He didn't bother to dodge it. Or perhaps he tried, but his body was too fatigued to process the maneuver. At any rate, the ice balls crashed into the golem, knocking him onto his back. Slowly, he rolled over, fighting his way onto all fours. Lucious flashed a sinister grin as he summoned another ball of ice, only this one was nearly three times the size of the golem. The ice hovered over him like an anvil tied to a rope. With a snap of his fingers, Lucious sent the ice ball plummeting, crushing the golem under its weight. The wall opened up, and the tournament attendants rushed in.

Virgil's blood was boiling as he stared at Lucious from the stands. "I'm getting really sick of that asshole."

"Why are you so worked up?" Olivia asked. "You said it yourself, you don't even know the golem down there."

Virgil turned towards Olivia. "That's beside the point." His voice was raised and full of frustration. "Lucious thinks that he can just walk around here and do whatever he wants. I'm sick of it."

"Just ignore him."

"That's a lot easier said than done," Aurelia said. "Virgil isn't the kind of person to just sit by and let bad things happen to people."

Virgil looked down at Lucious and they locked eyes. Lucious flashed that twisted grin Virgil had come to loathe. No words needed to be spoken between the two men for each to know just what the other was thinking.

"Aurelia," Logan said as he approached the group. "How did it go?"

"I did okay," she answered, her tone low and glum. "I'm moving on to the next round." Aurelia gasped as she turned to Virgil and Olivia. "I'm so sorry. I forgot to ask how you two did."

"You don't have to apologize," Virgil said, pulling his attention off of Lucious. "I made it on to round two, but Olivia lost."

Aurelia frowned. "I'm sorry to hear that."

"Don't be," Olivia replied. "I'm just happy to have made it here at all."

Another siren went off, and the lights in the coliseum went dim. "We have concluded the first round of the tournament," Roxanne announced. "Here are the next set of matchups. This time around, we'll be giving you an hour to make it to your designated arenas. Enjoy the extra bit of rest before your next match."

The group looked up to the holograms. Virgil was slated to battle with Angelica. He couldn't recall her name, but he definitely remembered her face. She had been among the crowd of people hounding him before the exam had even begun.

Then he noticed: with Paisley's defeat and Lucious's victory, Lucious would be Aurelia's next opponent.

"Damn, girl," Olivia said. "You just can't catch a break, huh?"

Aurelia let out a heavy sigh. "Apparently not."

Logan placed his hand on Aurelia's head. "Listen," he began, "if you don't think you can handle it, you don't have to fight."

"I'll be okay."

"It's not worth the risk. If you're not certain, you should back out now before—"

"Don't listen to Mr. Grouchy over here," Virgil interrupted. "As much as I would like to be the one to knock Lucious out of the tournament, I know you got this. Go ahead and show him who's boss."

Aurelia opened her mouth to speak, only Logan had beat her to the punch. "Pardon my forwardness, but you are in no position to be giving my sister any kind of advice."

Virgil groaned. "You know, you and your attitude are really starting to piss me off. I think Aurelia could use a little more love and support from her older brother instead of you constantly doubting her."

Logan stepped closer to Virgil. His fists were tight, and his nostrils flared. "You want to say that again?"

"Whoa," Olivia said, stepping between the two men. "Why don't we just calm down here for a second?"

"I'm perfectly calm." Virgil said folding his arms. "It's Logan who has the problem."

"I'm just fine," Logan replied. "You're the problem here."

"I'm the problem? You're the one being a shitty friend ruining everyone's mood."

Logan pushed Olivia aside, his face red with anger. "Let's get one thing straight," he said, his face mere inches away from Virgil's. "I'm not your friend. I never was, and I never will be. Every once in a while, my sister takes a liking to some stray. I don't like it, but it makes her happy, so I deal with it. Sooner or later, though, you all step way beyond your boundaries, and I have to clean up the mess. You're not special, Virgil. You're just this month's lost puppy."

The group was silent, so much so, you could hear a butterfly beat its wings. Virgil stood, tears ready to burst at a moment's notice. He trembled as he struggled to keep his composure. His every instinct beckoned him to cock back and slug Logan in his jaw. And yet, he couldn't find the strength to do so. His mind and heart were overflowing with a raging fury, but what he found most damning was that it wasn't for Aurelia, or even Logan. It was for himself, and how he could have been so utterly foolish as to think he could ever truly call somebody his friend.

CHAPTER
TWENTY-SEVEN

The tension in the air was unbearable. Nobody said a word. Virgil spun around and stormed off, unable to stand the silence for a second longer. He moved quickly, ignoring the calls of his name, desperate to get as far away as possible.

"You're an idiot," Virgil said to himself, his voice nearly cracking. "Why did you ever think you could make friends?" He picked up his pace. "Everything will be okay," he continued. "You've been alone before. You've always been alone. You know-"

A wooden wall erected from the ground in front of Virgil, forcing him to a halt. He turned around to find Olivia standing there. "You're not alone," she said as she recalled the blockade.

Virgil blinked back tears. "I am alone. I was a fool to ever think I wasn't."

"You're not a fool," Olivia replied, shaking her head. "And you're certainly not alone."

"I am."

"Virgil, you're—"

"You don't get it!" Virgil exclaimed. "All my life, it's been just me and my family, and they were ripped away from me. Since then, I've had no one. I allowed myself to believe that wasn't true anymore. I convinced myself I found people I could connect with, but I was just playing myself." Tears poured from Virgil's eyes, and his breaths became heavy. "You don't know what it's like, reaching for something that you'll never be able to touch again."

Olivia approached Virgil. "You're right. I don't know what that's like. Even so, I don't need to know what you've been through to feel the pain you're holding on to. I can see it when I look at you. I hear it when you speak. I can't imagine what life has been like for you up until this point, but you can believe me when I tell you, you are not alone anymore."

Olivia took Virgil into her arms. His every instinct urged him to pull away and leave her there, but he couldn't. He stood there, perplexed. His mind was a hopeless mess of confusion, worry, anger, and sorrow.

"I know we haven't known each other long," she continued. "I couldn't possibly begin to understand everything there is to know about you, but in the short time we've spent here on this island, you have been my only comfort. Even now, while I wish you weren't involved in this ordeal, I'd be lying if I said it didn't set me at ease knowing I don't have to face this alone." Olivia shook her head. "No. It's more than that. It's because I have you here with me. When I'm with you, I feel safe. I feel like no matter what happens, if you're there, I know everything is going to be all right. I want you to feel the same way when you're with me."

Virgil wrapped his arms around Olivia, utterly powerless to resist her embrace any longer. Her touch was warm, and her scent intoxicating. They pulled back just enough to look at one another. There they were looking up at him—those sparkling hazel eyes beckoning him to move in closer. He complied, and Olivia followed suit. They closed their eyes as they moved closer and closer, and then closer still.

The only thought remaining in Virgil's mind was the impending touch of Olivia's lips. His heart pounded away in his chest, so much so that it rang in the back of his ears. His skin was warm, and time seemed to slow down to encapsulate this one glorious moment. Their lips were merely a hair's breadth apart, and in that moment, for as brief as it may have been, nothing else in the world mattered.

"Celebrating already?" Lucious gloated as he approached the couple.

Virgil pulled away from Olivia, the tenderness of the moment completely drained from the air. He was so close he could nearly taste Olivia's lips, but now his first kiss felt as if it were in another dimension entirely.

Lucious walked past, not bothering to look in Virgil's direction. "You better not lose," Lucious said. "It would break my heart if you didn't make it to the semi-finals with me."

"Ignore him," Olivia said. "Just remember what we're here for."

Virgil's eyes were still fixed on Lucious. "Yeah," he said, his eyes narrowing. "I remember."

Virgil left Olivia and headed to his designated arena, his nerves much steadier than they had been before. As he waited outside the arena, he focused his mind on the task at hand. He had to determine if Angelica was working with the Scarlet Mage, and if not, finish their battle as quickly as possible.

The arena wall opened up. As Virgil walked onto the battlefield, his opponent did the same. The dark-brown woman was skittish, her eyes falling upon everything and everyone except Virgil.

That's odd, he thought. *She couldn't keep her eyes off me before the exam. What's changed?*

Virgil looked at the woman closer. He didn't even need to scan her aura to know how it would be. She was a nervous wreck, sheepishly twirling her fingers through her black curls. Still, he checked her aura, finding it turbulent like choppy water.

There's no way she's working with the mage.

Finally, Angelica looked at Virgil. They locked eyes, and almost immediately, she turned away.

Maybe she is working with him. She could feel guilty about it. Second-guessing herself. No. She seems more frightened than anything.

"The second round is about to begin," Roxanne called out. "If you would like to shake hands, do so now."

Virgil began walking towards the middle of the battlefield, and Angelica reluctantly followed suit.

What if she's being controlled by him? She could be bewitched. Or perhaps blackmailed.

"I-it's good to see you again, V-Virgil," Angelica stuttered as she extended her hand.

Virgil took it. It was cold and clammy, trembling in his grasp.

"Likewise."

"I know I could never beat you, but I-I'm gonna try my best, okay."

Virgil nodded. "Sounds good. I'll do the same."

The combatants turned their backs to one another and walked back to their starting positions.

I get it now, Virgil thought. *She's terrified. Terrified of me.* He smiled. *I can use that to my advantage.*

Virgil reached his starting position and turned to face Angelica. The siren blared, and Virgil focused his mana. Angelica raised her hands to Virgil, taking a battle stance, although it looked as if she could barely keep her knees from wobbling. Virgil turned his palm upward to the sky. The air became thick and saturated with an overwhelming heat. Angelica's eyes grew wide, and her arms fell to her side. A lustrous blue glow bathed the battlefield, all emanating from the ball of fire hovering in the sky. The blazing sphere was massive, and only growing more ferocious with each passing second.

"You, you'll kill us both," Angelica whimpered.

"We won't die," Virgil said, his tone stoic. "It's just gonna hurt a hell of a lot. Well, for you anyway. A good pyromancer can burn an entire forest down, but a great one will burn just a single little tree."

Tears poured from Angelica's eyes as she turned around to run. "I surrender!" she screamed, pounding against the metal wall. "I SURRENDER!"

TWENTY-EIGHT

Virgil took a deep breath as he left the arena. "Not my proudest moment," he said to himself. "But I finished early. That's what's important."

Virgil made his way back to the stands. He looked up, expecting to find Olivia sitting there waiting for him, but instead found nothing.

"Where could she have gone?" He looked the entire coliseum over, and still nothing. He closed his eyes. "Maybe she got a lead."

Virgil tuned his aura perception, searching for Olivia. Nothing. He expanded the search beyond the coliseum and found nothing still. He focused as hard as he possibly could. Sweat formed upon his brow as he scanned as far as his perception could reach, well beyond the walls of Akata Castle. Still, his effort turned up nothing. It was almost as if Olivia had never set foot on Akata Island at all.

"This is bad," Virgil said, his eyes shooting open as his shoulders tensed. "He must have gotten to her."

"Who must have gotten to who?" a familiar voice said from behind Virgil.

"Fynn." Virgil spun around, his guard extended. "What are you doing here?"

Fynn held up his hands. "Easy there. I come in peace. I promise."

"S-sorry," Virgil said relaxing his guard. "I'm just a little high-strung right now."

"I see. You're looking for Olivia. Right?"

"Yeah. Have you seen her."

Fynn nodded. "I passed her in the hallway not too long ago. It seemed like she was in quite a hurry."

"Thanks, Fynn," Virgil said, flashing a smile. "I owe you one."

Fynn returned the smile. "You don't owe me a thing. I haven't had a chance to thank you for what you did back in the Network, but don't think for a second it goes unappreciated."

"You're welcome, but I don't think I did you much good. Your friends still turned their backs on you."

"They were never my friends. I talked to my father when I got out of the Network. His business deals are falling through left and right."

"I'm sorry to hear that," Virgil replied.

"Don't be," Fynn said. "For a minute, I thought about how I could still take care of my family. I'm a Crusader now, after all. But as my dad laid into me, bitching about how I ruined everything, how I'm an embarrassment, how I'll never be a noble, I realized something. He's right."

"Fynn—"

"No, he's right," Fynn said. "I'm not a noble. I tried to be for a long time, but I can't do it. It's just not me. But I'll tell you what, I realized something else even more important."

"And what's that?"

"It's not my job to take care of my father." Fynn grinned. "I think I'm gonna do my own thing for a while. See where that takes me."

"Well, I'm glad you found peace with it."

Fynn turned his attention to Lucious and Paisley, sitting across the coliseum. "It's funny," he said. "Lucious tried to ruin my life, but all he did was set me free."

"Yeah," Virgil said slowly, Lucious's devilish grin sending an uneasy chill up his spine. "Is it just me, or does he seem awfully happy?"

"I know that look. He's up to something." Lucious waved Virgil over. "Be careful," Fynn said.

"Oh, don't worry. I'm not going over there."

Then it hit him. If Lucious was here, where was Aurelia? Virgil couldn't recall seeing her face in the crowd or feeling her aura in his search. He made his way over to Lucious, keeping his eyes fixed on him.

"What happened?" Virgil demanded, his nostrils flared, eyes narrowed to slits.

"Is that really the tone you should be using when asking for something?" Lucious replied.

"Don't make me repeat it."

"You know, I was truly shocked to see your big light show earlier. You must have scared that poor girl to death. Who knew you could be so cruel?"

Virgil exhaled as he balled his fists. "I'm beginning to lose my patience."

Lucious groaned. "I know you're dense, but do I really need to spell it out for you?"

"That bitch finally got what was coming to her," Paisley joined in, satisfaction evident in her tone. "Man, do I wish I could have been the one to knock her down a peg, but I'll settle for my hubby getting the job done."

"That's not fair," Lucious said as he turned to Paisley. "How's he ever going to learn if you give him the answer?"

Paisley ran her finger across Lucious's chin. "Sorry, sweetie. I just didn't think he would ever get it."

Virgil turned to walk away, confident in the fact that if he stayed any longer, he would do something he'd regret.

"Oh Virgil," Lucious called out. "One more thing." Reluctantly, Virgil turned around, fighting the urge to set Lucious ablaze. "They took her away screaming like a little bitch."

Virgil rushed back over to Lucious and snatched his collar. His skin was hot. Rage bubbled inside him like molten lava, begging, pleading, screaming to be unleashed.

"Go ahead," Lucious goaded. "Show us all who you really are. A bullheaded, good for nothing, low-class hunter."

Virgil's breaths were heavy and misty with steam. He looked

around the coliseum. Nobody had noticed them yet. Everyone's atten-tion was still fixed on the battles taking place. He took in a deep breath and walked away. Lucious continued on, no doubt continuing to provoke Virgil, but he might as well had been speaking in another language. Virgil had but one thought on his mind—getting to Aurelia.

It took but a moment for Virgil to lock on to Aurelia's aura signa-ture. It was faint and barely noticeable, but at least it was stable. Virgil rushed to her location. When he made it there, he burst into the room, only to be driven to tears. There she was, lying on the operating table. Her bloodied clothes sat in a pile on the floor, and a white sheet covered her delicate areas. There were cuts and bruises spread across her skin and frost-covered her body in patches. Even with the Saint's Breath spell enveloping her, she shivered uncontrollably. Each breath she exhaled, as feeble as they were, was icy and hung in the air.

Cordelia loomed over Aurelia, her glowing blue hands caressing Aurelia's body. She was hard at work healing her, so much so she hadn't even noticed Virgil had entered the room.

"How is she?" Virgil asked, finally mustering up enough courage to approach.

"Virgil!" Cordellia exclaimed spinning around. "You shouldn't be here!"

"I had to come and check on her."

"I know that," Cordellia replied as she resumed her work. "I mean you shouldn't see her like this. Once you've seen someone in such a broken state, it can be challenging to forget that image."

"I already know all about that." Virgil's hands clenched. A lump lodged deep in his throat. "Tell me. Is she going to be all right?"

Cordellia frowned. "Of course you would already know that. Forgive me. It's going to take some time, but it's nothing I can't fix."

Virgil smiled, but it didn't last long. His relief faded and his burning rage took hold once again, threatening to consume him like a lit match. *This is my fault,* he thought. *I pushed her to do this."*

"You're upset," Cordellia said. "That's understandable, but you mustn't let that anger fuel you."

"I'm not upset," Virgil replied, trying his best to temper his fury.

"I'm upset when I stub my toe getting out of bed in the morning. I'm upset when a hunt gets away. This? This is infuriating."

"Again, that's understandable, but—"

"But nothing!" Virgil exclaimed. "How can you just sit there? How are you not more enraged than I am? Why are you letting this asshole walk around here like he owns the place?"

Cordellia shot Virgil a look so cold he felt it in his bones. The Saint's Breath disappeared, and Cordellia's eyes glowed a brilliant blue. Ice began to coat the walls and furniture, and Virgil could see his breath before him as the temperature plummeted. He began shaking and his heartbeat slowed. His every instinct urged him to coat himself in a layer of thermal energy, but the cold dulled his senses, completely butchering his reaction speed.

"Nothing would please me more than to bury that little prick in a mountain of ice so cold his spirit would freeze over." Cordellia's stare was as sharp as an arrow. Her eyes returned to normal, and warmth returned to the room. "Sadly, that's not the way things work."

"W-what do you mean?" Virgil asked. "You're a king. Surely-"

"My power is great," Cordellia said. "But there are forces in this world far greater than I."

"No," Virgil replied. "My father always told me to avoid fighting with a king of the Crusaders at all costs. Even if you won, it wouldn't be worth the trouble."

Cordellia conjured the Saint's Breath over Aurelia again. "You flatter me, but the truth of the matter is the Crusader's Alliance would not exist if not for the aid of wealthy nobles such as Lucious and his family. As ugly as it is, that is a fact."

"It can't be worth it to have to deal with people like him. To allow them into positions that could influence so many people. It just—it can't be worth the trouble."

"We do our best to screen out as many problems as we can. We take those stones which are a little rough around the edges and polish them into fine gems. Much like what we're doing with you."

Virgil paused for a moment. "And what happens when your best isn't good enough?"

"Then we deal with the consequences of our failure."

"Where is she?" Logan demanded, bursting his way through the door, nearly ripping it from its hinges.

Logan looked past Virgil to find his sister lying on the table. Frantically, he rushed over to her side, nearly toppling Virgil over in the process.

"Aurelia," he whimpered as he took her by the hand. He then turned to Cordellia. His eyes were watery and shot red with anguish. "Please. Please tell me she's going to be okay."

"She'll be fine," Cordellia said. "I just need time to put her back together again."

Logan's tears began to slow. "Thank you."

Virgil stood there quiet, unsure of whether he should go or stay. He desperately wanted to be there for Aurelia. Then again, they weren't really friends. Logan had made that abundantly clear. Of course, she had been there for him when he needed her, and that was enough to keep Virgil rooted right there.

"Virgil," Logan said, his eyes still fixed on Aurelia. "I'm sure you can't stand to even look at me right now, and I know I have no right to do this, but I need to ask you for a favor."

"What is it?" Virgil asked.

"I need you to forfeit your next match."

Virgil's brow raised. "Excuse me?"

"You're fighting Lucious in the next round, right?"

Virgil shoulders tensed, and he clenched his fists. "Yeah," he said, his tone low and determined.

"Surrender your match, and that way I'll get to face off against him in the final round."

"You're joking. You expect me to—"

Logan turned to face Virgil. His eyes were hungry, desperate even. "Please, Virgil. This tournament is the only chance I have. If I go after him outside of the arena, I'll be disbarred for sure."

He began to tremble. At first glance, it might appear that he was frightened, but Virgil knew that expression all too well. He had seen that look reflected back at himself so many times before. Logan was commanding every fiber of his being to contain his fury. Virgil remained silent, struggling to find the words to say.

"I know I'm asking a lot," Logan continued, "but I don't have any other option."

Virgil proceeded to walk away. He opened the door and stopped. "I'll think about it," he said, glancing back. "I don't know if I can sit back and do nothing. But if we do fight, I swear to you, he will pay for this."

TWENTY-NINE

Virgil entered the arena. He tried to keep his mind focused on the task at hand, but all he could think about was Aurelia. Each moment they had shared played in his mind. He smiled, but thoughts of her broken and beaten flashed before him, reigniting the fire in his gut.

Could you live with yourself if you just let this go? he thought.

"Here we are," Roxanne called out. "The placement tournament semi-finals. If you would like to shake hands, do so now."

Although Virgil's gaze was fixed solely on Lucious, he couldn't get the image of Aurelia out of his mind. Each second that passed only added to the resentment building in his heart, until finally, Virgil took a step forward. *You have to make this right,* he thought.

"I have to hand it to you," Lucious called out as he made his way to the center of the arena. "I half expected to you to forfeit and tend to your little friend. Kudos on not being a total bitch."

Virgil didn't answer and kept walking, keeping his pace. Lucious held out his hand, but Virgil didn't take it. Instead, he cocked back and smashed his fist into Lucious's jaw. Lucious fell back clear on his ass. He held his cheek in his hand, bewilderment slathered across his face. The siren rang, but it was entirely unnecessary.

"Get up," Virgil demanded as his fists became engulfed in blue fire. His tone was cold, and his glare even more so. "I can't knock you down again if you stay on the ground."

Lucious summoned an ice wall around Virgil, breaking off his line of sight. Flames sprouted from Virgil's body, melting the wall away. Lucious made a hasty retreat, and placed his palms together, one over the other. Virgil threw his hand in the air, and a pillar of fire shot up from under Lucious. Smoke trailed from his feet as he just barely managed to get out of the way in time.

Lucious ground his teeth and his eye twitched. "I see you're ready for a battle," he said.

Virgil walked towards Lucious, summoning a ball of fire in his palm. "This isn't a battle. It's a massacre."

Virgil hurled his fireball at Lucious. With a snap of his fingers, Virgil split the ball into smaller chunks like a blast from a shotgun. Lucious erected a barrier of water around himself, but it proved to be pointless. Not a single ember came in contact with him. Instead, they hung in the air around him.

"I get it," Lucious said. "This is your signature sorcery. Right? Well, bring it on!"

Virgil laughed as he closed his fist and the fires grew exponentially in size. "This isn't even close to what I'm capable of."

The fireballs swarmed around Lucious, dancing around him. His eyes darted around as he fortified his barrier, waiting to see which one would strike first. One by one, the fires descended upon Lucious, and steam burst forth as they struck the water.

Amidst the chaos, Virgil flew forward. He closed the distance between them and threw another punch at Lucious. Once again, he aimed for his face. However, Lucious caught the strike. Virgil poured mana into his fist, and the flames surrounding it grew unruly. Lucious winced, hissing as he released Virgil's hand. Virgil followed up with another jab. His fist connected, but he wasn't satisfied. He threw another blow, and another. Blood trickled down Lucious's nose and his face began to swell, but that did nothing to quell Virgil's rage.

Virgil pulled his fist back, mustering everything he had into yet another blow. As he threw it, Lucious coated his face in a thick layer of ice. Virgil grunted, flinching as his strike landed. Lucious spun around, and planted his foot into Virgil's shoulder. Just like his face, Lucious coated his foot in ice. Pain shot through Virgil's arm as he stumbled backward, but he managed to remain on his feet.

Both men breathed heavily, seizing the opportunity to rest. Although it pained him to do so, Virgil flexed his shoulder, forcing it to stay fluid. Lucious wiped his nose and looked at the blood on his hand. When he saw it, he ground his teeth and looked to Virgil.

"Okay," Lucious said, his tone low and harsh. "I'm done playing games with you."

Virgil focused his mana, pooling it into his fists. Massive towers of fire rose into the air. They were ferocious, but they paled in comparison to the fire that burned within him. Virgil took flight, charging straight for Lucious, but he stood unwavering. He summoned a barrage of ice shards around him and threw them at Virgil. One after the other, Virgil weaved past them. As he approached Lucious, he prepared his strike.

An overwhelming force struck Virgil's gut as a pillar of ice shot out of the ground and into his stomach. Virgil gasped as the wind was ripped from his sail. The column rose in the air, lifting Virgil along with it, all while encasing him in ice.

Lucious placed his palms together, almost as if he were praying. As he closed his eyes, he recited an incantation. "Freeze where you stand. Glacial Wind!"

Clouds began to form in the air, and the temperature in the arena dropped. Despite being underground, wind started to blow, carrying a frigid chill. Virgil released a burst of fire around him, melting the ice holding him back. He breathed deep. His breath was as visible as smoke.

Damn it! he thought. *He has another signature.*

A stiff gust blasted Virgil, and the polar wind cut his skin like hundreds of tiny blades. He enveloped himself in a layer of thermal energy, but even so, the freezing gusts chilled his skin. His muscles tensed as he ground his teeth.

This is bad. At this rate, I'm gonna run out of mana before I can take him out.

"What's the matter?" Lucious shouted from the ground below. "Lost your nerve?"

Snow fell from the clouds in bulky clusters. One fell upon Virgil's shoulder, and he cried out as a piercing pain shot through his arm. It was like he was trapped in the artic without so much as a scarf to shield his body. A mound of ice sprouted from the spot where the cluster had landed and began spreading across his arm. Virgil engulfed himself in flames once again, managing to melt the ice. Only this time, it required much more mana to do so.

"This is it," Lucious gloated. "There's no way you'll be able to beat this technique. Your little friend certainly couldn't handle it."

Virgil's nostrils flared. The orange glow around him turned blue, and fire erupted from him. The fire kept growing, with no end in sight. Virgil's skin blazed as if it had been set on fire, but he didn't care. He charged at Lucious with everything he had. "Don't you dare talk about her!"

Lucious was unfazed. He raised his hand to Virgil and fired off a barrage of icicles. With a mix of fury and finesse, Virgil blew past the ice and snow. He hurled his fist at Lucious, focusing his fire into the attack. Had it connected, Virgil would have certainly crushed Lucious to dust, but Lucious pulled back just in the nick of time. Virgil's fist crashed into the floor. He grunted, pushing the pain flaring through his knuckles out of his mind. Fire shot out of the ground like a geyser. A blue luminescence glowed bright, and the clouds above them parted from the rising heat. Another snow cluster landed on Virgil's leg. He cried out once again as it crusted over with ice. He held his hand towards it, and melted it with another blast of fire.

Lucious laughed. "You should actually feel quite honored. I developed this ability just for you, and after testing it out on your little friend, I knew—"

Like a rabid dog, Virgil lunged at Lucious. "I TOLD YOU NOT TO TALK ABOUT HER!"

Lucious fired off more shards. One pierced Virgil's arm, and blood gushed from the wound, but it was as if a mosquito merely grazed him. Lucious froze, his eyes wide as Virgil took hold of his neck. He pinned Lucious to the wall, and a loud clang rang out as his back struck the metal.

Virgil channeled his mana into his fingers. Another cluster of snow fell upon his arm. He hissed, but kept his grasp. Ice spread over his arm. Still, his hand did not so much as budge from Lucious's throat. The pain was immeasurable, and the logical move would be to melt the ice as quickly as possible. However, that was the furthest thing from Virgil's mind. Instead, he allowed the ice to consume his arm and ignited his hand with fire.

Lucious shrieked as the fire scorched his neck. The pungent scent of sizzling skin flooded the air, making Virgil's eyes water. The ice crept up to his shoulder and onto his neck, but he continued pouring out fire as if the pain were gasoline. His breaths were heavy and elongated and accompanied by several pain-filled grunts. Still, he kept the fire burning with as much intensity as he could muster. The clouds in the sky disbanded, and the ice that covered Virgil's arm cracked. Finally, he released his hold on Lucious, and the ice coating his arm shattered into a pile on the floor.

Virgil stumbled backward, collapsing on the ground as he held his arm. It was cold to the touch, and stiff to move. His skin was as hard as stone, and so blue it was nearly purple. But his hand, his hand was charred, completely covered with varying shades of black, brown and white skin. Lucious, however, was writhing on the ground, his cries of agony incomprehensible.

Slowly Virgil rose to his feet. Although his body was trembling, it was impossible to tell whether it was due to the pain pulsating through his body, or the wrath coursing through his veins. "Get up," he commanded, his eyes teary.

Lucious didn't respond, the searing pain radiating around his neck clearly too much of a distraction.

"I said, GET UP!"

"I-I can't," Lucious cried.

Virgil walked over to Lucious, each step heavy. "No." He grabbed Lucious's shirt with his good hand. "You don't get to quit." Virgil pulled Lucious up and pinned him to the wall once again. "You don't get to surrender. Not after everything you've done."

Virgil's handprint was painstakingly burned into Lucious's neck, clear as day. Virgil looked into his eyes. They were sunken and pathetic, red with anguish and overflowing with tears.

Virgil shook his head, closing his eyes tight. "It's not enough," he said as he let Lucious go. "It's not nearly enough." He took a few steps back and raised his palm.

Lucious's eyes grew wide. Sweat formed upon his brow, and he cowered on the floor. "I'm sorry," he whimpered.

A fiery inferno swallowed Virgil's hand. "No, you're not," he said. "But you're going to be."

Lucious put his head down, raising his hands above his head. "I-I surrender. You win. Okay? You're the better sorcerer."

The wall opened up, and the tournament attendants rushed in.

"You think I care about petty shit like that?" Virgil exclaimed, his flames intensifying. "This has always been about you being an insufferable, conniving, just a fucking cunt of a human being. No. You're worse than that."

"You're right," Lucious pleaded. "I'm a horrible person. I'll never bother you or your friends again. I swear it."

Virgil looked down at Lucious, cowering like a frightened puppy. This was too easy. After everything he had done, it couldn't end like this.

"The match is over," one of the attendants said.

"Stand down, or you will be disqualified," the other joined in.

Virgil looked at each of them before returning his attention to Lucious. His heart was pounding so hard in his chest, it was a miracle the whole coliseum didn't hear it.

Clayton shot up from his chair. "That's enough, Truesdale! Consider this your final warning."

Virgil looked up at Clayton, and they locked eyes. Everything within him begged Virgil to finish what he started. He looked back down at Lucious and ground his teeth. He took a deep breath, rescinded his flames, and turned to walked away.

"Wait," one of the attendants said. "We have to treat your injuries as well."

Virgil didn't bother looking back. He left the arena, his pace slow and cumbersome as he walked through the halls. Although he had won the fight, he felt empty inside. Nevertheless, he headed straight to the infirmary, but it wasn't for his own benefit.

THIRTY

Virgil shambled his way into Aurelia's room. She was fast asleep, enveloped in the healing glow of Cordellia's Saint's Breath. Logan sat by Aurelia's side. Cordellia, however, sat in a chair along the wall, reading a book. As Virgil approached, she looked his way. A frown crept into her face, and she resumed reading.

"It's done," Virgil said as he held his frostbitten arm.

The room remained quiet. Logan stood up and walked towards Virgil.

"Did something happen?" Virgil asked.

Still no response. Logan walked past Virgil and left the room.

"What did I miss?" Virgil asked, turning to Cordellia.

"Nothing happened," she replied, although she kept her nose in her book.

"Then why are you both acting so weird?"

Cordellia closed her book and set it down on the end table next to her. "We're disappointed in you, Virgil. Albeit for two very different reasons."

Virgil scoffed. "Let me guess. Logan's pissed I didn't bow down for him, and you're upset that I'm upset."

"That more or less sums it up for Logan, but you couldn't be more wrong about me."

"Really? Because when we last spoke, it seemed like you wanted me to just bottle everything up and forget about all the bullshit I've been through."

"And that only furthers my disappointment in you." Befuddlement washed over Virgil, prompting Cordellia to shake her head. "Virgil, the purpose of my words was to relieve you of your frustrations. That's not to say that your anger isn't valid. You have every right to feel the way you do, but you also have every right to move on and be happy."

Virgil's shoulders tensed up. "So, what? Are you saying that I should just let it go? You think I should forgive him for all the terrible things he did?"

"Refusing to let anger consume you does not equate to forgiveness. Anger is a powerful force, Virgil. It can fuel you, drawing out strength you never knew existed within you. But anger is destructive. It can lead you to do terrible, indefensible things."

Virgil's eyes widened as his stomach began to knot. "I'm fine," he said, turning away. "My anger doesn't consume me."

"You don't believe that. It's written all over your face even now. You may not want to admit it, but deep down, you know it to be true."

Virgil remained silent, unable to think of a response. The longer the silence held, the more exposed he began to feel. He couldn't see Cordellia, but he could sense her looking at him. She wasn't glaring, and her actions certainly weren't malicious. Still. It felt as if he were caught under the lens of a microscope, and he needed something, anything, to put an end to the moment.

Cordellia let out a heavy sigh and stood up. "Take a seat." She gestured at her chair. "I'm sure you want to know all about your friend. I'll fill you in while we fix you up."

Virgil looked over to Aurelia as he limped his way over to the chair. She was looking much better, prompting him to smile. However, Logan's remarks shot into his mind, snatching away the happiness he felt. "We're not friends." He grunted as he slowly lowered himself into the chair. "Not anymore."

Cordellia looked Virgil over. Her gaze sank low, and she looked as if she wanted to cry. Virgil's face heated as he turned away, placing his focus on Aurelia.

Cordellia took a deep breath, and conjured the Saint's Breath on Virgil. "If you and her aren't friends anymore, then why are you here?"

Virgil remained silent prompting Cordellia to grin. "That's what I thought,"

Virgil shook his head. "Logan made it abundantly clear we were never friends."

"Of course he did," Cordellia said, rolling her eyes. "As much as I love molding you young Crusaders into upstanding warriors, you're going to work me into an early grave."

"Do you really like it that much?"

"I do, although I wager Roxanne enjoys it more than me. Anywho, try to take what Logan says with a grain of salt. He has some serious baggage, and he's going to take an abundance of patience."

"What kind of baggage? I swear he acts more like Aurelia's father than her brother."

"That isn't for me to say. The good news is, I think you are just the catalyst he needs to finally unload that baggage. I know it sucks. He's going to hurt your feelings, probably more than a few times. If you can bear through it, you can really help him and Aurelia both. But even if you and Logan never see eye to eye, you and Aurelia are certainly friends. Anyone watching you can tell that, so don't you ever take it for granted."

Aurelia turned in her sleep, prompting Cordellia to pick up her book, the title of which made Virgil blush and turn away. "Looks like she's waking up," Cordellia said as she began walking towards the door. "Why don't you get her up to speed on what's going on? I'll be just down the hall. Close enough to keep the Saint's Breath in effect, but far enough to give you two some privacy."

Virgil let out a puff of air then smiled as looked at Cordellia. "You knew this was all going to happen, didn't you?"

"Nope." Cordellia grinned. "I never use my talent during the placement tournament. I like to be surprised by how things turn out."

Cordellia left the room. As the door closed behind her, Aurelia drifted back into consciousness.

"Welcome back," Virgil said.

"Where'd I go?" Aurelia asked. Her voice was low and hoarse.

"Lucious knocked you out in your match. You don't have to worry, though. I cleaned his clock for you."

Aurelia shivered. "That explains why it's so damn cold."

"I can help with that." Virgil reached out for Aurelia's hand.

She took it, and her hand began to glow orange. The glow spread around her until it covered every inch of her body.

"You really are a space heater," Aurelia said with a smile as she cozied up in her sheet. "While I do appreciate your generous donation of heat, shouldn't you be conserving your mana? I hate to say it, but you look terrible."

Virgil looked his body over. The Saint's Breath was doing its job, but it still had a way to go. Cuts and bruises were no longer present, and his hand was beginning to look normal. Even so, his arm was still discolored despite regaining some feeling. "Yeah. It seems I can't keep myself from getting hurt. I'll be fine, though."

"Well, you're in good hands. Cordellia is an amazing healer. I mean, she's got us both wrapped in the Saint's Breath. I can tell you firsthand, casting it once is difficult."

"She is pretty great, huh."

"I'm guessing Logan is out going through his match."

Virgil nodded. "Try not to worry about him. Just focus on getting better."

"Oh, I'm not worried. He's going to win, and he'll be back here soon enough."

"Yeah. I'm sure you're right." Aurelia fell silent as she looked down. "Is everything all right?" Virgil asked. "I can run and get Cordellia."

Aurelia shook her head. "No. I, I'm fine."

"You know, I'm pretty sure I've mastered the art of deciphering when you're upset."

Aurelia giggled as she turned to Virgil, her head tilted slightly. "You think you know me that well?"

"Maybe. I could always just read your aura."

"That's true. Honestly though, I'm fine. I just, we really should talk."

"About what?"

"You know. What happened before between you and Logan—"

Virgil leaned back in his seat. "There's nothing to talk about."

"Yes, there is. Logan said horrible things to you and—"

"And I'm still here. Don't get me wrong. What he said hurt. Like really really hurt, but I understand he's going through a lot. I'm willing to overlook it. I mean, that's what a good friend would do. Right?"

Aurelia's face reddened. "I, uh, I didn't expect you to take this so well. Don't take this the wrong way, but you can be a little hot tempered."

Virgil chuckled. "Well, I did have some help putting things into perspective. In any case, you and I are friends, and that's something nobody can take away from me."

"You're damn right." Aurelia said. "Don't worry. I'll make sure Logan gives you an apology."

"Aurelia, that's really not—"

The doorknob turned, and Logan stepped into the room. "You're awake." He beamed.

"That was pretty quick," Virgil replied. "You didn't throw your match, did you?"

"Of course not," Logan said as he approached the hospital bed. "I just ended the match as quickly and efficiently as I possibly could."

Aurelia gasped. "Logan, you didn't."

"You know I did."

"Okay, I'm lost," Virgil said. "Just what did you do?"

"I merely broke the girl's hands," Logan said as he folded his arms. "It's nothing a good healer can't fix, and some of the best in the world are here on the island."

Aurelia sighed as she shook her head. "At least you both made it through to the next round." The room fell silent as each of them realized just what those words meant. Virgil and Logan looked to each other, not a word spoken between them. "You two cut that out right now," Aurelia snapped.

"Aurelia, I—"

"I don't want to hear it, Logan." Virgil couldn't help but chuckle as Logan began to blush, but a stern look from Aurelia put an end to it. "Logan, you have been incredibly rude and insensitive towards Virgil. Apologize to him this instant."

Logan remained silent as the siblings glared at each other.

"Aurelia," Virgil began, "you don't have to—"

"No, Virgil. My brother has been a complete ass, and he needs to apologize." Logan remained silent still, folding his arms. "Have you forgotten that Virgil saved your life? The least you can do is apologize for what you said to him."

Logan pursed his lips, and sighed as he turned to Virgil. "I hate to admit it, but my sister's right. I do owe you for what you did back in the Network."

Virgil shook his head. "I didn't save you for any type of reward. You don't owe me a thing."

"Be that as it may, my behavior as of late has been uncouth. Especially considering what you have done for me. Though I must admit I'm not really good at this sort of thing."

Virgil smiled. "Don't worry about it. I understand."

Aurelia groaned as she rolled her eyes. "I suppose this is as good as I'm going to get, huh. Listen, you two. You both have a special place in my heart. Logan, you are my brother. We're family, and I know you will always be there for me, just as I will always be there for you. And Virgil, I know we haven't known each other long, but we've been through a hell of a lot together. As far as I'm concerned, we're friends for life. Actually, fuck that. We're best friends. You two have helped make my dreams come true, and I will always be grateful for that. Don't let the stress of this exam tear us apart."

Virgil and Logan nodded before turning to one another. Virgil smiled, and proceeded to walk away.

"Where are you headed off to?" Aurelia asked.

Virgil glanced back. "Nowhere in particular. If Logan and I are going to be battling, we probably shouldn't be hanging out in the same room." He opened the door and waved back to Logan. "No matter what happens, no hard feelings, okay."

CHAPTER

THIRTY-ONE

"This is it," Virgil said as he walked through the corridor. "I made it to the final round of the tournament. I really wish I didn't have to fight Logan, but I guess that was always a likely possibility."

Virgil cracked his knuckles and stretched his arms. His muscles were still stiff, but he was close to being restored.

"This is going to be a tough fight," he continued. "His strength alone is going to be a problem, but then there's O'Drakka's Fist." Virgil groaned. "Just how exactly am I supposed to deal with this?"

He took a deep breath. "Remember what you're here for. You have to find a way to win. Making rook is your ticket to riding solo and tracking down Cecelia, and you know just where to start looking. I'm sure the Scarlet Mage . . ." Virgil's eyes grew wide and his heart skipped a beat as a terrifying thought echoed through his mind. "The Scarlet Mage. I was supposed to be looking for the Scarlet Mage. Fuck. I was supposed to be looking for Olivia!"

Virgil picked up his pace, only to slow back down as Cordellia rounded the corner ahead. "What incredible timing," she said. "I just heard the news and was coming to get you. We can't have you and Logan socializing before your match, after all."

"Right," Virgil replied, trying his best to keep his composure.

"Come along with me. I'll escort you."

"No," Virgil said abruptly. "I mean, you don't need to trouble yourself with me. You've already done so much."

Cordellia wrapped her arm around Virgil. "Oh, hush up. It's my job to take care of you, and you still have about ten more minutes until you're fully healed."

"Really," Virgil said, rubbing his neck. "I feel so good, though. I don't want to be a burden any more than I already am."

Cordellia stopped. "Okay, Virgil," she began. "What's going on? Are you really that nervous about fighting Logan?"

"Y-yeah," Virgil replied. "I'm just, I'm really nervous. I would feel a lot more comfortable working through it alone. You know?"

"Of course." Cordellia nodded. "Whatever you need to do to relax. As soon as you're finished healing, I'll get out of your hair."

"Great," Virgil replied, forcing a smile as they resumed walking.

Virgil closed his eyes and focused his mind. He prayed he'd be able to pick up a trace of Olivia, but just as before, he came up dry.

Damn it, he thought as he ground his teeth. *How could you be so stupid?*

"You really are stressed, aren't you?" Cordellia said. "Are you sure there's nothing else bothering you? I wouldn't have guessed you'd be this distraught, having to face off against Logan."

Olivia's words echoed through his mind. He had promised he wouldn't say anything to anyone. Of course, she was supposed to be there with him. Time was running out. No. It was nearly out. There was only one match left to go, and he was no closer to finding the Scarlet Mage than when he started. In fact, he had managed to lose the one person he knew he could count on.

"Virgil?" Cordellia said. "You can tell me what's wrong. I'm here to help you."

Virgil stopped in place. It was as if his heart and mind were competing to see who could race faster. His stomach was wound tight and sweat trailed down the back of his neck.

What's the right thing to do? Can I really handle this on my own? How would I handle this on my own? What if he already got his hands on the Crystal Catalyst? What if he captured Olivia? What if he killed her?

Cordellia placed her hand on Virgil's shoulder, and they locked eyes. "You look terrified," she said, worry plastered all over her face, her eyes heavy with concern. "What's going on?"

I can tell her, can't I? What if I do, and she's working with the Scarlet Mage? I'd have to fight her. She's an aquamancer. Fuck. She's a king. She'd kill me on the spot.

Cordellia gave Virgil's shoulder a gentle squeeze as she waited with bated breath. "Cordellia," Virgil began. "This is going to sound crazy, but I need you to hear me out."

"Of course. Whatever it is, you can tell me."

"The Scarlet Mage is here. He's after the Crystal Catalyst. It isn't safe."

Cordellia's face turned pale. The Saint's Breath coating Virgil vanished. Her mouth fell open and her eyes widened as she pulled her hand back. "How do you know the Crystal Catalyst is here on the island?"

"I, I can't say."

A moment of silence passed between the two as each of them seemed to be analyzing the other. Cordellia cleared her throat. "Well," she resumed, "I assure you, what you're suggesting is impossible. The kings have enchanted the island to ward off unwanted intruders. No one can step foot on this ground without being invited."

"That's just it." Virgil clenched his fists. "I think the Scarlet Mage has infiltrated the Crusader's Alliance somehow. Perhaps as an applicant."

"Again, that's impossible. Each of you has been vetted extensively. There's no way the Scarlet Mage has slipped past us. Now, where have you gotten this idea?"

"I'm telling you he is here, and he's after the Catalyst. If he manages to get it, a lot of people are going to die."

Cordellia sighed as she shook her head. "Okay. Let's just take a step back. I don't know how you came to know we've recovered the Crystal Catalyst, but it is securely kept under guard. It couldn't possibly be in a safer place. That aside, I doubt severely the Scarlet

Mage, as powerful as he may be, would be able to infiltrate our ranks."

"He's not alone, though. He's been working with witches, and—"

"We're aware of that as well. Even so, the likelihood of the Scarlet Mage successfully sneaking his way among us is just laughable."

Virgil paused for a moment as he looked down at the floor. "Your clairvoyance!" he exclaimed as he looked up again with a spark of hope. "You can look into the future, and we can know for sure nothing is going to happen."

Cordellia frowned. "It isn't as simple as that, Virgil. As I said before, none of what I see is absolute. I merely get a glimpse of the most likely possibilities, and from there, I can make an educated guess on what will happen."

Virgil's shoulders tensed, and he balled his fists. "That's still better than nothing."

"Virgil, I—"

"Please, Cordellia. I have an awful feeling this tournament is going to end terribly, and this could be the only way to keep it from happening.

Cordellia fell silent. After a brief moment, she closed her eyes and exhaled. "I'm not going to use my clairvoyance." Virgil opened his mouth to speak, but Cordellia quickly cut him off. "After spending most of the day healing our Crusaders, I simply don't have the mana reserves left to see anything of consequence. What I will do is have a team search the castle grounds. Will that put your mind at ease?"

"But what if the Scarlet Mage is one of the search team? He could be anyone, and—"

"And if that happens to be the case, then I will deal with it personally."

Virgil fell silent once again.

"Is there anything else?" Cordellia asked.

"N-no," Virgil stuttered. "Thank you."

"All right," Cordellia said as she wrapped her arm around Virgil once again. "Let's get you to your final match."

After walking Virgil to his destination and ensuring he was in tip-top shape, Cordellia left him to his own devices. Virgil stood outside the arena, trying his best to contain his anxiety. His body was tense and his nerves jumpy. He closed his eyes and scanned the castle once again.

"I still can't sense her," Virgil said to himself.

Finally, the arena wall opened up, and the combatants stepped through. Virgil looked across the battlefield at Logan. A fierce determination radiated from him as he kept his gaze fixed on Virgil.

I have to finish this quickly.

Logan cracked his knuckles and summoned O'Drakka's Fists.

Who am I kidding? There's no way this ends quickly.

"This is the final round of the placement tournament," Roxanne called out to the coliseum. "Given what we've seen from these two competitors, it is sure to be a match for the ages." The crowd was deafening with excitement. "If you would like to shake hands, please do so now."

Virgil's eyes widened. *That's it! I can surrender.*

Logan walked towards Virgil, and he followed suit. The two men shook hands and returned to their respective sides.

Virgil smiled. *Yeah. If I surrender, the match will be over, and I can focus on finding Olivia.*

He looked up to the kings and opened his mouth to speak, only to be interrupted by a violent eruption.

CHAPTER
THIRTY-TWO

T he entire island quaked, and an eerie green glow appeared. A barrier adorned with runes began to form and was quickly sealing off the coliseum.

"Everyone remain calm!" Roxanne called out as she summoned a void behind her. "It appears we are under attack. Remain here, and we'll be back for you once we have secured the island."

The kings left through the void, and the arena walls retracted into the ground. Virgil dashed for the exit, desperate to make it through before the barrier closed. His efforts, however, were entirely in vain. The barrier closed off just as he reached the threshold.

Virgil reached out towards the barrier. He could feel the malice oozing from it. He looked at the runes, and while he couldn't read what they said, he recognized them instantly. His heart skipped a beat, and his hands trembled. He closed his eyes and scanned as far as his aura perception could reach. There were several new auras spread out across the island. Each of them gave off a malevolent force so intense they sent shivers down Virgil's spine. However, there was one distinct aura signature he had encapsulated deep within his heart. Virgil opened his eyes. His fists were tight as he stared at the barrier. There was no other option. He had to escape the coliseum.

Virgil unleashed a flurry of blue flames upon the barrier only to have them be soaked up like water into a thirsty sponge. His jaw tightened as he prepared to throw another blast. However, a touch on his shoulder stopped him.

"Don't bother," Logan said. "Even I can tell that barrier's too strong for you to burn through."

"You don't know what I'm capable of," Virgil sneered as he turned to Logan, shrugging his hand off.

"Just step aside," Logan said, as he approached the barrier. He reached out with his gloves. As soon as his fingers touched the barrier, sparks erupted from it, and Logan flinched as he pulled his hand away. "This can't be," Logan said, his jaw wide. "Even if it's lost magic, O'Drakka's Fist should still have an effect on it."

"Well, it doesn't," Virgil replied. "Now move out of the way."

Logan turned back to Virgil. "Would you just stop for a second and think? Throwing fire at it over and over again is only going to waste precious resources."

Virgil clenched his fists. "I don't have time to sit here and argue with you. I'm going to bust through that barrier. Don't expect me to feel sorry for you if you get hurt because you're too stubborn to move out of the way."

"You think I'm stubborn?" Logan pointed to his chest. "You're literally trying to throw the same tired ass solution at the problem, expecting it to work as if it didn't just fail miserably."

"What if I joined in?" Fynn suggested as he, along with the other probationary Crusaders, approached the bickering men. "Perhaps if we attacked the barrier together, we could overpower it."

Logan shook his head. "There's no way we'll overpower it."

"And why not?" Mifune asked. "Among the nine of us here, we have someone from nearly every branch of sorcery. It seems to me like it's at least worth a try."

"Even with all of us combined, we couldn't break through."

"You just can't help being a wet blanket, can you?" Virgil replied.

Logan focused his attention on Virgil. "Look," he began, his tone stern. "No one wants to break out of here more than I do. My sister is out there right now, and while I can't sense it, that anxious look on your face tells me some seriously bad shit is going down. That said, if you stopped to think, you'd realize this barrier is a prison. Whoever is responsible for this waited until the final round of the tournament. Our forces are either injured or focused on the battle. This means this cage was designed to hold the strongest Crusaders on the island, and in case you failed to realize it, that includes the kings."

"Logan makes a fair point," Mifune said. "Assuming the intent of the barrier is to contain all of us plus the kings, there's not a chance in hell we'd be able to break it."

Virgil turned away. He didn't want to admit it, but Logan was right. Again. Still, he had to find a way out.

Astrid stepped up. Even though the fair skinned blonde was short, she stood tall, brimming with confidence. "All right. All right," she began, "Astrid's here to save the day." She waved her fingers, and a pink void appeared.

Virgil turned back to Astrid, his nostrils flared. "You know allostry, and you only just now said something?"

"I was enjoying the theatrics," Astrid replied. "Now, there is one little problem."

"And what's that?"

"I'm still a little shaky on spatial magic. I'm afraid I'm only capable of transporting three people a few hundred feet. After that, my manas pretty low."

"That's not a problem," Virgil replied. "If you can just get me outside of the barrier, I can manage the rest."

"Not so fast," Fynn jumped in. "Why do you automatically get to go?"

Because she's out there! Virgil thought. He cleared his throat as he folded his arms. "Well, because I'm the strongest one here."

"That has yet to be decided," Mifune pointed out.

Virgil groaned. "Whatever. Then Logan and I will go, and the rest of you can decide on the last spot."

"Umm, excuse me," Astrid replied as she raised her finger. "Don't you think I should have a say in how my magic is used?"

"You are absolutely correct," Logan said as he turned to Astrid. "This is your ability, and you have every right to decide how it is used." He took a small step towards her, and clasped his hands together. "Please allow me to use your void. I have to make it to my sister."

Virgil rolled his eyes and turned his attention back to the barrier. "We're just wasting time at this point. Let me know when you've made a decision." Virgil balled his fists as he stared at the barrier. "Let's see if this prison can contain white fire."

"Are you serious?" Fynn said, his jaw wide. "You're really skilled enough to produce white fire?"

"I don't know," Virgil replied, his eyes narrowing, "but I'm going to find out."

Astrid burst out into laughter. "So much drama. I love it!" She took a deep breath and placed her hands on her hips. "Now here's what I'm thinking. Despite being a total dick right now, Virgil is right." Virgil stopped and turned back to the group. As he looked at Astrid, his face heated and he rubbed his neck. "He and Logan did make it to the final round," she continued, "therefore, they will likely be the most useful outside. Unfortunately, neither of the runner-ups are here, so that leaves the C team." Astrid then turned her attention to Angelica. "I'm sorry to say this, but seeing as you folded under pressure in the second round, I don't think you're up for the task." Angelica's face turned red as everyone's eyes were fixed on her. She looked as if she wanted to speak, but as harsh as Astrid's words were, they were ultimately valid. "So, that just leaves me."

"Then it's decided," Virgil said. "And I'm sorry. I just—"

Astrid held up her hand. "Don't. Just go out there and show these assholes who they're fucking with."

Virgil nodded, and the trio approached the pink void. His skin was hot with anticipation, and his nerves felt as if they had been struck by lightning. A wide grin stretched across his face. It wouldn't be much longer now.

Virgil entered the void and reappeared into a pitch-black space. Not an ounce of light was in sight, making the darkness feel infinite and all-consuming.

"Logan?" Virgil called out. "Astrid? Are you there?"

"I'm here," Astrid replied in the distance.

"Where are we?"

"I don't know? My void should have placed us just outside the coliseum."

"Logan?" Virgil called out again. "Can you hear me?" Still, no response.

"I got a bad feeling about this," Astrid said.

"You and me both. Stay where you are. It'll be easier for me to make it to you."

"Y-yeah. Sure. Sounds like a plan."

Virgil closed his eyes to tune his aura perception. Before he could locate Astrid, the sound of her screaming echoed through his ears, springing him to attention.

"Who, who's there?" she shouted.

"Hold on!" Virgil shouted as he flew through the darkness, heading towards the source of Astrid's cries.

"Stay back. I said, stay back!"

Virgil pushed himself to go faster. He closed his eyes once again and locked onto Astrid's aura signature. His eyes burst open, and he came to a screeching halt. He narrowed his eyes, searching the darkness ahead for the slightest bit of movement. He took a deep breath, his hair standing on end.

"Virgil!" Astrid called out. "Where are you? I-I need your help!"

Virgil shrouded his fists in fire, lighting the darkness. Sadly, the light only reached a few dozen feet. "I don't know who you are, but you are not Astrid."

Everything fell silent. The darkness only seemed to amplify the sense of dread looming in the air. Virgil looked closer. It was faint, but there were two glowing slits in the distance. They were as red as freshly drawn blood. Virgil couldn't help but tense up and intensify his flames. His eyes widened as he shifted to the side. While his reflexes were sharp, they weren't nearly fast enough. He hissed, and blood began to trickle down his cheek from the freshly sliced patch of skin.

"Oh my," Astrid said. "I didn't expect that. I can usually get a clean shot. Right between the eyes."

"Who are you?" Virgil demanded.

"Who I am doesn't matter. After all, you'll be dead soon enough. Just like all of your little buddies."

"You couldn't be more wrong," Virgil scoffed. "If you're the Scarlet Mage—"

He jumped to the side, but it was no good. He flinched, grunting as a blade lodged in his arm.

"The Scarlet Mage," the voice sneered, but it was different from Astrid's. It was now deeper and full of contempt. "If only. You might have stood a chance then."

Virgil grasped the hilt of the blade. "That's too bad. Now, there's nothing to hold me back from roasting you alive." He yanked the blade out, wincing as the cold metal pulled against his flesh. As soon as the knife left his body, it disappeared from Virgil's hands. He held his palm over the wound, burning it shut. The pain was intense, and he hissed as the flames seared his skin, but of course, he was no stranger to being burned.

Virgil lifted his palm up and summoned a massive ball of fire. With a snap of his fingers, the ball dispersed into countless orbs. They spread throughout the darkness. The glowing slits of a creature's eyes became clearly visible. His skin was a pale blue and appeared to be as smooth as silk. He wore a black robe held together with red chains, and skulls were draped around his neck.

"You're a demon," Virgil said, his eyes narrowing. "Clearly not the friendly type."

"Ouch," the demon replied. "You sound so harsh. Careful. You might hurt my feelings."

"Like I give a damn about your feelings."

"Oh. Would you care if I looked like this?" The demon began to morph and change. Even his clothes shifted. In a matter of moments, the demon was the spitting image of Astrid.

"Why didn't you help me, Virgil?" the demon teased. "I'm dead now because of you."

Virgil tensed up, his shoulders stiffening. "You're lying."

The demon laughed as it shifted back into its original form. "Believe that if you want. To change my form, I need to drink the blood of my victims." The demon then licked his lips. "Trust me. I have quite the thirst."

The demon charged towards Virgil, and he followed suit. As the demon moved, he summoned a short sword in each of his hands. He drew in close and swung one of his blades. Without the darkness hampering his vision, Virgil could evade the strike. The demon swung his remaining blade, and again Virgil dodged the steel. He grabbed the demon's neck and pinned him to the ground.

"Like I said before, there's nothing to keep me from killing you."

"W-Wait," the demon gasped between choked breaths. "If you kill me, you'll, you'll never escape this place."

Virgil tightened his grip. "I'll figure something out."

The demon drove his blade down, only it didn't crash into the floor. Instead, it entered the shadow cast on the ground. A stinging pain surged through Virgil's shoulder. He hissed in pain as blood slid down his back. He couldn't help but release his grip on the demon.

The demon fell back, retreating to safety. "That was a close one," he said, relieved.

Virgil stood back up on his feet. He didn't bother trying to remove the blade. It was far too deep in his back for him to reach it anyway. "That was my mistake. I should have known you were an adept alloster. After all, you managed to reroute Astrid's void. Right?"

The demon smirked. "That was mere child's play. Your friend could really use more training. Oops. I suppose it's too late for that now."

Virgil forced out a laugh. "It's funny. I always imagined my first fight with a demon would be a lot different. I've heard so many terrifying stories."

"Oh," the demon replied, tilting his head "Am I not living up to your expectations?"

"Honestly, you're not even close."

The demon's eye twitched, and anger filled his face. He began to shift once more. He grew larger, and extra limbs sprouted from his flesh. His smooth skin turned nasty and rotten as if it had been slowly eaten away by maggots. A powerful odor emanated from the demon's body, and his eyes merged into one massive orb.

"How do you like me now?" the demon taunted. "Am I terrifying enough for you?"

Virgil didn't so much as blink as he looked at the monstrosity standing before him. "All you'll accomplish now is making a bigger pile of ashes."

The demon lunged at Virgil, but he simply closed his fists. The demon burst into flame and screamed. Despite his tearful wails, he swung his massive arms at Virgil, but it would have been nearly impossible for Virgil not to dodge his slow, brutish blows. Virgil cranked up the heat, turning his orange fire to a luminous blue. The demon stopped in place, his cries of anguish growing louder. He began to shrink. Virgil called off his fire as the demon knelt on the floor.

"I'll only tell you this once," Virgil said, his tone cold. "Let me out of this place, and I might just let you live."

The demon looked up to Virgil. Through the charred and seared flesh, it was difficult to make out, but it was clear looking in the demon's eyes, he had taken Olivia's form.

"Virgil," the demon uttered.

Virgil ground his teeth, his eyes narrowing as he closed his fist once more. "Wrong answer," he said, and a roaring inferno consumed the demon.

CHAPTER
THIRTY-THREE

Virgil recalled his fire. There was nothing more than a pile of ash on the floor. He exhaled, relaxing his guard. The room began to shake, throwing him off balance. The darkness shifted, and was replaced with the evening sky. Virgil was so high above the ground, he could see the edges of Akata Island.

He stabilized himself and looked around. Chaos surrounded him. Trees collapsed in the distance, and massive boulders flew around as if they were merely wads of crumpled paper. From the corner of his eye, Virgil saw a blur spiraling. He turned to face it and found Logan falling to the ground. Only he wasn't alone. With him was another demon, this one nearly twice Logan's size.

"Not this again," Virgil said as he took off. Virgil caught up to Logan and the demon, and threw a kick, knocking the demon away. "Grab on to—"

Before Virgil could even finish his sentence, Logan latched onto him. "What the fuck!" Virgil exclaimed, barely able to breathe.

"I, I'm sorry," Logan said, his eyes shut tight. "I'm afraid of heights."

"You've got to be kidding me. You were fine just a second ago."

"I had something to keep my mind off it. You have to get us to the ground safely."

"You know, I think I preferred this when you were unconscious." Virgil's eyes grew wide as a terrifying realization popped into his mind. "Wait a minute. If we both appeared in the sky, where is Astrid?"

Virgil closed his eyes and focused his mind, tuning his aura perception. With his attention diverted, they plummeted, prompting Logan to let out an ear-shattering scream. Virgil's ears rang as he slowed their descent. "Seriously, Logan. What the fuck."

"I-I'm sorry."

"You're lucky I found her."

Virgil looked over in Astrid's direction. She was a few hundred feet above them. Thankfully, she didn't have company with her. Unfortunately, it would be impossible to save her while Virgil still had Logan in his arms. Virgil looked down. A collision with the ground was imminent, and they would soon be approaching the treetop foliage of the forest biome.

"All right, Logan," Virgil said as calmly as he could. "I need you to listen to me."

Logan shook his head vigorously. "Why does it sound like you're about to hit me with some bullshit?"

"Listen to me. Astrid is falling over there, and I can't save you both."

"Yes, you can. Don't say that."

"Logan, I'm going to have to drop you."

"No, no, no, no, no, no. That's bullshit, Virgil. I knew you were going to come at me with some bullshit."

"Logan, I have to drop you. We're approaching the trees. I can slow down as much as I can, but I have to drop you, and you have to grab onto one of the branches."

Logan didn't respond but intensified his grip on Virgil.

"Oh, for fuck's sake." Virgil slowed down and shrouded his body in fire, keeping the flames just hot enough to force Logan to let go of him. "You can do it!" Virgil shouted as Logan fell. "Just reach out and grab a tree!"

Virgil turned his attention to Astrid. She was falling rapidly, but if he hurried, he could still make it. He took off, funneling his mana into flying. A shining pink light formed under Astrid. As she touched the light, she disappeared, and not long after, so did the light.

Virgil came to a halt. "She overcame her limitations." He then looked down at the forest below and frowned. "Sorry about that, Logan. I guess I could have helped you down." Virgil took in a deep breath and released it, closing his eyes. "Okay. Now, where is she?"

It didn't take long for him to find her again. He flew faster than he ever had before. Even so, it wouldn't be enough. He lit his fists and feet on fire, releasing streams of flames as if his limbs were jet engines. Dull pain pulsed in his back from his previous injury, and his mana was far from full. Still, his eyes were unblinking.

Danny. Danté. Both of them were plastered in his mind.

Virgil tried his best to shake away those thoughts. They would only serve to hamper him, dulling his senses when he needed them the most. Casting them aside was his best chance at coming out on top, and yet, he could see them both so vividly.

Danny. Danté. His family.

Virgil approached the grassland biome situated just beyond the forest. His chest grew tighter as the aura he despised so much became clearer. Time felt like it was slowing down with every breath he took. Finally, he saw her, and his heart skipped a beat. Virgil pushed himself, forcing his body to go even faster. The thought of delaying the moment for even a second longer was an indignity too great to bear.

Virgil landed on the ground a few dozen feet behind the woman. She kept her pace, unfazed by Virgil's arrival. For a moment, he paused. Surely she recognized Virgil's presence. How could she not? He waited for her to acknowledge him, his body tense and his stomach tied in knots.

He tried to keep his composure, but his nerves got the better of him. "CECELIA!"

She didn't respond. Virgil threw his hand into the air, summoning a massive wall of fire blocking Cecelia's path. She sighed and slowly turned around. "All right," she said, her voice smooth, almost soothing, "you have my attention."

Virgil grinned, his eyes narrowing "Finally. I've finally found you. This time things will be different."

"This time?" Cecelia replied. "Pardon me, but do I know you?"

Virgil's eyes widened as Cecelia's words echoed through his mind. There was no doubt within him. He had felt her presence even before escaping the coliseum. This was it. He had finally found her. "Do you *know* me?" he said, unable to gather his thoughts beyond those four words.

"Yes. You clearly know me, but I'm afraid you're not ringing any bells, sweetheart. Have we hooked up before or something? You certainly look like my type."

"You don't, you don't recognize me. Do you?"

Cecelia laughed. "Obviously not."

Virgil swallowed the lump in his throat. "You took everything away from me," he said, his voice hollow. "My brother. My father. You ruined my life, and you don't even remember who I am."

Cecelia placed a hand on her hip. "I've ruined a lot of lives. I'm afraid you're going to have to be more specific."

Virgil fell silent, entirely floored by Cecelia's response. His flames subsided, and his arms fell loosely to his side.

Cecelia rolled her eyes, her patience clearly waning. "Look. Now's really not a good time, so here's the deal. I can either kill you, or you can let me go. Normally, I wouldn't be so generous, but it's been a bit of a shitty day for me, so I'd rather not be bothered."

"You're never leaving this island," Virgil said, snapping out of his stupor. "I'm going to spend hours melting every inch of flesh off your bones."

Cecelia's eyes narrowed to slits. "Wait a minute," she said as her eyes trailed downward falling upon Virgil's neck. It was subtle, but her body tensed up. "I remember now. You're Vincent. Right?"

"It's Virgil."

"Whatever. You're Danny's brother. I remember you from that night all those years ago. You got that same hateful look in your eyes. Wait. No. It's much worse now."

Virgil balled his fist. "I'm glad it's all come back to you. Truthfully, I would have taken your life either way, but it warms my heart to know that as you die you'll understand why I'm burning you to ashes. You're going to pay for taking my brother and father away from me."

Cecelia's brow raised and she pursed her lips. For a brief moment she stared Virgil down, and then flashed a devilish grin. "You don't remember what happened. Do you?"

"I'm not falling for your tricks," Virgil said shaking his head. "You killed my brother. You cursed my father. If it wasn't for you they'd still be here!"

Cecelia let out a hearty laugh before holding out her hand. "Can't pull the wool over your eyes, huh. Nevertheless, it seems like my luck's turning around. So, here's the new deal. If you hand over the Fang of Kayveon, you get to leave here alive. Refuse, and I'll feed you to my demons. Oh, but not before enchanting your body of course. We wouldn't want you passing out during the feast!"

Virgil's skin ached with heat. He forced the pain down, and placed his left hand over his right wrist. "You're going to pay for every family you've ripped apart, starting with mine." Virgil's aura began to swell as he focused his mana into his right hand. "Hand of Destruction. Immolation!"

His right hand burst into flame. Only this time, it was different. His hand wasn't merely surrounded by an inferno. It *was* an inferno. The roaring fire lit up the night in an ominous purple glow. It was nearly impossible to distinguish just where Virgil's flesh ended and the fire began. A stark sensation overtook the air. Despite the fire roaring from Virgil's wrist, the air felt cold, as if Virgil's flame siphoned all of the heat from around him.

Neither Virgil nor Cecelia blinked as their eyes were locked on one another. Virgil took flight, charging directly for her. Cecelia appeared unfazed. In fact, she smiled with a sinister glint in her eye. Virgil drew in close. He reached for Cecelia, but quickly pulled backward, retreating to a safe distance. He wasn't nearly fast enough. A trail of blood spattered across the grass from his chest. He was losing blood fast. His hand returned to normal, and his breath became burdened. His mana reserves were nearly empty.

Virgil looked over at his assailant. A man stood in front of Cecelia, holding a blood-soaked sword. He couldn't have been taller than five foot eight, and he wore a red and black cloak with a lowered cowl. A black mask decorated with splatters of red paint covered his face. Slits in the mask revealed bronze skin and a pair of dark brown eyes. His hair was as black as midnight, and a mess of untamed curls sprouted in nearly every direction.

"Hmmph," Cecelia said, placing a hand on her hip. "Look at you, coming to rescue little ol' me."

The man remained silent, his attention fixed on Virgil. He raised his palm, and a red void formed behind him.

"He doesn't know," Cecelia said as she turned to walk away. "Make it quick before he figures it out."

Virgil waved his hand, summoning the mightiest wall of fire he could muster between Cecelia and the void, but given his current state, he could barely keep his legs from shaking, let alone conjure a decent wall. "N-no," Virgil said, his breath escaping him. "I've waited, I've waited too long for this. You're—"

Perhaps it was the blood loss finally settling in. Or maybe the man was just that fast. Virgil blinked and the man was in his face, slashing him across his chest once again. Virgil cried out as he stumbled backward. The wall of fire disappeared, and Cecelia stepped through the void.

"You," Virgil whimpered. "You're the Scarlet Mage. Aren't you?"

Just like before, the man didn't speak. The Scarlet Mage walked towards Virgil. His instincts told him to move, but his body refused. The Scarlet Mage reached out towards Virgil, grabbing hold of the Fang of Kayveon.

"That's mine." Virgil raised his hand to stop him, trying his best to conjure flames, but to no avail. "You can't. You can't take it."

The Scarlet Mage pulled the necklace over Virgil's head, and casually placed it around his neck. He placed a hand on Virgil's chest. "I expected better from you," he said, finally breaking his silence.

Virgil's eyes grew wide as the Scarlet Mage's words echoed through his ears. But it wasn't what the man said that rocked him to his core—it was the familiarity of his tone. The Scarlet Mage nudged Virgil, knocking him onto his back. He turned and walked towards his void.

Virgil closed his eyes. He had to confirm it. A quick scan was all it took to turn his worst fears into a horrifying reality.

Get up. You can't let him go. Get up.

Despite his desires, his body simply wouldn't obey. He could only lie there helpless, the dreams he had for so long slipping away.

His ears perked as he heard another familiar voice. "Stop!" Olivia shouted. "I'm placing you under arrest by order of the Crusader's Alliance."

GET UP! Virgil dug deep, finally summoning the strength to sit up. The Scarlet Mage turned to face Olivia.

"No," Virgil said.

Olivia raised her hands to the Scarlet Mage, summoning a massive wooden fist. It flew towards him, and the Scarlet Mage returned the favor with a conjured trident. As the trident hit the wood, it split it clean in two. Each half of the fist flew past the Scarlet Mage, bypassing him entirely. However, the trident didn't stop there. It kept going, plunging deep into Olivia's stomach. She shrieked as she stumbled backward. Blood began gushing onto the ground, and she gasped for air.

Virgil's screams grated his throat. Tears flowed from his eyes in a downpour. It wasn't too late. If he could just make it there, he could do something. Anything. His jaw tightened, and he pushed himself further. His body throbbed with the slightest bit of pressure. He grunted as he forced himself onto his feet. His muscles felt as if they were being shredded.

Virgil took a step. It was small, and his leg gave out from under him, but it was one step closer to Olivia. He looked over to her, and the Scarlet Mage snapped his finger. The trident began to spin like a tornado, completely eviscerating Olivia's insides.

CHAPTER
THIRTY-FOUR

The Scarlet Mage left through his void, leaving Virgil alone with Olivia. Virgil was mindless, his breath shallow and full of pain filled grunts. A mix of sweat and blood soaked his torn and ragged clothes. His only concern was reaching her. He forced himself up and took another step only to succumb to the pain shooting through his legs. Virgil fell to the ground, but still, he pressed forward, dragging himself across the grass.

"Olivia," he choked. "You, you have to get up."

Olivia didn't respond. Her open eyes lifelessly stared into the night sky. The trident was gone now, leaving a gaping hole in her gut. The pool of blood around her was extensive, and still warm to the touch as Virgil approached her body. The few entrails that hadn't been obliterated in the attack were scattered across the field in bits and pieces. Virgil reached out, his hand trembling as he placed his palm on Olivia's face.

"Please," he said, struggling to lift Olivia towards him. "You have to get up." Tears covered his cheeks. "No one was supposed to die. Not anymore. Not because of me. You have to get up."

Something touched his shoulder, but he didn't turn back. He

couldn't. Although it tore him apart to see Olivia in his arms, he couldn't bring himself to turn away.

"Virgil," Roxanne said, pulling his attention away from Olivia. "You can't stay here. It isn't safe."

Virgil looked Roxanne in her eyes. "It's my fault," he whimpered. "I did this."

Roxanne frowned. "As much as I would love to comfort you right now, we're still securing the island." Roxanne turned to Clayton. "Can you ensure Virgil makes it to Cordellia? It's a miracle he's still holding on."

"Of course." Clayton nodded as he approached.

Virgil turned back to Olivia's corpse. "We have to bring her," he said. "We can't leave her here alone."

Roxanne turned quickly, fiddling with her glasses. "She's gone, Virgil," Roxanne said, her voice choppy. "I swear to you we will mourn her later, but for now, you need to go with Clayton."

Clayton hoisted Virgil up, helping him back onto his feet. They began walking towards the white void from which Roxanne and Clayton had arrived. Every step Virgil took felt wrong. His mind knew he had to leave. His body knew it as well. However, his heart begged him to stay. With every pump, it pleaded for him to rush back to Olivia's side, even as Virgil stepped through the void and disappeared from sight.

When Cordellia saw Virgil, her mouth dropped. It was clear she was drained and running on fumes, but she immediately got to work nonetheless. Not a word was said between them. When her strength finally began to fail, Cordellia stepped out of the room. For several minutes, Virgil was alone. Although, nothing really changed. At that moment, he could have been in a room full of people and still felt as if he were the last man alive.

Aurelia stepped into the room. They locked eyes, and Virgil turned away. It was a brief exchange, and he hoped she hadn't seen the loss tugging at his heartstrings. The failure cascading over him. The shame bubbling inside him. Aurelia made her way over to the hospital table. Without speaking a single word, she took Virgil into her arms and held him tightly.

Virgil lay there. Trembling. It was as if the only thing keeping him together was her arms wrapped around him. He tried to keep his composure. To hold it all in. That didn't last long, though. The dam holding his tears back shattered, and he melted into Aurelia's embrace, his grip tight as he held onto her. He couldn't control his sobbing. She ran her fingers through his hair.

For hours, Aurelia remained with Virgil, even after she had finished restoring him. They talked, or rather, Aurelia did. Virgil mostly listened as she caught him up what had happened outside the coliseum. She told him how she and Cordellia fought to protect the injured Crusaders until reinforcements arrived. She gushed over how it was an honor to see Cordellia in combat, and she informed him that everyone had been released from inside the barrier unharmed. Eventually, her words slowed.

"I noticed you're not wearing your necklace," Aurelia said. "They took it, didn't they?"

"Y-yeah," Virgil muttered. "Slipped it right off my neck. I was powerless to stop them."

Aurelia reached over and placed her hand over Virgil's. "You were in a bad position and did the best you could. You're still alive, and that's what matters."

Virgil forced a smile. "I know you're right, but—"

"But nothing. We're going to get your fang back. It's only a matter of time before whoever attacked us shows up again. When they do, we'll be ready."

Virgil looked to Aurelia. There was so much conviction in her eyes it spilled over into him. It filled him with a confidence he thought abandoned him the moment the Fang of Kayveon was removed from his neck. He smiled, much more genuinely this time around. "I don't know what I ever did without you."

Aurelia gave Virgil's arm a playful nudge. "Of course not. Didn't you know I'm one of a kind?"

The door flung open and in walked Clayton, Roxanne trailing close behind him. "You're making a mistake," Roxanne insisted. "It's far too soon."

"No," Clayton argued. "You and Cordellia are mistaken. We've given Virgil more than enough time. We need to know what they are planning, and he's our best shot at achieving this."

"Who's they?" Aurelia asked.

Clayton turned his attention to Aurelia. "Leave now, Fairbanks."

"It's Bryant," Roxanne quickly corrected.

"R-right," Clayton stuttered. "My apologies, but what we are about to discuss is classified information. I need you to leave immediately."

Aurelia stood, only for Virgil to take hold of her arm. "Why does she have to go? We're both probationary Crusaders, so I fail to see what's okay for me to hear, but not her."

Clayton's eyes narrowed as he looked at Virgil. "Excuse me?"

Virgil opened his mouth to reply, but Roxanne beat him to it. "We'll have to reveal this soon enough, Clayton. Does it really matter if she knows now or later?"

Clayton looked at Roxanne, and paused. It looked as if he were searching for an excuse, but he merely sighed after a moment of silence. "I suppose not." He turned back to Virgil and Aurelia. "Go ahead and get comfortable. We have a lot to talk about."

Roxanne turned to Virgil. "If at any point this becomes too much to handle, we can stop and reconvene at another time."

"He's a grown man," Clayton scoffed. "Stop treating him like a child."

"This grown man just witnessed the murder of someone he cared for. It doesn't matter how old you are, you don't just brush that off."

"Of course you don't. I'm not as callous as you think I am. However, the Scarlet Mage is still at large and now equipped with the equivalent of a magical warhead. I hate to say it, but right now, his feelings are irrelevant." Clayton turned his attention to Virgil, locking eyes with him. "Speaking of magical warheads, just how did you manage to lose the Fang of Kayveon?" Virgil remained silent, his face turning red from embarrassment. "I can understand not using it before," Clayton continued. "A weapon of that caliber shouldn't be used on people you would soon enough be calling your allies. But this. I struggle to see why you wouldn't call upon its strength to defend us."

"I couldn't use it," Virgil replied, his tone just as low as his eyes.

"And why is that? Why would you withhold—"

"No. I mean, I don't know how to use it. My father never taught me. I've tried to tap into the Fang of Kayveon before, but I've never been able to."

Clayton closed his eyes, placing his palm over them. "Unbelievable. One of the most powerful magical weapons, reduced to nothing more than a flea market trinket."

"It's okay," Roxanne said. "It isn't easy to wield a catalyst properly. Especially a Dragon's Treasure. Please forgive us for being so forward."

"No," Virgil replied as he looked back up. "Clayton's right. I should have worked harder to use the fang. If I knew how to use it, we wouldn't be here. I would have killed her, and Olivia would still be alive."

The room fell silent. A brief moment passed before Roxanne broke the ice. "You said 'her.' I'm assuming you're talking about the witch in the green dress."

Virgil nodded. "Her name is Cecelia Holland."

Clayton folded his arms. "That's interesting. The woman is a complete mystery to us. How have you come to know about her?"

Virgil paused as thoughts of Cecelia flooded through his mind, and then it dawned on him.

"What is it?" Roxanne asked. "Do you need a break?"

Clayton groaned, grinding his teeth as he looked at Roxanne.

"I'm fine," Virgil answered. "I just, I've hated Cecelia for so long, but I've only just realized I really don't know much about her. This is only the second time I've ever even seen her."

"Then tell us what you do know," Roxanne said.

"Well, she's as old as dirt. The first time I saw her, she was transferring her soul into the body of a younger woman. Who knows how old she truly is?"

"That's lost magic," Aurelia muttered. "How could someone actually stoop so low?"

"You're a Crusader now," Clayton said. "Get used to it. We may be civilized enough to leave such barbaric sorcery in the past, but don't count on our enemies to return the favor."

"What else do you know about her?" Roxanne asked.

Virgil shrugged. "Beyond the fact she killed my father, nothing really."

"And what of your other family?" Clayton asked.

"What do you mean?"

"He means your brother and mother," Roxanne answered. "Our record of your family isn't exactly the most accurate. Is Cecelia connected with them in any way?"

"No," Virgil replied. "Well, not my mother. She died when I was young. I don't even remember what she looked like. My brother, though," Virgil paused as his shoulders tensed and he looked down. "He left home at eighteen to go out on his first solo hunt. He, he never came back."

"Was he hunting Cecelia?" Clayton asked.

"Yeah." Virgil nodded.

"And what became of him?"

"I'm sure you know what happens to hunters who don't return home."

"Okay," Roxanne said. "It's not much, but we have a basis to start from."

"What's this all about?" Aurelia asked.

"Nothing you need to worry about at the moment," Clayton said. Roxanne shot him a look, compelling him to rub his neck. "They call themselves Nobody. From what we can gather, they are led by Cecelia."

"They appear to be a new group on the scene," Roxanne said. "But considering how well they executed their attack, I sincerely doubt they're amateurs."

"You're giving them far too much credit," Clayton said. "They got lucky."

"We got lucky, Clayton. If Cordellia hadn't happened to use her clairvoyance and warn us, we wouldn't have been able to keep them from, well, you know what."

"What is you know what?" Aurelia asked.

"I'm sorry," Roxanne said, "but that truly is classified."

THIRTY-FIVE

The following day, the Crusaders gathered in the coliseum. Virgil sat alongside Aurelia and Logan, but not a word was spoken among the trio. Roxanne, Clayton, and Cordellia were in the boxed seating with Roxanne leading the announcements, per usual. She began by informing the probationary Crusaders about Nobody and what exactly had transpired the previous day. Virgil heard her words, but they were little more than noise echoing in his ears.

"Unfortunately, we have not driven back our assailants without sacrifice," Roxanne said. She waved her hand and a white void appeared in the middle of the battlefield. When the void dispersed, a pile of wood stacked in a pyramid was left behind. Virgil tensed up. A top the pyramid was Olivia's body, wrapped in elegant white linen, and arrangements of white flowers were scattered around her. "It pains me to inform you all that Olivia Abernathy has been taken from us."

Virgil swallowed the lump in his throat, fighting hard to keep his body from quivering. A warm hand fell upon his shoulder. He looked over to find Aurelia smiling at him, and he instinctively returned the expression.

"In taking our Crusader's Exam," Roxanne continued, "you each put your lives at risk to become a part of something greater than yourselves. You knew the risks involved and bravely entered the fire anyway. To lose someone who still had so much to learn. So much more to grow. So much more to contribute. It is beyond devastating and she will surely be missed."

Tears began to fall down Virgil's face, and he quickly wiped them away. Aurelia rubbed his back as she placed her other hand over his and gave it a gentle squeeze.

"As Olivia leaves behind no relatives, we will be the ones to set her soul to rest." Roxanne turned her attention to the trio. "Would you like to do the honors, Virgil?"

Virgil nodded as he stood up and held his hand towards the pyramid. Blue fire swirled around his hand, and as he clenched his fist, the pyramid erupted in a surge of flames. A radiant blue glow lit the coliseum, captivating the crowd's attention. The inferno raged for several minutes, and no one dared speak until the last ember was extinguished.

"All right," Roxanne began again. "Let us move onto business. I'm sure you are all wondering how we will be proceeding with the placement tournament, seeing how our final round was interrupted. We've discussed it and have decided that we will forgo the remainder of the tournament. As such, we are awarding both combatants of the final round the position of rook. Please join me in congratulating Logan Bryant, and Virgil Truesdale." A flurry of applause echoed throughout the coliseum before the crowd simmered back down. "As I mentioned before, this final phase of the exam will be a mentorship. You will each be grouped into teams and assigned a rook or queen Crusader. For our tournament champions, you will have the option to work alone and merely report to an assigned queen. However, to progress further in the rankings, you will need to work on a team at some point. Take time today to figure out which path you would like to follow. For the rest of you, you are free to form your own teams; however, if you are unable to do so, we will group you together into a team of at least three."

Virgil looked to Aurelia and frowned. *I'm sure she'll want to group up*, he thought.

"You feeling okay?" Aurelia asked.

"Y-yeah," he said, turning back to Roxanne. "I'm good."

"To ensure you are assigned the proper mentor," Roxanne said, "each of you will be conducting the Crystal Divination ritual. This ritual will gauge your physical aptitude, your current mana reserve, your potential for learning new branches of sorcery, et cetera et cetera."

She held her hand out towards the coliseum floor, and a white void appeared. As it disappeared, it revealed a massive crystal held up by a steel harness. The gem was so clear, an observer might fail to see it with a quick glance.

"This will be useful," Virgil said. "If I'm lucky, I'll have an aptitude for aquamancy. Then I'd be able to patch myself up for a change."

Virgil paused, expecting a reply from Aurelia, but heard nothing. He turned to her and his heart skipped a beat. She was pale and her expression was blank as she stared at the crystal.

Right, he thought as a frown took over his face. *How could I forget?* "Aurelia," he said. Again, she didn't respond. Virgil slid in closer and nudged her arm.

"Hmm," Aurelia uttered nearly robotically.

"Are you all right?"

"Yeah..."

Virgil placed his hand on her shoulder. With a careful tug, he pulled her towards him so their eyes would meet. "Are you sure? You seem really distracted. Worried even."

Aurelia's eyes were sunken. "I'm fine," she replied, her tone low.

Virgil paused. It was clear that something was amiss. A quick glance at Aurelia's unique aura revealed she was a swirling mess of anxiety, fear, and doubt. "Aurelia. I know that you're—"

"Everything's okay," she said sharply. "Honestly. I'm good."

Virgil bit the inside of his lip. His mind was like a game of tug of war, debating whether he should press the matter further, or give her space. He took a deep breath and gave her shoulder a gentle squeeze. "All right," he said. "But know I'm here for you if you need it."

Aurelia smiled, but as soon as she looked at the crystal again, her smile faded.

"Will Fynn O'Hare come down," Roxanne called out. Fynn stood up and made his way down to the crystal. "For those of you who have no idea how Crystal Divination works," Roxanne continued, "you should pay close attention."

"All right," Fynn replied. "How do I do this?"

"Simply place your hand upon the crystal. The ensuing reaction will reveal everything we need to know."

Fynn nodded and complied with Roxanne's instructions. In a matter of seconds, the rock began glowing a bright red. In the middle of the gem, the insignia representing pyromancy shone brightly, and fire began to shoot into the air in a roaring blaze.

"It appears you are a pyromancer through and through. While you can learn other branches of sorcery, it would undoubtedly be an arduous journey to do so. Other than that, it looks like you have quite the well of mana."

One by one, the probationary Crusaders were called down to the crystal. For the first three or so rituals, the crowd's attention was fixed on the ceremonies. With each one that passed, however, interest seemed to die down a little more.

"Would Logan Bryant please step down," Roxanne called out.

Logan stood up and made his way down to the crystal. Virgil turned to Aurelia. She looked even worse than she had before. She was sweating, and nervously twirling her cross between her fingers.

"Aurelia," he said again, trying to get her attention, but to no avail.

Logan placed his hand on the crystal, and nothing happened. A brief moment passed, but there was still no change in the crystal.

"Logan," Roxanne said. "It looks like you have no mana whatsoever. It is a rarity, but not unheard of. After all, we have a number of Crusaders who serve dutifully without the use of magic." The crystal trembled. It began to crack. Fissures spread throughout the rock. "Although, it does seem—" Before Roxanne could finish, the crystal shattered into hundreds of pieces. "Like you have tremendous physical strength. I don't believe we've ever had someone with such raw brute strength."

"Thank you, ma'am," Logan replied. "And I'm sorry about the crystal."

"Don't worry about it," Clayton said, raising his fist. His hand began to glow, and the crystal started to repair itself within the harness.

Logan walked back to his seat.

"Will Aurelia Bryant please come forward," Roxanne said.

Virgil took another look at Aurelia. She was trembling. Virgil called to her again, but she simply stood up, utterly oblivious to his attempt at grabbing her attention. She walked, but it looked as if her legs would collapse at any moment. She passed Logan on the stairway, and he placed his hand on her head. She stopped, and he leaned in close to her. After whispering something, he patted her on the head. Aurelia nodded and continued her descent towards the crystal.

"What did you say to her?" Virgil asked as Logan sat down next to him.

"Forgive me," he replied, his gaze fixed on his sister. "But this is really a private matter. Please understand."

Virgil turned his attention to Aurelia. By no will of his own, he held his breath as she placed her hand upon the crystal.

The gem began to flash a spectrum of colors. It moved from black to green, to red, to yellow, to white, then back to black again. As the crystal cycled through each color, the insignia present inside the rock shifted as well. Virgil breathed a sigh of relief, as did Aurelia. The gem continued its glorious light show and began to shoot out a mix of water, flower petals, fire, stones, and swords.

"Well," Roxanne said, awe evident in her eyes. "You are an omni-mage capable of learning any branch of sorcery without restraint. It has been quite a long time since we've had one in our ranks. Congratulations, Aurelia, and thank you for choosing to serve the Crusader's Alliance."

Before Aurelia could respond, something peculiar began to happen. The flames emitting from the crystal dispersed. The water evaporated. The flowers withered. The stones crumbled into dust, and the swords shattered. The gem became muddled, clouded with thick black shadows. They were few in number at first, but within seconds, the crystal became filled with darkness. Aurelia took a step back, her body trembling once again. Her eyes widened as they darted around the coliseum.

The crowd exploded in a collection of gasps and whispers as everyone was focused on Aurelia. Virgil's heart skipped a beat, and he ground his teeth as he analyzed the crowd. He saw a mixture of emotions. Fear. Pity. Anger and disgust. Worst of all were the looks of hatred.

"I knew something was wrong with her!" Paisley yelled as she rose to her feet. "She's a fucking demon!"

"Everyone calm down," Roxanne commanded, trying to regain control of the situation.

"How could you let that thing take the exam?" someone called out.

Roxanne continued trying to get everyone's attention, but it was no use. Everyone was in an uproar, their attention focused on the demon in their midst. Aurelia looked like a puppy cowering in the corner of a cage as beasts rampaged outside the bars. Virgil had only one thing on his mind: rushing down to Aurelia.

Virgil stood up simultaneously with Logan. The two men locked eyes with one another. "This doesn't concern you," Logan said, his voice stern. "If you know what's good for you, you'll—"

"THAT'S ENOUGH!" Roxanne shouted. Her eyes glowed white and her voice sounded almost primal. Her aura intensified, and the room shuddered, rendering the crowd silent. She then looked to Aurelia. "I'm truly sorry—"

Aurelia took off running, stumbling as she hastily left the coliseum.

"I'm warning you," Logan said. "Stay out of this, or else."

He ran off after his sister. Virgil paused. Aurelia was his friend just as much as she was Logan's sister. Making up his mind, Virgil proceeded to chase after them.

"Let's get back on track," Roxanne said, her tone and eyes

returning to normal. "Will Virgil Truesdale please, ah, I see you are already on the way."

Virgil groaned and hastily walked down to the crystal. He placed his hand on the gem, barely able to keep his palm steady. The crystal began to glow a vibrant red, and a pillar of flames shot high into the air.

"My word," Cordellia said, covering her mouth with her hand.

"Forgive me," Virgil replied as he removed his hand, "but I must be going."

"Hold on a moment," Roxanne said. "The ritual has not finished yet."

A collection of swords appeared and began dancing around the flames. The crystal alternated between red and white light, and the insignias switched between pyromancy and allostry.

"It appears you have a dual aptitude. Given that I am an alloster myself, I hope you consider exploring this branch of sorcery."

"Thank you," Virgil said abruptly. "But I have to—"

"Hold on," Cordellia said, standing up. "There's something else going on in the crystal."

A bright light began to shine from the core of the gem. It was small, but lustrous like a star in the night sky. There was another light, and then another.

"What is that?" Roxanne said, peering deeper into the crystal.

The crystal exploded, leaving a cloud of fine dust looming in the air. The crowd was speechless, the coliseum eerily silent.

"This is unfortunate." Clayton stood up and walked next to Roxanne. "But I suppose it was bound to happen eventually. We have been using this same crystal for decades now, and I'm sure being shattered didn't help. Let's take a short recess while we secure another one. Everyone report back here in one hour."

Virgil hadn't the slightest clue what was going on. Even so, it didn't bother him one bit. The only thing present on his mind was reaching Aurelia. He turned and left the coliseum.

CHAPTER
THIRTY-SIX

Virgil walked through the corridors of the castle. There wasn't a moment to lose.

"Wait a minute," Clayton called out behind him.

Virgil rolled his eyes and stopped. *I don't have time for this!* "I thought you were off getting another crystal," he said as he spun around.

"Roxanne is headed to the Aetherial Realm as we speak. We need to have a little chat."

Virgil's shoulders were tense, and his breaths were quick. "With all due respect," he said, "can this wait until later? I kind of don't have time now."

"No, it can't. Tell me, Virgil. Where is your family from?"

Virgil's eye twitched, and he couldn't help but clench his fists. "You already know that. It was in my application. I'm sure it's in my record, too."

"Yes, but as we said yesterday, our record of your family isn't complete. Apart from what you provided, we have next to nothing. I just—"

"And?" Virgil said with a shrug, trying with all his might to temper his frustration. Clayton huffed, clearly irritated by Virgil's interruption. Virgil sighed. "I'm sorry, but I'm kind of in a tight spot here. Aurelia is out there, probably more terrified than she's ever been, and I fail to see the problem in what you're saying. Hunters are private people, and as I'm sure you know, many of them don't like your organization."

"That's not good enough," Clayton said folding his arms. "Your family history, it's—"

"What do you want from me!" Virgil exclaimed. "We were a small family from Arythbelle. Why does it even matter anyway?"

Clayton opened his mouth to speak, only he didn't say a word. He just looked at Virgil before turning around. "N-never mind," he said. "Go on and tend to Aurelia. And forget I said anything."

Virgil returned to the surface. He stopped in place and began to focus his aura perception. He found Aurelia, and his heart sank. Her aura was a raging vortex, much worse than before.

He made a mad dash for her location. As he drew closer, the presence of Aurelia's turbulent aura was more intense. He entered the northernmost courtyard and found her with Paisley. She was on the ground, and Paisley was towering over her. A conjured wall of stone blocked Aurelia from running away.

"Why are you doing this?" Aurelia cried.

Paisley dug her foot into Aurelia's back. "You know damn well why I'm doing this. The world doesn't want your kind!"

"Please," Aurelia pleaded. "I don't want any trouble."

"Knock it off!" Virgil shouted as he approached the two women.

Paisley looked back at Virgil. She waved her hand, and a rocky prison appeared around him. Virgil held out his hands and began pouring out flames in an attempt to break free.

Paisley turned her attention back to Aurelia, her face lit with anger. "Look at you down there. I can't believe I ever compared the two of us. You're nothing but a stain to be wiped away from this world."

Aurelia whimpered. "I just want to be left alone. Please—"

"Bullshit!" Paisley reached down and picked Aurelia up by her hair. "I bet you led Nobody right to us, didn't you? Why don't you stop pretending to be a human, and show us what you really are?"

Aurelia tried to break free, but Paisley's grip was too tight. "This is it, isn't it?" Paisley said as she took hold of the cross around Aurelia's neck. "This is the seal locking all that evil away."

Paisley yanked the necklace from around Aurelia's throat. A foreboding sense of dread shot out from around Aurelia in an enormous wave. The air in the yard became thick, so much so, it was nearly tangible. Although her aura was still distinctly hers, it had morphed into something else. It was dark, twisted, and full of bloodlust. Aurelia's gray eyes changed to a bloody red. She looked up at Paisley, and Paisley released her hold.

"Don't look at me like that," Paisley said, taking a step back. She was quivering, her voice shaky.

Aurelia let out a shrill giggle, and Paisley tensed up. "What's wrong, Paisley? Isn't this what you wanted?"

Aurelia darted toward Paisley and placed her hand over Paisley's face. The prison she had summoned crumbled. "W-wait," Paisley whimpered, the force on her face clearly making it difficult to breathe.

"Wait," Aurelia taunted. "You wanted this. Right? We can't stop now."

"Aurelia," Virgil called out. "This isn't you. You have to let her go."

Aurelia looked over at Virgil. "Unless you're going to help me skin this pasty bitch alive, this doesn't concern you." She giggled once again. "Pasty Paisley! It's got a nice ring to it. Doesn't it?"

Aurelia doubled her grip on Paisley's skull, and she fell to her knees. She screamed, writhing in agony as she clawed at Aurelia's grip.

Virgil approached Aurelia, slowly raising his hands. "You have to stop this before it's too late."

"My god, Virgil. You're right." Aurelia released Paisley, and she collapsed onto her knees. "If I bust this bitch's grape, she'll die too soon. Where's the fun in that?"

Aurelia cocked her foot back and kicked Paisley in her chest. Paisley tumbled across the courtyard, leaving a trail of blood before finally stopping several yards away. Virgil held out his hand towards Paisley's body and erected a barrier of blue flames around her.

Aurelia turned to Virgil. "Do you honestly think that will stop me?" she snarled.

Virgil's heart sank as he looked at his friend. "I know you don't wanna do this," he said, his throat tensing up. "You may be a demon, but that doesn't define who you are."

Aurelia's hands began to glow a deep, dark blue as she twisted her fingers together. "Aquatic Serpent. Hydra!" An assortment of snakes comprised entirely of water sprouted out of her back. There were nine in total, each of them tremendous in size and hissing angrily. "Don't be silly." She grinned. "Of course that defines me."

Aurelia charged at Paisley. Her speed proved to be much greater than Virgil had anticipated. With a swing of her arms, she sent her snakes barreling towards Paisley. Virgil's barrier blocked most of them, but a few slipped through. They sank their fangs into Paisley, and she screamed in pain. Virgil summoned another barrier. Only this time, he made it much more powerful.

Aurelia whipped around towards Virgil. "Why won't you just stay out of this?"

"You know I can't do that," Virgil said as he walked towards Aurelia.

"You can, and you will, or else I'll—"

"Come on," Virgil exclaimed. "This isn't you."

Aurelia scoffed. "The Aurelia you know is a lie. This is who I really am. This is who I've always been. It's all I'll ever be!"

Virgil shook his head. "I know you're strong enough to beat this. I just need you to know that as well."

The watery serpents began to rage and wave violently. "You don't know a damn thing about me!"

Aurelia charged at Virgil. He readied himself. They clashed, and bursts of water and fire spread around the courtyard. As the minutes went by, the courtyard became more and more damaged. Aurelia fired off a blast of water. It smacked Virgil's shoulder, knocking it out of its socket. He flinched and sucked in a breath as he stumbled backward.

"What's the matter?" Aurelia said. "You're getting sluggish."

It was true. Perhaps if his efforts weren't so fractured, he'd be able to keep pace. With each minute that passed, Virgil's movements and reaction speed got just a little bit slower. If he didn't put an end to this soon, Aurelia would.

"It's not too late to call this off," Aurelia said as she held her hand up. "We both know you're not going to fight me seriously."

Virgil looked into Aurelia's eyes. He swallowed the lump in his throat and sighed. "You're right," he confessed, relaxing his guard. "I don't want to hurt you. Still. I can't just—"

Aurelia dashed forward. She covered her fist in a ball of ice and struck Virgil's stomach. The sheer force of her strike lifted Virgil into the air. Every bit of breath he had stored in his chest was forced out of his lungs. Aurelia pulled her fist back, and Virgil's stomach began to ice over as he fell to his knees.

Aurelia reached down, lifting Virgil's head up. "Do you understand now?" she asked. "Or do I have to kill you for you to finally get it?"

Virgil looked up at Aurelia. Her eyes were a raging storm of red. The anger she felt was as clear as day, but underneath all of the ferocity was something else. Something Virgil knew all too well.

Virgil's breaths were heavy. "You won't do this," he said, blood trailing off his lip. "You're not going to kill me, or even Paisley."

Aurelia laughed. "Are you willing to bet on it?"

Virgil took a deep breath and recalled his flames. A devilish grin stretched across Aurelia's face. She tightened her fists, and the snakes moved in. They crept around Virgil. He kept his eyes locked on Aurelia. Even as the snakes twined mere inches from his neck, he didn't budge. The only sound in the courtyard was violent hissing as the two friends stared each other in the eyes.

After a moment, Aurelia bit her lip. Tears welled up in her eyes. She let go of Virgil, and the ice coating his stomach began to melt.

"I know you don't want to hurt me," Virgil said, struggling to get back up on his feet.

"You don't know anything," Aurelia snapped. "I'm not this sweet, lovable person you think I am."

"You're wrong," Virgil said shaking his head. "You're not the monster you think you are."

Aurelia stepped backward, retreating into herself. "I. You. You don't know who I am."

Slowly, Virgil walked towards Aurelia. "I know exactly who you are. You're Aurelia. You are kind and compassionate, loving and considerate." Aurelia fell silent, her guard lowering. "I had to fend for myself for a long time. I had forgotten what it feels like to have someone care for you. To worry about you. To pick you up, no matter how many times you fall flat on your face. I wouldn't be standing here right now if it weren't for you. Do you really think a monster is capable of that?"

"P-please," Aurelia said. "Just leave me here. I'm going to hurt you. I always hurt the people I care about. It was stupid of me to think this time would be different."

Virgil reached out towards Aurelia, wrapping his arm around her. The snakes pounced, sinking their fangs in Virgil's flesh. His shoulders. His back. His ribs. His arms. He hissed and flinched as blood dripped onto the ground. The pain was searing. Still, he kept his hold, took a deep breath and smiled as he rubbed the back of Aurelia's head. "You of all people should know, if there's only one thing I'm good at, it's taking a beating."

Aurelia whimpered as she grabbed onto Virgil, burying her face in his chest. She sobbed, and the snakes retreated. "Virgil," she said, her voice partially muffled by his shirt. "I'm so sorry. I—"

Gently, Virgil pulled Aurelia's head back and looked her in her eyes. He opened his mouth to speak, only to be interrupted.

"Where is her cross?" Logan asked as he approached them.

"Logan," Aurelia said, her knees trembling.

"I think Paisley still has it," Virgil replied.

Logan checked Paisley's body. His demeanor was calm and collected, as if he had done this before. He made his way over to his sister and placed the necklace back around her neck. The demonic aura that had drenched the courtyard was sucked back into the cross. The snakes dispersed, and Aurelia's eyes returned to their gray hue.

Aurelia looked over at Paisley, weeping. She rushed over to the motionless body, scattered with a medley of cuts and bruises, and turned Paisley over to assess the damage. "She has a pulse, but it's faint. Several of her bones are shattered. I'm so sorry," she cried, as blue light began to emanate from her hands.

"Is anyone else injured?" Logan asked, his eyes fixed on Paisley.

"No," Virgil answered, holding his arm.

Logan's brow raised as he turned to Virgil. "You don't look too good."

"Don't worry about me."

Aurelia kept her focus on healing Paisley's most life-threatening injuries. As she worked, not a word was spoken between the trio. After a while, Paisley's eyes began to open. Upon seeing Aurelia, she fell into a panic. Despite her injuries, Paisley frantically pulled herself away, fighting against the pain.

"Get away from me," Paisley barked.

"Please don't run away," Aurelia pleaded. "You have a lot of critical injuries and—"

"I'll find another healer. Just stay the fuck away from me!"

Paisley whimpered away like a wounded street dog, her tail firmly between her legs. Aurelia sat on the ground, despair oozing from her. Logan walked over and placed his hand on her shoulder before helping her to her feet. She turned to face Logan. It looked like there were a million words she wanted to say, but she couldn't bring herself to speak a single one.

"You don't have to say anything," Logan said, patting Aurelia on her head. "None of this is your fault." Aurelia's lip trembled, and she turned away. "Please don't be upset. We've sealed up the demon before any real damage was done. Paisley will be fine."

Despite Logan's attempts to quell his sister's anguish, Aurelia's aura was more turbulent than ever. Logan tried to reach out to comfort her, but she pulled away at his touch. "You just don't get it! All you ever do is sweep me aside and lock me away. I could have killed her, Logan."

"But you didn't, and even if you did, it wouldn't have been you. The demon—"

"You really don't understand." Virgil interrupted.

Logan glared at Virgil. "Stay out of this," he snapped. "Although it wasn't warranted, I appreciate your help in stabilizing my sister, but this is really a private matter so—"

"It isn't a private matter if I lose it and kill somebody!" Aurelia exclaimed.

"That will never happen so long as we keep the demon sealed away."

"There isn't some demon living inside her," Virgil said. "Aurelia is a demon. No matter how you try to rationalize it or hide it away, that is a fact. Sealing away her demonic aura does nothing but repress her power and emotions until they explode like this. Your sister doesn't need a chain around her neck. She needs help."

Logan walked toward Virgil, the ground nearly trembling with every step he took. "You're trifling with matters you couldn't possibly understand. My sister is sick. She has a disease flowing through her, and the only thing keeping her in check is that chain. You may not like it. Hell, the entire world might think I'm an asshole, but none of you have the slightest clue what's best for my family."

"You're right about one thing," Virgil said as he stared at Logan. "I don't know what's best for Aurelia but I know damn sure you have no idea what's best for her either."

Logan curled his fists. "What did you just say to me?"

Virgil coated his hand in flames. "You heard me. I'd rather not fight a friend, but if fighting me will knock some sense into you, then so be it."

Logan took a firm grip on Virgil's collar. "I told you once before. We are not friends."

"STOP!" Aurelia shouted.

Logan turned to his sister. The look on her face was unmistakable. "Aurelia—"

"Just go."

Logan let go of Virgil, turning his full attention to his sister. "But I—"

"I said go, Logan."

Aurelia shot Logan a stern, demanding look. For a moment, he stood there, clearly in shock at his sister's response.

"I, I can't do that," he said, finally breaking his silence. "I need to protect you."

Aurelia didn't respond. She simply turned her back to him. Without saying another word, he left the courtyard, leaving Virgil and Aurelia alone.

THIRTY-SEVEN

Aurelia walked across the quiet courtyard to the stone wall. She plopped down alongside it, and Virgil slowly made his way over.

Aurelia curled up into herself, tucking her knees into her chest. "You don't have to stay here," she said, keeping her gaze away from Virgil.

Virgil winced, sitting down alongside her. "I know." He grunted as he placed his back to the wall. "I want to."

Aurelia shook her head. "God, I'm such an idiot," she said. "Let me take care of you. I'm sorry, but could I have you lie on the ground? I don't think I can conjure the Saint's Breath right now."

"Of course," Virgil said as Aurelia helped him lie down. "But really, this can wait. I've been through a hell of a lot worse than this."

"It's the least I can do."

Aurelia worked diligently on healing Virgil. While his injuries weren't life threatening, she took great care in repairing the damage she had caused.

"So," she began, her tone somber and low. "Now you know the truth."

"Yeah," Virgil replied. "I suppose I do."

"Can I ask you a question?" Aurelia asked, a hint of hesitation in her voice.

"Shoot."

"You don't seem shocked, or upset, or anything at all, really. I always imagined if you found out, well, you would hate me." Virgil laughed, and Aurelia began to blush. "I'm serious, Virgil."

"I know," Virgil said pulling himself together. "I'm sorry. It's just, why would I hate you?"

Aurelia paused. "Well, for deceiving you for one, or for just flat out being a demon."

"You're adorable," Virgil said, smiling. "I never asked if you were a demon. Keeping something to yourself is not deceiving me."

"I suppose it isn't exactly, but that doesn't explain why you weren't surprised."

Virgil huffed. "Geez. I swear it's like you want me to be stoked or something."

"N-no," Aurelia said, her face turning redder still. "I just, you're being way too nice about everything. It doesn't make sense."

Virgil took in a deep breath. "The truth is," he said, "I'm not surprised, because I've known you were a demon since the day we met."

Aurelia fell silent. Although she had prodded Virgil for the information, it appeared she hadn't prepared herself for the reality his answer would bring. "You knew this whole time?"

Virgil tilted his head. "Well, I guess it would be more accurate to say I suspected it."

"How?" Aurelia asked, her tone shaky and full of doubt. "How could you possibly have known?"

"The day we first met, I could feel your aura, and it felt off. I feel it now actually. I can tell your aura isn't complete, like a piece of it has been ripped away."

"You can really feel that?"

Virgil nodded. "From there, it was just a process of elimination. Demonic aura is the only aura type I can imagine anyone would want to seal up."

"But even knowing that, you still bothered to be my friend?"

"Well, yeah. I mean, I'm not gonna lie. It took a while for me to get the hang of this friendship thing, but that's just because I'm a scrub. You've been nothing short of amazing."

Aurelia pulled back her healing hands. Virgil turned to her. She looked as if she were about to burst into tears. "What's wrong?" he asked.

"Why?" she cried. "Why would you do that? Why would you be so nice to me knowing what a horrible creature I am?"

Virgil sat up and placed his hand on Aurelia's knee. "Because you are not a horrible creature. Aurelia, I wasn't trying to just get you to snap out of it earlier. I meant every word I said. You're a demon, sure, but that doesn't define who you are. You are who you choose to be, and the Aurelia I know is a kind-hearted and compassionate woman."

"And what about when I hurt people? I injured you." Aurelia choked up. "I almost killed Paisley."

"Let's be honest. She has been asking for it since day one, but we all make mistakes. Sometimes even big ones. Ultimately, we just need to pay for them, learn what we can, and move on."

Aurelia paused for a moment before looking Virgil in his eyes. "Before my brother showed up, you were going to say something. What was it?"

Virgil began to blush as he rubbed his neck. "It was nothing really."

"Tell me. I wanna know."

"Do I have to?" Virgil said, squirming in his seat.

"Yes."

"Fine," he said with a pout. He then took a deep breath. "I was going to tell you that everything was going to be okay, and I was gonna say that I was your best friend and, well, I was there to pull you out of the darkness."

Aurelia grinned. "Really?"

Virgil's face was hot, and his stomach felt queasy. "I know." He rubbed the back of his neck. "It's cheesy as fuck. I swear it sounded a lot more profound at the moment."

Aurelia giggled as she placed her hand over Virgil's. "I think it's lovely, and you're amazing, not just for what you did back there, but for being such a good friend to me. No one has ever done for me what you have."

Metal shackles appeared around Aurelia and Virgil's wrists, binding their hands together. They had been so entranced in their conversation, they hadn't even noticed Roxanne enter the courtyard. "You two will be coming with me," she said as she approached.

"What's going on?" Virgil demanded as he rose to his feet.

"You're both being brought in for questioning regarding the recent incident. So long as you cooperate, you have nothing to fear." Roxanne opened up a void and gestured Aurelia and Virgil to step through it.

"Why do I get the feeling the Alliance is about to fuck us over?" Virgil said as Aurelia stepped through the void.

"As I said, cooperate, and you have nothing to worry about."

Virgil stepped through the void and found himself in the same drab and dreary room used for the second phase of the exam. Only this time, Paisley and Aurelia were also in attendance.

"Have a seat," Clayton said, gesturing Aurelia and Virgil towards two open seats across the table. "Now that we're all here, the hearing can commence."

"Excuse me," Virgil said, raising his cuffed hands. "But are these really necessary?"

"I suppose not," Roxanne replied. With a wave of her hand, the shackles around Virgil's hands disappeared.

"And what about Aurelia?" Virgil said rubbing his wrists. "Aren't you going to get rid of hers?"

"Given the circumstances, it would be in everyone's best interest her shackles remain on."

Virgil shot a glance at Paisley. "Is that so? Tell me, why she isn't shackled then? If we're concerned about safety here, little miss princess over there should be sporting some iron."

"Are you kidding me?" Paisley protested. "I'm lucky to be alive right now."

"It's fine," Aurelia said, nudging Virgil's arm. "I don't mind the cuffs if they make Paisley feel safe."

Paisley rolled her eyes.

"If we're done with the chitchat," Roxanne said, "let's get this hearing underway. Our workload is extensive enough as it is."

"Tell us exactly what happened," Cordelia said. "We'll start with you, Paisley."

"Well, Aurelia and I were having a disagreement and—"

"You call that a disagreement?" Virgil interrupted.

"Allow her to finish giving her statement," Roxanne said.

"I would if she wasn't full of shit."

"That has yet to be determined. You'll each have a chance to give us your account of what transpired."

Virgil sat back in his chair in a frustrated silence. As Paisley gave her testimony of the event, he fought back the overwhelming desire to speak out. Every snide comment did nothing but pour gasoline on the fire raging inside of him. When it finally came time to give his testimony, Virgil tried his best to refute Paisley's claims. Perhaps it would have been better if Aurelia had tried to defend herself a bit more. Of course, Aurelia being Aurelia, she was a lot more concerned with everyone else rather than her own well-being.

Roxanne turned to Paisley. "Well, I'm certainly sorry you were injured—"

"Injured?" Paisley exclaimed. "I nearly lost my life!"

Roxanne waved her hand, and a sheet of metal wrapped around Paisley's mouth, muffling her words. "As I was saying before you so rudely interrupted me, I am truly sorry you were injured. However, you brought that suffering down upon yourself." Roxanne's eyes were cold and as sharp as steel as she stared at Paisley. "If it were me in that courtyard, there wouldn't have been a force in this world that could keep me from sinking my fangs into you. I believe we all know how best to proceed. Virgil, given your role in this event, you won't be punished. Although I would like to remind you that you are still just a probationary Crusader. Your act to intervene and keep people from getting hurt was indeed a noble effort, but at your level of development, it was foolish. In the future, you are to seek out a licensed Crusader to deal with the situation."

"Are you serious?" Virgil said. "Do you really expect me to have left them there to go get one of you?"

"Yes," Roxanne said bluntly. "You are an incredible sorcerer and are extremely talented, but a professional Crusader would have been able to subdue Aurelia without taking nearly as much damage as you did."

Virgil opened his mouth to speak, but Clayton beat him to it. "We shouldn't be so hard on him."

The room fell silent in shock. For a second, Virgil was sure he had misheard him.

"I spoke with Virgil during the recess," Clayton continued. "I asked him to tend to Aurelia, as I felt he was the best man for the task. Frankly, I believe he did an excellent job." He turned his attention to Paisley, giving her a menacing scowl. "After all, the only thing seriously hurt here is Miss Alderidge's pride."

Cordellia smiled as she turned to Clayton. "That isn't like you."

Clayton folded his arms as he leaned back in his chair. "I haven't the slightest idea what you're talking about. I gave a subordinate an order. Same as I've always done."

"W-well," Roxanne began, clearly flustered, "just try to be more cautious next time, Virgil. We'd hate for anyone to be injured." She looked at Paisley and then Aurelia. "As for you two, I'm afraid both of you will be expelled from the Crusader's Exam effective immediately. Per expulsion rules, you will be barred from reapplying for the exam for no less than five years provided you have a willing sponsor."

"Wait a minute," Virgil said as he perked up in his chair. "You're expelling Aurelia too?"

"That is correct," Roxanne confirmed.

"I'm sorry," Virgil said shaking his head. "Perhaps I missed it, but I fail to see why Aurelia's being let go."

"The condition for allowing me to take the exam was that I keep my demonic aura in check," Aurelia explained. Her voice was shaking, just barely above a whisper, and tears ran her cheeks.

"It is quite unusual for someone of Aurelia's heritage to take the Crusader's Exam," Roxanne added. "Not all demons are evil and will go on to commit heinous acts, but there is no denying the propensity of demon-kind to be seduced by evil intentions. Let us not forget the Blood War waged upon us by the demon lords of old. That being said, we live in far more progressive times. The Alliance deemed it satisfactory to allow Aurelia to take the exam so long as she swore to keep her demonic aura in check."

Virgil's face burned with anger, and he clenched his fist. "So, you knew. You knew she's half-demon, and you made her perform the ritual in front of everyone anyway."

"We considered having Aurelia perform the crystal divination ritual separately from everyone else," Clayton began, "but we decided against it. We felt doing so would alienate Aurelia, and thus, defeat the purpose of allowing her to take the exam in the first place."

Virgil ground his teeth. "Well even so, what happened isn't Aurelia's fault, and if you couldn't tell, she's beating herself up for it enough as it is."

"That may be," Roxanne replied. "But it doesn't negate the damage she caused. I'm afraid we have no choice."

"Don't give me that. You always have a choice. You have all the control here. You get to say who comes and who goes. Who is worthy of being a Crusader and who isn't. You don't have to expel anyone here. You shouldn't expel anyone here."

"I agree with Virgil," Cordellia said. "We could simply put this behind us. I'm sure everyone here has learned a valuable lesson."

Roxanne exhaled. "The situation is unfortunate, but—"

"I don't know," Clayton said. "We mustn't forget, Aurelia is an omni-mage. There can only ever be five living at once, and it would serve the Alliance well to have such a powerful sorcerer on hand."

There it was again. Virgil knew he could count on Cordellia to back him up, but Clayton? Just where was this coming from? The two men locked eyes briefly, before quickly turning away.

"You don't think I know that?" Roxanne's eye twitched. "I hate the decision we have to make, but rules are rules."

"Look," Cordellia said. "Why don't we shelve this conversation until another time? We do still have the mentorships to discuss, and the tension in the room is getting pretty thick."

Clayton folded his arms and shook his head. "No. We need to nip this matter in the bud as soon as possible."

"Agreed," Roxanne said as she summoned a white void in the room. "I believe we have everything we need from you three. You'll find that this void will take you each to your respective rooms. You can expect a definitive answer from us tomorrow when we discuss the mentorships."

THIRTY-EIGHT

Virgil collapsed onto his bed. His mind was exhausted, and he wholeheartedly welcomed the relaxation a night's rest would afford him. He lay there for what seemed like days, but he simply couldn't find the path to dreamland. Counting sheep. Studying the stone tiles in the ceiling. Holding his breath. Nothing helped.

Several times, he came close, but each time his mind finally drifted off, it snapped back to the same sick and twisted thought. Every time he closed his eyes, he saw Olivia. Her body lying in the open field. Her entrails spread out around the dirt. Her dull, lifeless stare. No matter how hard he tried, he couldn't shake those images.

A knock echoed on Virgil's door, and he perked up. "Just a minute," he said, dragging himself out of bed.

He opened the door to find Aurelia standing in the hallway. She was alone. Her eyes were red and watery. She must have been crying for hours.

"Can I come in?" she asked, rubbing her arm.

Virgil gestured her inside. "Of course. What's wrong?"

Aurelia took a seat on Virgil's bed. "I don't really want to talk about it. I just. I need a place to lie down in peace."

"Sure, sure. You go ahead and take the bed. I'll sleep on the floor."

"What? No." Aurelia stood up. "I don't want to kick you out of your bed."

"I used to be a hunter" Virgil laid down on the floor. "I'm used to sleeping outside on the ground. This is luxurious by comparison."

"Virgil, I can't just—"

Virgil waved his hand. "Yes, you can. Consider it my gift to you."

"Fine," Aurelia pouted. "If you insist on giving it to me, then I'll gladly take it." Virgil burst into a fit of laughter. "What?"

"Nothing."

Aurelia giggled as she rolled her eyes and laid down. "Shut up. You knew what I meant."

Virgil simmered down and wiped a lone tear from his eye. "Are you sure you don't want to talk about what's bothering you?" he asked. "Don't get me wrong, I appreciate your company and all, but it isn't really like you to be knocking at my door at this time of night."

"It's a long story."

"Then I guess it's a good thing I have time then."

Aurelia turned on her side and looked at Virgil. "Do you really want to know?"

"No, I just love hearing the sound of your voice. Yes. I wanna know why my friend needs a peaceful place at, uh, what time is it?

"It's three in the morning."

"Shit, it's really that late?"

"It is, and okay, but don't say I didn't warn you. I guess to give the full context, I have to start at the beginning. I was born Aurelia Alexandria Fairbanks."

"Was it also a dark and stormy night?" Virgil asked.

Aurelia tossed a pillow over, hitting Virgil in the face. "As I was saying," she continued, forcing down a grin, "my parents were once well-respected members of the Crusader's Alliance. My mother was even a queen at one point."

"Really? I don't recall ever hearing much about the Fairbanks."

"That's because nobody ever talks about us. After what happened, we've pretty much been wiped from the history books." Aurelia paused, and Virgil waited with bated breath for her to continue. She sighed. "My mother and father worked together on the same team. It's how they met actually. The funny thing is they were actually talking about retiring from the Alliance. Logan was growing up, and they were missing so much of his early life. However, the Alliance needed them for one more mission. It was supposed to be simple—suppress a demon uprising in the Cario Mountains of the Amber Nation. It wouldn't have been the first mission like that for them."

"Sounds like things didn't go too well."

Aurelia shook her head. "My father nearly lost his life, and my mother, she was captured by the demons. They, they violated her in the worst possible way."

Virgil was taken aback, trying his best to keep his composure. "I'm so sorry to hear that," he said. "If you want to stop, I completely understand."

"No. This is actually the first time I've ever told my story to anyone before. In a way it's liberating."

Virgil flashed a smile. "Well, I'm here to listen so long as you want to tell it."

Aurelia nodded. "The Alliance rescued my mother after a few days, but that was more than enough time to break her. She never returned to the field. Neither did my father. A couple months after they retired, my mother realized she was pregnant. Given the time frame, there was no doubt. My mother was carrying a demon's baby. The Alliance wanted her to abort me, but my mother believed that all life, no matter its origin, is sacred until the day it proves otherwise. She wanted me to have a chance at a normal life, and that desire ultimately proved to be her last."

"You mean she didn't make it?"

Aurelia nodded. "She died giving birth to me."

"And what about the Alliance? What did they have to say about it?"

"They weren't pleased with what happened, but they left us alone at least. It was my birth father who gave us trouble. He sent his minions after us. He believed that I was his property, and he intended to take me. We stayed on the move, Logan, my father, and I. We always managed to stay one step ahead of them. That is, until the night they found us."

"What happened?"

"I'm not entirely certain. I was only eight at the time, so I don't remember it all that well. Logan was thirteen, but with such a traumatic event, he only remembers bits and pieces of it. I remember my birth father finding us with his group of demons. I remember my father fighting hard to protect us, and ultimately failing. And I remember Logan having to step up and kill the demons."

Virgil was taken aback once more, his eyes wide from shock. "He killed them?" he asked. "Demons? At thirteen?"

"He did," Aurelia replied. "That was the same night he received his gift. We don't know how it happened. His mana had never been too impressive, but that night, it just left. Suddenly, he had god-like strength. I don't think even he knows the limit to it." Aurelia frowned. "Logan saved me, but I know he beats himself up for not being able to protect our mother and father. It's why he takes his promise so seriously."

"And what promise is that?"

"With my father's dying breath, he held both of our hands. He made me promise to always be the ray of sunshine my mother wanted me to be. And Logan, he made him promise to always protect me."

"Okay." Virgil nodded. "That certainly explains a lot, but how does that relate to now?"

"Logan is convinced that joining the Crusaders was a bad idea. He believes my demon aura would have never been released if we hadn't come here."

Virgil rolled his eyes and sighed. "Okay. Logan convinces himself about a lot of things. That doesn't make him right about everything."

"I know. I know. Logan can be so frustrating, and I just. I just don't feel like arguing with him anymore. Really, I feel like if he can't learn to loosen up, then it may be time for us to spend some time apart."

"I can understand that. I'd hate to see you two split, but perhaps it would be best if you went your separate ways. At least for a little while. You need space to be your own person. Shit, so does Logan. Time apart might be just what both of you need."

The room fell silent as Virgil waited for Aurelia to reply. After a moment, he spoke up. "You still there?"

"Y-yeah," Aurelia stuttered, her face flustered. "I was just, I got lost in thought, is all." She turned her back to Virgil. "We should get some sleep."

Virgil yawned. "You're right about that."

He closed his eyes, attempting to lull himself to sleep. While Olivia didn't come to mind, there was something else gnawing away at him. He tried to ignore it, but every time he tucked it away, it bubbled back up to the surface. After several minutes of wrestling with himself, Virgil finally spoke. "Aurelia," he said softly. "Are you still awake?"

"Yeah," she replied as she rolled back over.

"I know you probably want to team up for our mentorship—"

"That's assuming I'm even still here tomorrow."

"They'd be crazy to let someone as wonderful as you go." Aurelia didn't respond, instead flashing a smile. "But for the mentorship, I'd like to work alone. It's nothing against you. I just. I need to—"

"Virgil, it's fine. It's not like I'm your girlfriend or anything."

Virgil exhaled, relief washing over him. "Okay. Thank you for understanding."

"Just promise me one thing."

"Anything."

"Promise me you'll stay safe, and you'll call me when you find her. You shouldn't have to face Cecelia alone."

Aurelia reached down, and they held hands.

"I promise."

CHAPTER
THIRTY-NINE

The following morning, the Crusaders gathered in the banquet hall. Per usual, it was noisy with conversations and clinks of dinnerware. After making their plates, Virgil and Aurelia sat down together eating what would be their final meal in Akata Castle. It wasn't long before Logan joined them. He didn't say much, leaving most of the conversation to Aurelia and Virgil. It was hard to tell whether he was still angry, or just his usual untalkative self. At any rate, their table seemed to garner the attention of the other Crusaders. The trio tried their best to ignore it, but it was clear that everyone had their eyes on the demon in their midst.

"Damn, I'm gonna miss this," Virgil said, the taste of buttery eggs dancing across his palette.

Aurelia giggled. "Take it easy. They're just eggs."

"You lie. These eggs are divine. The gods themselves couldn't have cooked up a better meal."

Aurelia scoffed. "I admit, the food's been pretty good, but the chefs here got nothing on me."

Virgil tilted his head. "You can cook?"

"Cook? No. More like create culinary masterpieces."

"Right." Virgil chuckled. "I'll believe it when I see it."

"I'm serious. Ask Logan. He'll tell you."

Virgil turned to Logan. "Yeah, right. Like he's a reliable source." Logan flashed a smile before taking a sip of his coffee. "Well, look at that. Someone's actually in a good mood today."

"It's a beautiful day," Logan replied as he set his cup back down on the table.

Aurelia nudged Virgil's arm. "Don't change the subject."

"Are you still on about that? I'm sorry, but I just can't picture you in the kitchen."

"Oh really. See, I was gonna say you have to let me make you dinner sometime, but now I think you don't deserve to eat my cooking."

Roxanne, Clayton, and Cordellia entered the banquet hall. To Virgil's surprise, Clayton was leading the charge. Several additional people accompanied the kings.

"Good morning," Clayton said, greeting the crowd. "I trust you all are eager to meet your new mentors." The crowd remained silent, unsure of just how they should respond. "If you have formed your groups, go ahead and gather up now. On the other hand, if you would like us to assign you to a group, then come up to the front, and we will sort you accordingly."

Virgil stood up. Shock washed over Logan's face when Aurelia stood up as well.

"What are you doing?" Logan asked, his voice stern.

"I don't want you to be upset," Aurelia said. "But I'm going to have the kings assign me to a team."

"That wasn't the plan, Aurelia. We were supposed to work together."

"I know, but . . ."

Virgil walked closer to Aurelia. He took her by the hand, giving it a gentle squeeze. Aurelia turned towards Virgil, and their eyes met.

Logan stood up, his fists tightly woven into balls. "And just what exactly is this?"

"I think we should spend some time apart," Aurelia said, her voice emboldened as she turned back towards her brother.

"So, what? Are you telling me you're ditching me to party up with him?"

Aurelia huffed. "No. If you were actually listening to me, you would have heard I'm going to have the kings assign me to a team."

Logan shot Virgil an angry look. His brow was furrowed, and his nostrils flared. "You—"

"I'm glad you're all together," Roxanne said as she approached the group.

"Oh, Roxanne," Aurelia said as she spun around. "I was just about to go see Clayton."

"Don't bother. I actually need to speak to the three of you." Roxanne walked away, gesturing the trio to follow her. "Let's find a quiet place to talk."

No one said a word. Virgil tried his best to ignore it, but Logan was staring holes through him. Aurelia looked nervous, as if she expected to be thrown off the island at any moment. The four of them reached an empty corridor, and Roxanne gestured the trio to sit down on a hallway bench.

"All right," Roxanne began. "There isn't any easy way to say this, so I'll just come out and say it. The Alliance is very hesitant about your presence here, Aurelia."

Aurelia looked down, tensing. It was clear she was holding back her tears. "I understand. I'll leave immediately. If you could just send me to the nearest city—"

Roxanne raised her hand. "Just hold on a minute. Nobody's kicking you out."

Aurelia perked up. "I can stay?"

"You can, but there are conditions."

"What kind of conditions?" Logan asked.

"For starters, I will be mentoring her."

"Are you serious? Surely you must have more important things to do."

"Everything we Crusaders do is important work, but at any rate, this is what we agreed upon as the best course of action. It was a tough decision, but we agreed it would be best if I take on the responsibility, given that Aurelia is already so proficient in aquamancy and Clayton isn't exactly the mentoring type. And then there is the other condition as well."

"What's the other condition?" Aurelia asked.

Roxanne paused for a moment as she looked Aurelia in her eyes. "If you ever lose control like that again, I will kill you on the spot."

The trio fell silent as Roxanne's words hung in the air. Virgil swallowed the lump in his throat as he looked at Roxanne. He studied her face, checking for the slightest hint that she may have been bluffing. He found nothing but conviction.

Roxanne turned to Logan and Virgil. "That goes for both of you as well. I know you are a tightly-knit group. I've seen you bond quite a bit throughout the exam thus far. But if things go off the rails and you stand in my way, then I will not hesitate to put each of you down."

Again, the group fell silent, the magnitude of the situation overwhelming. "Of course, you don't have to agree to this, Aurelia," Roxanne continued. "We understand that we are asking you to place yourself under a tremendous amount of pressure. If you think it is too much to handle, then you are free to leave the Alliance now. However, if you decide to stay, you will have the kings' full support. I won't lie to you. It's going to be hard. You saw how people responded yesterday, and I've seen the looks you've garnered today. It's going to take time to win over their hearts and minds, but it can be done."

Aurelia nodded, a fierce determination in her eyes. "I'm going to stay, and I would be honored if you taught me everything you know."

Roxanne smiled. "I figured you'd say that." She turned her attention to Virgil. "Again, there's no easy way to say this, so here it goes. You're coming with me as well."

"What?" Virgil asked, befuddled. "I thought as a rook, I'd be able to work on my own."

"Normally, yes. But as the kings discussed things yesterday, we came to the realization that you will, let's say, require greater supervision."

"And why is that?" Virgil sneered as he tightened his fists. "You think I'm not capable of working on my own?"

"Quite the contrary, but given the current state of affairs, it will be foolish to leave you to your own devices, trusting you to simply check in with your superiors."

Virgil paused as he ground his teeth, searching for the proper words to vent his frustrations. "In that case—"

"Let me finish before you shoot yourself in the foot. Aiden and I are the heads of a joint task force in charge of capturing the Scarlet Mage. In fact, Aiden's absences throughout the exam are due to the work he's been putting into this operation. Based on recent revelations, we're expanding the scope of our forces to include Cecelia and her organization. I want you on my team for two reasons, Virgil: to help us put an end to Nobody, and to help you reach your fullest potential as a sorcerer. Your abilities are unlike anything we've seen before, and it would be a crime if we didn't develop them into everything they could be."

Virgil was floored, his mouth hanging open. "Well, I-I suppose that would be all right," he stuttered. "Thank you for the opportunity."

Again, Roxanne smiled. "Don't make me regret it." Finally, she turned to Logan. "That just leaves you. Honestly, we don't have any qualms with you. You are free to work alone or join a team. We are confident that no matter which path you choose, you will excel. However, we also know about the bond you share with Virgil and your sister. Thus, I'd be more than willing to take you on as well. The choice is yours."

Logan looked over at Virgil, locking eyes with him. "I wouldn't have it any other way."

CHAPTER

FORTY

After their discussion, Virgil, Logan, and Aurelia went their separate ways to gather their things. As Virgil walked through the hallway, he stopped to the sound of a familiar voice.

"Ummm, Virgil," Paisley said. "Can I talk to you for a minute?"

Reluctantly, Virgil stopped and turned around. "What do you want?"

Paisley was clearly nervous. She kept her eyes low, and twirled her hair between her fingers. "I just wanted to thank you. You know, for what you said last night. The kings are going to let me stay and, well, I know we haven't exactly seen eye to eye, but thank you."

Virgil scoffed. "If you want to thank someone, then go thank Aurelia. I only said no one should be expelled because that's what she wanted. I honestly don't care what they do to you." Paisley, obviously shocked, said nothing. "But let me make one thing perfectly clear," Virgil continued, his tone turning stern as he stared Paisley in her eyes. "If you ever so much as look at Aurelia the wrong way again, there won't be a healer in this world capable of fixing what I'll do to you."

He turned and walked away, not bothering to wait for a response. When he finally made it to his room, he quickly packed his things and made his way back to Roxanne. Once everyone had arrived, Roxanne summoned a void, and they stepped through it.

The group reappeared in front of a colossal brick house. Two massive pillars holding up a stone awning adorned the front door. There were numerous windows, although it was impossible to see through the black drapes hanging on the other side of the glass. The lawn was manicured to perfection, not a single blade of grass out of line. Rows of bushes lined the path leading up to the house, and there was a single oak tree equipped with a tire swing on the front lawn. The tree stood just as tall as the house. A massive fence surrounded the house on all sides, and the nearest house was acres away.

"My apologies," Roxanne said as she walked up the path. "But my wife gets quite annoyed with me when I void into our home."

"This is your house?" Virgil said, unable to conceal the awe he felt. "This is amazing."

Roxanne slid her key into the door. "Thank you. This is my sanctuary. The one place nothing in the world can bother me."

Roxanne opened the door and entered. "Riley! Peyton! I'm home!"

"Mama," a young voice called out from the other room. "Is that really you?"

Before Roxanne could answer, a small boy peered into the room. He wore a pair of jean shorts and a t-shirt, and was the spitting image of Roxanne. Upon seeing her, his face lit up with joy.

"Mama!" he exclaimed as he ran up to Roxanne.

The boy tripped, but as he fell to the floor, Roxanne summoned a void under his body. The boy disappeared and then reappeared in the air in front of Roxanne. "You have to be more careful, Peyton," Roxanne said as she reached out and caught her son.

Peyton reached out and gave Roxanne a firm hug. "I'm sorry, Mama. I just missed you so much."

Roxanne grinned. "And how much is that?"

Peyton pulled back and extended his arms out. "It's thiiiiiis much. That's a whole lot. Isn't it, Mama?"

Roxanne lowered her son to the floor. "It sure is, and I missed you too. Where's mommy?"

"In the kitchen." Peyton looked past Roxanne, finally noticing the extra people accompanying his mother. Slowly he inched closer to his mom.

Roxanne laughed. "It's okay, pumpkin. These are a few of my subordinates. They're going to be staying with us for a few months or so."

Peyton's eyes lit up even more intensely than they had before. "You mean you're gonna stay?"

"Yeah," Roxanne nodded. "I'm going to be working from time to time, but I'll be here with you and mommy."

Peyton erupted in excitement. He jetted down the hall towards the kitchen. "Mommy!" he called out. "Mama's home!"

"I heard, pumpkin," another woman said, rounding the corner.

Riley stood in the hallway, her jet-black hair tied up in a loose ponytail. She wore a casual orange dress fastened with a wide belt around her stomach. She had an apron tied around her waist, and while it was clear she had washed her hands, she still had some flour sprinkled across her sand-colored skin. "Welcome home, babe."

Riley walked over to Roxanne, and they took each other in their arms. Their lips touched. For a moment, they stood there, reveling in each other's embrace, as if they might never get the chance again. Riley pulled back and gently slapped Roxanne on the arm.

"What?" Roxanne said.

"You didn't tell me you were coming home, and on top of that you brought guests."

Roxanne blushed. "Well, it all kind of happened suddenly. We only just decided on things early this morning. At least I didn't void into the house this time. Right?"

Riley looked Roxanne in her eyes, which only served to make her blush more. "I suppose that is an improvement," Riley said, smirking. "Well, don't just stand there. Introduce me."

"Y-yeah, sure," Roxanne said as she turned to Virgil, Logan, and Aurelia. "This is Virgil Truesdale, and Logan and Aurelia Bryant. They're probationary Crusaders, and I'll be mentoring them for the next few months."

"Forgive us for dropping in like this," Logan began. "If it's any trouble—"

"Oh, it's no trouble at all," Riley replied. "I'm just starting to prep dinner, and it would have been nice to know we were going to have company. I'm afraid I don't have enough ingredients to serve everyone, but that's nothing a trip to the store can't fix." Riley turned to her wife. "Go ahead and get our guests settled in upstairs. When you're finished, I want all of you to report to the kitchen."

Roxanne nodded and planted a kiss on Riley's cheek. "All right," Roxanne said as she walked towards the stairs. "Follow me, and I'll show you where you'll be rooming while you're with me. While we're at it, you can all change out of those tracksuits. I'm sure you're probably sick of them by now."

The group headed upstairs. Roxanne's home was just as magnificent on the inside as it was on the outside. The floors were all covered with plush dark blue carpet, and the walls were painted in comforting earthy tones. Beautiful crystalized lights hung from the ceiling, and the decor had a modern, yet homey feel to it.

Each of the trio was given their own room: Logan on one end, Aurelia in the middle, and Virgil on the other side. Virgil opened the door to his room. It was huge, equipped with a queen-sized bed, two dressers, a vanity mirror, a TV, and a desk.

"Please make yourself at home," Roxanne said as Virgil stepped through the doorway.

Virgil turned back towards Roxanne. "I will. Thank you for your hospitality."

"You're welcome," Roxanne replied as she began to close the door. "Don't be long now. As I'm sure you've noticed, my wife isn't the type to keep waiting."

Virgil walked over to the bed and laid down his bag. He rummaged through its contents, eager to finally be rid of that horrid tracksuit. He stripped down and tossed the clothes off to the side before slipping on a pair of black jeans and a light gray t-shirt. As Virgil looked in the mirror, a frown crept onto his face. The Fang of Kayveon had always accentuated this outfit so well. He sighed and left the room to walk downstairs to the kitchen.

"There you are," Riley said. "Come on over here and lend me a hand."

"O-okay," Virgil stuttered. "But I have to warn you. Cooking isn't really my thing."

"Nonsense. How many times have you cooked before?"

"Never. Unless you consider roasting mcat with my hands cooking."

"You'll be fine. By the time you leave my home, you'll be a master chef."

"Are you sure you don't want me to do something else? I'd hate to burn dinner, or get anyone sick."

"I've already sent Logan and Roxanne off to the store for extra ingredients. That leaves you and Aurelia to help me prepare dinner." Riley pointed over to the sink. "Go ahead and wash your hands, and start with dicing up those tomatoes."

Virgil complied with Riley's request. As he stood over the cutting board, he reluctantly picked up a tomato along with a large kitchen knife. He was more than willing to help, but this was far beyond his comfort zone. He laid the tomato on the board and began cutting. Juice oozed from the fruit as Virgil pressed the blade into its flesh.

"And there's Aurelia," Riley said.

Virgil looked up at the kitchen doorway to find Aurelia standing there. She wore a pair of blue jeans and a baby blue blouse. Her hair was tied up in a long ribbon that matched the color of her jeans. "Is there anything you need me to do?" she asked.

"Why, thank you, dear. I was just about to ask you to dice up that onion over there."

"I'll get right to it." After washing up, Aurelia walked over and stood next to Virgil. "I guess you get to see me cook after all."

Virgil continued cutting his tomato. "I guess so. Are you sure you got the skills for it?"

"I don't know. You tell me."

Aurelia grabbed the onion and a knife and quickly skinned it. First, she cut it in half straight down the middle. Then she cut along the onion halves in a crisscross pattern, taking great care not to slice all the way through on the far side. Aurelia took one of the halves and held it firmly against the cutting board. Her blade rocked back and forth with swiftness in an almost rhythmic fashion. When she finished, she grabbed the other half and cut through it just as gracefully as she had the first.

Aurelia turned to Virgil, her eyes beginning to water. "What do you think of that?"

"I'll admit. I'm impressed, but this is nothing you should cry over."

Aurelia rolled her eyes. "I'm not crying. It's the onions." She picked up a towel off the countertop and carefully wiped her eyes. When she opened them again, she gasped. "What have you done to that tomato?"

Riley rushed over and peered around Virgil's shoulder. "You weren't kidding when you said you were no good at cooking."

Virgil looked down at the cutting board. The tomato looked more mashed than cut.

Aurelia moved in closer to Virgil. "You're pressing too hard. Here. Let me help you." Aurelia reached over and placed her hands over Virgil's. "The trick to cutting a tomato is to be firm, but gentle. Let the knife do the work." Together they rocked the knife back and forth, gently caressing the tomato's flesh with the blade. "See," Aurelia said as she pulled back. "That wasn't too hard, was it?"

Riley, Aurelia, and Virgil worked harmoniously in the kitchen while Peyton sat at the table, his nose deep in the pages of a coloring book. Virgil and Aurelia focused their efforts on making pasta. Riley worked on the other dishes to be served. It didn't take long for the kitchen to be overrun with smells. The sweet and savory scent of simmering spaghetti sauce danced around the air. Fresh biscuits baked in the oven, and the crisp popping of pork chops hitting hot oil echoed throughout the room.

Aurelia took a teaspoon and dipped it into the sauce. She brought it to her lips and softly blew on it. Her eyes lit up as she tasted it, and she squirmed with excitement. "This just might be the best sauce I've ever made."

"It can't be that good." Virgil said.

Aurelia grabbed a new spoon and dunked it into the sauce. She held it out in front of Virgil's face. He leaned in to have a taste, only for Aurelia to pull the spoon back. "You have to blow on it first," she said. "It's really hot."

Virgil flashed a blank stare. "I can literally breathe fire."

"That doesn't mean you can't burn your tongue."

"Fine," Virgil said before puckering his lips.

He blew on the sauce covered spoon and Aurelia gently placed it in his mouth. His eyes widened. It was as if each of his taste buds were being massaged by the various flavors all at once. The onion. The oregano. The pepper. The garlic. Everything blended together in a beautiful symphony of deliciousness.

"Okay," Virgil said. "That just might be the best spaghetti sauce I have ever tasted." Aurelia burst into a fit of giggles. "What? I mean it. I may have doubted you before, but now I see the light."

Aurelia grabbed a towel off of the counter. "I'm glad you've come around," she said as she reached towards Virgil's face. Carefully, she dabbed Virgil's mouth with the towel. They locked eyes with one another. For a moment they stood there, neither of them saying a word.

"Thank you," Virgil said, breaking the silence between them.

"Y-you're welcome," Aurelia replied, her cheeks reddening before turning away.

Roxanne entered the kitchen. "We're back," she said.

"And we have another guest," Riley replied.

Virgil looked around Aurelia to find Roxanne and Logan accompanied by a familiar nymph. "Orlando!" he exclaimed.

The nymph waved. "Fancy meeting you here."

"I take it you already know him?" Aurelia asked.

Virgil walked over to Orlando. "Know him? He sponsored me for the exam." Virgil held out his hand. "You know, I never thanked you for that."

"It was my pleasure," Orlando said as they shook hands. He then looked to Riley. "Oh, and sorry to drop in so unexpectedly. I have to debrief Roxy on some stuff. It's kind of important I do it in person."

"You know guests are always welcome here," Riley said. "But you know the rules. Family time comes first, so work will have to wait till after dinner."

CHAPTER
FORTY-ONE

The dinner table was lively with conversation, although it remained clean as Peyton was present among them. With the time difference, it had only been a few hours since Virgil, Aurelia, and Logan had eaten breakfast, so they made their plates light. Virgil limited his to a small helping of spaghetti and a biscuit, and had an ice-cold glass of tea to wash it down. As he ate, he couldn't help but smile. The food was even more delicious than he had thought it would be.

As dinner wound down, Orlando stood. "Everything was wonderful, as usual. If you would excuse me, though, I'm going to go out back for a smoke." He tapped Virgil on his shoulder. "Why don't you come out with me? Keep me company."

"Sure thing," Virgil said as he stood up. "Please excuse me, everyone."

Virgil followed Orlando out into the backyard. As the door closed behind him, Orlando pulled out a cigarette.

"All right." Orlando lit up. "Fill me in. I want to know everything that happened in the exam."

Virgil grinned. "I thought we weren't supposed to talk about the exam. Past, present, or future."

Orlando returned the gestured as he lightly slapped Virgil on the shoulder. "You're a Crusader now. That rule only applies to sponsors and applicants."

Virgil spent the next several minutes recalling his experiences on Akata Island. He left out no detail, even the ones painful to dig back up.

Orlando exhaled a cloud of smoke. "Sounds like you've been through a hell of a lot, but it's certainly made you stronger. You look like a new man."

"Yeah. I'm a totally different person now." Virgil chuckled. "I've gotten my ass handed to me more times than I care to admit. I can't remember a time I've ever sucked this hard."

"Okay," Orlando said. "Way too personal there."

Virgil chuckled as he shook his head. "Shut up. I meant metaphorically."

"Yeah, yeah." Orlando smiled. "Whether you want to admit it or not, Akata Island has had a positive effect on you. Either that, or it's that pretty young thing in there."

"I guess you can say that. Aurelia and I have bonded quite a bit throughout the exam."

Orlando placed his palm on Virgil's shoulder. "Just be careful. You don't want to mix your feelings for Olivia with Aurelia. I know it might seem like things are over on account of Olivia being dead and all, but emotions. They don't die so easily."

Virgil blushed. "What do you mean? Aurelia and I are just friends."

Orlando shot Virgil a droll, unconvinced look. "I get it. Logan is her brother, right? I suppose I'd keep it on the DL too if that behemoth was staring me down every day. But if you're serious about romancing Aurelia, sooner or later, you're going to have to tell him."

"No. I mean it. She's my best friend. Nothing more."

Again, Orlando shot Virgil that same look, only this time, his eyes dropped shortly after. "My god. You're not kidding."

"I'm not. Two people can be friends without being romantically involved. In fact, it was Aurelia who encouraged me to pursue Olivia in the first place. Without her, I wouldn't have stood a chance."

Orlando took another draw from his cigarette. "You're completely right. You certainly can just be friends. However, the way that girl couldn't keep her eyes off you at dinner, she's definitely into you."

"You're wrong." Virgil shook his head. "I sort of told her I didn't think she could cook. I'm sure she was just checking to see if I really enjoyed the meal."

Orlando raised his finger. "First off, never tell a woman she can't cook. Even if she can't so much as melt butter, you eat whatever it is she makes and smile like it's the best damn thing you've ever eaten. Second, if Aurelia doesn't think the two of you could be more than friends, I have gravely lost the ability to understand women. And since that simply isn't possible—" The back door opened, and out stepped Roxanne, Logan, and Aurelia. "Roxy. I take it you're ready for that debriefing."

"I am." Roxanne waved her hand, summoning a white void. "However, given that we have new members on the task force, I think it would be best if we pull in the other members as well."

They stepped through the void and were instantly transported to a large, bunker-like room. The floors and walls were made of metal, and there wasn't a single window in sight. Numerous LED panels embedded into the ceiling lit the room. There were two floors. Furniture was sparse on the bottom floor. Apart from the bookshelves spread along the walls, the only other furniture present was a huge rectangular table sitting in the middle of the room, and several chairs surrounding it.

The upper level, on the other hand, was much homier. Or, at least as homey as a bunker could be. There were six twin-sized beds. Nothing too luxurious, but it certainly beat sleeping on the floor. A fridge sat in the corner of the upper level, and next to that was a small electric stove.

Roxanne gestured to everyone to take a seat at the table. Naturally, she took the spot at the head. As she sat down, the table lit up, revealing a keyboard and screen in its glossy surface. She began typing away. Before long, she had two projections up, sitting in the chairs as if they were there in the room with them.

One of the projections was that of a plump elven woman. She had orange skin like a summer sunset, and bright red hair which her lips perfectly matched. Her eyes were an amber gold. She was dressed casually in a long gown clearly meant for sleeping, and her hair was tied up as if to avoid tangling as she slept.

The other projection was the complete opposite of the first. The golem was tall and slender and had deep brown skin similar to wet dirt. Her eyes were cold and black, and there didn't appear to be a sliver of hair on her. The golem was dressed in a pair of jeans and wore an open vest, revealing a rocky set of muscles.

"Please forgive me for contacting you so late," Roxanne said. "I was going to do this tomorrow morning, but Orlando has some information to divulge, so I figured we can just get it out of the way now."

The elf yawned as she rubbed her eyes. "Sure thing, boss." Her voice was soft and sleepy. "No need to apologize to us."

"It is very discourteous to yawn in the presence of your commanding officer," the golem sneered. "Must you always be so uncouth?"

"Cut me some slack. Some people enjoy getting some rest from time to time."

"How can you find time to rest with such important work to do?"

"Easy. When I feel myself getting irate like you, I usually stop and think to myself, 'Hey, Lilith. You should go lie down. Nobody likes an old stick in the mud like Ash.' And then I go to sleep. Simple as that."

"I am not a stick in the mud." Ash grumbled as she crossed her arms.

"Ladies, if you are done squabbling," Roxanne said, "can we get this show on the road?"

"Yes, ma'am," the two women said in unison.

"Good. Then I will start with introductions. I'm sure you have noticed we have company with us." Roxanne gestured her hand towards the trio. "Allow me to introduce you to Logan and Aurelia Bryant, and Virgil Truesdale. Virgil and Logan tied in this year's placement tournament and have joined our ranks as rooks, and Aurelia has placed as a knight."

"It's a pleasure to meet you," Lilith said with a wave of her fingers.

"My name is Lilith Talson, otherwise known as the Smoldering Sunset. I'm a rook as well. Normally I report to Ash here, but since joining this group, I've been reporting to the big boss herself."

"And my name is Ash Zobel, the Frigid Wood. I'm ranked queen and report directly to Roxanne alongside Orlando. If there's anything I can do to assist you in getting acclimated to our team, please do not hesitate to ask."

"Thank you," Virgil said. "I look forward to working with you all."

"Likewise," Aurelia joined in.

Logan simply nodded as he crossed his arms.

"All right." Roxanne turned to Orlando. "You have the floor."

Orlando stood. "So, I got good news and bad news. The bad news is Nobody is in the wind again. Their hideout was mostly abandoned when I got there, and I have no clue where they could have relocated to."

"That's okay," Lilith said. "We suspected as much after their attack on Akata Island."

"What's the good news?" Ash asked.

Orlando reached into his vest pocket and pulled out a peculiar looking notebook. It was bound with black leather that looked to be centuries old. There were a series of runes sewn into the leather, and a silver clasp held the book shut.

"What is that?" Roxanne asked.

"That," Orlando said as he tossed the book onto the table, "is a grimoire I managed to recover from their hideout. Of course, I had to fight through a horde of demons to get it, but—"

"Are you serious?" Ash said in shock.

"As serious as I am fine as hell. So yes. I am very serious."

"Excellent work," Roxanne exclaimed.

"I don't understand," Virgil confessed. "Why does recovering one of their grimoires matter so much?"

Logan groaned. "If we know what kind of magic they are capable of producing, we might be able to discern their next move. We may even discover their motive for attacking us."

"Precisely," Roxanne said, "especially considering the great lengths they went through to obtain a catalyst."

Virgil fell silent, looking down at the table. He hadn't forgotten about the Fang of Kayveon being stripped away from him, but the mere mention of it was enough to dredge up every negative feeling he was trying so hard to bury. He felt a warm touch on his arm and looked over. Aurelia had reached over and given his arm a gentle squeeze. For a brief moment, they locked gazes, prompting them both to smile.

"So," Roxanne continued. "What does the grimoire say? Are there any leads in it?"

"Oh, I have no clue." Orlando sat back down. "The damn thing nearly disintegrated me when I tried to open it."

Roxanne sighed. "Of course. We can't expect everything to go so smoothly, right?" She turned toward Virgil. "Can you scan it for me?"

"Sure thing," Virgil replied. "Anything I'm looking for in particular?"

"Yes. I want you to tell me if you detect any imprints of aura related to lost magic."

The room fell silent at the mere mention of those words. Virgil nodded and complied with Roxanne's request. His body tensed and his heart skipped a beat. "Yeah," he said, opening his eyes. "The book has been sealed up by Cecelia using lost magic."

"I had a feeling," Roxanne said as she picked up the grimoire. "We have to find out what's inside here. I'll have Cordellia take a look at it, and Ash, I want you to work with her on this. I'm sure between the two of you, you can break whatever enchantment is protecting it."

"As you wish," Ash replied. "I'll reach out to her in the morning and schedule a rendezvous."

Roxanne turned to Lilith and Orlando. "While we wait for the results, I want you two to begin researching Cecelia Holland. Thanks to Virgil, we have a name now. I want everything you can find on her."

"You got it, Roxy," Orlando replied.

"You can count on us," Lilith added.

Roxanne stood up. "One last thing, before I dismiss you. My

focus for the foreseeable future will be on getting our new recruits up to speed. They have incredible talent and potential, but they aren't quite ready to be out there in the field. However, I will always be available for contact, should you need me."

Both Lilith and Ash stood and saluted Roxanne before their projections cut out.

Roxanne turned towards the trio of recruits. "As for you three, we will be operating out of my home in Fenmont. This room, however, is one of my own creation. It is a dimension entirely split from our world. So as long as I draw breath, this room exists and is impenetrable."

She walked over to one of the bookshelves and grabbed a small box. From it, she took out three crystals, each no bigger than a golf ball.

"Once you two learn allostry, these teleportation crystals will be a lot less useful. Until then, use them to enter this dimension. Should you need a safe haven, consider this bunker your refuge."

With that, Roxanne returned the group to her home. Orlando said his goodbyes. As the rest of the group proceeded to turn in for the night, Virgil pulled Roxanne to the side.

"What is it?" she asked. "I hate to be rude, but tonight is the first night I'm able to sleep with my wife in months, so please be quick."

"R-right," Virgil said, his face flushing. "I'll just be a minute. I want you to teach me allostry—"

Roxanne turned to walk away. "Of course. Didn't you hear me earlier?"

Virgil took hold of Roxanne's arm. "No. I mean. I need to get stronger. A lot stronger. I imagine whatever training you went through to get where you are must have been grueling. Even so, I want you to put me through the same." Roxanne laughed. "I'm serious. No matter how painful it is or how long it takes, I'm willing to devote everything I have to training."

"Virgil, if I put you through the same training I underwent, you wouldn't survive the first day."

Virgil's face fell. "But I—"

Roxanne placed her hand on Virgil's shoulder. "You worry too much. No one deserves the level of hell I went through, but I assure you, you will get stronger under my tutelage."

But will I be strong enough? Virgil thought.

CHAPTER
FORTY-TWO

Virgil lay in his bed. His brain was ready to get up and start the day, but his body had yet to find the motivation to comply.

A wave of cold washed over him and wetness splashed all over his body. His eyes burst open in a panic as he couldn't breathe. Each gasp for air came along with a gulp of water while his mind raced. Virgil looked around, only to find darkness surrounding him in every direction. His lungs were beginning to ache, and his heart pounded so vigorously it felt as if it would leap out of his body. He shrouded himself in flames, and the water around him evaporated. Virgil fell to the ground, desperately struggling to fill his lungs with oxygen, but it was no use.

With his flames glowing bright, he could see he was in a metal box, barely big enough to hold him. The room was airtight. His strength began to falter as his eyesight drew weary. Virgil placed his palm on the floor and focused what little of his mind was still working. Pouring his mana into his hand, he released a stream of blue fire that tore away the metal floor. Before long, he fell through, landing flat on his face.

Virgil coughed, spitting up water. Each breath felt like shards of glass sliding down his throat as he heaved in air. He lay on the ground, his chest rising and falling as he savored each pain-filled gulp of air.

"Let that be a lesson to you," Roxanne said. "Never be late for training."

"What, what do you mean?" Virgil uttered between breaths. "We never established when we'd be starting."

"I am aware of that. This exercise is an insight into what will be your punishment should you turn up late."

Virgil looked around. He was in an open field. There was nothing but grass and blue skies for as far as he could see. "You call this an exercise?" he asked.

Roxanne snapped her fingers, and Virgil felt a crushing weight upon his back. It was as if a massive boulder had been placed upon him, and yet, no such thing had occurred. He opened his mouth to speak, but the pressure on his body was far too high, pinning his chest to the dirt.

"And this is what happens when you question my methods," Roxanne continued. She scoffed as she crouched down to look Virgil in his eyes. "When I was training, my master would teleport me to the cold vacuum of space without so much as a moment's notice. He'd leave me there until I was so close to death I could taste it, or until I learned how to void myself back to Earth. Do you have any idea how long it takes for a deity to reach the brink of death in such conditions?"

Again, Virgil opened his mouth to speak, but to no avail.

"You have tremendous potential, but do not confuse potential for strength. Over our time together, you will come to hate my very existence. You will loathe the mere mention of my name, but when everything is said and done, you will thank me for the warrior you will become."

Roxanne stood up and summoned a void behind her. "I've transported you to another one of my dimensions," she said as she walked away. "This one I've created solely for the purpose of training without any restraints. Your training will begin every morning at six o'clock sharp. If you are still asleep when I come for you, you will find yourself punished in the same manner you were just now. For every infraction, you can expect the punishment to worsen. Your training today will consist of trying to get up from that spot. Assuming you can get up before noon, lunch will—"

Roxanne turned around to face Virgil. He was struggling to lift himself off of the ground. His body trembled as energy surged through his body and he pushed his hands into the dirt.

Roxanne chuckled. "That's quite a valiant effort, but I—"

A luminous blue fire erupted around Virgil's body. The flames swirled ferociously. Gradually Virgil pulled himself to his feet. His breaths were heavy and elongated, but he set his jaw with determination.

"Well, okay then." Roxanne dispersed her void. "I admit I didn't expect you to be able to pass that test so soon."

Virgil doused his flames and took in a deep breath. "I told you before. I'm willing to do whatever it takes to get stronger."

"Fair enough," Roxanne said. "Let's move on then. Go ahead and show me your signature." Virgil paused, his shoulders tensing up. "If you're afraid you'll hurt me—"

"I'm afraid I'll kill you," he confessed.

Roxanne laughed. "I assure you, I'll be fine."

Virgil pointed off to the side. "Summon a barrier over there."

"Is that really necessary?" Roxanne said, fixing her glasses.

"If we're gonna do this safely."

"All right then." She waved her hand. A glowing metal wall appeared about ten feet away. "I'll bite."

Virgil turned his attention on the barrier and placed his left hand across his right wrist. "Hand of Destruction. Immolation."

Virgil's right hand turned entirely into a shimmering purple flame. The air became cold causing Roxanne to shudder a bit. Virgil placed his hand on the metal barrier, but it didn't catch fire. Instead, it began to disintegrate, slowly rotting away as if the metal were eating itself. In a matter of seconds, it was gone.

Virgil turned to face Roxanne, and his hand returned to normal. He opened his mouth to speak, but his legs collapsed from under him, causing him to fall back onto the ground.

Roxanne grinned. "That was impressive. The amount of mana it must take to convert your physical flesh into raw magical energy is just, it's insane."

Virgil gasped for air. "Yeah. I only ever get one shot, but anything I touch—"

"Is completely destroyed."

"Yeah."

"Again. The sheer mana needed to cause that level of destruction. It's—"

"Insane."

"Precisely." Roxanne stroked her chin inquisitively. "Are you sure you're human?"

Virgil laughed. "Yeah. I'm sure."

"I'd expect a signature such as this to belong to a more magically adept race such as an elf or a dragon. To think a human could pull off such a feat. I shudder to think of the kind of power you'll wield once we teach you how to use a catalyst."

Roxanne snapped her fingers, and again Virgil felt a tremendous pressure cascade over him, pinning his body back to the ground. This time, however, the gravitational force was much more robust. "I've doubled the force this time around," Roxanne said as she turned to walk away, summoning another void. "Given your fatigued state, I doubt you can make it up before lunch. However, I hope you won't stop impressing me."

The pressure was intense, so much so, Virgil could barely summon the strength to breathe. And yet, he couldn't help but grin as he watched Roxanne walk away.

By the day's end, Virgil was a wreck. He stumbled to the kitchen table, and collapsed in a chair. He had used the last bit of his strength bathing himself and finding his way to the kitchen. "Is there any way you can just blend dinner into a smoothie?" he whined.

Aurelia walked over with two plates in her hand. "Oh, hush up. I found the energy to come back in and help with dinner. The least you can do is chew your own food."

She sat a plate down in front of Virgil. He perked up at the sight of the seared pot roast and steamed veggies. "Well," he began as he picked up his fork, "that just means Roxanne's pushing me harder than she's pushing you."

Aurelia sat down next to Virgil. "I doubt that. I know this is just the first day, but learning allostry is pretty tricky. You have no idea how much of a headache you get trying to create a rip in space."

"Are you serious? She has you trying to create voids already?"

Aurelia laughed. "Trying is the perfect word. What? Aren't you doing the same?"

Virgil rolled his eyes. "I wish. I spent the day trying not to get crushed to death. I swear it feels like my body's been through a hydraulic press."

"I'm sorry to hear that. After dinner, come by my room and I'll patch you up." She winked. "You know I'll take good care of you."

Virgil smiled. "Thank you. If tomorrow's anything like today, I'm gonna need it."

"I don't know about your room, but I have a TV in mine. I'm sure we can find something to watch together while I heal you."

"Yeah, I'm sure that would be some decent training too."

"Huh?" Aurelia said, her brow raised.

"Remember back in Akata Castle? Cordellia was able to keep up the Saint's Breath while reading, having a conversation, hell, even from another room entirely."

"Oh." Aurelia frowned. "Y-yeah. This will be great training."

This quickly became a routine for the pair. Each day, Roxanne would put them through the wringer, and every night, Aurelia restored them, prepping them for the torment the next day would bring. Before Virgil knew it, an entire month had gone by.

FORTY-THREE

Virgil zipped around the training space. The gravity was intense as usual, keeping his body about ten or so feet off the ground. A white void appeared just yards in front of him. He channeled his mana into his flight, trying desperately to come to a stop. As Roxanne stepped through the void, Virgil fell to the ground, crashing hard at her feet.

"I see you're getting the hang of maneuvering in such intense gravity," Roxanne said. "You continue to impress."

"Thank you," Virgil groaned as he stood up. "Oh. Hey, Logan. I didn't see you there."

Logan waved.

"All right," Roxanne said. "I think it's time we take your training to the next level."

"Wait," Virgil said. "You're going to have us train together? How would that work?"

Logan cracked his knuckles. "What? Are you afraid of going toe to toe with me?"

Virgil rolled his eyes. "Absolutely not."

"You won't be fighting one another," Roxanne said.

"That's a disappointment," Logan replied.

"Then what will we be doing?" Virgil asked, trying his best to ignore Logan's comment.

"As I said before," Roxanne replied, "we're taking your training to the next level. You will begin sparring today, but not with each other. I want you both to come at me with all you got." Neither of the two men replied. "Is that going to be a problem?"

"No," Virgil said hastily. "I just, I've been looking forward to learning allostry. When you said we'd be moving on to the next level, I kind of assumed that's what you meant. It's been a month, and we haven't even started yet. Aurelia's been learning—"

"I've put each of you on different paths catered to your individual needs. I appreciate your enthusiasm to learn the craft, but we'll get there when we get there. Right now, we are focusing on bolstering your mana reserves and teaching you to use your mana more efficiently."

"R-right." Virgil nodded. "I'll just be patient then."

Roxanne disappeared, reappearing several yards away. She removed the gravitation hold held on the field, allowing everyone to move unrestricted.

Logan stepped forward, placing his hand in front of Virgil. "I'll go first," he said. "Just sit back and take notes."

Virgil was taken aback. "But Roxanne wanted us to—"

"You're not needed here."

Virgil looked at Logan as he approached Roxanne. In his gut he wanted to speak out, but ultimately shrugged and took a seat on the ground. "Whatever. Knock yourself out."

"This isn't what I instructed," Roxanne said as Logan took his battle stance. "Do you honestly think you can take me on alone?"

Logan nodded. "I don't need his help."

Roxanne crossed her arms. "All right, then. I guess I'll just scale things back a bit. We'll consider this portion of your training complete when you can knock me off of my feet. Feel free to come at me whenever you're ready."

Logan charged towards Roxanne. To Virgil's surprise, he was much faster than he ever had been before. Logan pulled his fist back and struck Roxanne's jaw, only to hiss in pain. Roxanne didn't so much as flinch as his fist collided with her face. He didn't even shift her glasses.

Roxanne placed her hand over Logan's. She struck his gut, and he grunted as his eyes widened. The force from the blow lifted him high into the air. Had she not been holding onto him, Logan surely would have been sent flying. Roxanne released Logan, allowing him to fall to the ground. He clutched at his stomach as if his entrails were in danger of leaking out.

Virgil stood. "Well, that was quick."

"Are you sure you don't want to wait for him?" Roxanne said.

Virgil took a battle stance and ignited his fists. "He seems like he's going to be a minute."

"Very well, then," Roxanne said with a sigh. "Whenever you're ready."

Virgil closed his fists, calling forth a multitude of fiery pillars scattered across the battlefield. They stood about seven feet tall, and while they were in no particular pattern, they surrounded Roxanne. With a snap of his fingers, the pillars began to mobilize in a frenzy. Virgil joined the crowd of flames moving seamlessly between them. Roxanne studied her surroundings, looking for Virgil among the roaring fires.

Virgil darted from out of the fire, swinging his foot towards Roxanne. She raised her guard, taking the brunt of the strike with her elbow. Virgil hissed and Roxanne slid backward, her feet leaving trails in the dirt below. Virgil fell to the ground, and all the fire he had conjured vanished. He clutched at his leg. It felt as if he had just kicked a steel pole. Roxanne, on the other hand, was unscathed, apart from the look of utter disappointment plastered on her face.

Damn it, Virgil thought. *She has the allostry talent. No wonder she didn't flinch when Logan punched her. She can make her bones as hard as metal.*

"Do you still insist on doing this separately?" Roxanne asked.

Logan stumbled back to his feet. "I told you once already, I don't need his help!"

He charged at Roxanne once again, while Virgil struggled to get back up. His leg was throbbing, but at least it wasn't broken. He fought against the pain as he put pressure on his leg. A massive force knocked him over again, pinning him to the ground.

"Would you please get off me?" Virgil said, barely able to speak under Logan's weight. Logan didn't respond as he pushed off of the ground. "Thank you." Virgil pulled himself up. "Now, if you're done dicking around, perhaps we can . . ." Logan took off towards Roxanne, paying no attention to Virgil. "I guess not."

Virgil took flight, dashing forward to join the battle. He circled around Roxanne, examining the fight between her and Logan. Finally, he saw a chance to hit in Roxanne's blind spot as Logan approached from the opposite direction. Virgil concealed his aura, attempting to hide his presence as much as possible before going in for the attack. He dove in and swung for Roxanne, waiting until the last possible second to ignite his fist in blue fire.

As calculated as the attack was, it was utterly useless. Before his fist could connect, Roxanne disappeared, leaving Virgil's blow to land on Logan instead. His fist slammed into Logan's chest, and a burst of blue fire erupted around Logan.

"I'm sorry," Virgil said as Logan flailed, desperate to dispel the fire with his Dragon's Treasure.

"This is getting tiresome," Roxanne said as she reappeared. Before either of the men could respond, Roxanne took Virgil by the collar and threw him into Logan. She waved her hand and summoned a massive metal cage around the two of them. "Listen up. Your behavior today is completely unacceptable."

"Wait," Virgil began, "I can—"

"You've had your chance!" Roxanne shouted, her eyes turning a bright white. "Now I don't know what's gotten into the two of you, but it stops now. I don't care if you have to talk, hug it out, or just beat the hell out of each other. If you don't have this shit resolved by the time I get back, then I'm expelling both of you."

Virgil opened his mouth to speak, but the look on Roxanne's face crippled the words in his throat. She left the two men alone in the cage.

"Okay," Virgil said as he took a seat. "Do you want to talk about what's bothering you?" Logan remained silent. He sat down, folded his legs, and closed his eyes. "Hey," Virgil said, waving his hand. "I'm talking to you."

"I know," Logan replied. "I'm not talking to you. See the difference?"

Virgil took a deep breath, his eye twitching. "In case you missed it, we're both gonna be expelled unless we—"

"I'm aware of the situation. Everything will be fine if you just stay out of my way. You can manage that, right?"

Virgil exhaled, and lay back in the grass. "Whatever. Come and talk to me when you're done being an asshole." With nothing else to do, he began studying the clouds.

An hour or so went by as Virgil droned on in his mindless task.

This is bullshit, he thought. *I'm going to be expelled over some bullshit.* He glanced over at Logan. He hadn't budged since sitting down. *What the fuck am I supposed to do? I can't make him not be a dick.*

Virgil exhaled deeply as he sat up. "Look," he began, not entirely sure of what exactly he wanted to say, "we, we need to talk about this?"

"There is nothing to talk about," Logan said sharply.

"Well, Roxanne and I disagree."

Logan opened his eyes. "Your opinion doesn't mean shit to me, and Roxanne is just as caught up in your hype as everyone else. Since nobody wants to be the one to tell you this, allow me to inform you that you are nothing special, and you never will be. Now, if you excuse me, I'm trying to enjoy a moment of peace."

Virgil paused, unsure of how to process Logan's words. There was no hesitation in the way he spoke. It was clear he meant every word of what he said. "Dude, what is your problem?"

"You. You're my problem, Virgil."

"This is because of Aurelia, isn't it?"

"What else would it be about?" Logan said with a roll of his eyes. "You've been nothing but a pain in the ass since the day I met you. I've tried to be nice and give you a chance for Aurelia's sake, but once again, I have to be the bad guy because she doesn't know what's good for her."

"Logan, you have to—"

"Don't sit there and try to tell me what I have to do! Especially not after what you've done. You're lucky I haven't plucked every bone from your sorry-ass hide, but things are different now. If we weren't Crusaders in the Alliance, I would have beaten you to a bloody pulp by now."

"What are you talking about?" Virgil asked, perplexed. "Just what have I done?"

Logan's face turned red. "Don't play stupid with me. You know damn well what you did."

"I really don't, but it's obviously upset you, so why don't you tell me and—"

"YOU FUCKED MY SISTER!"

CHAPTER
FORTY-FOUR

Logan's words left Virgil's jaw low and his eyes wide open. "I what?" he replied.

"You heard me," Logan grunted. "And the look on your face says it all. Did you really think I wouldn't notice? Your visits to her room at night. The hand-holding. Her damn near feeding you all the time. You must think I'm an idiot."

"Logan, I promise you I—"

"To hell with it," Logan said as he stood up. "The Alliance can throw me out. It'll be worth it to beat you senseless just one good time."

Virgil stood up as well. He didn't want to fight, but if he had to, he'd rather not take a punch sitting down. Especially from Logan. "Listen, you've got it all wrong. I'm not sleeping with Aurelia. We're just friends. I swear. We are just friends." Logan summoned his gloves as he cracked his knuckles, completely ignoring Virgil's attempts to reason with him. "You have to listen to me. Nothing is going on between us."

Logan began walking towards Virgil. "How long has it been?" he asked, his glare intense. "How long have you been giving it to my sister?"

"I'm not. I haven't been giving anything to her."

"Stop lying to me!"

Logan charged at Virgil and threw a punch. Despite the ferocity in his strike, his movements were brutish, making evading child's play for Virgil. Logan hit the metal bars of the cage, and Virgil floated to the ceiling.

Logan ground his teeth as he looked up at Virgil. "You're nothing but a coward and a cunt. Have some decency, come down here, and accept your retribution like a man."

"I'm not going to fight you, Logan."

"Whether you fight back or not is irrelevant. I'm going to beat you down regardless, and don't think just because you can fly, I can't get my hands on you."

Logan leaped into the air, but to Virgil's surprise, he didn't make it far. He struggled to clear even half of the distance between them.

Virgil exhaled in relief. "Will you please just chill for a minute and listen to me?"

"Fine," Logan said as he knelt down. "I'll just knock you out of the sky." He pressed his fingers into the dirt, attempting to dislodge a chunk of rock from it. When that failed, he struck the ground and grunted as he flinched. Virgil looked down at Logan, and bewilderment washed over him.

The fuck is going on? Logan could shatter stone just by looking at it if he really wanted to. Perhaps it's this dimension? No. The dirt's still dirt as far as I can tell.

Slowly Virgil descended to the ground. "What's going on? Are you hurt?"

Logan smirked as he approached Virgil. "No, but you're going to be."

"Are you sure? You're not acting like yourself."

"Like you would know," Logan sneered. "All you care about is banging my sister." Tears were forming in his eyes. "She's the only family I have left, and you're trying to take her from me."

Logan cocked his fist back and swung at Virgil. As he caught Logan's fist, his palm stung from the impact, but Virgil knew full well his bones should have shattered.

Virgil looked the troubled man in his eyes. "I just want what's best for both of you. I think you have depended on each other for so long, you've never really had the chance to exist separately. You shouldn't be defined solely as Aurelia's protector, nor should she be defined as your responsibility."

Virgil let go of Logan's hand, and it promptly fell to his side.

"You don't get it," Logan said shaking his head.

For a minute, Logan paused as he looked at Virgil. He seemed so desperate to speak, but his words simply wouldn't comply.

Virgil nodded, and gave a reassuring smile. "Go ahead and let it out. I promise you'll feel better when it's out in the open."

"It's. It's my fault our father died."

"Logan, you can't hold yourself responsible for—"

"No," Logan said, his gaze tilting to the ground. "It truly is my fault. He's dead, and it's all my fault."

Virgil placed his hand on Logan's shoulder. "You were still just a kid when he passed. You couldn't possibly—"

"I let them in," Logan cried. "I let them in." In a matter of moments, his cheeks were flooded with tears, and his breaths were long and heavy.

Virgil helped Logan to the ground. "Okay. One step at a time. What do you mean you let them in?"

Logan took a deep breath. "I hated Aurelia so much when we were little. For a long time, I blamed her for our mother's death. I thought. I just thought. The demons were supposed to just take her and go."

Virgil sat, shocked into silence. Logan covered his face with his palms. Perhaps it was to hide the shame, or maybe it was a futile effort to hold his tears back.

"I was stupid," Logan continued. "I was young and stupid and foolish, and I wasn't thinking. I wanted to be rid of that burden. To not have to move around anymore. To be able to walk down the street and not watch my back."

"Okay," Virgil said, finally breaking his silence. "I admit that is quite traumatic but you can't let that hold you back. Like you said, you were young. We all make mistakes, especially when we're young enough to think we have all the answers. Hell, I was older than you were when I disobeyed my father and followed him on his hunt for Cecelia. Had I not been with him, he'd surely still be alive today."

Logan sniffled as he lowered his hands. "Then you should know the shame and dishonor that hangs on my heart."

"I do, but that also means I know how destructive your actions are right now. I'm not going to pretend like our pain is the same, because it's not. But one thing you have that I didn't is someone to share the pain with. I know you want to protect Aurelia from everything that can hurt her, but if you keep holding onto her the way that you are, you're going to cause the very suffering you're trying to prevent, and she's going to hate you for it. I know it's hard to hear, but it's the truth, Logan."

"I-I know. But it's too late now. I failed her, and she's replaced me with you."

Virgil laughed. "I can't replace you. You're you. You're her older brother. Her hero. When she speaks of you, she talks about all the good times you've shared. How you make her feel safe. You haven't failed her, and you haven't lost her. Now, I'm not gonna lie, you came pretty damn close, but it's not too late to fix things between the two of you."

Logan wiped his tears away as he finally began to settle down. "How do you know? How do you know she doesn't hate me already?"

Virgil chuckled. "It's Aurelia. She isn't capable of hating anyone."

"Yeah," Logan said with a nod. "She's always been my ray of sunshine."

"Now that you've calmed down, are you sure you're okay? Not that I'm complaining, but catching your fist back there should have shredded my bones to dust." Logan paused as he looked down at the dirt. After a brief moment, Virgil spoke. "If you don't want to tell me, that's cool. But know that whether you want to admit it or not, we're friends, and friends are there for each other for stuff like this."

Logan took in a deep breath. It was clear he was nervous, his quivering muscles a testament to that fact. "The night I let Aurelia's father into our home is the same night I was gifted my strength. I realized my error in judgment, but not before my father was slain. I fell to my knees and prayed. It was all I could do. I was just thirteen. I had no chance against all those demons. I prayed to the gods for someone to help me, but what they did was far greater."

"And just what did they do?"

"They offered me a contract. All it cost me was my soul and my mana, and they promised to bestow upon me strength far beyond the comprehension of mere mortals." Logan chuckled. "Or at least that's how they put it."

Virgil was shocked, but deep down he knew that if he was presented with the same situation, he would've taken the deal in a heartbeat. "You sold your soul," he said. "Does that mean you've been without a soul this whole time?"

"No, I still have my soul for now. The deal was that I relinquish my mana then, and when I die, my soul is theirs to do with as they see fit. So long as my will remains strong and my faith true, my strength will not fail me."

"Well, that certainly explains a lot."

Logan nodded as he exhaled. "Yeah. I haven't exactly been in the best state of mind, but I'm beginning to feel a lot better about things. You're not as bad of a guy as I thought. Perhaps, I mean, if my sister was to date, I suppose I don't mind if—"

Virgil exhaled. "For the last time, Aurelia and I are just friends."

"Right," Logan laughed. "I get it. I'm sure Roxanne wouldn't appreciate that. I promise I won't say a thing."

Virgil rolled his eyes. "Why does everyone keep suggesting this? Don't get me wrong—your sister is an amazing woman. She's kind and thoughtful and funny and compassionate and—"

"Everything you'd want in a woman?"

Virgil cleared his throat. "Well, yes, but we're just friends."

"Whatever you say. If it were up to me, Aurelia wouldn't even know the opposite sex existed. So, if you're really not a thing, it's no skin off my back. But if you do hook up, I'm not going to kill you for it. Unless, of course, you break her heart. Then I'll have to hunt you down."

"R-right." Virgil paused. A troubling thought crept into his mind.

For a moment, he debated whether he should share it, until finally, he found the conviction to do so. "Logan, I hate to sour such a good moment, but you know sooner or later, you're going to have to tell Aurelia what really happened all those years ago."

Logan frowned, and he looked down to the ground once again. "Yes. I know."

"If you want, I can help you do it. That way—"

Logan shook his head. "I appreciate the offer, but this is really something I should do on my own. I just need to find the right moment."

CHAPTER

FORTY-FIVE

The kitchen was flooded with the smell of fresh cinnamon and vanilla, making Roxanne's cozy home feel even homier. Per usual, Riley and Aurelia were hard at work preparing meals for everyone. Virgil sat down at the table next to Logan, who was deeply engrossed in a blend of coffee and newspaper headlines.

"I think today's the day," Virgil said, smiling.

Logan folded his newspaper over and set it down on the table. "You've been saying that for months now."

"When you say it like that it sounds like it's been forever. We've only been joint training for two months."

"True, but two months is still months. Plural."

Virgil groaned. "Fair enough."

"I do think we'll get her any day now," Logan said, smiling as Aurelia approached with two plates in her hands.

"Here you go," Aurelia said as she placed the plates in front of Logan and Virgil. Virgil's eyes grew wide as Aurelia took a bottle of syrup and covered the powdered toast on his plate. She turned to Logan. "Do you want some, too?"

"Just a smidge."

Virgil took his silverware, his palate eagerly awaiting the sugary delight resting on his plate. Everything seemed to fade away as the fluffy goodness melted in his mouth.

"So," Aurelia said. "How do my boys like their breakfast?"

"It's amazing," Virgil exclaimed, his words muffled as he chewed.

"Don't talk with your mouth full," Riley scolded from across the counter.

Virgil swallowed. "I'm sorry." He took another bite, squirming in place as he swallowed. "I swear these are even better than what they were serving in Akata Castle."

Aurelia smiled as she reached over and tussled Virgil's hair. "I'm glad you like it. This is actually the first time I've made it. I remembered how much you liked them and I thought I'd try to make them for you."

"Thank you. You did an amazing job."

"It was nothing. Riley really helped me out. I'm just glad you love my cooking so much."

"Is there something in my hair?" Virgil asked.

"N-no," Aurelia replied, her cheeks flustering as she pulled her hand away. "I mean, not anymore. I got it."

"Well, good morning, everyone," Roxanne said as she walked into the room, Peyton in her arms.

"Roxanne," Virgil said, his words muffled once again.

"You're not supposed to talk with your mouth full," Peyton said. "Right, Mama?"

Roxanne set Peyton down. "That's right."

"Sorry, little man," Virgil replied. "I promise I'll do better next time."

"We'll be done soon," Logan said. "Five minutes. Tops."

"Yeah," Virgil agreed. "I hope you're ready because today we're going to—"

"You can take your time," Roxanne said. "We won't be training today."

"What?" Virgil said, damn near dropping his fork. "Why not?"

"You all have been working hard these past few months. I think you've earned a day off, and frankly, I would love to spend some time with my family."

"Thank you," Virgil said, his face falling. "But I'm good to keep training. I've been improving so much, and I'd hate to break my momentum." Virgil turned to Logan. "I suppose we can just do some training on our own."

Logan nodded. "As long as you're willing."

"While I appreciate your enthusiasm," Roxanne said, "you two should really take advantage of this opportunity. Days like this will be few and far between."

"We appreciate it," Virgil replied. "But we're good to keep going. Before you go, can you send us to your training dimension?"

"You two really don't want to rest, huh?"

"Not really. It's only a matter of time before we have to face Nobody again. If I'm gonna get my fang back, I need to get as strong as I can before that day comes."

"My motives aren't so personal," Logan said. "But nevertheless, Nobody is a threat, and we need to be ready to deal with them when the time comes."

Roxanne opened her mouth to speak, but Aurelia beat her to the punch. "Don't worry." She wrapped her arms around Virgil. "I'll make sure these guys get the R&R they need."

"You should come to the beach with us," Peyton exclaimed. "It's going to be so much fun!"

"That does sound like loads of fun," Aurelia replied. "But we wouldn't want to intrude on your family outing."

"Nonsense," Riley said. "We'd love it if you joined us. Isn't that right, babe?"

Roxanne nodded. "Of course. Today's the summer solstice, after all, and I know the perfect beach in the Onyx nation. It's like the sun is shining directly on the island."

"Hold on a second," Virgil said. "I don't even have any swimwear."

"Neither do I," Aurelia said. "We can run out really quick and grab some. Roxanne, do you mind waiting on us until we get back?"

"Of course not."

It didn't take long for the group to finish breakfast and obtain suitable swim attire. Once they were all ready, Roxanne summoned a void, transporting everyone to the sandy beaches of Ozryn Isle, located deep in the Onyx nation. The crowds were massive, but given the beach's size, there was more than enough sand and water to go around.

There wasn't a single cloud in sight, making the heat intense. With every second that passed, the cool glistening water looked more appealing. Virgil looked around. He had never seen such radiant blue sands before. There were trees scattered everywhere, sprouting high into the air, and numerous birds hovered over the beach.

The group found a spot and laid out a large blanket to claim it as theirs. Peyton could barely contain his excitement. One after another, he tossed his outer layer of clothes off, letting them fall carelessly on the ground.

"Come on, Mama," Peyton squealed. "Let's go build a sandcastle!"

"Hold on a second, pumpkin," Roxanne said. "You have to put on your sunblock first."

Peyton was a swirling ball of energy, fidgeting in place as Roxanne coated him head to toe. When she finished, Peyton stepped away. "Okay," he said. "Now, you and Mommy go. And you have to hurry!"

"Don't worry," Riley said. "It will only take a second."

In all of the commotion, the trio had already shed their clothing. Aurelia had helped her brother cover his back with sunblock, and he was off to enjoy the water. Virgil, on the other hand, sat atop the blanket, his eyes fixated on his palm. He was summoning balls of blue fire above his hand and swirling them around in a whirlwind.

"And just what are you doing?" Aurelia asked as she approached him.

"Nothing really," he replied. "Just practicing some fire manipulation."

Aurelia sighed as she walked in front of Virgil. She crouched down and looked him in the eye. "We're here to have fun. Remember?"

"Yeah, I know. I just . . ." Virgil trailed off as he noticed Aurelia was wearing a two-piece swimsuit. It was blue with white frills that trailed along her waist and bustline. More noticeable, though, were

Aurelia's breasts. They were right there, just a couple of feet away. Perhaps it was the lack of clothing covering them or the way her swimsuit seemed to perk them up together. Nevertheless, they were something he hadn't noticed before. Quickly he raised his eyes, realizing where they had fallen.

"You're right," he said, blushing. "Let's have some fun."

Aurelia smiled as she turned around. "That's more like it. Now rub some sunblock on my back."

Virgil's face grew redder still. "Are you sure you wouldn't rather have Roxanne do it? Or Riley? I'm sure Peyton wouldn't mind."

Aurelia giggled as she sat down in front of Virgil. "I'm not gonna bite you. Well, not unless you're into that kind of thing."

"Wha-what?"

"You know. A little nibble on the neck. I promise not to leave a mark."

Virgil fell silent. His heart thumped in his chest as he struggled to find the right words to say.

Aurelia broke the silence. "I'm joking, Virgil."

Virgil forced out a laugh as he picked up the bottle of sunblock and poured some into his hands. "Right. That was just a joke."

Aurelia began undoing the string holding her swimsuit top in place.

"What are you doing?" he exclaimed as he turned away, shutting his eyes.

Aurelia burst into laughter. "You can't apply it properly with this string in the way. Don't worry. My breasts are still covered. Nobody can see my naughty bits."

Reluctantly, Virgil turned back to face Aurelia. Her skin looked smooth and soft to the touch. Slowly he placed his palms upon her back. It was even more supple than he had imagined. He rubbed his hands across her gently, carefully spreading the white liquid.

"Don't forget my lower back. If you don't get it, I'm afraid I'll get a terrible sunburn."

Virgil swallowed the lump in his throat as he poured more sunblock into his palm. He placed his hands on the small of her back, and she quivered at his touch.

"I, I'm sorry," Virgil said hastily as he pulled back.

"You're fine," Aurelia replied, looking back behind her shoulder. "I just like the way it feels when you touch me."

"You do?"

Aurelia smiled. "Of course," she replied, her tone playful and inviting. "Don't you like touching me?"

"N-no," Virgil said quickly, his face flushing, his body hot. "I mean, I don't mind it."

Virgil continued on, moving lower and lower down her back. His shorts became tighter with each inch of skin he covered. "Okay," he said, pulling his hands back and clearing his throat. "You're all set."

"Already," Aurelia whined, as she began tying her swimsuit back up. She spun around to face Virgil and flashed a smile. "My body thanks you."

"It was nothing," Virgil said, trying his best to casually place his hands over his lap.

"Well, whether you want to admit it or not, you're my hero." Aurelia gestured to Virgil to turn around. "All right. Now, let's do you."

"N-no," Virgil said sheepishly. "I mean, I don't need it. I'm a pyromancer. Applying sunblock for us is like putting a floaty on a fish."

Aurelia pouted. She then grinned as she stood. "In that case, let's hit the water."

"Sure thing. You go on ahead though. I'll be right behind you."

CHAPTER
FORTY-SIX

Virgil flew through the water. A quick glance behind him confirmed Aurelia was still hot on his trail. He pushed himself to go faster until he felt a strong current ahead of him, drastically reducing his speed. He looked back once again to find Aurelia reaching for him. She grabbed him and charged towards the surface.

"I got you," she exclaimed as they shot out of the water.

"You cheated," Virgil replied. "You used your magic to hold me back."

"You were using your magic to swim faster."

"Well, I, that's different. I'm not an aquamancer."

Aurelia giggled. "Whatever makes you feel better. All I know is I'm a shark, and you're a little fishy, and you're mine now." She looked down and held onto Virgil tighter. They were hovering over the water, several hundred feet in the air. "I guess I overdid it, huh."

Virgil laughed. "Maybe just a little. I'll make sure we get down safely."

He began lowering them towards the water before Aurelia stopped him. "Wait."

"What's wrong? Don't tell me you're afraid of heights, too."

"What?" Aurelia asked. "No. Who's afraid of heights?"

"You mean you don't, uh, never mind. It's not important."

"Okay," Aurelia said slowly. "What I was going to say is, I've never seen a view like this before. The beach looks so beautiful from this high up."

"Say no more." Virgil positioned her on his back. "Just make sure you hold on tight, okay."

Aurelia rested her arms around him, and Virgil tried his best to ignore the gnawing thoughts compounding in his head. The warm feeling billowing in his chest. Her soft and supple body pressed so firmly against his back. Her breasts. Good god, her breasts. He tried to push those thoughts and feelings aside. After all, they were just friends. Best friends, but friends nonetheless.

They flew around the beach, taking in the sights. Everything looked so minuscule. They could barely see the people down below. The sun glistened off the water, giving it a crystal-like appearance. They could see the many jungles that covered Ozryn's inland, and the various villages that rested between the foliage. Everything looked sublime.

"Look at that." Aurelia reached over and pointed to the side. Her body shifted, causing her to abruptly tighten her grip on Virgil, drawing them even closer together. "I'm sorry," she said hastily, her face hugged tightly against Virgil's neck.

Despite their aquatic frolicking, Virgil could still smell the sweet scent of peaches looming off her. Butterflies swirled in his gut as he placed his hands onto Aurelia's thighs, further securing her on his back. "It's all right. Even if you fall, I promise I'll catch you."

Aurelia ran the tip of her finger across Virgil's chest as if she were drawing hearts in his skin. "I know. That's one of the things I love about you. You always make me feel so safe. Like no matter what, we'll always be okay and I can really be myself with you."

Aurelia's touch sent a shiver through Virgil's body, and he could feel her breath gliding down his neck with each breath she took. It was exhilarating, and his mind surged with thoughts. Again, he tried to cast them out, but he might as well have been asking the sun to stop its radiant glow.

Okay. Everyone was right. No! You're just friends. Her finger slipped! Yeah. She wouldn't do that. Not intentionally. Yeah. Stop being weird, Virgil. You are just friends. FRIENDS!

"You still with me?" Aurelia asked.

"Y-yeah. What is it you wanted me to see?"

"Those trees over there. To the east."

Virgil turned his head. "Oh yeah, I see them. From up here, they look like, like a heart."

"I know, right!" Aurelia gushed. "They're two beings coming together to form one heart. Isn't it just so romantic?"

"I suppose it is."

Yeah. Right. You know that was the most romantic thing you've ever seen. And she pointed it out. Why would she do that? Wait. Is this a date? Am I on a date right now? No! We're just here to have fun. Fun with friends. Only it's just us. Alone. Looking at this romantic heart. Fuck! This is a date. But then again, what if it's not?

Aurelia gave Virgil a gentle squeeze as she placed her cheek against his neck once again. "Thank you," she whispered. "You don't know how much this means to me. I promise I'll never forget this moment with you."

Virgil smiled. *It does feel good when she holds me like this. If we were a couple, we could do this all the time. I think I'd like that.*

"Yeah," Virgil replied. "Neither will I."

Aurelia sighed. "It must be nice. You get to see things like this all the time."

"I suppose it is pretty amazing when you think about it. When you're so used to flying, I guess it's easy to forget that."

"What's it like? Flying, I mean."

"You should know by now. We've been up here for a while."

"You're flying," Aurelia giggled. "I'm just along for the ride. I meant what's flying like for you? What's it like to not be controlled by anything? To be able to just get up and go where you want, when you want?"

"Well, you pretty much hit it right on the head. When you're up here, nothing can bother you. It's liberating."

"Is it hard?"

"It's about as hard as breathing. Well, at least for me anyway. Just because you're born with a talent, doesn't mean you're born with the ability to use it. It could take years to master."

"How long did it take you?"

"I don't really know. I've been flying since I can remember. My father used to scold me for floating for no good reason. Apparently, it was a hard habit to break." Aurelia giggled once more. "You just pictured a little version of me floating around, didn't you?"

"Maaaybe," she replied, her tone elongated and playful. "What if I did?"

Virgil chuckled. "I don't know what I'm going to do with you."

"Well, whatever you decide, can it include lunch, preferably of the fried variety?"

Virgil turned his attention to the pier. "I think we can make that happen."

The pair flew over and slowly descended upon the pier. After a brief wait in line, they had their lunch in hand: chicken tenders, a basket of fries to share between them, and frozen smoothies to wash it all down. They sat down at one of the many patio tables spread about the pier.

"So," Aurelia said after taking a sip of her drink. "Are you having a good time?"

"Definitely," Virgil replied. "I can't remember the last time I've had so much fun. Thank you for that."

Aurelia reached over, plucking a fry from the basket. "You're so welcome, oh bestie of mine."

Virgil smirked. "Oh, so I'm 'bestie' now."

Aurelia winked. "For now."

"I see. I should be careful before I get kicked to the curb."

"I would never do such a thing. Not to you."

"You say that now, but . . ."

Aurelia paused, awaiting Virgil to finish his sentence. However, his attention was drawn elsewhere. "Virgil," she said, waving her hand in front of his face. "Are you still there?"

"Excuse me." He stood up abruptly, knocking over his chair. "I'll be right back."

Virgil fought his way through the crowds of people. His mind was focused on one thing. She was a short elven woman with hair as black as midnight, and her skin was a powder blue. Her white sundress fell just shy of her knees, and her hair was tied up in a ponytail. She was walking along the pier, heading inland.

"Excuse me, miss," Virgil said as he placed his hand on the woman's shoulder. Startled, the woman turned around. "I'm sorry," Virgil continued. "I didn't mean to frighten you. I just. You. Do you happen to be related to Olivia Abernathy? You look like you could be her sister."

"N-no," the woman said, shaking her head. "I'm afraid I have no idea who that is. Is she a friend of yours?"

Virgil frowned. "She used to be."

"Oh. Well, I'm sorry to have gotten your hopes up."

"Don't worry about it," Virgil said as he turned to walk away. "I'm sorry to have bothered you."

Virgil walked back to the table with Aurelia and sat down.

"Find something you like?" she asked, dragging a soggy fry through a pile of ketchup.

"That's good," Virgil said. "Keep pretending to be mad at me."

Aurelia scoffed. "Done."

"When I tell you to, take your drink and dump it on me. Then I want you to storm off and go get Roxanne and Logan. Meet me at the heart-shaped trees. If I'm not there in fifteen minutes, have Roxanne evacuate the island."

Aurelia raised her brow. "Okay," she began. "Now you're starting to scare me. What's going on?"

"I'll explain later." Virgil placed his hand on Aurelia's.

"Don't you try and kiss up to me now!" Aurelia stood up. "I can't believe you would do this to me after all I've done for you!"

Aurelia grabbed her drink and tossed it into Virgil's face. Turning her nose up, she turned and stormed away. Virgil wiped the frozen drink from his face. Although he had known it was coming, that didn't make it any more pleasant. The stares from the other beach patrons didn't make it any better either. Nevertheless, he promptly cleaned off the table, and proceeded to leave the pier.

CHAPTER
FORTY-SEVEN

As Virgil approached the heart-shaped trees, he saw Logan, Aurelia, and Roxanne standing there. Logan was stern and calm, his arms folded. At first glance, Aurelia appeared to be just as relaxed as her brother, but Virgil had come to be able to tell how she really felt inside. Her nervous, shifting eyes confirmed her anxiousness. Roxanne, however, stood just a few feet away from the siblings. She had her phone up to her ear and was deep in conversation.

"Understood," Roxanne said. "I'll mobilize the task force immediately."

"What's going on?" Virgil asked.

Roxanne turned her attention back to the group. "That was Aiden. Nobody's on the move again."

"What? Is he sure?"

"Absolutely. The Scarlet Mage has been sighted in the Amber Nation, and he's not alone. Aiden's forces are in pursuit as we speak. I'm going to assemble our team and join the hunt. If the attack on Akata Castle taught us anything, it's that the Scarlet Mage is not to be trifled with, and that was before he got his hands on a dragon's treasure."

"We got this," Aurelia said. "If we all work together, I'm sure we can take him down."

Roxanne paused. She looked at the trio and took a deep breath. "I'm leaving you three behind."

"What?" Logan asked, his jaw nearly dropped to the ground.

"I don't understand," Aurelia added. "I thought you wanted us to help stop Nobody."

"I did," Roxanne said, "I mean, I do. I thought we'd have more time but—"

"But you think we can't handle it." Logan finished.

Roxanne pursed her lips and let out a heavy sigh. "Look, the truth of the matter is that none of you are ready for this. You've each made incredible strides since I've been working with you, but as it stands right now, the odds of you surviving this battle are just too unfavorable to risk it."

"But—"

"I'm sorry, Aurelia. I know you three have been putting your all into this, but I'm not willing to put you three in danger when I don't have to." Roxanne then turned to Virgil, who had yet to say a word. "Are you okay?" she asked. "I expected you to be the most upset of all."

Virgil looked at Roxanne. "Frankly, I couldn't be angrier with you, but I'll live. I mean, that's the point. Right? I can't be a good dog if I'm dead."

"Virgil, I—"

"Don't bother. After all, this is the life I signed up for. Being told what to do and when to do it." Everyone fell silent as Virgil turned to walk away. "If you don't mind, I'll make my way back to Fenmont on my own."

"You can't be serious," Logan said. "The Diamond Nation is several thousand miles away."

"I know. I'll have to stop here and there, but I'll make it back eventually. I could use a nice long flight right about now."

Roxanne nodded, and Virgil walked away.

"Wait," Aurelia said as she followed behind Virgil. "I'll come with you."

"No," he said, not even bothering to look back. "I'd prefer to be alone right now. Please understand."

Virgil left the group and returned to the beach. He slipped back into his normal attire and left Ozryn.

Or at least that's how he made it seem. Once he was sure he wasn't being followed, he returned to the pier. It had been nearly an hour since he was last there, but in all that time, he kept his aura perception focused on the elven woman.

He began his journey deep into the island's inland and stumbled across a remote village. The buildings were small, appearing to be made out of a mixture of straw, bamboo, and leaves the size of blankets. Virgil had stopped seeing paved roads, and the natives were mostly nymphs. He stuck out like a sore thumb, and he didn't know the first thing about speaking nymph. Fortunately, he had a clear trail to follow.

He stopped, and panic began to set in. Virgil tuned his aura perception as high as he could manage, but it was no use. The woman was gone, as if she had simply vanished off the island.

A large hand grabbed his shoulder. "Okay," a familiar voice said, "that's far enough."

"Logan!" Virgil spun around. "How did you find me?"

Logan pulled out a cell phone. "Aurelia and I both agreed you were acting weird, so we devised a plan to tail you." After dialing a number, Logan pulled the phone to his ear. "You can join us now."

"I don't get it. I made sure I wasn't followed. I didn't sense any aura."

Logan smiled as Virgil's eyes grew wide. "Shortly after Roxanne brought us back, we left Fenmont. We told Riley we were going out to catch a movie. Not sure if she bought it, to be completely honest, but that's neither here nor there. After Aurelia transported us to Ozryn, she left, leaving me to wait for you. The one person who could tail you without you even realizing it."

A blue void appeared, and Aurelia stepped through. She was livid, her face red and her fists balled. As she approached Virgil, he opened his mouth to speak, only for his words to be slapped right out of his mouth. He held his face in shock. Aurelia's eyes were glistening, and it looked as if she would burst into tears at any moment.

"Aurelia, I—"

"Why did you do it?" she asked, her tone low as she cut Virgil off.

"I. It's. It's complicated."

"Then un-complicate it."

"Aurelia. You don't understand. I—"

"Make me understand!" she blurted out, tears falling down her face. "Please. Just make it make sense. I thought I meant something to you, but you just left me behind. Why? Why would you do that to me? You promised you would call for me. You promised we'd face this together."

Virgil fell silent, floored by her outburst. Again, he opened his mouth to speak, only this time, he failed to find the words to say.

Aurelia turned away trying her best to wipe away her tears. "I can't even stand to look at you right now."

Logan reached out and patted his sister on the head. "I'm sure he has a good reason," he said as he looked to Virgil. "Right?"

"R-right," Virgil nodded as he swallowed the lump in his throat. "You see. I. On the pier. I caught a glimpse of someone who looked kind of like Olivia. Not strange, I know, but when I looked at her aura, it was a dead match."

"That's impossible," Logan replied. "Auras are as unique as someone's fingerprint, and Olivia died at Akata Castle. You burned her body yourself."

Virgil tensed up and his stomach lurched at the thought of her burning corpse. "I know, but, I mean, I know what I felt. I swear the auras are a perfect match. I don't know how it's possible, but something isn't right. Don't you find it odd that the Scarlet Mage would appear mere moments after I spoke with this woman?"

Logan stroked his chin. "I admit it. That is quite the coincidence. Let's say Olivia is alive somehow. That would mean she likely faked her death at Akata Castle. If so, there's a good chance she's been a spy for Nobody all along. It would certainly explain the assault on the island."

Aurelia turned back around still fuming with anger. "That doesn't explain why you left me!"

Virgil's gaze fell to the ground. "You're right." He took a deep breath. "I left you behind because I didn't want to drag you down with me. If I'm right about this, then that means the task forces are chasing a ghost. Once the Alliance finds out what I've done, I'll be lucky if all I'm facing is expulsion. It's always been your dream to be a Crusader like your parents. I didn't want you to be punished for my actions. This is my fight, and if anybody should suffer for it, it should be me."

Aurelia reached over, placing her hand on Virgil's cheek. Gently, she raised his head up. They locked gazes. Her tears had finally ceased. "I appreciate the thought, but this isn't just your fight anymore."

Virgil looked over to Logan.

"It's true," Logan agreed. "And besides. How are they going to kick out the Crusaders who put an end to Nobody?"

All Virgil could do was smile. Words simply couldn't express the warmth he felt surging through his heart. The trio of friends pressed onward, traveling deeper into Ozryn's jungles. As they moved, they formulated their plan on how they would attempt to subdue their targets.

After an hour or so, they came to a halt.

"What is it?" Aurelia asked Virgil. "Do you sense Olivia again?"

"No," he answered. "But there are a handful of people nearby. Based on their positions, and the last place I sensed Olivia's aura, I'm guessing their hideout is close by."

"That sounds like a fair assessment," Logan said, flexing his muscles. "All right. I'll try to make this quick."

Virgil gave Logan the coordinates of the guards. Logan nodded and summoned O'Drakka's Fists. "I'll send a text once I've cleared them out. If you don't hear from me in ten minutes, come on in, guns blazing."

Logan darted off, leaving Virgil and Aurelia alone. Virgil walked over to a nearby tree and leaned against it as he sat down. He took in a deep breath, and exhaled even more deeply.

"How are you feeling?" Aurelia asked as she sat down next to him.

"Ignorant. Foolish. Stupid." Virgil flexed his knuckles, but his movements, were stiff and rigid. "Most of all, I'm angry. I'm trying hard not to lose it again, but I don't know if I can keep it all in."

"That's understandable. Olivia fooled us all. Hell, I pushed you to go out with her. I'd love to just hit the bitch in the face one good time."

"It's more than that, Aurelia. I've never told this to anyone, but when I get angry, like really really angry, I lose focus. It gets harder and harder to control my fire, and well, I can't even protect myself." Virgil tensed up, hanging his head low as he frowned. "It's pathetic, really. A pyromancer burned by his own flame."

Aurelia wrapped her arm around Virgil and rested her head on his shoulder. "Don't do that. You're an amazing sorcerer. This may be an issue now, but I'm sure you'll overcome it one day. And I'll be right here by your side cheering you on when you do."

Virgil began to tear up. "That's why I'm scared. With the battle we're about to get in to I don't think I can keep it all together." He looked down at his trembling hands. "Even now, I feel like I'm going to explode. I don't care if I hurt myself. I could burn down to the bone, but if I hurt you—"

"You won't," Aurelia said. Her words were simple. Definitive.

"H-how do you know that?" Virgil said choking up.

"Because I'm here with you."

Virgil sniffled. "Does that mean you'll keep me from burning us all to the ground?" he asked.

Aurelia shook her head. "It means I'll be there to pull you out of the darkness."

Virgil couldn't help but smile as he rested his head on Aurelia's. "I know you're tired of hearing this by now," he said placing his hand over hers, "but thank you. You've been nothing short of an angel to me, and I promise I'll never leave you behind again."

There was a brief moment of silence between the two of them. "I know this is a terrible time to say this," Aurelia began, her tone shrouded in uncertainty, "but I'm afraid if I don't say it now, it might never come out."

"What is it?" Virgil asked. Once again, Aurelia paused. Virgil turned to her. Gently he caressed her cheek, guiding her eyes to meet his. Her cheeks were flushed red, and it looked as if a thousand words were echoing through her mind. "What is it?" he asked again.

"Do you think that we, I mean, Could you and I . . ."

A loud vibration echoed in Aurelia's pocket. She sat upright and pulled out her phone. Sure enough, it was Logan giving the all-clear.

Aurelia stood up. "It's time."

"Wait," Virgil said as he stood up as well. "What were you going to say?"

"It's not important. Besides, there's no time for it now."

Aurelia proceeded to walk away, but Virgil took hold of her hand. "We'll make time for it. Right here. Right now. I don't want you to ever feel like you're not important in my life."

Aurelia smiled from ear to ear. "I'll tell you what. When we make it through this, I promise we'll lay everything out on the table."

CHAPTER
FORTY-EIGHT

Virgil and Aurelia emerged from the trees in front of Logan. Before they could speak, their attention was drawn to the structure behind him. It was huge, but it was more wide than tall. It was made of stone and metal and covered with ancient runes. It was easy to see that the building had been magically constructed.

"Let's go," Virgil said. "It's only a matter of time before they notice us."

Logan and Aurelia nodded, and the trio entered the building. There was only one room, and as they entered, the lights sprung on, revealing a demon as tall as a house. His skin was lime green, and he was draped in a tattered brown cloth. He was sleeping, but with the room now lit, he was beginning to wake up.

"I'm sorry, mistress," the demon said, wiping his eyes. "I couldn't help but fall asleep. It's been so boring, just sitting here. Do you think I could maybe come down below with you?" He was unarmed, but his sheer size alone would prove to be troublesome. "Wait," the demon said blinking erratically. "You're not Mistress Cecelia."

Virgil tensed up, burying the fury raging in his heart.

The demon leaned in closer, his attention fixed on Virgil. "You!"

he said, his tone growing deeper as he stood up. "I know you. Mistress told me. You killed Berraal!"

Thoughts of his battle on at Akata Castle looped through Virgil's mind. "You mean the demon who attacked us? I'm sorry, but he didn't leave me much of a choice."

"He was my brother!" The demon swung his fist towards Virgil.

With a flash of light, Aurelia summoned an enormous blade in the air and sliced the demon's arm clean off. As quickly as the blade appeared, it was gone, and blood began pouring from the severed limb like a broken faucet. The demon opened his mouth to scream out in pain, but Aurelia summoned a metal box around his skull. It was airtight, completely muffling the demon's wails into unintelligible grunts. He sat down, desperately trying to pull the box from off his head. With each passing moment, he grew weaker, fighting less and less, until finally, he lay still on the floor. Aurelia reduced the box to merely a muzzle, and bound the demon to the ground with shackles and chains.

Virgil closed his eyes, scanning the structure. Now that he was within its walls, he could feel several auras present throughout the stronghold. Even so, all that mattered to Virgil was that Olivia was there, along with the Scarlet Mage and Cecelia.

The group entered an elevator. The ride underground was lengthy as they descended deeper and deeper into the Earth. With each minute that passed, Virgil's nerves became more and more unstable. His skin was growing tighter, and his body hotter. His mind continually shifted focus, bouncing like a pinball between killing Cecelia, capturing the Scarlet Mage, and confronting Olivia.

After five minutes, the elevator stopped. Virgil looked over to Logan and held up two fingers. The doors slid open, revealing two men. One stood frozen in shock while the other summoned a wall of fire, trapping the trio in the elevator.

Logan smirked as he reached through the flames, absorbing it into his gloves. He took hold of the men's faces. "You should have gone for the kill."

Before they could respond, Logan knocked their heads together, crashing them into one another with incredible force. Both men lost consciousness, and Logan tossed them into the elevator. Aurelia incapacitated the men just like the demon, ensuring that they wouldn't be able to send for help should they come to.

Virgil peered down the hallway. "We're close. They're in a room, maybe a few corridors away. But they're not alone. There are ten people in total. Perhaps they're in a meeting or something."

"That's unfortunate," Logan said. "It would have been a lot better if they were separated."

"Are there other people here?" Aurelia asked.

"Yeah. They're scattered about."

"They're likely posted up as guards," Logan added. "Or maybe they are patrolling a set area."

"Can you navigate us around the guards?" Aurelia asked. "It would be best if we conserve our energy for the main objective."

"I don't know," Logan said. "We have the element of surprise at the moment. With Virgil's ability to sense auras as well as he can, we could easily knock off all the stragglers. That would minimize surprises during the main battle. And let's not forget we are entering a fight three against ten. It'd be best if that didn't snowball further."

"Yeah, but—"

A siren began blaring throughout the hallway, accompanied by flashing lights. "Well, that decides it then," Virgil said. "I'll hurry ahead."

He took to the air and darted off, leaving a trail of fire in his wake. His intense training over the last few months had vastly increased his flight speed. He rounded a corner and came across a guard. With a swift kick Virgil pinned the guard to the wall and a fiery cage trapped him. Virgil continued on, disposing of each combatant he came across with speed and efficiency.

At his extreme speed, it didn't take him long at all to reach his destination. He entered the room, and his heartbeat quickened. The massive room was mostly empty. Cecelia, the Scarlet Mage, and Olivia stood behind a stone altar. Seven demons were tied to floor with vines and roots. There were candles lit everywhere, and runes painted with blood scattered across the floors and walls. A skull sitting upon the altar emanated an ominous, foreboding presence that filled the room.

It looked to be centuries old and clearly wasn't human. It had horns curved into spirals, sharp fangs, and three eye sockets.

Cecelia turned to Olivia with a sneer. "I thought you said he wouldn't follow you!"

"Obviously, I was mistaken," Olivia replied. "I thought you said your diversion would throw them off."

Virgil looked at each of the individuals standing before him. He didn't know who to focus on. Olivia, the woman who toyed with his heart. Cecelia, the woman who stole everything from him. Or the Scarlet Mage, the man with his aura signature. He took a deep breath, suppressing the urge to burn everything to ashes, and focused on the Scarlet Mage.

The Scarlet Mage raised his hand, summoning a red void behind him. "Grab the remains and go," he said.

"Just kill the boy as you should have done before," Cecelia snapped. "I've waited far too long for this."

"Then what difference does a little while longer make? Are you really so shortsighted that you'd risk everything now, when we are so close to realizing our dreams? I'm sure Virgil is only the first to make it here, and reinforcements will be descending down upon us at any moment."

Cecelia sighed before reaching over and tussling the Scarlet Mage's hair. Virgil's blood began to boil, and he wound his fists into balls. "You're right," she replied. "What would I do without my rock?"

"You'd be dead," the Scarlet Mage replied, his tone even and low.

Cecelia laughed. "Of course." She turned to Olivia. "I'll trust you can clean up this mess."

No," the Scarlet Mage said, "he's my responsibility."

"You had your chance. Now come on before I—"

"Nobody is going anywhere!" Virgil erupted, unable to remain silent any longer. His hands burst into flames, and he summoned a wall of fire, cutting off their escape route. "You all are going to answer for what you've done," he said, smoke trailing off his body.

With a flick of his wrist, the Scarlet Mage summoned a series of blades that sliced through Virgil's fire, dispersing the flames. He turned to walk away. "For a second there, I thought you had made significant progress." The Scarlet Mage scoffed. "Sadly, you're still not good enough."

Cecelia collected the skull from the altar and started to leave with the Scarlet Mage. As futile as it was, Virgil tried to erect another barrier. Olivia fired off a barrage of wooden spikes towards him. He pulled back, easily dodging the strike, but put a considerable distance between himself and his fleeing targets.

"You should really focus on not dying," Olivia taunted.

Cecelia and the Scarlet Mage left, leaving Olivia and Virgil alone. For a moment, the two of them stood staring each other down. There were a million words Virgil wanted to say, but he ultimately decided on just five. "Was any of it real?"

"Was any of what real?" Olivia replied, her tone condescending.

"Us. The time we spent together. The laughs we shared. When we looked into each other's eyes. Did you really feel nothing for me?"

Olivia let out a shrill laugh. "Of course not. I kept you close because you were our contingency plan. If we couldn't get the Crystal Catalyst, we would settle for the Fang of Kayveon. It's as simple as that."

Virgil's shoulders tensed, and he ground his teeth. "I saved your life."

"You saved nothing. What you fell for was a magical double hosting a fragment of my soul. I was never truly on Akata Island."

Virgil paused as Olivia's words sunk in. His body felt hot, and his breath was heavy. He tried to calm down, but his flames were growing rapidly.

"How does it feel?" Olivia said. "How does it feel, knowing that it will be your failures that plunge the world into darkness?"

Virgil snapped back into the moment. "Don't celebrate just yet."

Olivia rolled her eyes. "And why not? Do you honestly think you have a chance of stopping us?" Virgil grinned, causing Olivia's expression to sour. "You don't get it, do you?" she continued. "We've already won. You and your friends have no chance of leaving here alive. We have everything we need to bring the Alliance down to its knees, and claim what is rightfully ours."

Virgil pointed towards Olivia. "You're the one who doesn't get it. Or have you not noticed the void still behind you?"

Olivia turned, and her eyes grew wide at the sight of the red void. She spun back around, to find Logan and Aurelia entering the room.

"Sorry we're late," Logan said.

"Did we miss anything?" Aurelia asked.

"Nothing much," Virgil answered. "You guys remember the plan?"

Logan cracked his knuckles. "Of course."

"You can count on us," Aurelia added as she readied herself.

Virgil nodded. "Watch out for the demons. I don't think they're willing participants in whatever was going on here."

"You're insane if you think I'm going to—"

Before Olivia could even finish her sentence, Aurelia dashed forward with blinding speed. She drove her fist into Olivia's mouth, knocking her to the ground.

Aurelia smiled. "Boy did that feel good." She made her way to the void, and Virgil followed suit.

Olivia reached out, encasing the void in a wooden cube. Logan walked over and placed his foot on Olivia's back. She squirmed, crying out in pain as he increased the pressure on her spine. The wooden cube crumbled, and Aurelia stepped through. Virgil approached the void, but stopped as he heard Logan scream. He turned around to find Logan stumbling backward, a wooden spike piercing his stomach.

"Logan!" Virgil shouted, his fists tightening.

"Don't worry about me!" Logan replied, leaking blood onto the ground. "Continue the plan!"

Virgil raised his palm to Olivia. "The plan didn't include you taking a wooden spike in the gut!"

"Damn it, Virgil! If you don't leave now, this will have all been for nothing!"

Olivia stood and took a deep breath. She exhaled, blanketing the seven bound demons in thick green mist. "Hear my call," she said. "Fungal Subjugation."

The vines shackling the demons released. They stood up, their eyes turning a bright green. Moss coated their bodies, and they glared at Logan.

"What are you waiting for!" Logan shouted.

Virgil snapped to his senses, turning his back to Logan. "Please," he said, his voice shaky. "Please make it through all right."

"You're not going anywhere!" Olivia exclaimed as she raised her palm towards Virgil.

Logan released a downpour of blue fire from his gloves, burning Olivia's hand. Reluctantly, Virgil stepped through the void, leaving Logan to fend for himself.

CHAPTER

FORTY-NINE

Virgil appeared in the desert sand a few feet away from Aurelia. The sun was beginning to set, turning the hot orange sand to a cooler, almost blue color. She had the Scarlet Mage bound in chains; however, Cecelia was nowhere to be found.

"I'm sorry," Aurelia said, careful not to take her eyes off the mage. "I couldn't keep Cecelia from making an escape."

Virgil stepped ahead of her. "That's all right. I'm much more concerned with him." He paused for a moment, a single question burning through his mind as he looked at the Scarlet Mage. "It's you. Isn't it?"

The Scarlet Mage didn't respond. Virgil's eyes began to well, his nose sniffling. "Of course, it's you. I'd know your aura signature anywhere."

Again, the Scarlet Mage said nothing.

"How could you do it?" he continued. "Don't you know what she's done?" He ground his teeth. "You have to know. You've been with her this whole time. Haven't you?"

Still, the Scarlet Mage remained silent.

"Dad's dead. He died looking for you. But you, you were fine. You chose to be with her. The woman who cursed him. You chose to be with a witch over your own flesh and blood."

Virgil stared at his brother, desperate for a response. Just the slightest bit of acknowledgment would do. Still. Nothing came.

"SAY SOMETHING!" he shouted as he threw his hand towards Daniel.

He closed his fists, and the mask covering Daniel's face burst into flames. In a matter of seconds, it was reduced to nothing but ashes collecting in the sand. Daniel's eyes were sunken and low, cold and unfeeling.

"What would you have me say?" Daniel began, finally breaking his silence. "Would you like me to apologize for Danté's death? Do you want me to grovel and beg for forgiveness?"

"I want you to care."

"Believe me, I care. I wanted Danté to see my dreams come true, to see that I was better than he could ever be. I wanted him to hold on to his pathetic life until that day came, but I suppose that was too much to ask for."

Virgil fell silent. His breaths were heavy, and his hands were trembling.

Calm down, he thought. *You have to stay in control. Don't lose control.*

The Fang of Kayveon began to glow around Daniel's neck. In one quick motion he burst out from the chains binding him. "It's been twice now I've allowed you to live," he said, "and yet, you keep interfering with my plans." He summoned a pristine sword in his hand. It looked sharp enough to slice through diamonds. "Honestly, you aren't worthy to perish by my blade, but since you insist on being a problem, you leave me with no other choice."

Virgil took a battle stance. "You know me. I was always the stubborn one."

The two men dashed towards each other. Virgil covered his fists in blue fire. His body was surging with heat, his rage ready to burst like an overfilled balloon. All he could think about was his brother, but not this imposter. No. Virgil thought of Danny, his older brother who had been taken from him.

Virgil struck Daniel in his chest, releasing a barrage of fire. Daniel sucked in a breath as he flew back and planted his feet in the sand. He swung his sword, and the flames were gone, extinguished by the force of his swing. Daniel's chest was scorched, and his flesh was exposed. Despite this, he stood unfazed, as if he hadn't been damaged at all.

Virgil hissed, blood trickling into the sand. He hadn't seen it, but during their exchange, Daniel had slashed his arms. Once. No, twice. No, three times.

Daniel burst forward once again, and Virgil raised his hand. A wall of fire surrounded Daniel, but he leaped into the air, clearing it with ease. Again, Daniel cut away at Virgil, leaving another six lacerations before Virgil could land a blow.

The battle raged on for several minutes, intensifying with each strike the men traded. Virgil was beginning to grow sluggish. Individually, his wounds were nothing more than an inconvenience, but collectively, they were proving to be catastrophic. The sands were stained with his blood, and it was getting worse with each passing minute. It wouldn't be long before he succumbed to the blood loss and slipped out of consciousness.

Daniel, on the other hand, showed no such weakness. He stood firm, each of his movements calculated and deliberate. It seemed like the blistering pockets of skin bubbling in the night air meant nothing to him. He kept going, inching closer and closer to landing a lethal blow.

Virgil took in a deep breath. Smoke trailed from his body, and his skin ached with burns that coated his arms. However, there was no room for pain in his mind. He was too busy fighting back the disgust seething inside him. "What has she done to you to make you like this?" he asked as he stared down his brother.

Daniel laughed. "You think I'm bewitched? You seriously believe I could fall victim to her spell? I assure you, my thoughts, feelings, and actions have always been my own."

Virgil raised his hand towards Daniel. "You're lying. This isn't you, Danny."

Daniel dashed forward and took hold of Virgil's neck, piercing Virgil's leg with his blade. Virgil tried to scream, but the grip on his throat was far too tight. "You're mistaken," Daniel said as Virgil collapsed onto his knees. "I am who I have always been. This fantasy you hold of a perfect life and perfect family is just that. A fantasy."

Daniel released his hold and pulled his blade from Virgil's flesh. Slowly, he raised his steel, preparing to deliver the final blow, as Virgil struggled to regain his breath.

"You're wrong," Virgil said, his voice strained, yet full of vigor. He looked up at Daniel and tightened his fist as his aura began to swell. "You. Dad. Me. We weren't perfect, but we were happy. Brother, you were happy."

Daniel's face grimaced. He doubled his grip on his sword, and the Fang of Kayveon grew even brighter than it had before. "YOU ARE NOT MY BROTHER!"

Daniel swung his sword at Virgil, his blade aimed at Virgil's neck. Virgil released his fire in defense, although his flames weren't blue anymore. Pain surged across his hand as golden fire erupted into the air, and Virgil couldn't help but scream out. Despite the agony plaguing his flesh, he pumped his mana into his blast. Daniel hissed and his eyes narrowed as the inferno seared his flesh. Nonetheless, he kept his blade in motion.

A flash of white light shone, and a loud clang echoed through the air as Daniel's sword was knocked back.

Virgil looked back towards Aurelia. "I'm sorry," she said, tears falling down her face. "But I couldn't just stand here waiting anymore. I don't know what's going on, but I know you're better than this. If you die here, I'll never forgive you."

Virgil swallowed the lump in his throat, and smiled. "Right," he said as he forced himself up onto his feet. "I wasn't thinking clearly. Thank you."

Daniel turned his attention to Aurelia, pointing his blade in her direction. "You just couldn't wait your turn, huh."

Virgil reached over, placing his hand on Daniel's sword. "We're not done yet." Virgil's hand ceased to be, replaced with purple fire.

Daniel fell back. His blade began to deteriorate, and he tossed it onto the ground.

Virgil and Daniel locked eyes. Virgil's left hand turned to flame just like the other, while Daniel summoned two more swords. Virgil's gaze fell to the Fang of Kayveon, and his eyes narrowed.

There's only one way we come out of this alive, he thought.

Virgil and Daniel charged at one another. As quickly as they leaped, the clash was over. Both men stood in the sand motionless. Daniel smirked as Virgil trembled, grunting as blood spilled into the sand. One of the swords was falling apart in Virgil's hand, but the other was plunged deep into Virgil's stomach.

"You missed," Daniel said.

Blood ran down Virgil's mouth. "No. I, I didn't."

Daniel looked down and his eyes grew wide. Virgil held the Fang of Kayveon in his hand.

A burst of light erupted from the black tooth, and it began to disintegrate. Virgil reached for Daniel, prompting him to quickly retreat.

Virgil laughed, fighting through the pain. He grabbed the sword left in his gut. "I wasn't going to touch you," he confessed. The blade disintegrated from his body. He held his hand over the hole in his gut and hissed as he quickly cauterized the wound. He trembled, and he wanted desperately to give in to his body's desire to shut down, but instead he smiled as he looked at Daniel. "I'd never do that to my brother."

Daniel's face grew red, and he ground his teeth. He took a deep breath, and ran his fingers through his hair. "I underestimated you," he said. "That won't happen again." He raised his hand towards Virgil. "Allow me to show you just how strong I've gotten over the years."

The blood in the sand began to glow, causing Virgil's eyes to grow wide. He covered himself in a fiery barrier, but it was no good. Throughout their battle, Daniel had been methodically wearing Virgil down all while setting the stage for the killing blow. Dozens of spikes erupted from the blood, piercing Virgil's body. He screamed in agony.

In a panic, Virgil grabbed the spikes one after the other in an effort to disintegrate them. But for every one he destroyed, two more sprang forward, lodging itself deep into his flesh. The blood began to coat Virgil's body, encasing him like a caterpillar in a cocoon. It became harder and harder to move, until it simply wasn't possible at all.

I have to go further, Virgil thought. *My entire body. Everything I have left. I. I can't. I can't die.*

Virgil's eyes began to flutter, and his heartbeat faltered.

Aurelia charged at Daniel, quickly summoning a sword. She swung, but he parried with a blade of his own.

"Let him go now!" Aurelia cried.

Daniel didn't respond, instead, pushing Aurelia back. She didn't let up. She swung, again and again, each time putting everything she had into her strikes.

"How could you do this to your own brother?" Her voice was boisterous and full of rage. "You two are the only blood you have left!"

"He's not my brother!" Daniel replied as he pushed Aurelia back once again.

Aurelia dispersed her sword as she touched the tips of her fingers together. Her eyes were fierce, lit with a mix of anger and determination. "Cerulean Effigy!"

Four clones of Aurelia sprouted from her body. Daniel took a step back as Aurelia and her clones approached. "Release Virgil, or I'm going to kill you," she threatened, as she and her clones summoned blades.

"I won't," Daniel replied. "But you do have a choice here. You can spend your time fighting me. Or you could spend your time saving him."

Aurelia stopped in place. For a moment, she stared at Daniel before shaking her head and rushing over to Virgil. He was nearly encased in the bloody cocoon. "Just hold on," she cried. "I'm going to get you out of there."

Virgil opened his mouth to speak, but the crystalized blood wrapped around his head, cutting off his words. He couldn't see, but he could hear Aurelia rustling outside of the cocoon.

Although that didn't really matter. His body felt cold, and breathing became cumbersome. Virgil tried with everything he had to hold on, but his efforts were in vain, and darkness overtook him.

CHAPTER

FIFTY

T ender memories filled every crevice of Virgil's mind. He was in his childhood bedroom. The door opened with a creak and in walked Danté, but not the feeble old man Virgil remembered dying before him. No. This was the young, vibrant Danté Virgil had always admired. Alongside Danté was another younger man. He looked to be about the same age as Virgil and wore a pair of black rugged jeans, a turtleneck sweater, thick black boots, and a long black trench coat. However, Virgil was much more concerned with his father rather than the man accompanying him. He stood up, speechless, his eyes fixed on Danté.

"Virgil." Danté raised his arms. "Come here, my son."

"Dad." Virgil approached his father. "Is it really you?"

Danté nodded, wrapping his arms around Virgil and holding him tightly.

The man proceeded to take his leave. "You have fifteen minutes. Make them count."

Danté smiled. "Thanks, Sam. I will."

With teary eyes, Virgil held onto his father. "Dad, I'm so sorry."

Danté rubbed Virgil's head. "You have nothing to be sorry for."

"That's not true. You hate me. Don't you?"

"What?" Danté chuckled. "I could never hate you."

Virgil trembled as he held on tighter. "But I joined the Crusaders. I couldn't kill Cecelia. I couldn't stop Danny. I-I destroyed your treasure."

Danté pulled his son away from him and looked him in the eyes. He reached over and wiped the tears from Virgil's cheek. "Crusader or not, you are my son. No matter what happens, I will always love you."

Virgil's tears had ceased, but now Danté began to tear up. "It's me who owes you an apology," he said.

"For what?" Virgil asked.

Danté shook his head as he took a deep breath. "I was a fool for the way I raised you. I wanted you and your brother to grow up big and strong and fearless. It's a cold, terrifying world out there, and I wanted you and your brother to be able to care for yourselves when I was no longer around, but I failed. Danny is lost, and you've lived a life of loneliness, anger, and hatred."

"You did the best you could. And I'm not alone anymore." Virgil couldn't help but smile as he thought of Aurelia and Logan. "I've made friends. Really good ones."

Danté returned the expression, his chest swelling with what could only be pride. "I've seen."

"You have?"

"Of course. What? You think your old man wouldn't be watching over you? You've cultivated quite the family. I'm proud of you."

Virgil exhaled, his father's words like a warm blanket on a cold winter's day. "Thank you."

Danté began making his way over to the bed. "Virgil," he said as he sat down. "I want to ask a favor of you. Actually, it's more like a promise."

"What is it?" Virgil asked as he sat down alongside his father.

Danté paused as he looked down. He opened his mouth, but failed to speak.

"Whatever it is, Dad, you can count on me."

Danté took in a deep breath, and turned to his son. "I want you to stop your pursuit of Cecelia and Danny."

Shock overtook Virgil. He sat, stunned in silence, unsure of what he just heard.

"Did you hear me, son?"

"What? What do you mean?" Virgil asked.

"I want you to stop pursuing Cecelia and Danny," Danté repeated.

Hearing his father's words a second time didn't make them any less foreign. "I don't understand," Virgil said, his voice shaky. "Why would you say that? If I don't stop them—"

"It's not your job to stop them. Nobody should be forced to fight their own family, and Cecelia has taken enough from us as it is. The world will be fine without you taking on that burden."

Virgil stood up, taking a few steps towards the door. "No," he said, shaking his head. "That isn't right. I can't just sit back and do nothing while good people suffer. It's not what you taught me."

"What I taught you is going to get you killed," Danté exclaimed as he stood up. "I'm not saying turn your back on those in need. You can continue to help others. You can even be a Crusader if you want. I just don't want you to throw your life away trying to clean up my mistakes."

Virgil looked at his father. He didn't know what to say, or even where to begin.

Tears began to pour from Danté's eyes. He opened his mouth to speak, only to wipe his eyes and turn away.

"Dad—"

The door sprang open, and a blinding light flooded the room. Virgil reached for his father, but it was no use.

"Dad!"

Danté was gone, along with the room. All that remained was an all-consuming light for as far as Virgil could see.

Virgil's eyes burst open. He looked around to find he was in his room at Roxanne's home. He was tucked in bed, barely clothed, his injuries nothing more than a memory. Aurelia lay at his bedside, a blanket wrapped around her as she slept. Roxanne sat in a chair off to the side and perked up as Virgil awakened.

"Welcome back," Roxanne said.

"How long was I out for this time?" Virgil asked, his voice hoarse as he rubbed his eyes.

"Four days."

"It feels like it." Virgil paused as he realized what Roxanne's presence really meant. "I take it, you already know everything then?"

"Not everything, but enough to know what a disappointment you've been." Virgil fell silent, bracing himself for what was to come. Roxanne forced a chuckle. "It's funny. I've had ample time to consider just how to have this conversation with you, and I still have no idea where to begin."

Virgil swallowed the lump in his throat. "You should know," he began. "Aurelia and Logan had nothing to do with what happened. They were actually trying to stop me and—"

"Spare me the bullshit," Roxanne said, her tone stern. "I'd have to be a fucking moron to believe that, and besides. Your friends already informed me you all came to this decision unanimously."

Virgil pursed his lips. "I see. Even so, you shouldn't expel them. I fully accept whatever punishment you see fit, but please don't punish them." He looked over at Aurelia. "Especially her. She's wanted to be a Crusader more than anything in the world. Please don't take that away from her."

Roxanne crossed her arms and sighed. "Nobody's taking anything away from anybody."

Virgil paused, unable to hide his astonishment. He had hoped for Aurelia and Logan to be spared from the kings' wrath, but he didn't expect himself to be so lucky.

"Don't be too excited," she added.

"I'm sorry," Virgil replied. "I'm just, you're really not going to punish us? Like, at all?"

Roxanne smirked. "Oh, you'll be punished. If you thought your training was brutal before, you have no idea what I have in store for you. For now, though, you should take a look at the dresser over there."

Virgil looked over to find an envelope. He reached over and picked it up, carefully pulling the paper apart. Within the envelope, he found a Crusader's license, freshly minted with his name and picture, and a diamond rested in the corner of the card. "The Blighted Flame," he said.

"Yup. That's the code name you've been assigned now that your probation has been lifted."

Virgil shook his head. "I don't understand. I failed. Miserably. I disobeyed orders. I don't, I don't deserve this."

"You can't disobey orders you weren't given. Of course, the Alliance doesn't agree with what you did, but the bottom line is you foiled Nobody's plan. While Cecelia and the Scarlet Mage did escape, we did manage to apprehend quite a few of their members. And most importantly, no one lost their lives due to your actions. With all things considered, we are willing to continue working with you. We still believe we can guide you on the right path."

Tears began rolling down Virgil's face as he looked down at the shiny metal card in his hands. "Why would you do that for me?"

"We are more than just a military force, Virgil," Roxanne said. "We are a family. Always remember that." Virgil looked up at Roxanne and smiled. "Now that we've gotten that out of the way, I can fill you in on the finer details we've uncovered. Given what we found at the stronghold and what we've recovered from the grimoire, we now know what Nobody's goal is."

"Are you serious?" Virgil said, his eyes wide with excitement. "You got into the grimoire?"

"It took quite a while, but Ash and Cordellia managed to break the curse warding it. I hate to admit it, but Cecelia is a powerful witch. Likely an elder. At any rate, Nobody is planning to resurrect someone. Or perhaps something."

"That makes sense," Virgil said with a nod. "They had a skull placed on the altar at their hideout. I suppose the demons they had tied up were meant to be sacrifices then."

"You saw the remains?" Roxanne exclaimed. "What did they look like?"

"It was just a skull, but it had horns curved into spirals. It was big, with sharp fangs, and it had three eyes." Roxanne let out a heavy sigh, and a frown crept onto her face. "What? Do you know who that is, er, was?"

"Yes, and it is just as we feared."

"Why? Whose remains were those?"

"Agramel, the Devourer."

"Agramel," Virgil said, "as in the Demon Lord Agramel? The one who sparked the Blood War?"

Roxanne nodded. "The very same."

Virgil ground his teeth as he looked down at his hands. "I'm sorry," he said. "I should have destroyed the remains. I could have—"

"There's no way you could have known what they were, and who knows if you would have even been able to reach them in the first place. You've bought us valuable time. According to the grimoire, the resurrection ritual must be performed on a solstice and with a catalyst. And not just any catalyst will do. It has to be a Dragon's Treasure. Speaking of which, I know it must have been painful destroying the Fang of Kayveon. It was the only thing you had left of your father."

Virgil tensed. "I'll be okay. After all, there was no other option. If I hadn't done it, Aurelia and I would have been killed for sure."

"Well, the Alliance sincerely appreciates your sacrifice."

Virgil paused as he thought of Daniel. Their fight played out in his mind. Every cut. Every jab. Every chance he missed, because he wasn't strong enough.

"Is everything okay?" Roxanne asked.

Virgil nodded. "I know I have no right to ask you this, especially after what I've done. But if I tell you something, will you promise not to tell Clayton or Aiden?"

"I'm afraid I can't guarantee that. They are our allies and your leaders."

"I figured you would say that."

"That being said, I would still like you to tell me what is troubling you. It is my job as your king and mentor to assist you in whatever way I can."

Virgil exhaled, and looked Roxanne in her eyes. "My brother, Daniel, he's the Scarlet Mage."

"He's what!" Aurelia shifted in her sleep to the sound of Roxanne's raised tone. She lowered her voice to a whisper. "I thought you said your brother was dead."

"I believed he was," Virgil replied. Roxanne fell silent, stroking her chin as she processed the information. "I need to get stronger. If fighting Daniel made one thing clear, it's that he's prepared to do whatever it takes to reach his goals. A lot of people are going to die if Nobody isn't reined in."

Aurelia turned in her sleep once more, this time with more vigor.

"We'll talk more about this later," Roxanne said as she stood up and walked towards the door. "Enjoy this rest, because it's the last you'll see of it for a while." Roxanne opened the door. "By the way," she said, looking back, "she's slept by your side every night. We've barely been able to tear her away to take care of herself."

Roxanne left the room, leaving Aurelia and Virgil alone. Gently, he placed his hand on her shoulder and gave it a light shake. Slowly she pulled herself up and wiped the sleep from her eyes.

"I was only resting my eyes, Virgil," Aurelia opened her eyes frantically, nearly bursting into tears as she saw him.

"Don't cry," Virgil said. "I'm al—"

In one quick motion, Aurelia leaned over and planted her lips onto Virgil's. Shock washed over him, leaving his eyes wide open. "I-I'm sorry," she said, her face flushed red. "I shouldn't have—"

Aurelia fell silent as Virgil reached over and placed his hand on her cheek. They drew in closer to one another. As they did, their eyes closed as if on instinct. Their lips touched, and they melted into one another. Each second that passed wasn't nearly enough. Again, and again, they pulled back, only to reposition and lock lips once more.

Virgil's senses were ablaze. The sweet smell of peaches flooding his nose. The quickening pace of his heartbeat ringing in his ear. The smooth touch of Aurelia's skin pressed against his own. The divine taste of her lips. His mind stripping away every last article of clothing wrapped around her body.

The doorknob turned, prompting Aurelia to pull back into her seat. "You're awake," Logan said as he stepped into the room. "Aurelia, you were supposed to come and get me when he woke up."

"S-sorry," Aurelia said hastily. "I, I forgot."

"No worries. I'm here now."

"I'm, uh, I'm glad to see you're okay," Virgil stuttered. "Olivia didn't give you too much trouble, I hope."

Logan placed his hand over his stomach. "She got a few shots in, but I managed to take her down. She was nothing compared to the Unbreakable Fist."

"I suppose that's your code name," Virgil replied. "So, you two have been lifted from probation as well?"

The siblings nodded in unison as they pulled out their licenses.

"I'm the White Lotus," Aurelia said.

"Well," Virgil replied, showing off his license, "I definitely have the coolest code name, that's for sure."

Logan scoffed. "In your dreams, maybe."

Virgil paused, thoughts of his father flooding his mind.

"Is something wrong?" Aurelia asked. "You're not hurt anywhere, are you? I can cast the Saint's Breath again."

"No," Virgil answered. "I'm fine. I was just remembering a dream I had."

"Was it a good dream?"

"I think so." Virgil smiled. "Listen, guys. I have something to share with you. The Scarlet Mage is my brother. Daniel."

Logan took a seat on the edge of Virgil's bed. "Your brother? I thought he was dead."

"So did I."

"How do you feel about it?" Aurelia asked. "I can't imagine what you must be going through."

"It might sound odd, but I'm actually okay. That wasn't my brother. Not really."

Logan's brow raised. "I'm confused. You just said—"

"I meant he's not the brother I knew," Virgil explained. "He's different now. I wanted to believe he had been bewitched, that he was being forced to do what he's done." He chuckled as he shook his head. "Even though I never sensed such a thing in his aura, I convinced myself that it was true. I don't know what he's been through, or how he's gotten to where he is now, but he's not Danny anymore."

EPILOGUE

The air was dense. Thick. So much so, it was hard to breathe. Between the mist, trees, and grass, visibility was terrible at best. Nonetheless, Roxanne led the way through the forest.

An immense pressure cascaded upon Virgil. Each step felt heavy, as if his feet were weighted down. Had it not been for his previous training with Roxanne, the forest would certainly have crushed him the moment he stepped foot into its borders. He slipped. His knee thumped against the ground, and he grunted as a shooting pain surged through his leg.

Roxanne glanced back. "It's not too late to turn around."

Virgil took a breath. "I wouldn't dream of it," he said, as he pulled himself back to his feet.

Roxanne nodded, and the two of them continued on. They moved closer and closer to an immeasurable aura off in the distance. The two cleared the forest and found themselves in an enormous field. White flowers stretched across the plain, and the sky was as gray as steel. Most notable, however, was the tremendous tiger that lay sleeping. It had white fur and long blade-like spikes sprouted from its back along its spine.

Roxanne approached the tiger. "Father, I've come to see you."

Slowly, the beast woke up, turning its attention to Roxanne. It yawned, and a gust of wind nearly toppled Virgil over. "Roxanne," Ateus replied. "It's good to see you." Ateus tilted his head down, and an irritated scowl washed over his face as he looked at Virgil. "I see you've brought a guest as well. You do remember that mortals are forbidden in the Aetherial Realm, don't you?"

"Forgive me, but I need to ask a favor of you." Roxanne turned to Virgil, giving him a nod.

"Ateus." Virgil stepped forward. "I come seeking your guidance."

Ateus leaned in closer to Virgil. His eyes were as white as cotton, and he glared with an intensity that eclipsed the sun. "Those merely seeking my guidance need only pray to me. You, a mere mortal, have invaded my home. You have stepped foot on holy lands. Laid eyes upon that which you are not worthy to behold." Ateus groaned. "You want a lot more than my guidance, boy."

Virgil swallowed the lump in his throat. "I'm sorry," he began. "You're right. I do want, no, I need a lot more from you. If you would be so kind, please teach me allostry."

END

THANK YOU!

First and foremost, I'd like express my appreciation to you for picking up my book. In the sea of content published out in the world, it truly warms my that you decided to pick up something I wrote and give it the time of day. Thank you, and I hope you enjoyed the ride!

If you'd like to share your thoughts and opinions on my story, please feel free to leave a review. Doing so is a great help not only to get my work out to more readers, but it also helps me improve by utilizing your feedback. To help make things simpler, scanning the QR code below will take you to your Amazon product review page.

WANT MORE FROM ME?

Had fun and want to keep the good times rolling? Check out some of my other works.

Fantasy:
    Covenant of the Ashen Wolf Vol. 1

You can also join my newsletter to stay up to date with projects I'm working on, receive free goodies, and gain access to exclusive content.
https://bit.ly/papena-newsletter

ABOUT THE AUTHOR

P. A. Peña is an author writing adult science fiction and fantasy novels. He discovered his passion for writing as a child, however, he initially planned to be a mechanical engineer leaving writing as merely a hobby. It wasn't until he made it to college and received a push from his wife that he decided to seriously pursue his passion. Patrick currently resides in Michigan where he was born and raised. If he isn't writing, he is likely playing video games, watching anime, reading, or spending time with his wife and daughter.

For more information, visit patwritesbooks.com

www.ingramcontent.com/pod-product-compliance
Lightning Source LLC
Chambersburg PA
CBHW051313250626
47155CB00007B/2304